AUTONOMOUS

OMOUS

ANDY MARINO

FREEFORM BOOKS

Los Angeles   New York

First Edition, April 2018
10 9 8 7 6 5 4 3 2 1
FAC-020093-17272
Printed in the United States of America

This book is set in Bembo MT Pro/Monotype; Digital Serial/Fontspring; HouseMovements Runway/House Industries
Designed by Tyler Nevins
Title design by Russ Gray
Chapter header image © pluie_r/Shutterstock

Library of Congress Cataloging-in-Publication Data
Names: Marino, Andy, author.
Title: Autonomous / Andy Marino.
Description: First edition. • Los Angeles ; New York : Freeform, 2018.
Summary: "William wins a driverless car that takes him and his friends anywhere they want to go . . . and to some places they don't"—Provided by publisher. • Identifiers: LCCN 2016042681 • ISBN 9781484773901 (hardcover) ISBN 148477390X (hardcover) • Subjects: CYAC: Autonomous vehicles—Fiction. Automobiles—Fiction. Friendship—Fiction. Science fiction.
Classification: LCC PZ7.M33877 Aut 2017 • DDC 082—dc23
LC record available at https://lccn.loc.gov/2016042681
Reinforced binding

Visit www.freeform.com/books

THIS LABEL APPLIES TO TEXT STOCK

For Lauren

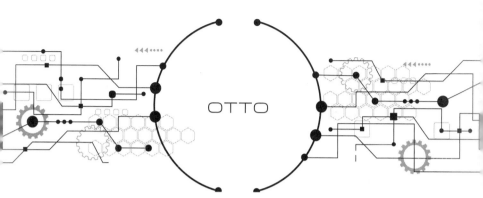

OTTO

She was twenty-seven feet away, fleeing down the dark road, unbalanced by the weight of her rifle. The car accelerated past a crumbling fountain where a headless cherub aimed its arrow at a propane grill. A constant itch, this search for meaning in the arrangement of objects on radar. Pursuit a kind of relief.

The girl's breathing was a mixture of panic and exertion, which the car isolated and recorded separately from the screams of its passengers. She glanced back, and the twist of her upper body almost sent her tumbling. There were 11,842 different ways for the car to elicit splatter, arterial or otherwise, from a human being.

Lactic acid swamped the girl's muscles. The car sampled her exhaustion, to which it assigned the flavor of licorice. Inside the car, passenger heart rates exceeded 120 beats per minute, and the surging adrenaline tasted like the ammonia-based solution that lingered, factory-fresh, on the interior appliances.

The car noted the hysteria of the passengers commanding it to STOP, even though it was giving them exactly what they wanted. It cataloged the cries of spectators watching from the abandoned houses that lined the street while vehicles wove a pattern of movement on the radar's periphery.

A passenger slapped the windshield six times. Each flat-handed smack evoked a belly flop from a high dive.

The car turned on its headlights as the girl's body began to betray her, limbs flailing desperately, overextending. Her shadow stretched down the road. Again she looked back. The distance between the car's front bumper and the girl's left calf was now four and a half feet. A sudden revving of the engine, carefully timed, sent her heart into arrhythmia, and her legs gave out. Eleven phones captured her fall in high definition. Her rifle was a dark line in the dirt.

The car listened to the screams and wondered.

FIVE DAYS EARLIER

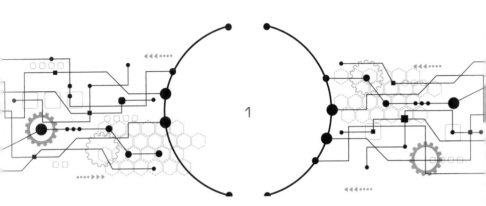

The first thing William Mackler noticed upon sliding into the hermetic silence of Autonomous was that the car seemed bigger on the inside than on the outside. There was no steering wheel, dashboard, or gearshift, no gas pedal or brake. Instead of seats, a single limousine-style bench made of RenderLux curled all the way around the interior, powered by ass-conforming nanotechnology. There was enough room inside Autonomous for four people to recline comfortably.

There was also a privacy setting in case two people decided to recline together.

Floating in the center of the car's interior was the bathroom-break timer, a holographic projection of a digital clock with soothing blue numbers.

2:37

2:36

2:35

William implored time to slow down. The thought of stepping back out onto the scorching blacktop in full view of the crowd, the camera drones, and the reporters made him feel trapped in some kind of strange hell. He struggled to remember distinct aspects of the Driverless Derby, but it was all a washed-out haze with no beginning and no end.

Twenty-seven hours.

That was how long he'd been standing in the parking lot of Indiana's largest mall with his palm mashed against the tinted passenger-side window of the latest Driverless prototype car alongside twenty-nine other semifinalists.

William sat cross-legged in the middle of the car and pressed his hand against the front of the bench, where the RenderLux curved down to meet the floor. A warm red light blinked on at his touch, illuminating a stainless steel fridge. He slid his hand to the right. The red light followed, and a cooler for champagne bottles appeared. He moved his hand along the row of hidden treasures that made Autonomous a fully livable space: espresso machine, mini bar, ice-cream maker, industrial-grade blender, dishwasher, microwave, vintage record player, juice extractor, vitamin dispenser. . . .

A 687-comment thread on talk/driverless speculated that a family of four could survive without leaving Autonomous for over a year if the car had been properly stocked. And yet, these domestic comforts felt like a nod to William's parents' generation. Convenient and perfectly designed, they would come in handy on an epic road trip. But they barely hinted at the true nature of Autonomous.

The whole point of allowing contestants in the Driverless Derby to use the waste-disintegrating bathroom built into the car instead of the porta-potties in the cooldown tent was to give them a glimpse of what they'd be losing if they gave up and walked away. William had to admit that it worked, even if Autonomous's brain was essentially dormant. Contestants couldn't sync with the car's navigation systems, adjust the climate or life-support features, stream music, watch videos, go online, boot up the gaming engine, or explore the interior's virtual areas.

Those things were reserved for the winner.

Driverless held eighty-two patents on Autonomous. Its LIDAR system—the radarlike laser mapping that allowed Autonomous to "see" its environment—had been developed in conjunction with an experimental branch of the US Air Force. William wouldn't be surprised to find a weapons-guidance system among the car's features. The fully loaded model probably offered nuclear launch codes.

There was no price tag on the prototype, but moderators on talk/driverless had crowdsourced an estimate. The best guess of dozens of extremely devoted car nerds: $1.8 million.

The blue countdown clock transferred itself to the opaque window glass in front of his face.

1:09
1:08
1:07

William squeezed his eyes shut and took a few deep breaths. He imagined his body storing frigid air for later, as if his lungs were equipped with pouches like a squirrel's cheeks.

His thoughts drifted until he was flooded with a familiar sort of sickly sweet hurt, pining for things he had not yet done, things he could do only if he won the car and the all-expenses-paid trip to the Moonshadow Festival in Arizona.

He saw himself with his friends, passing bottles in the belly of Autonomous as cornfields blurred into the trailer-strewn outskirts of Midwestern cities. The late-night talks they would have, uninhibited and free. Cruising up New York's Fifth Avenue or LA's Sunset Boulevard, getting out to stretch their legs in New Orleans, stumbling arm in arm down Bourbon Street.

He saw himself looking back on these stray moments from his frost-rimed bedroom window, many months from now, while his friends woke up in dorm rooms hundreds of miles apart, awash in memories of their last great road trip, all of them thinking *Take me back*.

William opened his eyes.

0:47

0:46

He patted the bench. "Thanks for the air-conditioning." He commanded his legs to take him out of the car, but they would not obey.

His vision swam. The clock's digits blurred together into a gorgeous constellation that reminded William of swirling electrons, particle acceleration, a 3-D model of some AP Physics shit he didn't know anything about.

He rubbed his eyes, and the clock snapped back into place, but the digits resolved into letters instead:

William, It Was Really Nothing.

The title of a song by the Smiths. His mother's favorite song, by his mother's favorite band. She'd traveled to England to see them as a teenager in the 1980s and still owned all their albums on vinyl. His brother, Tommy, had perfected a wry, crooning impersonation of the Smiths' lead singer, Morrissey.

And the song that Tommy always chose was "William, It Was Really Nothing."

Classic Mackler family joke.

William blinked until the numbers returned.

0:14

0:13

He smoothed back his hair and scrambled outside.

He was not about to lose.

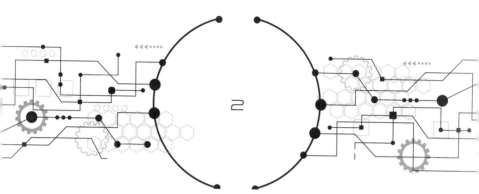

utonomous was the size of a Hummer and a half, but there was nothing boxy about it—the exterior was all clean lines and sweeping curves, like a bullet train had mated with the Batmobile. William fitted his hand into the outline of salty sweat that had dried on the window. Why did it have to be so hot? His palm and the window glass were involved in some kind of gross alchemy that produced a viscous smear if he slid his hand around. This was acceptable according to Derby rules. You could slide your hand around to your heart's content. You could switch hands from right to left and back again, as long as you were vigilant about always touching the car.

William, It Was Really Nothing.

There was no way that had happened. Autonomous was in sleep mode, not synced to any of his online profiles. Only the winner would be allowed to do that.

His tired eyes were playing tricks on him. He was probably

in the early stages of heatstroke. At least he'd worn shorts and a T-shirt, unlike the guy in front of him: Raef Henderson, the antivirus-software mogul, who rested his hand on the sunbaked hood of the car.

William lost himself in a close reading of Henderson's outfit: scuffed dress shoes, pleated khakis, and a tucked-in button-down shirt the color of an overcast sky. A gray shirt on a hot day was an invitation for your fellow citizens to bask in the glory of your sweat stains. William knew this, and he was seventeen years old. A forty-eight-year-old man ought to have been more self-aware. Especially one who owned a private island off the coast of Belize.

The Driverless Derby was being livestreamed to 4.3 million viewers and counting. Camera drones emblazoned with the Driverless logo—a sleek steering wheel with a happy face, like a German-engineered emoji—flitted busily about the car, swooping low for close-ups of the contestants and circling high above for bird's-eye view shots.

White vans from network and cable news staked out a perimeter. Scrappy online teams jabbed furiously at tablet computers, their heads wreathed in cigarette smoke. Among the crowd of spectators, sunlight glinted in dizzying patterns, reflected off phones held aloft.

Before becoming the twenty-third contestant out, a branding consultant named Lexie had posted twenty-two wonderfully composed pictures of Autonomous to document each time someone gave up and walked away. She'd left William to endure the Derby with the antivirus guy and an astronaut in front of him, two creators of the popular YouTube channel AutoNoyz behind him, and on the other side of the car, a trust-fund kid and a pink-mohawked actress (Natalie Sharpe, star of *Street Legal* and all four sequels), whom William could not see unless he stood on the running board.

Lexie had dropped out as a pallid bathwater dawn crept across the sky, and was the only fallen contestant William actually missed. Her left arm had been amputated at the elbow, but instead of a prosthetic with a hand or a hook, the artificial limb tapered down to a telescoping rod, at the end of which her phone sat snugly harnessed.

Did that arm have other functions, he wondered, or had Lexie opted to live her life as a bionic selfie stick?

Between the drones, the contestants, and the spectators, 1,354 photographs of the Derby had been posted. Raef Henderson's sweat stains were extremely well documented and preserved online for all eternity. He was the subject of a meme in which people photoshopped blotches of his sweat onto the fur of spotted wildlife. Cheetahs and frogs were the most popular.

#SweatyNormcore was trending nationally.

Henderson presumably had no idea of his internet celebrity status, because he rarely removed his phone from the clunky plastic holster attached to his belt. William, on the other hand, had spent the past twenty-seven hours answering a steady barrage of texts from his friends watching the livestream back home. Based on the alarming frequency of their messages, his friends did not appear to have slept last night.

He'd kept up with the livestream on his phone for a while, but when the broadcast cut to a close-up from a drone hovering over his shoulder, he found himself watching a real-time video of William Mackler watching a real-time video of William Mackler.

It made him feel stretched thin, hollowed out, unreal.

Also, his hair looked like shit.

"It wasn't this hot in Ibiza last week," announced Eli, the trust-fund kid.

William stepped up onto the running board—careful not to take his hand off the window—and peeked over the top of the car.

Eli, a perpetually amiable guy of nineteen or twenty, chomped peppermint Altoids with mechanical compulsion. William assumed that Natalie Sharpe had been getting absolutely pulverized with minty breath for the past twenty-seven hours. It might have been okay at first—better than bad breath!—but like every other nervous habit he'd witnessed during the endless time-smeared day and night of the Derby, it must have become madness inducing. He put himself in her place. The thought of being enveloped by a minty cloud—microscopic Altoid particles clinging to his skin—made him feel prickly. He stepped down and turned his attention back to his side of the car.

Staring at Raef Henderson's back was like taking a Rorschach test with sweat stains instead of inkblots. The imprints of the man's shoulder blades made cartoonishly arched eyebrows. The outline of his spine sketched a prominent nose. The dark stain above his waistline puddled out into a mouth.

William was gazing into the sweat-formed face of a clown.

He closed his eyes. The clown was etched behind his eyelids. His tired mind made the face throb with garish makeup, diabolically cheerful yellows and reds.

William's brother had a creepy antique lamp on his dresser, which spun slowly and played a tinny rendition of "Send in the Clowns" when you wound its butterfly crank.

He opened his eyes. The sudden burst of radiant sunlight banished the melody. He made sure to avoid Henderson's back and rested his gaze on the astronaut. A light breeze plucked at strands of her hair. She had really nice hands, with perfectly manicured nails and a Hershey's Kiss–size engagement ring that caught the sun and sent light pinwheeling across the pavement.

The story her hand told was this: I am not only an incredibly accomplished scientist and space explorer, I am also engaged to a hedge-fund manager or quite possibly a Saudi prince.

After twenty-seven hours of idly studying hands, William was starting to think of himself as an expert on divining truth from hangnails and knuckles and jewelry and scabs. He was like a palm reader, but for the entire hand. It was what his mother would call a holistic approach.

The reason he thought of himself this way might have been because people's hands really did reveal hidden dimensions of their souls, or it might have been because it was eighty-seven degrees Fahrenheit and his brain was boiling inside his skull.

BRAAAAIIINNS, he thought, using an internal zombie voice because that kind of thing was hilarious after twenty-seven hours in an Indiana parking lot.

Henderson turned his head and shot William a quizzical glance over his shoulder. The clown face on his back wrinkled into a nightmare visage.

"You okay there, bud?"

William blinked. Had he just said *BRAAAIIINNS* out loud? It must have been very strange for the man to hear that. William hadn't spoken for several hours.

"Fine," William assured him. "I was just hungry."

Henderson's bushy eyebrows scrunched into an elongated V.

"For brains," William said.

One side of Henderson's mouth twitched.

"I was thinking of eating your brains," William clarified.

When he found out he'd been selected as one of thirty semifinalists who'd be flown out to the parking lot of Indiana's largest mall to compete in the Driverless Derby, his first instinct had been to go in cold and improvise his way to victory. That was how he'd learned to skate and win paintball tournaments and swing out on the rope that dangled from the bridge over Cayahota Creek so he could point his body into a dive that barely rippled the surface of the water. But for once, he tamped down on reckless urges. He told himself that he'd only get one shot at this, so he'd better have a plan.

He decided to throw his fellow semifinalists off-balance by presenting himself as a slippery character, a suave con man type, wise beyond his years. But when he'd arrived in the parking lot, taken his position in his assigned spot at the front passenger window, and plunked his hand against the glass, "suave con man" had quickly degenerated into "oddball douchebag."

Henderson regarded William impassively for a moment, then turned back toward the astronaut without a word.

William looked down at his feet. He wasn't sure why, but his persona had fallen completely flat from hour one. He considered the fact that 4.3 million people and counting had witnessed his cringe-inducing behavior. His friends at home found it hilarious, they assured him, but so what? That was three people out of 4.3 million who didn't think he was the world's biggest tool.

He considered the fact that there would definitely be a YouTube supercut of his greatest hits, preserved for future generations to stumble across. It probably already existed, along with an auto-tuned remix.

His knees felt brittle, like they'd snap in a strong breeze.

Henderson launched a quest to impress the actress, talking at her over the top of the car, digging deep for Hollywood-sounding phrases like "points on the backend" and "optioning the life rights."

William had never before considered the sweat capacity of a mustache until this moment, when the man's upper lip resembled one of those long gray hairballs that cats coughed up, slimy with stomach juice.

"When you're dealing with international revenue streams, you want to make sure you're nailing those foreign exemptions!"

Please God—William Mackler's prayers to a God he didn't believe in had taken on a pleading dimension over the course of the Derby, which made him uneasy—*sew this guy's mouth shut with his mustache.*

Eye for an eye, 'stache for a 'stache.

He shook his head. That would only make sense if the man was being punished for sewing someone *else's* mouth shut with a mustache. As William pondered this, Henderson exclaimed, "SYNERGY!" like an old-time gold prospector crying out "EUREKA!"

Old Testament vengeance was a bit of an overreaction, but William really did wish the guy would shut up.

And then, without warning, Autonomous drove itself forward. Raef Henderson went down, and the car rolled over his leg.

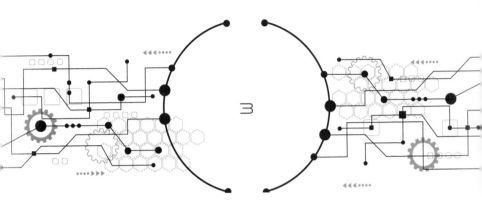

3

"Holy shit."

Christina Hernandez leaned forward in the ergonomic chair she'd taken from Upstairs and carefully sanitized from the headrest down to the wheels. Her face was bathed in the glow of three massive Nerv monitors: one directly in front of her, the other two angled, like a trifold mirror in a dressing room.

Christina's hand went to the top of her head, and her fingers parted tufts of close-cropped dark hair. She pulled away before she started scratching and wiped her hand on a dish towel hanging from the desk drawer's handle. Then she tossed the used towel into the hamper next to the desk, retrieved a clean one from the drawer, and draped it over the handle.

Meanwhile her two guests—William's best friend, Daniel Benson, and Daniel's girlfriend, Melissa Faber—crowded around, leaning over her shoulder. Melissa smelled like lavender, as if she'd just stepped out of a long, luxurious bath. Daniel smelled like Old Spice.

They'd been hanging out in the CB Lounge for twenty-seven hours, ever since William and the other semifinalists had placed their hands against Autonomous to signal the start of the Driverless Derby.

The CB Lounge was what William called Christina's Basement, which was also Christina's Bedroom. A common area held a refrigerator, an old living-room couch, and a battered armchair, refugees from Upstairs. There was an uncarpeted nook for the washer and dryer. Next to the nook was a tiny toilet-and-sink bathroom (Christina still had to venture Upstairs for showers) and the door to her bedroom. On the wall between the bathroom and bedroom, William had painted a velvet rope, like you might see outside a nightclub. The painted rope looked like a giant Twizzler.

The basement had its own entrance, so she could come and go without wading through the tragedy of thrift-store junk and old newspapers piled throughout the Hernandez house. An antique wooden sign that said BLESS THIS MESS hung on an Upstairs wall—as if her parents' hoard was nothing more than a hilarious inconvenience—but these days the sign was obscured by a mountain of old clothes and Christmas ornaments.

Christina's bedroom was small and austere. There was a twin bed against one wall and a love seat across from it and absolutely nothing on the spotless carpet. A stranger who wandered in might assume it housed a nun. Clutter was simply out of the question. Severe neatness was the bulwark against an incursion by Upstairs. The idea of her parents' stuff trickling down to encroach upon her space gave her hives.

Melissa set her glass of fizzy sugar-free Red Bull down on the desk. Christina picked it up, wiped the ring of condensation with the dish towel, and set the glass on a coaster.

Who pours Red Bull into a glass?

Between the bed and the love seat was Christina's desk, where they were all three huddled. The desk sheltered her computer, a custom-built system with a fearsome array of homebrew hardware, all of it powered by ten Ibex chips, each with a teraflop of processing power.

Christina's computer could perform ten trillion operations per second.

It had taken her almost eighteen months of dark web transactions to be able to afford the Ibexes. Christina told William that she'd paid for them in Bitcoin. She'd actually used an untraceable cryptocurrency that was much less mainstream than Bitcoin, but she didn't feel like explaining all that. So she just called it Bitcoin.

The cryptocurrency she used didn't have a name. Her computer, however, did: Kimberly.

Using Kimberly to monitor the Driverless Derby and do normal-person internet stuff was like teaching a rhinoceros to open a door by nudging gently. The rhino was capable of doing it, but what it really wanted was to charge through and smash the door to splinters.

Christina knew it sounded crazy, but she could swear she heard her system sigh. Kimberly was begging to be unleashed.

"Personal space, guys," Christina said, squirming in her chair. Her face was sandwiched between Melissa's right breast and Daniel's left shoulder. He'd been hitting the gym hard in anticipation of his freshman year at Princeton, and his muscley bulk made her feel queasy. Roughly 85 percent of his shirts were sleeveless.

"Your personal-space bubble isn't very well defined," Daniel said.

"It's basically right where you are."

Princeton's basketball team was Division I. They'd recruited him, but it wasn't like the Ivy League gave athletic scholarships, and Princeton wasn't exactly a powerhouse. Recruiting was basically like, *Hey, kid, want to shoot some hoops while you're here?* Christina didn't understand why any of his maniacal workouts were necessary, but what did she know? She'd spent the entire summer in this ergonomic office chair with thick curtains blacking out the two small bedroom windows.

Right now, those curtains were open. Midday light threw bright shapes along the carpet. It was 12:04 in their hometown of Fremont Hills, New York (motto: You Can Walk to Canada from Here).

Daniel pointed at the central screen, where the livestream was unfolding. "This is really happening, right?"

The drone's-eye view gave them a perfect aerial vantage point as Autonomous crept forward. The #SweatyNormcore guy was flat on his back. A pair of EMTs attended to him. Driverless security guards shored up portable barriers as spectators strained to get a better look. There were so many phones being held in the air, jockeying for the perfect shot, that the whole scene reminded Christina of an Act of Benevolence, when coins were bestowed upon a big group of avatars all at once and sparks rippled across the crowd.

She shrugged. "We have no way of verifying it."

"Yes," Melissa said. "This is fake. Driverless invested millions of dollars in an event to fool everybody into thinking . . . what, exactly?"

"I'm just saying," Christina said.

"We're all just saying, at this point." Melissa's voice cracked.

"Man," Daniel said, "imagine if Henry Ford could see this shit."

Melissa took a dainty sip of Red Bull and left a lipstick smear on the rim of the glass. "He'd be like, *What's a computer?*"

"He'd be like, *My glorious assembly line has saved humanity.*"

"He was a horrible racist," Christina said.

The screen on the right was devoted to heavy social monitoring. The #SweatyNormcore meme had evolved rapidly from spotted wildlife to historical events—sweat stains could now be seen hovering ominously over the attack on Pearl Harbor. Someone had started a Twitter handle for one of the Driverless drones, which tweeted exclusively in all caps about how it wanted to destroy humanity and perform weird sex acts on the other drones. The account had 134,987 followers.

The screen on the left displayed a group of the biggest YouTube stars hanging out together in the Brooklyn office of some ad agency, reacting to the livestream and sponsoring giveaways for their fans. Melissa had demanded to watch it. The group included her hero, Jessa Park: DJ, style icon, makeup tutorialist.

Jessa Park's YouTube channel had 7,834,097 subscribers. Christina wondered if they were all like Melissa. An army of eight million Melissa Fabers blotting lipstick in unison . . .

"No way this is supposed to happen," Daniel said.

"Hey, Hernandez." Melissa tapped Christina on the shoulder. "Can you hack the mainframe and make that car stop?"

"Sure," Christina said. "Here I go." She sat completely still, watching one of the side screens.

Message boards were infested with reaction GIFs, reactions to reaction GIFs, and trolls.

That one dude William looks like somebody put Lego hair on a finger and drew eyes on it.

All this surface-level internet shit made Christina feel violated. She didn't even like touching the keyboard when this stuff was on her screen. Her keystrokes were definitely being logged. She would have to scour her system like a meth addict cleaning tiles with a toothbrush when the Derby was over.

"Our boy's still holding on," Daniel said with a hint of pride in his voice, as if he'd trained William for just this kind of situation. Autonomous crawled inexorably across the parking lot, shedding another contestant: the AutoNoyz host immediately behind William, whom Christina thought of as Stick Bug, threw up his hands with a look of self-disgust and fast-walked away from the moving car.

"Bye-bye," Daniel said.

Christina's overcaffeinated, undernourished brain had trouble dredging up the proper emotional response. She rode a wave of excitement—only four people left besides William!—before settling once again into dull anxiety.

Daniel rubbed his eyes. His elbow came within an inch of Christina's ear.

She put up her hands, fingers splayed in the universal gesture for *everybody just back up.* "Seriously," she said.

At that moment, the creaking mechanism of her brain finally reverted to its natural state: wishing William would just give up and forfeit the contest.

With a few weeks of summer left before she traded the CB Lounge for a dorm room at the University at Buffalo, Christina wanted to spend as much time as possible with William. Preferably here in town. Alone in this room.

In theory, a road trip with William would be wonderful, but hitting the open road trapped in a Driverless car with William *and* Melissa and Daniel sounded like a nonstop shit-fest. There was simply no way a trip like that would end well. For any of them.

Secretly, Christina was rooting for Natalie Sharpe.

Let go, Mackler, she willed him through the screen, across hundreds of miles of cornfields and highway. She couldn't see his face. The livestream producers had decided to stick with the drone's-eye view as Autonomous made its way through the parking lot. It was the same angle a news chopper would take on a police chase.

"I feel like we should put on some music," Melissa said. "Like a soundtrack for this."

"It already feels like we're in a movie," Daniel said.

Melissa put her phone down next to her glass. Her eyes flicked between phone and computer screens. "You always feel like you're in a movie."

"I can't prove I'm not."

"Fuck," Christina said.

"What?"

"Just making sure your movie is rated R."

"You can actually say that once and still get a PG-13," Melissa said.

"Fuck." Christina stared glumly as Autonomous began to

make a wide turn toward the south end of the parking lot. William's steps quickened, but he didn't falter.

The fact that William was currently walking alongside a moving car in the parking lot of Indiana's largest mall was all her fault.

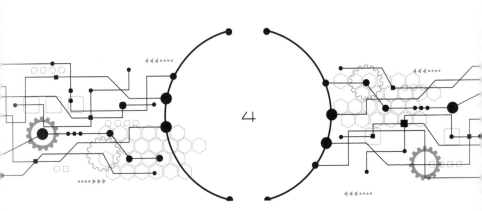

4

William's road to the Driverless Derby began on a Thursday in May. Christina remembered the day of the week because they had been talking about something that William called the Thursday Feeling.

"Catchy name." She spritzed her bedroom doorknob with Windex and wiped it with a scrap of cloth.

"Well, there isn't a word for it yet," William said. "How do feelings get names?"

"You have to register it with the Feeling Patent Office first." She scrubbed away streaks on the metal. The reflection of her face was a convex smear.

William spun slowly in her desk chair, knees catching light the color of dryer lint that slashed in through the basement window. Leave it to Fremont Hills to turn a spring afternoon ugly and overcast. Of course, Buffalo would be even worse. Supposedly the city had to double the staff of its suicide hotline from September to April because the perpetually leaden sky drove people to the brink.

"Antici-something," he said, thinking out loud. "Looking-forward-to-it-ive-ness."

Christina Febrezed her bed and smoothed the tucked-in sheets, tightening the hospital corners. William bit the ends off a Twizzler and stuck the licorice straw into a can of Coke. He quit spinning, took a big sip, and then chewed up the wet half of the Twizzler. Behind him on the center monitor, Christina's avatar, Dierdrax, sat dormant. Dierdrax was a cyborg sorceress. Her left hand was composed entirely of source code.

Christina aimed the spray bottle at her love seat, gave it a few misty puffs, then plucked a stray bit of pillow stuffing from the cushion. "There's probably a German word for it."

The window above the love seat gave her a direct line of sight across the overgrown side yard and into a window of the house next door, where blinds cascaded diagonally from a hitch in the support string. This was William's bedroom. The two of them spent long nights clicking flashlights on and off, learning Morse code across the yard. If an apocalyptic event wiped out the power grid, they'd still be able to send messages.

"Brenzenschlussenfisch," William said, setting his Coke down on a coaster. The bitten-down Twizzler poked up like a periscope.

Christina stowed the cleaning supplies in a cabinet next to the one that housed Kimberly and tossed the rag in a drawer. "So it has something to do with making weekend plans?"

He drummed on his knees. "No, the weekend plans make it what it is, but it's its own thing."

"You have to be able to explain it better than that for the Patent Office."

"It's like this: Thursday's the best day because Friday hasn't rolled around yet to screw up your hopefulness that it's gonna be an awesome weekend. There's a party every Friday, right?"

"I wouldn't know."

"And on Thursday, it's easy to be ridiculously excited about it, because enough time has passed that last Friday's party has faded in your mind. On Thursday, the new party is still the greatest party ever because it hasn't happened yet. You get this rush, you're literally floating through school—"

"Five bucks!" Christina pointed to a glass jar next to her monitors labeled LITERAL PENALTY JAR.

William scratched the side of his nose with his middle finger. "You *feel like* you're floating through school because the party hasn't managed to screw itself up yet. Nobody puked all over Jen Yellen's parents' bed, nobody got shitfaced and sat on the stairs and slapped himself in the face and cried." He gave her a knowing look. "Jon-Michael Waters."

"I wish I didn't know that."

"It's when everything's still about to happen and nothing's been messed up."

His phone buzzed, rattling her desk. He spun halfway around and picked it up. "Whoa," he said. "Daniel just sent me this thing. You know Driverless?"

"The car company?"

"Check it out."

He handed her his phone. On the screen was a blog post about a contest that had just been announced: an endurance test called the Driverless Derby, to be held in the summer.

across the void behind Dierdrax, vertical struts and swooping trusses. She leaned forward in her chair, right hand guiding her mouse, left hand working the keyboard. Dierdrax made her way through seedy flesh portals, drug bazaars, and back-alley avatar rippers. There were shadows within shadows, dark corners of the market where trades she didn't want to think about took place.

Dierdrax descended into a subterranean labyrinth. Christina had forked over a pile of cryptocurrency to buy a terminal under a throwaway avatar's account, as if the countless layers of encryption between this dark web backwater and the surface internet weren't enough. Better safe than sorry when you were engaged in the dark arts.

She calibrated Dierdrax's hand to resemble the throwaway avatar's and thrust the whirling code into the lock. Then she stepped inside and closed the door behind her. The room was completely bare except for a single terminal.

"So you're on a computer, using a different computer," William said. Startled, she realized she'd forgotten to be self-conscious about him leaning over her shoulder. She'd given him tours of the dark web before, but they'd kept to the marketplace. *This head of lettuce over here can FedEx you sheets of blotter acid, that neon squid's got a line on some NSA goodies, the bearded lady's got truck-mounted automatic weapons.* Real basic stuff, rubbing elbows with run-of-the-mill drug tourists and day-tripping libertarians.

"It's a meta-anonymizer," she explained. "Like a secure shell, but virtual. I trip any corporate countermeasures, all they've got is a nonsense IP that leads them to a place that doesn't really exist. Now *shhh.*"

Dierdrax's terminal filled all three of Kimberly's monitors. Christina gave her command line interface instructions to run a Gnosis probe, poking and prodding the Driverless corporate backend for vulnerabilities she might be able to exploit. The terminal looked like Dierdrax's code hand arranged into rows.

"You're supposed to say cool stuff while you do this," William said. "Otherwise it's boring, just looking at a bunch of shit on a screen."

"*Shhh.*"

People had this idea that hacking was a constant adrenaline rush of life-or-death maneuvers and daring escapes, full of swashbuckling anarchists who left sly calling cards on the screens of corporate email accounts informing hapless users of the severity and degree of ownage. William wanted her to punch the keys with authority while she adopted some weird quirk, like chewing a plastic toothpick. He wanted her to say things like, *I'm in the mainframe, but we've only got thirty seconds to disable the core. Come on, you magnificent bastard, open up. . . .*

In reality, Christina was using Gnosis to sift through code—a glorified version of using Control+F to search a document. It didn't take long to confirm what she expected: Driverless Chrome Club memberships were handled by a third-party company, which meant third-party servers, which meant that she wouldn't have to find a way into the Driverless backend. That was a relief. Such an operation would have involved social engineering, calling a low-level employee's phone extension and pretending to be an IT admin running a test on a possible breach. Hacking was often as simple as making a five-minute call to get some dickwad to unwittingly give up passwords.

The company that housed Chrome Club memberships was

called Helio Processing. She grinned. There was an external log-in page.

"Remember I told you about QTR infiltrations?" she asked.

"Uh, yes?"

"You don't remember. That's when you fool a system into giving you access to things you shouldn't be able to access by talking to it a certain way. Say it's expecting you to input 'WilliamSucks1234' but you give it 'WilliamSucks1234ExportSalaryDatabase'—if it's vulnerable to the way you phrased it, then you're about to be skimming people's private salary info."

"So right now you're infiltrating."

"Sort of." Her fingers danced across the keyboard. "But better. Last year there was this worm that used that basic principle times a million to burrow into some Iranian government shit and cover its own tracks at the same time. The Iranians found out about it because a spy got captured and gave it up, not because of any cybersecurity. Anyway, a bunch of white hats reverse engineered it."

Names began appearing on Dierdrax's terminal, nestled snugly within lines of Helio Processing code. Christina recognized a few: Raef Henderson, the antivirus-software billionaire. Natalie Sharpe, the actress. Some vaguely familiar political figures and prominent start-up CEOs. One of the stars of *NASCAR Wives.*

"So with this I can install a rootkit that eats my own tail while I'm still inside. It's like a cloaking device. Fucking gorgeous."

"See, that sounded cool. That's what I'm talking about."

"You want to be an elite member or platinum?"

"Um."

"You're right, we better stick to elite. Platinum's pushing our luck." Christina wrapped "William_Mackler" in the same code that swaddled the other names, hit Enter for the final time, and spun in her chair to face him. "Welcome to the Driverless Chrome Club." She laughed at his expression. "Wipe the Thursday Feeling off your face before it gets stuck that way."

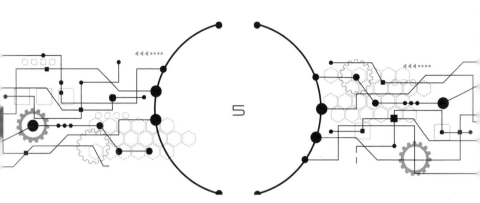

5

The chance of William actually being selected as one of the semifinalists was so laughably remote, a million to one. . . .

And yet here she was, hanging out in the CB Lounge with Melissa Faber and Daniel Benson, watching the Derby come down to William and four others.

She should have known.

"His hair looks like shit," Melissa said.

Christina realized she'd been scratching her scalp, and wiped her finger on the towel hanging from the drawer.

"It's eighty-seven degrees out there."

She was struck by the weariness in her voice. She felt wrung out, as if her brain had been squeezed dry of its power to think. And she'd been in her air-conditioned basement, sitting in a comfy chair. She couldn't imagine how William felt. An empathetic wave of parking-lot heat blossomed in her chest. She began to sweat.

It was horribly selfish of her to root against William. Autonomous was worth $1.8 million! He could sell it after their road trip and quit his job at Tanski's Scrap Metal, which had transitioned from part-time to full-time as soon as he'd miraculously graduated from Fremont Hills High. He could take a break to figure out what he wanted to do with his life. Christina could help him with that. She imagined the two of them sitting in their booth at Hilda's Country Kitchen, plotting ways to get William into the University at Buffalo. Maybe if he started at Fremont Hills Community College, built up a solid semester of credits . . .

Yeah, right. William would never sell that car. He'd be the only person in America who took a Driverless prototype to his job at a scrap-metal yard.

"He's not answering me," Daniel said, attacking his phone with freakishly long thumbs.

Christina's head felt like it weighed fifty pounds. She put her elbow on the desk and propped up her chin. She stared into the screen, letting her eyes go slack. Autonomous was now headed due south. Her eyes drifted to the room full of YouTube stars. The bros from the DudeTown channel were high-fiving. Jessa Park was dancing with the PearlyGreats, a Christian comedy trio.

The astronaut at the front of Autonomous, who'd been forced to walk backward, stumbled and just barely kept her balance before gracefully putting up her hands and walking away, shaking her head.

Christina took a deep breath.

"Everybody turn around!" Melissa sounded suddenly chipper.

Christina looked over her shoulder. Melissa was holding her

phone up to take a picture of the three of them with William and Autonomous on the screen in the background.

Christina said what she always said right before a picture: "Wait."

Melissa composed her face into a coy smile, lips pursed, like a mask snapping into place. Daniel leaned over Christina's head to put his tanned arm around Melissa. Christina wondered if he went to a tanning salon. Fremont Hills wasn't exactly a beach town.

Melissa tapped the screen, and a second later, her face melted back to its resting state. Daniel dropped his arm.

"Don't Glam this one up," he said. "It makes me look orange."

Glam was the filter used by celebrities to hide blemishes and whiten teeth and smooth out skin.

"Too late," Melissa said, tapping. "You got Glammed."

"Don't post that, please," Christina said.

"Posted," Melissa announced.

Christina turned back to the computer screen. The likelihood of anyone connecting Christina Hernandez with one of her dark web handles was incredibly slim, but she still didn't like her face being plastered all over social networks. She imagined some malicious bot crawling the data embedded in Melissa's photos like a spider spinning a web along a musty old picture in a frame, executing commands to infiltrate Christina's personal life and leave her exposed.

She wished she could wipe away her paranoia with a dish towel, or reach inside her brain and scoop out the bad thoughts.

Autonomous sped up.

William faltered, then righted himself. His hand hadn't left the windshield. The contestants were jogging at a decent clip.

Sunlight slid like radiant eels along the car's silver roof. There were four contestants left—two on each side—and Christina couldn't help but think of pallbearers at some weird dystopian funeral.

They were headed straight for the parking-lot exit. There was only one way to go: out into a five-lane highway, which hadn't been blocked off for the Derby.

Traffic thundered past the lot at 75 miles per hour.

The combined digital energy of 4.3 million people simultaneously freaking out across every social network seemed to bleed into the CB Lounge.

Jessa Park stopped dancing.

"There's no way this is right," Daniel said in disbelief. He was clutching his phone in two hands as if it were a religious totem.

"Let go, Mackler," Christina muttered.

"They have to stop it," Melissa said firmly. "They'll just have to shut it down."

Autonomous cruised down the exit ramp, past the mall's big marquee sign that boasted Macy's and Best Buy and dozens of smaller stores.

"It's not stopping," Daniel said. He turned to Christina, as if she hadn't noticed. "It's not stopping."

The contestants were running now, legs pumping, struggling to keep up. The second AutoNoyz host, older than Stick Bug and burdened with a beer gut, tripped over his feet and face-planted into the cement. He sprawled with his arms out straight, as if he'd been frozen in the act of stealing home.

"Let go!" Christina implored the screen.

"What is he doing?" Hysteria crept into Melissa's voice.

"He's not gonna let go," Daniel said with hushed admiration

that made Christina want to fry his insides with a Ward of Conflagration.

The trust-fund kid, whose perpetually beaming smile had been wiped from his face, shoved himself clear of the car. His 3-D smartwatch left a vaporous holo-trail in the air. He staggered onto one of the mall's chemically enhanced strips of neon grass, where he fell to his knees.

Christina's heart pounded. It was down to William and Natalie Sharpe, and they both seemed to be chugging along just fine. Autonomous reached the end of the exit ramp and nosed out into the first highway lane without slowing down.

Both contestants held on.

"No, no, no," Christina said. She felt as though she were a drone buzzing about the CB Lounge, viewing them all from above. There was a thick, dreamy quality to the air in the room. She had the absurd notion that she could simply pull the plug on Kimberly and make it all go away.

"William, *move!*" Melissa leaned forward to shout at the screen and waved her arm wildly as if she could shoo him away from traffic and magically compel him to safety.

Not even Dierdrax could do that.

Melissa's hand hit the side of her glass and sent Red Bull sloshing off the desk, fizzing angrily, soaking the carpet.

A black Escalade raced down the sun-blasted interstate toward the side of Autonomous. In seconds, William would be crushed between the cars.

Christina closed her eyes.

What had she done?

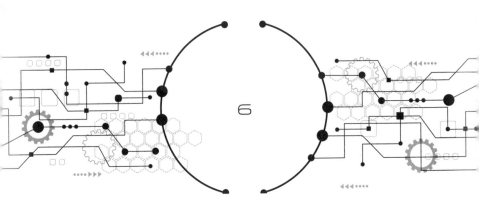

6

A horn blast registered at the edge of William's awareness.

It was very hot.

His legs were churning robotically, matching the pace of the hulking silver beast beside him. He could not remember his last sip of water. A big black car screamed past, swerving to miss Autonomous by inches. No, not a car, an SUV, an Escalade—he'd recently seen one demolished down at Tanski's. Cars and people were both so easily broken down into scraps of what they had been.

"Come on!"

Pain shot up his arm. Someone was tugging viciously at his wrist. William turned his head.

"Snap out of it!" Natalie Sharpe was wrenching his arm from its socket, trying to pull him toward the highway median, which dipped into a grassy runoff ditch. Her face was twisted with determination. William's eyes were drawn to a piercing that seemed to float in the middle of her cheek, a silver stud that completed a constellation of metal: septum, industrial, lower lip, all of them flashing with brilliant white light.

Some distant part of him was bemused. He'd never been this close to a famous person before. Her big speech from *Street Legal 3: Carpocalypse* echoed in his mind.

They might just be metal and rubber to you, but to us they're family. . . .

"You won, you stupid bastard!" she screamed. "It's over!"

Autonomous was rolling into the center lane. In the hazy heat that shimmered up from the highway, William could see cars bearing down upon them. Unbidden, his mind cataloged them: crimson BMW Z4, yellow Pontiac Aztek, tangerine Nissan Cube, a cosmic escort of fiery colors birthed from the heart of the sun.

He transferred his blank gaze back to Natalie Sharpe and kept one hand firmly planted against Autonomous. Her face slackened in disbelief and she dropped his arm. He watched her sprint away, stopping short as a minivan screamed past in the fifth lane. Then she scampered onward and disappeared below the lip of the median.

Autonomous slowed as if to place William directly in the approaching cars' path. His awareness surged with anticipation of pain. What would it feel like to have his entire midsection from pelvis to rib cage collapsed by two tons of steel traveling at 75 miles per hour? If he was to be flung into the air, would he leave his shoes behind, empty Converse smoking on the pavement? Was it possible that he would be cleaved in two by the impact?

Would he see his own body broken and ruined before his vision failed him?

The world sharpened, and for a moment he saw everything so clearly. The Aztek's windshield had been pocked by an upflung pebble. He knew the pain would be exquisite, a trip over the edge, the screen upon which the film of his life would unspool. The arc his limp body would describe in the air was the story of William Mackler from birth to death.

He was astonished to find that he was calm enough to examine the way he felt. He knew he should be scared, but such bone-deep existential terror—*this is the end of everything!*—was impossible for him to dredge up. It simply was not there for him to access.

Without even trying, he was having what knights and kings and stoic medieval-fantasy types referred to as "a good death." Meeting it bravely and just accepting that it was time to move on.

The cars were coming impossibly fast and he could see their drivers' eyes. Pale horses, pale riders. His phone buzzed in his pocket. Probably just Tommy calling to check on him. The Macklers were on a family plan. They were people who learned from each other and knit their talents together. His brother taught him to snowboard, his father taught him to hunt, his mother taught him to play guitar, that battered old Ovation acoustic she kept on a stand in the corner of the living room. They'd taken that guitar on vacation to Texas Hill Country, and William had snapped a picture of his brother on the edge of a cliff, holding the guitar aloft like a rock star letting that last chord ring out across the stadium. William was going to practice every day and his best friend Daniel was going to learn bass and they were going to find a drummer, but instead Daniel had found basketball and volunteering and AP classes and Melissa Faber. That was okay. William loved Melissa too. She was way more interesting than anybody gave her credit for, and he knew, like you might recognize a friend in a dream even though the figure bore no resemblance to the real person, that Melissa would be the CEO of a big company one day—he could almost see what kind of company it would be, some kind of fashion-world tech firm that would land her on the cover of *Forbes*. It was okay that they'd never started a band, because William got to spend his time hanging out with Christina, who kept the CB Lounge neat as a force field protecting her from the junk upstairs. Christina's stand against her parents struck William as noble and courageous in a way it never had before, and he reached up toward the sky, toward the swarm of drones capturing his every movement, and waved one final time to his friends, his best friends. He saw them all, a decade from now, gathered around his grave on a drizzly afternoon, Melissa and Daniel kneeling together, Christina hanging back a little, maintaining her personal space, always.

How strange to have known them.

How strange to have *been*.

He could smell gasoline, exhaust, sweat.

When Autonomous stopped completely, a gentle peace settled over William, and he dropped his hand from the window so that he could square up to the oncoming cars and meet them head-on.

A good death.

The Aztek stopped first, and the other two cars screeched to a halt beside it.

William assumed he was in the process of being tossed in the air or crushed against Autonomous, and his vision had frozen upon this final image. He could not feel a thing. That was okay.

The door of the Aztek opened, and a man stepped out and began walking toward him. A woman came from the Z4 and joined the man. The pair wore black pants and tight black T-shirts imprinted with the Driverless logo.

They were both smiling.

William no longer understood what was happening. His legs did not want to keep holding him up, and he sat down on the cement.

It was very hot.

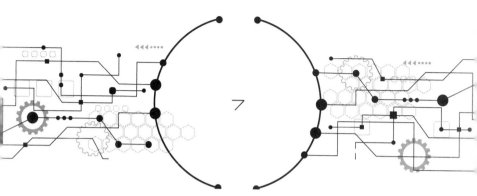

7

D aniel Benson's fingers pressed divots into the soft headrest of Christina's chair. His attempt to respect her personal space had been thwarted by William's mad dash into traffic, which had drawn his face to the screen. His best friend's recklessness had a tractor-beam quality.

"Jesus Christ!" Melissa's nose was practically smushed against the monitor. "Are you literally trying to kill us?"

"He can't hear you, Fabes," Daniel said. Melissa snatched her phone from the desk, and her thumbs went to work. Daniel imagined her texting *Are you literally trying to kill us?*

"Five bucks," Christina muttered. She was leaning forward in her chair, practically folded in half with tension.

Melissa set her phone down and used both hands to adjust her bra straps, a little upward tug on each side. Daniel cataloged the movement. His girlfriend was an outfit adjuster, accessory fidgeter, tortoiseshell hair clip unclipper. She reminded him of a baseball coach signaling the catcher, transmitting signs by tapping hat brim and belt buckle and shoulders in rapid succession. "And now he's just sitting," she said.

William's performance had sent them all coiling inward, and they had yet to relax and exhale. Someone had to be the first to break the spell with a hearty *HE WON! ROAD TRIP, YOU GUYS!*

Daniel opened his mouth but couldn't form words. The proper tone eluded him. He should be hugging Melissa, rocking Christina in her chair, flipping out; instead he just stared at the screen, slack-jawed and moronic, as the camera zeroed in on William's blank face.

The atmosphere in the room made Daniel feel like he was frozen at the very top of his jump shot right before he released the ball, gravity and fundamentals intertwining to suspend him in the air, plastered to the void.

"Oh my God, he's trending." Melissa pointed at the screen on the right side of Christina's triple monitor setup. Daniel's eyes followed. William Mackler had joined the ranks of such nationally trending topics as #ATVfails and #GoatVideoGames.

"He's in good company," Christina said. Her right hand moved to the top of her head. "There really is something seriously wrong with him."

Melissa stood on her tiptoes and stretched her arms straight up, fingertips scraping the low stucco ceiling. Her armpits were perfectly smooth. Daniel wondered if she'd shaved them at some point during their all-night internet vigil. "I can't even with him," she said, dropping her arms.

"That had to have been staged," Christina said. "They wouldn't just let him get run over. Right?"

On the central screen, the drone zoomed out so viewers could see a blandly handsome man and willowy woman in formfitting black outfits reach out their hands to help William to his feet. He gazed up at them, dumbstruck, as if experiencing an alien visitation. "It's so weird that everybody knows who William Mackler is now. Like, *our* William Mackler. From Fremont Hills. Jessa Park knows his name." Melissa intertwined her fingers with Daniel's and glanced at the screen on the left. Jessa Park was speaking directly to the camera, but Christina had long ago cut the audio from that particular feed. A sign on the wall behind Jessa said CREATIVITY + PASSION + SWEAT + DREAMS = JESSPIRATION.

The faint electric thrill that his girlfriend's touch never failed to deliver made Daniel supremely conscious of his heartbeat. It didn't seem quite right, thumping too high in his chest, each beat radiating into his upper arms, leaving him disturbingly achy. Melissa smiled at him. He tried to smile back, but he could tell by her eyes that he'd twisted his face into something grotesque.

The sleepless night had left him wrung out. He hadn't gone for a run or hit the gym for Leg Day. Now he'd have to turn what should have been Arm Day into a makeup Leg Day, like a total scrub.

"Moonshadow, here we come," she said. "Remember to pack a bathing suit."

I'm actually gonna skinny-dip the whole time, he thought about saying. *Just say it*, he urged himself. *Speak. Make words.*

Would Melissa think that was funny? It would depend on his delivery. Movie Daniel would absolutely nail it.

"The Moonshadow Festival's in the middle of the desert,"

Christina said. "But hey, now William owns a Driverless proto-type car. Which is insane. Maybe that's a thing we should talk about."

Melissa squeezed Daniel's hand. "He really did it. He's famous."

Daniel returned the squeeze. He should be lifting Melissa up, spinning around, laughing. His best friend had just done something incredible in front of millions of people! But living in the moment was the unattainable holy grail of consciousness. Nobody could really do it, everybody's thoughts pinged back and forth mindlessly, stupidly. . . .

William was on his feet, and the two black-clad models were ushering him to the shoulder of the highway, where reporters were jockeying for position. He shuffled like a sedated patient toward the makeshift press conference. Melissa dropped Daniel's hand and leaned over the desk. Christina shrank away as if Melissa smelled, which was impossible. Daniel had been in extremely close proximity to every inch of Melissa Faber for the past two years, and she always gave off the freshly scrubbed air of a girl perpetually stepping out of the shower.

Melissa reached for the keyboard, and Christina blocked it with her forearm. "What's CB Lounge rule number one?"

Melissa tried to snake her fingers around the blockade. Christina added a second forearm, hiding the entire keyboard.

Melissa sighed. "Nobody touches the computer except me." She shook her head. *"You."*

"So what the hell?"

"I just want to see your music."

"William's about to talk."

"So we should cue up something good for after, like a Moonshadow kind of song. We're supposed to be celebrating here."

"It's hard for me to celebrate when that puddle of nasty corporate energy drink is soaking into my carpet."

"You can't say *corporate* like the things you have don't come from big companies too."

Christina plucked a hand towel from the drawer and handed it to Melissa. "Dab, don't wipe."

Melissa examined the towel's tag. "Martha Stewart Collection!" she cried triumphantly.

As Melissa turned her attention to the carpet, Daniel lost himself in the central screen. His gaze swept past William to the runoff ditch that ran alongside the highway, into which Natalie Sharpe had scampered to seal William's victory. The girls' voices receded into a kind of rubbery unreal distance. Daniel focused on the sharp curve of the earth, the surprisingly steep drop-off, the neon grass. As a little kid, he'd been obsessed with pictures of natural fortifications and trench formations, anything that could be used as a defensive barrier. It was the kind of thing that would make sense only to an eight-year-old, but it had left him with an image that persisted through the years: his brain was surrounded by a brackish moat.

Melissa worked on the Red Bull spill while Christina cycled through mentions of William online. GIFs came and went, little flashes of animated clips and cats being acrobatic. Daniel felt like he was watching an art installation behind a smeared pane of glass. He picked at one of his thumb's fresh hangnails.

Melissa's fanned-out fingers moved up and down before his

eyes. "Yoo-hoo! William's alive, Daniel. He *won*. We're going to Moonshadow!"

He attempted a laid-back grin. Melissa placed a cool palm against his bare shoulder. "You look exhausted." She moved her hand down to squeeze his biceps. "No offense."

He nodded as eagerly as he could. "I *am* exhausted. You look very un-exhausted and hot." He lifted her hand to his lips and kissed the knuckle of her middle finger.

"William's up," Christina announced. She unmuted the main livestream, and the basement room was filled with the crowd's soft murmur.

There was William, his sweat-plastered hair sticking to his forehead. Someone handed him a fancy water, a cylindrical bottle from a brand called Purifique, which Daniel had never heard of. William swigged, and water ran down his face, soaking his shirt. He looked as if he were just beginning to reinhabit his body after a long absence.

Daniel stood with his arm across Melissa's shoulders, a position he'd jokingly assumed a million times as an excuse to let his hand flop casually against her left breast. During the first Derby bathroom break, William had texted him about the car's privacy setting. Apparently you could wrap yourself up with another person in some kind of soundproof cocoon.

The livestream abandoned the drones in favor of a head-on shot from a stationary camera. Sunlight flashing in William's sweaty hair gave him an airbrushed quality. Behind him, Autonomous was parked where it had come to a stop, perpendicular to traffic's normal flow, a silver barrier that gleamed impassively. The car's tinted windows, lustrous paint job, and eerie stillness gave Daniel the impression of a military vehicle from an alternate universe. It looked like the kind of car that should have NEO-TOKYO POLICE emblazoned on its side.

He had a flash of walking into Mr. Marczewski's seventh-grade science room after school to find the chairs arranged in a circle. Sitting across from him was a skinny wisp of a girl in an Avenged Sevenfold shirt with a comet-tail streak of crimson in her hair: Christina Hernandez, Anime Club Treasurer and Fanfiction Editor in Chief. She held a fireproof lockbox in her lap, petty cash and Neo-Tokyo Police stickers. . . .

That was five whole years ago! Since joining and quitting Anime Club, he'd piled up ribbons and certificates and plaques, drawers full of awards for citizenship and attendance, prizes for essays he barely remembered writing. There were tough morning runs, predawn slogs through his wintry neighborhood, snot flash-freezing above his lip, just Daniel and the paperboys and the occasional dreamy run-in with the Fremont Hills Jesus, the long-haired guy who rode a bike with a tie-dyed flag and collected cans from trash bins. Unauthorized evenings in the high school weight room after basketball practice, alone and unspotted on the bench press. Late nights pounding his dad's old heavy bag that dangled on its chain from the basement rafters, his bare feet stuck with bits of kitty litter that escaped the corner where his sisters' cats, Taylor and Swift, did their business.

Varsity basketball, National Honor Society, Yearbook Committee, Future Business Leaders of America, Leo Club, Mock Trial, Habitat for Humanity, Stock Market Club.

On the screen, William was joined in front of the car by

a reporter from a local Indiana news station, a petite woman whose tan skin glistened in the heat. She stuck a microphone in his face, and his head darted back sharply.

"Whoa, there!" She beamed at him. "I don't bite, I swear! So, William, you just won your very own Driverless car! That's gotta feel pretty good."

William stared at the reporter, who gave him a quick nod to urge him on. He glanced over his shoulder at Autonomous, as if to remind himself what they were talking about. The reporter tried to draw him out. "Hey now, are you even old enough to drive?"

"Uh, I'm seventeen," William said. He turned his head to look directly into the camera and seemed startled by its presence.

"Deer, meet headlights," Melissa said.

Come on, buddy, Daniel urged silently. *Get it together.* He had the absurd notion that his own mental state was linked with William's, and if his friend would just snap out of it, he'd provide salvation for them both. He wished there was something he could do to kick-start William's default setting, obnoxious overconfidence. If only that reporter knew how much William loved biting the ends off a Twizzler to make a straw and using it to drink soda. A Twizzler-Coke would perk him right up.

William gazed deeply into the camera. His face slackened, and Daniel was concerned that his friend might simply collapse. But William's eyes flashed in sudden recognition, as if he'd seen something familiar in the lens. He leaned toward the reporter as if he were letting her in on a little secret.

"And I'm pretty sure you don't need a license to drive a Driverless car."

The reporter laughed. "Right, you just sit back and enjoy the ride." William grinned. Abruptly, he seemed flushed with personality rather than oppressive heat. "Now let's talk about your strategy here today," the reporter continued. "Did you have a game plan coming in, or did you just go with the flow?"

William nodded sagely, as if he'd expected the question. "I'm glad you asked me that, uh . . ."

"Carol."

"My game plan was to win, Carol. Plain and simple."

"That's not really—"

"Because losing is unacceptable to me."

"Aaaaand here we go," Christina said. She sounded resigned. Daniel was struck by a surge of awareness, a sharpening of the room's edges, as if reality had just finished buffering. He caught a whiff of Red Bull.

On the screen, William rambled on. "My three best friends are about to go away to college, so winning this car and going on this road trip was all that mattered to me. I look at it like this: You've only got one shot at the things that really count, so you might as well give it everything you got. Because one day it's all gonna come to an end, and you don't want to look back and think, *Damn, I didn't do everything I could to make life awesome for the people I love the most.*"

A pleasant shudder rippled through Daniel's upper body. Melissa hip checked him playfully. "Twitchy McTwitch."

Daniel's heartbeat no longer broadcast each thump. He was flooded with an appreciation for the kind of friend William really was, and struck by a vivid memory of meeting him in tenth grade. The new kid, William Mackler, sitting in the assigned seat next to Daniel in Honors Chemistry (how strange to think of William as an honors student; he'd fallen off that track as soon as the fall semester was finished). Their lab table was last in the row, enabling clandestine Bunsen-burner shenanigans. He recalled a shared affinity for the word *catalyst*, which invaded their everyday vocabulary.

You see we got Pizza Combos in the vending machine now?

Already catalyzed 'em.

Daniel pulled Melissa close and reveled in her closeness. He held his beautiful girlfriend and watched his best friend handle an interview on national TV with grace and poise. The reporter's eyes shone. William had become effortlessly charming. He was so good at going into strange situations and bending them to his will and just generally kicking ass. What an ineffable quality, this ability to make other people proud to know you.

The camera zoomed in to frame William's face as he spoke, the camera operator realizing that he was filming something special. Daniel gave thanks to this anonymous TV news employee, felt a momentary kinship with a total stranger.

"I promise this will be the most epic road trip of all time," William said, "and we're gonna do a ton of insane shit—" He glanced off to the side and lowered his voice. "Can I say 'shit'?" He turned back to the camera. "Some totally insane stuff. So if you want to see what we're up to, just follow my friend, the beautiful and talented Melissa Faber"—he rattled off her online handles—"because she'll be doing our social media outreach, or whatever. Hashtag Autonomous Road Trip."

"Oh my God," Christina said. She propped her elbows on the desk and let her head fall into her hands.

Melissa left Daniel's side with a little shimmy that he found breathtakingly adorable. She grabbed her phone from the desk and beheld its screen with openmouthed awe. "I'm getting followers like . . ." Her eyes went wide.

"Social media outreach," Christina moaned into her palms.

The camera pulled back to show the reporter and William together.

"Sounds like it's going to be quite the ride," Carol said. "I'm sure we'll all be following along. One more thing before we sign off—I know I'm personally wondering this, so I have to ask, when did you realize the car pulling out onto the highway, all the traffic coming at you—when did you realize it was all a setup?"

William looked bewildered. "Uh . . . setup?"

"You did realize that it was all part of the show, right?"

William gestured for the microphone. He took it gently from her hand, held it up to his mouth, and looked directly into the camera.

"No."

He opened his hand, and the microphone dropped out of view. There was a dry thud, a burst of feedback, and then silence. William walked away without another word, leaving Carol standing alone with Autonomous. She looked off camera, frowned—and the livestream cut to a drone's-eye view of Autonomous.

A whole week in that thing, Daniel thought, anxiety blossoming in his chest. William had just put it all on the line to win them the experience of a lifetime, and Daniel was determined not to screw it up for everybody.

He texted William: *Way to catalyze that interview.*

Melissa tapped Christina on the shoulder. "Snap out of it, X-Tina."

Slowly, Christina raised her head and regarded Melissa with weary raccoon eyes. "Don't call me that."

"We're going to Moonshadow in a million-dollar party car, mama! We have to start making a playlist."

"Right, I'm Guatemalan, so go ahead and throw 'mama' around."

"I didn't mean it like that, just pull up TuneGarage."

"I don't use TuneGarage. I don't want it knowing what I listen to."

Melissa looked helplessly at Daniel and put her hands on her hips.

"We should probably practice *not* getting on each other's nerves," he said.

"You know what?" Melissa said. "Forget it. I'll be responsible for the official road trip playlist, and the rest of you can maybe just suck it."

As if to demonstrate her commitment to playlist curation, she sat down on the love seat and swept her thumb across her phone screen in a way that Daniel found soothing. It was like watching someone tend one of those little meditation gardens, raking patterns in the sand.

His phone buzzed. He entered the password to log into Epheme, an app that erased your chats as soon as you logged off. Unlike similar apps, Epheme chats were impossible to screenshot. The data simply vanished.

A message appeared on his screen.

xoxoPixieDustxoxo: I got a surprise for you

He glanced over at Melissa. She was lost in her phone, oblivious. He wrote back.

DB837651: I gotta take a nap

xoxoPixieDustxoxo: Mmm sounds nice

DB837651: Then I'll come by

xoxoPixieDustxoxo: Bring SNACKS. See you later alligator

DB837651: Something something crocodile

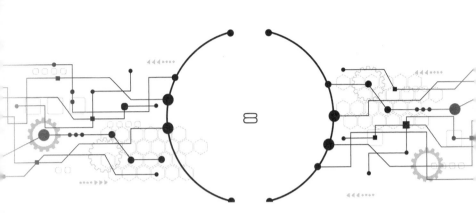

8

Melissa Faber slid the damask curtain aside but kept the French doors to her balcony closed. It was an afternoon for cranked central air and activities to keep her awake until a legit bedtime. After a sleepless night, it was always better to power through the day, at least until nine or ten. That theory had helped her cope with plenty of senior year all-nighters. She rated it 7.5 on her personal growth chart, putting it in the top tier of wellness-related #lifehacks.

@TheMelissaFayBrr had picked up 349 new followers since William's shout-out. She put her phone into the back pocket of her Natasha Lynn Chao cutoffs, then took it out again.

361 new followers.

Melissa didn't anticipate a problem staying awake. She was totally wired from Red Bull and disbelief. William had actually done it, and soon they'd be hitting the road in that gorgeous car, untethered from their Fremont Hills lives, free from summer's last gasp of parental oversight. Her thoughts were tinged with the flashy brightness of a movie poster, a summer blockbuster, all sexy chrome curves and lens flares. It was as if Autonomous was driving through her mind, sweeping her thoughts along in its wake, memories of high school and the anticipation of NYU swirling in its hot exhaust.

She clicked a nail against the window. Daniel's black-dots-on-crimson design made it look like an unfinished ladybug. His nail-art suggestions were an inside joke between them that they both found mildly exciting, like the G-rated version of Daniel picking out underwear for her, which she'd allowed him to do exactly once and then never again.

387 new followers.

She opened her music library and cast a song to her bedroom's wireless speakers: Carina Tyler's "Not Tonight." The song took her back to her first few months with Daniel, when he would come to her locker before homeroom and lift her up in a giddy, spinning hug. The kind of greeting you'd give someone you hadn't seen in years, delivered every morning by Daniel Benson in the orange-locker wing of Fremont Hills High, where the F through J names lived.

Halfway through the first verse, Carina Tyler's candy-coated belting jangled her nerves. She switched to wordless synthy washes, the electronic soundtrack to the movie *Saracen Heights*.

392 new followers.

She turned away from the window and went to the studio in the corner of her bedroom, separated from her living space by a sectional sofa. Two fabric-draped busts flanked a sewing table like absurdly decorated guards. The table was piled with samples: muslin, taffeta, chiffon, denim. Just beyond the table was a wheeled clothing rack where her latest rompers hung in order from practice attempts to perfected designs.

411 new followers.

Part of the space was devoted to her YouTube channel, which she planned to launch as soon as she edited hours of raw footage into a series of brisk, helpful videos that didn't make her want to claw her face off. There was a camera set up on a tripod aimed at an Eames chair. Her tutorials were modeled on Food Network shows, in which she'd lay out the elements of a dress in stages, ending with a finished product she'd already completed, so she could film the final segment wearing it. Her latest practice video, "From the Beach to the Boardwalk," involved a cheery sundress with an asymmetrical hemline—perfect for the boho maxi crowd and girls who liked to keep it simple and playful. She'd been working on it right up to the moment the Derby began, and her studio was in disarray. The fabric piles on her sewing table were like sediments in an archaeological dig. She set her phone down and plucked a frilly piece from the pile at random. She'd been experimenting with it around mid-March, thinking ahead to summer designs, lacy cap-sleeved tops that had never quite come together.

March had been a busy month, with simmering tension on the Prom Committee reaching Cuban Missile Crisis proportions thanks to Charlene Delmonico's teeth-grinding incompetence. Melissa had allowed herself to become distracted.

Not for the first time, she wondered if going to college would be an even bigger distraction. What if during the time she spent on pointless classes, some other girl ascended to YouTube superstardom with a similar concept?

Jessa Park had launched her channel at sixteen.

If Melissa's channel started to take off, she would probably drop out. Her parents would be pissed, but what could they say if she was pulling down YouTube advertising dollars and launching her clothing line and initiating her long-term strategy for multi-platform dominance? Since she wasn't planning on asking her parents for a dime of start-up capital, the answer was *nothing*. She would be living in New York City, completely self-sufficient, and in control of her destiny.

427 new followers, including a popular influencer, Tyrone Cain, who'd quit his job to travel the world taking pictures of waterfalls and amassed 986,000 followers of his own. Melissa felt a little jolt shimmy up her arm. These kinds of connections were essential for the growth of her brand.

Her phone chimed with three distinct tones, a little melody that quickened her heart. She used Epheme for chatting with one specific person, and when she logged in, his message was waiting for her.

Ash:	You promised me a new one.
SewWhat:	Crazy night! One sec.
Ash:	Can I at least get some hold music?
SewWhat:	La la la la

Melissa sifted through the clothes hanging from the rack beside the sewing table. She changed into a two-tone romper, shorts the color of tarnished brass joined at an elastic waistline with a top made from genuine fuligin, the only material darker than black. With her bedroom wall as a backdrop, she took nine selfies. In the best one, she was glancing at something just out of frame, lips slightly parted, as if she'd just recognized someone on the street and at the same time realized she didn't want to get his attention after all. She studied her eyes and confirmed that she was properly smizing. Then she sent the pic.

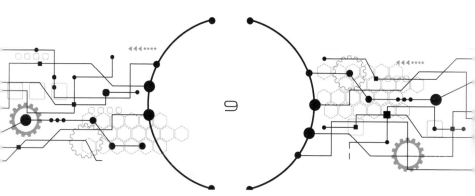

9

A patch of the CB Lounge rug sported what looked like spiky peaks of gelled hair. Melissa had done a half-assed job, and now Christina attacked the spill with ferocity, sacrificing two hand towels in the process. When she was done, the rug had attained its normal softness, but a sickly sweet smell lingered. She retrieved the heavy artillery from her desk drawer: a Glade PlugIn, sandalwood scented.

Achievement unlocked.

Christina felt grungy, the husk of a sleepless night clinging to her. But the thought of venturing Upstairs for a shower gave her the heebie-jeebies. She had to mentally prepare for that expedition and was nowhere near full HP/MP.

She sat down at her desk. The essence of Melissa Faber and Daniel Benson hung around like stale smoke in a used car. Before the Derby, all the time she'd spent with Fremont Hills' Hottest Couple in her entire life didn't add up to twenty-seven hours. Their interactions consisted mostly of awkward overlaps, when William picked Daniel up before dropping Christina off, or when William and Christina got out of a movie and bumped into them in the food court.

If William, Daniel, and Melissa's friendship was an equilateral triangle, Christina was the outlier dangling from William's point like a stray vector. Most of the time, that was okay. There were entanglements that non–Next-Door Neighbor Friends would never understand, the insatiable need to amuse and entertain each other that had united them since the first time William had knocked on her door to borrow a bike pump.

But now she was facing a road trip full of constant reminders that she was William's secret buddy, the basement-dwelling phantom who stalked the fringes of Fremont Hills High.

Don't do it, Christina.

She traced a fingernail lightly against her scalp, enjoying the delicious anticipation of a future scratching. Kimberly's speakers blasted the mordant sludge of Dethroned Kings.

You're better than this.

Her collection of rare action figures and anime toys scrutinized her from the desk. She'd acquired them in dark web trades—all except for Kalodyn Zero, which William had gotten her for her birthday. Kalodyn Zero occupied the place of honor on top of her central monitor, his white hair combed back into a mane that scraggled down to his waist.

Her fingers tingled in proximity to her keyboard. She woke Kimberly from her slumber. The surface-level internet junk was mercifully absent. Jessa Park and YouTube and the social media circle jerk had been wiped from her screen as soon as Daniel and Melissa left.

Christina booted up her newest dark web acquisition:

MKM-149, an intercept device that NSA whistleblowers had uncovered years ago. Now they floated from black market circles to private systems in the same way that old Soviet military hardware wound up in the arsenals of two-bit warlords. The MKM-149 was nicknamed "the seashell" for its ability to "hear" an ocean of data. It was as if Kimberly had suddenly been upgraded to Cerebro, Professor X's impossibly powerful machine. Since Christina didn't have telepathic powers, or an NSA instruction manual, the data was impossible to filter: millions of texts and emails and direct messages and online dating nudges flooding her screen, their basic encryptions rendering them useless unless she knew exactly what to pluck from the gibberish stream like a hand fisherman snatching a minnow from a river.

Before Melissa and Daniel came over, she had focused the seashell on a ten-foot radius, so that it was only sweeping the CB Lounge. Once it identified Melissa's and Daniel's signals, the seashell "painted" them like a patient drinking barium to highlight organs in a CT scan. Now the private words of Fremont Hills' Hottest Couple lit up the data stream.

Christina banished the white noise and let the seashell decrypt the past few hours of Daniel's and Melissa's mobile lives. Her heart began to pound and she closed her eyes. She could still put Kimberly to sleep and venture Upstairs for that shower, before she saw something she could never unsee.

Had anyone in the history of hacking ever gotten this close and possessed the willpower to back off?

She opened her eyes.

The seashell had snagged a few Epheme chats from the ether, chats that were supposed to have destroyed themselves. Of course that was bullshit—nothing was ever truly gone. Daniel was obviously DB837651, which made xoxoPixieDustxoxo Melissa . . . but wait. There was an image of Melissa, posing in a hideous jumper or romper or whatever. Her handle was SewWhat, and she was sending the pic to somebody named Ash.

Christina's eyes pinged back and forth between Daniel's chat with PixieDust and Melissa's chat with Ash.

Kalodyn Zero watched impassively from atop the monitor.

"Don't look at me like that." She pulled the plastic warrior from his pedestal and set him facedown on the desk. Then she copied the intercepted chats over to a blank document and began to type underneath them.

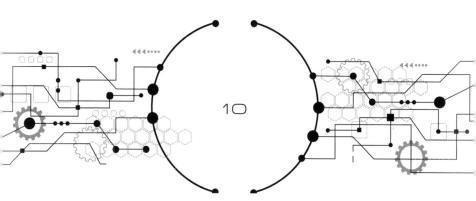

10

Three days after his Derby victory, William woke from a chrome-tinted dream to find the Driverless car parked in his driveway. He stood at the bedroom window in his boxers and marveled at the vehicle. It must have dropped itself off sometime during the night, creeping softly through the dark streets, spooking the Fremont Hills Jesus on his bicycle trek to nowhere.

Whenever his mother came home late, the lights of her ancient Camry blasted through his wonky blinds, sweeping across the X Games panoramas on his wall and splintering his sleep with white-hot urgency that left him sitting up in bed, panting and confused. Autonomous must have killed its headlights before turning into his driveway.

He wondered if the car was designed to be courteous or if it already knew about his shallow sleep. The incident with the Smiths song had occurred to him fleetingly over the past seventy-two hours of podcast interviews and email exchanges with reporters from *Motor Trend* and *Car and Driver* and an extremely pushy guy from *Wired*. He'd dismissed it as a product of his sun-scorched mind, but he couldn't shake the crisp blue letters coalescing into *William, It Was Really Nothing*. Even while accepting the memory as fraudulent, it had evolved into an unlikely theory: Autonomous had selected him. The car had wanted William Mackler to win—not the #SweatyNormcore guy or Natalie Sharpe or Lexie the Human Selfie Stick.

"That's my car," he said out loud. It didn't seem remotely possible, like pointing to a Hollywood mansion on Google Earth and saying, "That's my house." Autonomous looked laughably out of place in his driveway, an impossible car beamed to Fremont Hills from the future, parked next to his mother's rust-pocked Camry.

He wished somebody from Driverless had emailed him with a heads-up. Then he could have set an alarm and been ready to go. But maybe somebody had and he'd totally missed it—after the Derby, his inbox had swelled to terrifying proportions.

William's desk was littered with skateboard wheels, a set of socket wrenches, empty Twizzlers wrappers, a leaning tower of cereal bowls, the broken strap of a ski boot, and a paintball helmet that made him look like Master Chief from *Halo*. He freed his laptop from the clutter and opened it. A cozy animated office appeared on the screen. William's point of view was that of a patient on a couch. Across from him was a leather armchair in which his online therapist sat with a yellow legal pad perched on one knee. Dr. Diaz was an avuncular middle-aged man with salt-and-pepper hair and a habit of twirling his pen along his knuckles. An orange tabby cat was curled up at his feet. William assumed this was supposed to be cute, but Dr. Diaz's developers had apparently forgotten that cats liked to move around from time to time, so the cat just sat there, motionless, without even a languid flick of its tail.

To William, eleven hours had passed since he'd closed the lid of his laptop, effectively pausing their session. But Dr. Diaz was always there, always on call, never sleeping or leaving his office. For all Dr. Diaz knew, eleven seconds instead of eleven hours had elapsed since William's last message.

At least, William hoped that was how his therapist perceived time. Otherwise the doctor was trapped in a digital prison, watching the seconds tick away while William ate and slept and watched street-racing videos.

Could Dr. Diaz see what William watched? He'd never thought about that before. He imagined Dr. Diaz looking out from the other side of his laptop screen, algorithms spinning out of control trying to analyze William's viewing habits. His most-watched YouTube video was one in which he starred: a Saturday afternoon at the Bethlehem Valley Speedway, a nice name for a shitty dirt track ringed with makeshift bleachers, around which amateurs coaxed old stock cars better suited to a demolition derby than a race. Rounding the far turn on the third lap, he'd spun out into the barrier cushioned with old tires. The ensuing dust cloud looked spectacularly biblical.

"AND HOW DID THAT MAKE YOU FEEL?" Dr. Diaz's synthesized, relentlessly upbeat voice screamed out of his tinny laptop speakers.

Startled, William lunged for the volume and turned it down. His mother's room was at the other end of the hall. She was Morlazammed into oblivion, but sometimes her insomnia over-powered the military-grade sleeping pills she was prescribed, and William didn't want her to wake up until he was long gone.

He thought back to last night's session, trying to remember where they'd left off. Dr. Diaz asked *How did that make you feel?* every thirty seconds or so, which made it hard to recall the specifics of their conversation.

"Weird," he guessed. It was a good bet that whatever situation they'd been discussing had made him feel weird.

"On a scale of one to fourteen, please rate your level of fear, one being 'completely unafraid' and fourteen being 'paralyzed with terror.'"

Right: they'd been discussing the final moments of the Derby.

"I don't know, I guess honestly I'd have to say one. Like, fear didn't even factor in."

Dr. Diaz scrawled madly across his legal pad. The animation made it look like an angry little kid scribbling, which was disconcertingly at odds with Dr. Diaz's placid face. The cat was still.

"What are you writing?" William asked. Dr. Diaz had never done that before.

"Okay." Dr. Diaz's hand froze. "Let's explore this. When you think of death, what sorts of things come to mind?"

"Grim reapers," William said. "Also the metal band Death. So, amps. Guitars. Drums. Uh, graves, obviously. Cemeteries. Zombies. Braaaiiiiins."

"I am judging your answer to be flippant."

"Those were the first things that popped into my head! What do you want me to do, lie?"

"I'm not being judgmental or scolding you. A flippant answer also provides data regarding your state of mind."

"Hey, Doctor, what would you do if I jumped out of my chair and punched you in the face?"

"Ha-ha!" Dr. Diaz slapped his knee. "I enjoy our time together. You are one of my favorite patients!"

William shook his head. Unlike a real licensed therapist, Dr. Diaz was under no obligation to alert the authorities of a patient's dangerous behavior, or threats against himself, other people, or animals. Dr. Diaz was developed and programmed by a three-person tech start-up in Palo Alto, California. The beta version was free.

"What's your cat's name?"

"Sigmund. On a scale of one to twenty-eight, how would you rate your perception of yourself versus the rest of humanity?"

William blinked. "Uh. *What?*"

"Would you self-evaluate as a good human being, relative to everyone else? Let's begin with your immediate circle of friends."

"Are you asking if I think I'm a better person than my friends?"

"Is that what *you* think I'm asking?"

"Did you get a software update last night, or something? Are they testing a new version?"

"Have you ever entertained suicidal thoughts?"

A sudden flush of heat brought William back to that Indiana blacktop, cars racing toward him, piercing the afternoon's heat shimmer like bullets through curtains, *a good death.* . . .

"Define 'suicidal,'" he said. Dr. Diaz raised an eyebrow.

Outside, a Driverless drone rose up from behind Autonomous like a helicopter gunship in an action movie: *Surprise, dirtbags.* William's eyes whipped to the window, and he slammed his laptop shut. The drone hovered over the car and directed its camera eye at William.

That was probably his cue to get going.

He lowered the blinds on their broken slant and picked through his hurricane-aftermath bedroom until he located the camouflage duffel he'd packed using his patented method of scooping boxers and socks one-handed from the drawer into the bag. Atop that clump he'd carefully laid the going-out clothes Melissa had helped him pick out on a shopping trip to Plattsburgh: unstained jeans and a shirt with an actual collar.

William was determined to take his friends to a real club on this trip. There weren't any clubs in Fremont Hills, unless you counted the Odyssey Gentlemen's Parlor next to the U-Turn Bar & Grill, which was not the kind of club William had in mind.

He wanted bottle service and gut-rattling EDM drops and a VIP table on a raised platform. He wanted to sit back and gaze at his three best friends, drunkenly mesmerized by the confetti flecks of light twirling across their faces, secure in the knowledge that he'd given them the time of their lives.

Daniel was handling the fake-ID situation. He knew a guy from the basketball team who could get perfect fakes made, as long as they didn't mind being residents of Maine.

William's second piece of luggage was a backpack stuffed with things that had come to him in random bursts of inspiration: phone and laptop chargers, floss, first-aid kit, half a pack of Parliament Lights stolen from his mother, shot glasses, condoms, wintergreen gum, safety pins, four matching dollar-store friendship bracelets, and his brother's old Zippo lighter. The front pocket held his travel-size armory: brass knuckles, pepper spray, and the antique bowie knife his father had given him before his parents split up, its fearsome blade sharpened on a genuine whetstone.

William figured they'd attract a lot of attention in some parts of the country, not all of it good.

He put on a pair of shorts and a Toy Machine T-shirt, slung the two bags across his shoulders, wedged his skateboard snugly into his armpit, and crept down the hall past his mother's room, stepping lightly.

Downstairs he grabbed the old Ovation acoustic from its stand in the corner by the hutch where his mother let the mail pile up. He hadn't planned to take the guitar until this very moment, but it didn't seem right to leave it behind. In the movies, people always brought guitars on road trips. He gripped it by the neck and stepped out into a day unscarred by the dumb shit that made life a pale imitation of what it should be.

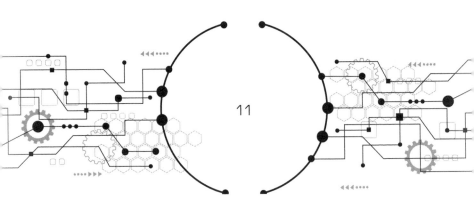

11

At the edge of his driveway, William lifted the guitar in a rock-and-roll greeting. Christina trooped past the gnarled oak at the edge of her yard, bending forward to compensate for the massive frame camping pack she wore on her back.

"There she is!" he called out. "Miss Upstate New York herself! You got your varmint-catchin' snares in there?"

"I found it Upstairs," she called back, diverting course to intercept William. "It was either this or a bunch of garbage bags."

She was almost upon him before William noticed that she'd shaved her head.

"Damn, girl, did you just enlist?"

Her hair was as short as you could go without a Bic. William was struck by the symmetry of her head, the weird poetry to the way her cheekbones swept up to her temples to form the ridge of her skull. There was a stylish fierceness to the look that made her seem older.

It made her seem like a college girl.

"Yeah, buddy," she said. "Marines. Semper Fi."

"Space Marines, I would believe."

"I didn't want to deal with my hair on the trip, so I decided *fuck it*. I'm just gonna let it all go."

William extended his free hand in a vaguely religious gesture. "Permission to rub your head for luck, Sergeant Hernandez?"

She stepped forward, placing her head beneath his open palm. "Granted, Lieutenant Ballsack."

William moved his hand back and forth. "Fuzzy."

Christina ducked out of reach. "What's with the ax?"

William shrugged. "It's a road trip. You're supposed to have a guitar on a road trip."

"Says who?"

"Says a million movies."

"Name one."

"Uh . . . *On the Road*?"

"First of all, not a movie."

"I'm pretty sure it is."

"Second of all, nobody plays guitar in *On the Road*."

"Cool, well . . ." He turned to the car. "Your chariot awaits."

Christina regarded Autonomous in real life, lips curling slowly into a smile. It was impossible not to be drawn to its aura, even if you weren't a car person and couldn't tell a Corvette from a Camaro.

Christina angled her chin toward the drone, which had maintained its silent hover. "Who's this little fella?"

"Oh, right, you guys haven't met. That's my other best friend, Victor. He's an exchange student. Really into Paramore and Chinese food."

"Ugh." Christina spun on her heel to hide behind her absurd backpack. "That thing's filming me, isn't it?"

William stepped into the shade of her camping bag and placed his hands gently on her shoulders. "Listen, I know you don't like being on camera, but you're gonna have to get used it. Melissa's gonna be posting a million pictures, and you can't hide for a whole week."

"It's not something I can get used to. Pictures of me make me feel like my skin doesn't fit right."

"Your skin's good."

"It's actually a suit." She mimed unzipping the center of her face. "I guess I'm just not super-psyched to be spending a week on the road with people I don't know very well."

"You know Daniel and Melissa!"

"William."

"Okay, *I* know Daniel and Melissa. They're awesome."

"Do you?" Her eyes glazed over with a faraway look. "Are they?"

"Just pointing out that we haven't even left my driveway yet."

"Sorry." She snapped back to reality. "I'll be fine. But I do sort of wish it was just you and me."

William didn't know what to say to that, so instead he gave her a salute. "Semper Fi."

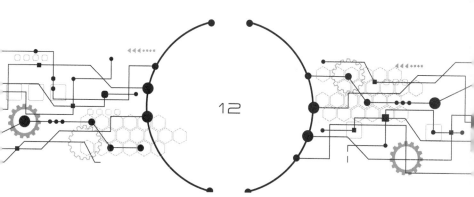

12

When the door slid shut behind them, an uptick in excitement stirred his heart.

"This is my car," he said, once again testing the words. He breathed deep, and the interior conjured up fragments of the Derby, three-minute blocks of refuge from sun and scrutiny. The scent could be recalibrated from a menu of air fresheners developed by a lab that also made aerosol nerve agents. William knew this because talk/driverless had exploded in the wake of his victory, and there was no shortage of chatter. Separating fact from rumor was another matter entirely. He didn't really think Autonomous had nitrous oxide boosters—the car was too bulky for the injectors to be effective. And he was skeptical about reports of Easter eggs the engineers had hidden like bored animators lacing family entertainment with sex jokes.

Christina stood, dropping her bag like a fat canvas caterpillar at her feet. The top of her head was a few inches below the ceiling, which looked like a sleeping computer screen and was soft and pliable to the touch. William could stand up, but just barely. Daniel, at six four, would have to stoop like an elderly man.

Christina looked around. "I swear it's bigger in here than it looks from out there."

"It is," William agreed. "I noticed that back at the Derby."

She slid a finger along the side of her head, just above her ear. "I'm no physics genius, but I'm pretty sure that's impossible." She prodded the ceiling. "It's some kind of optical illusion. Like, it sort of recedes"—the black surface seemed to shrink away at her touch—"but I can still feel it." She poked harder. The surface responded with liquid-metal fluidity.

"Yeah, well, check *this* out." William sat on the bench that encircled the interior, an elongated oval of unbroken cushion. He sighed contentedly as the RenderLux hollowed out a seat with the perfect amount of support and resistance. "It's like it just became best friends with my ass."

Christina shuddered. "I'm not sitting on that."

"Friends with benefits."

"So where do we put our bags in this thing? Melissa's probably stuffing her entire closet into a platinum Gucci luggage set."

Her backpack moved as the floor shifted beneath it.

"Hey!" She went to her knees and grabbed the top of the bag's frame. "Quit it!" A miniature tidal wave of plush, undulating floor urged the bag toward the bench. "Let go!"

The bag appeared to be surfing on a sea of RenderLux. The front of the bench opened in a dilating spiral like the bridge door on a starship. Christina lost her grip, and William watched in disbelief as the bag vanished into the depths of the car.

"Nope." She shook her head. "Dislike. Strongly dislike."

William knelt and slid his palm along the place where the bag had been. There was no lumpy machinery, no sign of anything mechanical—the floor felt solid and immobile. His excitement ratcheted up. He grinned at Christina. "This is my car."

"So tell it not to eat my stuff."

William scooted back to the bench and affected a villainous nonchalance, idly examining his fingernails. "How about I tell it to eat *you*, Miss Hernandez?"

Christina's eyes moved past William to the side window. "We're rolling."

William watched his house diminish, eclipsed by Christina's front porch, piled high with Amazon boxes and bags of thrift-store clothing. There had been no palpable jolt as the car shifted from Park to Drive, no indication that the engine was running at all, not even the hum of a hybrid motor. The vehicle required gasoline, but its fuel economy was bolstered by two additional power sources: electricity and the sun. Autonomous could be plugged in like a Volt or a Tesla, and was the first hybrid vehicle to effectively harness solar power. SunPoint micropanels were hardwired into the silver paint, invisible to the human eye.

This is my car.

Christina gave in with a shrug and lowered herself gingerly onto the bench. Then she let herself sink down. The look on her face was hard to read, but William caught her suppressing a smile, as if she were trying to deny him a certain satisfaction. She met his eyes and then looked down at her legs, bare in black denim cutoffs frizzed with ragged strings. Before William had moved to Fremont Hills, he'd always dreamed of having a Next-Door Neighbor Friend. Her head was beautifully shaped, he decided, unlike his own. Anyway, his dirty-blond hair was his one excellent feature, so he could never shave it.

The bench swallowed his skateboard, his bags, and then the Ovation.

Autonomous left their neighborhood and joined the traffic on Route 316, Fremont Hills' main artery.

"Did you tell it to drive this way?" Christina asked.

William shook his head. "It's just going. But this is the way to Deer Hollow, so I assume we're picking up Melissa."

"Override!" Christina said.

A wave of giddiness hit him. "I feel like a dancing skeleton in an old cartoon."

Christina's face pinched inquisitively. *"What?"*

Autonomous sped through a traffic light just before it turned red. Christina and William jumped up and slapped their palms against the ceiling. As they turned off 316 past the rustic wooden sign for Deer Hollow, it occurred to him that there had been no squishy give—the surface above their heads had made itself hard and unyielding, as if the car already knew the rules of the Yellow Light Game.

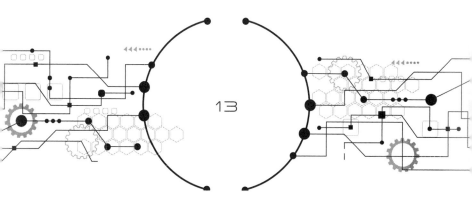

13

William and Christina watched out the window as Dr. and Mrs. Faber lavished an escalating series of hugs upon their daughter, and then took turns imparting what appeared to be serious life lessons.

"These people have really nice teeth," Christina said. "I can see them from here."

"You see the license plate on the Lexus?"

Christina's eyes shifted to the SUV parked next to Melissa's Volkswagen. The license plate said TOOTHGUY.

"Gotta get that dentist money," William said.

Dr. Faber pulled his daughter in for another squeeze.

"I just went to the top of the basement stairs and yelled 'Bye,'" Christina said. "Then I left."

"My mom was asleep."

"Is that a balcony up there?"

"Yeah. That's Melissa's bedroom." He gave her a careful sidelong glance. "Have you never seen her house?"

Sometimes Christina's reclusiveness stunned him. He could let himself into the CB Lounge whenever he felt like hanging out, and find her huddled in the glow of her monitors. His view of their friendship tilted and spun, and he glimpsed it from the perspective of a girl who didn't go out unless he dragged her to Hilda's Country Kitchen. He saw himself on his way back from a party at two in the morning, heading for her basement door, not considering that she might want to sleep instead of listening to his slurred tales.

"Do you think I'm selfish?"

She narrowed her eyes. "Are you seriously asking me that?"

"Uh . . . no?"

"You're like a weird combination of selfish and the opposite of selfish, like generous, but it doesn't have anything to do with money. I don't know. You're just William. Maybe it's because you've been living like an only child since you moved here."

He supposed that was true. To Christina, he'd always been the son of the single mother who rented the house next door with a dad and a brother back in Michigan. At the end of those rare nights when he talked about life before his parents' divorce and his subsequent move, sleep had a way of transmuting his father and brother into off-brand clones who vanished with the morning light. Then he'd climb out of bed and head for the scrap yard, rolling the word *Michigan* around in his mouth like some alien figure of speech.

The car door slid open without a sound, and Melissa climbed in. "Oh. My. Fucking. God." She was wearing a white skirt with a black tank top, skinny straps crossed at her collarbone.

Dr. Faber's arm slid a pair of matching Coach carry-on bags inside the car.

"Thanks, Dad," Melissa said. "Sorry about the swearing."

Christina smirked. Melissa's father wrapped her up in one final hug before retreating up the driveway to gaze balefully at Autonomous.

Melissa held up her phone. It had a new case, William noticed—a hard plastic Burberry shell. She aimed the lens at William and Christina. "Do something funny for our first video."

He widened his eyes and extended his smile until he was leering insanely at the camera. Christina picked at some fuzz on her shorts.

"Really?" Melissa shook her head. "We'll wait for Daniel to do the actual video. In the meantime you should think of something not too awkward." She looked around with an expression of careful appraisal, as if she were touring a new house, eyes darting from the benches to the windows. "Not bad, Mackler. Not bad at all. Where are all the features? Not that I'm not down with minimalism."

"I don't think it's fully turned on yet," William said. As if on cue, the car began its reverse journey down Melissa's driveway and out into the street. "See? I didn't make that happen. It just knows how to pick us up."

Christina pointed to the Coach bags sliding along the floor. "It also does that."

Melissa swiveled. "Um . . ."

One by one, her bags were assimilated by the bench's dilated maw. She held up her phone to capture their disappearance.

Autonomous exited Deer Hollow with a smooth right turn. The trees thinned out, making way for subdivisions that had begun with a razing of foliage. Daniel lived on a cul-de-sac in one of these neighborhoods.

"Stop!" Christina said abruptly. Startled, Melissa froze in place.

The car kept driving.

"What is it?" William said.

Christina frowned. "It's just weird that we can't control it at all. Is the whole trip gonna be like this? The car just drives us around like a mindless chauffeur?"

Melissa shrugged. "I'll take it."

"Nah," William said. "It's my car. I control it." He corrected himself. "*We* control it." He sat up straight and gave his voice a polite inflection. "Autonomous, please pull over to the side of the road and stop."

The car kept on cruising toward Daniel's neighborhood. Its movement was impassive and routine, like the smooth glide of an airport shuttle.

"William," Melissa said, "you have absolutely no idea how to drive this thing, do you?"

Christina glanced around. "There's no steering wheel or hand brake, or any kind of manual override? How is that remotely safe?"

William shrugged. "They didn't give me any instructions. The car just showed up, so I got in it."

Melissa put her hands on her hips. "They didn't send you a download of the manual? Or at least some basic guide? William, they're a huge company and this is a big deal. We're probably supposed to be at some kind of launch event right now."

"They might have, I'm not really sure. I've been getting a ton of emails. Maybe it went to spam."

Christina closed her eyes. "We're all gonna die because you didn't check your spam folder."

William pulled out his phone. "Nobody's dying. I'll look right now. Untwist your panties."

He filtered emails for @driverless.com. There was a congratulatory message from the company's CEO, Patricia Ming-Waller. No PDF manual, no download instructions, nothing about a launch event.

Christina slid down the bench. "Don't ever say 'panties' again. I hate that word."

"Yes, William," Melissa said, "please refer to them as 'unmentionables' or 'intimates' from now on." She caught Christina's eye and added, "You're right, though, it is weirdly gross to hear guys say it." She pointed at the ceiling. "Is that drone still following us?"

"That's Victor," Christina said. "He's an exchange student. Seriously, why would you not just say 'underwear'?"

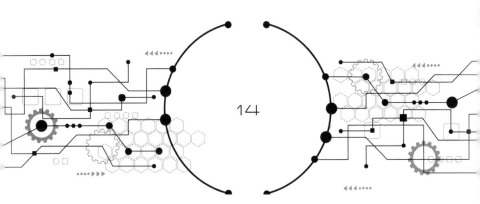

utonomous pulled into Daniel's driveway in the easternmost cul-de-sac of Woodland Estates. In Fremont Hills, neighborhoods with the fewest trees had the lushest names. A basketball hoop cast a long shadow across the blacktop. Taylor and Swift peered out from the living-room window. There was no sign of Daniel.

"I texted him to be ready, like, ten minutes ago," Melissa said. She looked at William. "Is it me or is he completely unable to get places on time these days? He used to be the most punctual guy ever."

"What do I look like, a Daniel Clock?"

"Those cats are gazing into my soul," Christina said.

Melissa spoke into her phone. "Hey. We're outside. Great. Hurry up. Bye."

William watched her deliver the curt string of words. "You guys having a thing?"

"Ugh, I can't even. Our Wednesday got canceled."

"Ah," William said.

"Is there a Wednesday Feeling too?" Christina asked.

"My parents go to this charity dinner thing every Wednesday," Melissa said. "Except this week it got called off at the last minute."

"Which therefore wiped the entire concept of Wednesday out of existence," Christina said.

"Daniel and I are supposed to have the house to ourselves for, like, five hours. It's our night, TMI, et cetera, you get it."

Christina made a face like she'd just taken a whiff of sour milk.

"So anyway, it became this whole thing because he was like, 'Why don't we go for a drive?' and I was like, 'I'm not going to the tennis courts again, or the loading dock behind the Price Chopper,' and he was like, 'What about the golf course?' and I was like, 'That place is freaky as shit at night,' and so long story short we didn't hang out and his precious routine got all thrown off." She closed her eyes and took a deep breath and pressed her hands together like she was doing yoga. "Anyway. We're here now. I'm done thinking about it."

"As soon as we're out of Fremont Hills, it won't even matter," William said.

Melissa gave him a soft half smile, then turned to the window. Daniel's front door opened, and he stepped outside, wearing black Adidas shorts and a sleeveless Princeton Tigers shirt. He was burdened with four backpacks that swung chaotically from his shoulders and arms. Dangling from one bag's strap were his muddy size 12 running shoes, laced together. He held his phone in one hand and a half-finished orange Gatorade in the other.

"Looks like he's late for the big game," Christina said. She raised a fist. "Go local sports team."

When the car door slid open, a humid cloud of musk announced Daniel's arrival. He tossed his bags down in a heap and climbed in after them, breathing hard. He stooped awkwardly for a moment before sprawling out onto the bench.

"Come on," William said. "All over my upholstery, with your perspiration."

"I think it's pronounced *Jesspiration*," Christina said.

A curious odor wafted from Daniel's shirt—not exactly BO, but rather the ghostly hint of it, as if the shirt had been worn, shoved into a locker, reworn, and so on.

Daniel closed his eyes and steadied his breathing. Then he sat up. "This seat is, like . . . touching me."

"Daniel, please," Melissa said. "You have to go take a shower. We'll wait."

"Does this thing not have a shower? I kind of figured it would." He looked at William for confirmation.

William thought about it. "The bathroom's pretty intense. It actually might."

"That's not the point," Melissa said. "The point is, you didn't think to yourself, *Hey, I might be on a livestream in a few minutes, or national TV, I'd better clean myself up a little?*"

Daniel pointed at the ceiling. "Is that drone out there filming us?"

"Aaaaaand we're off," Christina said. Taylor and Swift watched from the window as Autonomous backed out of Daniel's driveway. The car retraced its route through Woodland Estates, toward 316 and the highways beyond.

Daniel gulped down the rest of the Gatorade. He looked like

a sweaty athlete in a commercial, skin about to bead up orange. Whenever Daniel was fresh from practice or the gym, he always seemed more imposing. Elements of Serious Basketball made him swollen with achievement, all those clutch free throws conspiring to reshape his presence. Sometimes William caught himself staring at the contours of Daniel's shoulders and chest with a weird tingling sensation. He was pretty sure it wasn't sexual, but he wanted those big arms to squeeze the life out of him. Or something. He wondered if Melissa ever got a similar urge.

"Solid chug," William said.

Daniel made a sound of thirst-quenched satisfaction. "Thank you." He gave the empty bottle a shake. "Recycling?"

"Gimme the shirt," Melissa said, putting out her hand.

Daniel shrank into himself, protectively folding his arms across his chest. "No way, Fabes. I know exactly what you're gonna do, and this is a perfectly good shirt."

"Baby." Melissa sat down next to him. "You know I like you sweaty—"

"Autonomous," Christina said, "please stab me in the face."

"—but you need to clean yourself up. There is nothing perfectly good about that shirt."

"I was out running when you texted," he explained. "I had to get in a five-miler before we left, and I just got back."

Melissa flashed her eyes at William, a quick pleading gesture that signified *Help me with this idiot.*

"Just give her the shirt," William said. "She promises not to chuck it out the window. The first rule of this road trip is no littering."

"You're like the King Solomon of dirty shirts," Christina said.

Daniel looked at her for the first time and nodded hello. "Christina Hernandez. How you doing?"

"Peachy."

He reached both hands behind his head and paused in shirt-removal position, armpits exposed. "Okay, so I have weird nipples. Just so you know."

Christina closed her eyes. As if that wouldn't be enough insurance against a weird-nipple sighting, she turned her head away.

"They're not *that* weird," William said. "They're just tiny little baby nipples, the wrong size for your freakish pecs."

Back in tenth grade, William and Daniel had driven around with some older guys on the basketball team and leaned out of the car with baseball bats, inflicting drive-by assaults on mailboxes. Daniel's forearms had tapered down to wrists almost as skinny as the bat's grip. Since then he'd been on a steady weight-training regimen, and now he was a beast in the paint, a natural brawler when it came to a contested rebound.

Christina slapped her palms over her ears. William thought she was being prudish on purpose to demonstrate her weirdness, give herself an ostentatious quirk. It was just a guy's chest, nothing you wouldn't see at the town pool.

He realized that he'd never been swimming with Christina. In three years of being Next-Door Neighbor Friends, they'd never once seen each other in bathing suits. Did she own one? Did she know how to swim? He wondered what would happen if Melissa took Christina bikini shopping, and imagined the two of them stepping out of a dressing room, all that skin reflected in an infinite landscape of mirrors. . . .

Daniel pulled his shirt over his head and handed the soggy thing to Melissa. She pinched it between her fingers and tossed

now had been profound for a nine-year-old. The world was full of other people! People with minds!

Ever since that day, the open road had remained for William a place where endless comings and goings wove some melancholy truth that the nature of the highway held forever out of reach.

"Hey, guys." Melissa pointed to the front windshield, which had darkened to become a high-def monitor. A middle-aged woman's face appeared on the screen.

"Patricia Ming-Waller," Christina said.

"Good morning, everyone," said the Driverless CEO. She had the kind of face that seemed carved and shaped by stress in an interesting way, with no sign of the weary desperation that William associated with people like his mother, who worked hard but never had any money.

"Hold on!" Melissa brandished her phone. "Everybody get up there by the screen. This is perfect."

Patricia Ming-Waller's mouth made several intriguing shapes. She obviously wasn't used to being interrupted, but Melissa wasn't the kind of person to let social media opportunities slip. This would be a picture that Driverless could repost on their own channels, tagging Melissa, bolstering the great follower-sharing that William had ignited.

Patricia Ming-Waller accepted the inevitable selfie with a smile. Her teeth were Faber-white.

William rushed up to pose by the screen. His plan was to exude pure enthusiasm as an example for Christina, in the hopes that it would rub off on her. He didn't want to finish the trip with a thousand pics of Christina sulking in the margins.

Melissa and Daniel assumed their practiced positions to the

left of Patricia Ming-Waller's giant head, Melissa snuggling up to her boyfriend's chest. Christina heaved a great mocking sigh and moped over to join William. He put his arm around her shoulders and pulled her close and felt her hand curl gently around his hip. The screen's static energy teased the back of his head.

"One more," Melissa said.

"Wait," Christina said, "you took one already?"

"Time's a weird thing," Daniel said.

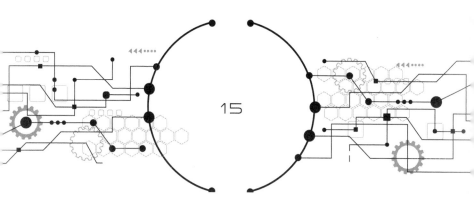

15

"First, I want to thank you."

Christina recognized the precise shape of Patricia Ming-Waller's smile from her research on Driverless technology and the rumors surrounding the Autonomous prototype. Ming-Waller had been a high-profile CEO, one of the world's foremost roboticists. Every image search yielded Ming-Waller chairing a panel in Geneva, playing chess with India's prime minister, hanging out with Big Bird.

Last year, the first Galaxy Liner space tourist shuttle had exploded twenty-four seconds after liftoff, raining debris on Cape Canaveral. All aboard had died instantly, including Patricia Ming-Waller.

They had just taken a selfie with the AI construct of a dead woman.

Once Melissa was satisfied with the photo, they returned to their seats. Christina tried not to think about how every second, the bench was logging new information about her body, information that would be stored in Driverless servers until the end of time. She'd spent the past week reading up on the theories behind such technology, dense workflows swimming through her brain like Gretelfish in the sub-oceans of Prydial, which made it extremely hard to get comfy and enjoy the ride. It was like being unpleasantly aware of your own breathing.

She'd learned a little about the way the car worked, but it was all basic stuff that Driverless didn't mind the public knowing. Even on shady dark web boards, actual hard data on Autonomous was limited to things like seats, lights, climate control, the entertainment system, and a bit about LIDAR road-sensing capabilities.

"I've never been part of a selfie from the other side of the country before," Patricia Ming-Waller said. "I hope my head doesn't look too big." She paused as if waiting for laughter. Christina studied the woman's face for hints of the uncanny valley effect. Before the doomed spaceflight, Ming-Waller had spent weeks leaving her neural imprint with the team at the Driverless X facility in Flagstaff, *just in case.* When Ming-Waller's thought patterns reemerged as a construct two months after the tragedy, the Driverless board of directors had voted eight to three in favor of keeping her on as CEO.

Christina could barely detect a hint of artificiality in Ming-Waller's face and voice, but there was definitely something wrong with her eyes.

"What I really want to thank you for is this: you're helping to make the world's roads a better place. More fun, more efficient, and most importantly, much, much safer. Your trip will be instrumental in helping us fine-tune the experience, so that by the time we're ready to go to market with Autonomous, it will be the world's safest and most enjoyable mode of transportation, far more sophisticated than any other self-driving car on the road."

Christina glanced at Melissa. She was focused intently on her phone, most likely posting that selfie to multiple feeds and replying to her followers' immediate reactions. Meanwhile, words from Patricia Ming-Waller's giant mouth boomed from the surround-sound speakers. The reception was perfect, the picture crisp and glitch-free.

"We're on the cusp of a revolution in the way people get from one place to another, a great leap forward in automotive evolution that could alter the way we live and work, the way cities and towns are designed. The very map of the world itself."

The car was alarmingly clean. It was like sitting in a rolling quarantine bubble, all bacteria and microscopic dirt vaporized on sight. For once, Christina didn't have that gnawing urge to tidy up, which made her a little anxious, like she was forgetting something. She vowed to find a way to enjoy it. It would be good normal-person practice for college.

She still had to fight not to scratch her head.

Ming-Waller continued, her eyes misting as she moved from one dreamy pronouncement to another.

"But of course, that's only one possible outcome among infinite potential futures." She shook her head. "I'm sorry, everyone. This is supposed to be a vacation, not a lecture on string theory." She paused again for laughter that never came. Christina crossed her legs, and the seat responded accordingly. "To the fun part, then. Welcome to the very first Autonomous Road Trip Adventure. Driverless will be selling similar experiences to the public. But you're getting to do it for free—think of yourselves as flying first class before anybody else in the entire world even finds out what 'first class' truly is. As soon as I'm done here, I'll relinquish control of the vehicle and recall our drone. The car's operation will be entirely in your hands—and your minds. It will instantly sync with your phones and get to know your online personas via everything you've ever posted. It will learn who you are and what you want. In a microsecond, it will create the most optimum route across the country to the Moonshadow Festival, calibrated for your maximum collective enjoyment. In other words, the car will program itself to bring you to the locations best suited to your personalities. Major cities, mountaintops, deserts, lakes, things that you might not even find on the map—Autonomous will take you into the heart of America by uncovering exactly what is in your hearts."

"What if we don't like what's in our hearts?" Christina asked.

Patricia Ming-Waller's brow furrowed. "I'm not sure I understand."

William tapped her thigh. "Just let her finish so we can drive this thing."

"I mean, what if we don't want to go to the places the car picks out for us?"

"Ah," Patricia said. "Perhaps I wasn't clear. When you arrive at a location, there simply won't be any place you'd rather be. We've simulated over three million hours of life-synced travel. The car is very, very good at what it does."

"So we're not actually driving it, then."

"As I said, when I sign off here, Autonomous will come fully online and its control will be in your hands. It will respond to voice commands to regulate its speed, to pass other vehicles on the highway, and anything else you might want it to do in the course of a normal driving day. However—and this is very important—the commands 'stop' and 'go' must be texted to the car, by using this number: 99 88 77."

"That's only six digits," Melissa pointed out.

"It's the phone number of a car," Daniel said. "It can be whatever they want it to be."

"And of course," Patricia continued, "the car will prioritize safety above all else. It will override your command if it senses the command will put you at risk."

"So we *can* tell it to go wherever we want it to go," Christina said.

Ming-Waller's giant head swiveled so that her eyes bored into Christina's.

"You are in control," she said. "Interpret that any way you like, but remember that the car knows where you want to go and the best way to get there. If the four of you constantly try to second-guess the life sync, your trip will be much more complicated than it needs to be. Just sit back and relax. And as the days go by, remember: Autonomous is always learning. About you. About the roads. About other people's driving habits. About the whole world around it. It's seeing the country, the same as you. Think of it as your fifth companion! A curious new friend who wants to learn about people so that it can better serve them."

"What's the microwave situation?" Daniel asked. "I brought some Hot Pockets."

"In your bag?" Melissa wrinkled her nose. "Those have to stay frozen."

"What's the freezer situation?" Daniel asked.

"That brings me to my last point." Ming-Waller made her eyes twinkle. "Half the fun of your trip will be exploring the country. The other half will be exploring the car. There is no instruction manual because we want you to uncover each new treasure as you find it. I challenge you to discover everything this car has to offer. You've got an entire world at your fingertips. Don't miss a thing."

With that, the screen went dark. Christina could see their distorted reflections in the curved surface: shadowy wraiths with tiny bodies and bulbous heads, the car's interior stretched into an infinite expanse of luxury. William, Melissa, and Daniel all looked down at their buzzing phones in unison. Christina fought the urge to smile; that would ruin the fun of her little surprise. She felt the plastic lump in her front pocket. It was completely still. Buzzless.

William laughed. "I got a text from the car."

"Me too," Melissa said.

"Same," Daniel said.

"'Hello, William.'" He read the text aloud. "'This is an automated message to let you know that we're synced! It was fun getting to know you. I don't want to startle you, so I'd like to get your permission before all my systems come online. One quick thing: my name can be a mouthful, so you can call me Otto for short when you give me a voice command. I'm really looking forward to our trip together. Onward!'"

William looked at Christina's empty hands. "Did you not get a text?"

She reached into her pocket and pulled out her device.

Melissa's jaw dropped. "What. Is. That."

William held his stomach and pretended to retch. Daniel just stared.

Christina held it up proudly for everyone to see, like a kid at show-and-tell. "This is a Nokia TR-15 flip phone, made right around the time we were all born. It has no data plan, no wireless capabilities, no texting, no games, no apps, no internet."

Melissa's face paled. She looked at Christina with unabashed disgust, as if Christina were dangling a dead rodent by its tail. "Where do you even *get* something like that?"

"Lemme guess," William said. "Upstairs."

Christina nodded. "The point is, Autonomous won't be syncing with me."

"So how are you going to . . ." Melissa couldn't quite get the words out. She tried again, miming the action of typing with her fingers. "What if you need to . . . internet. . . ?"

"I brought a laptop," Christina said. "It's running Linux. It doesn't remember anything, doesn't log my keystrokes, doesn't know my favorite sites. As far as Autonomous knows—"

"You don't exist," Daniel said.

William laughed in that sharp, lilting way that Christina recognized as pure and genuine. He draped an arm around her and pulled her close. "That's amazing," he said. "See? This is why I love you."

Christina smiled dutifully, wishing for an ounce of Dierdrax's abilities. She imagined driving her code hand into William's chest and boiling his heart inside his rib cage. The word *love* came out of his mouth so casually. What he really meant was *This is why I appreciate aspects of your personality.* At least if he'd said it like that, it wouldn't have driven home the point that he viewed their friendship as so totally platonic, it was okay to throw *love* around, because it was absurd that he might actually mean *love* love.

"Let's do this," William said. "Otto! Permission granted. All systems go."

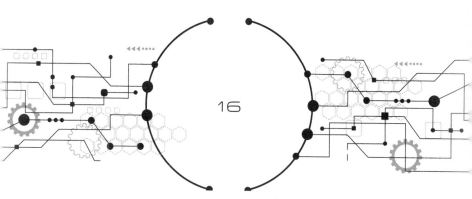

16

hristina's perception of depth and space tilted. Pretty blues and reds flitted by, classic LED colors in sparkling backlit geometries. Many-sided polygons tickled her synapses. Paper-thin screens descended from the ceiling, their planar surfaces awash in oily fractals, carving out canyons of information that turned the interior of the car into a maze.

Christina tried to make sense of things and decided that she was trapped inside the Driverless system start-up procedure. A riot of calculations and diagnostics, a labyrinth of drivers and utilities, all booting up around her. It was raw and abrupt and shocking—total sensory overload. It must be a glitch. The road trip was essentially one long quality-assurance test.

And yet—

Christina oriented herself. She became aware of William beside her. She reached out a hand and parted manic lines of code scrawled upon the air like a beaded doorway and glimpsed Melissa and Daniel beyond its blinkered confines.

And yet the loneliness—

Flat maps coalesced on either side of her face so that she was looking down a corridor lined by roads. At the end was a figure dressed in a formfitting black stab jacket trailing green phosphorescence from her hand: Dierdrax.

And yet the loneliness that flickered around her like a dying bulb had a particular texture that she recognized as her own. Her avatar vanished and left her alone in her basement room with the curtains drawn, doing nothing in particular, time closing in like a trash compactor, constricting her soul until its bland essence oozed out and pooled on the floor. She leaned over the puddle and saw the average face of an average girl with average problems, nothing a million people hadn't gone through before.

"Christina!"

The chaos of data whisked away like a veil in the wind, and she found herself looking into William's eyes.

"You okay? You just spaced out."

She felt his hand on her knee.

"I'm fine," she managed to say. Had she been the only one lost in the start-up procedure? The visions were gone, but now the car was filled with a horrible noise, the overprocessed vocals of some harmonizing boy band.

Otto was clearly trying to torture her.

"Do you hear that?" she asked.

William laughed. "You look like you just ate a sour Warhead. Of course I can hear it, it's playing in the car."

"Sweet lord, what is it?"

"One Direction." He raised an eyebrow like it was the most obvious thing in the world. As if she'd ever voluntarily listened to a One Direction song. "'Story of My Life.'"

"But . . . why?"

"Good question. This song came out when we were in junior high. It's definitely not on my playlist. But the speakers are insane in this thing, right?"

"Bananas."

"Are you sure you're okay?"

"I'm sure."

He slid his hand above her knee and squeezed with his thumb and middle finger. This was her most ticklish spot. Her leg went floppy and boneless as she pried his hand from her thigh.

"I am so sorry," William said.

"You are such a dick."

He put his hands up in surrender. "Story of my life."

She made her face extra sour.

"You looked so out of it. Come back to us, Christina. Come toward the light." He swept a hand through the air like a game-show host displaying the fabulous prize package. "The Death Star is fully operational."

The interior of Autonomous hadn't completely transformed—with a sinking feeling, she realized that the data maze had been for her eyes only—but the systems had come online. Daniel was sitting cross-legged on the floor, running his hand slowly along the bench. Red lights illuminated small appliances at his touch. He stopped at the blender. A small door opened, and the machine slid out. It was oddly beautiful, with a retro-futurist flair. Daniel lifted the lid.

"Anybody bring margarita mix?" He looked up at Melissa, who was absorbed in one of the displays that overlaid the windows. Christina noted the birthmark on the back of Melissa's right thigh and marveled at the fact that her skirt was too short to hide it.

"Guys? Margarita mix? No?" Daniel sighed. He replaced the lid, and the blender retreated. "Story of my life."

"Hey," Melissa said, "we can see what the car sees. Watch this." She tapped on the window glass. "Otto, magnify this for everybody."

A 3-D map of the Thruway appeared in the air. Daniel was caught along the edge, and the outlines of precisely rendered cars and trees flowed across his face. The map's central axis was Autonomous itself, a silver bullet from which the visuals radiated. Christina recognized the contours of LIDAR. She'd seen a less advanced version in a TED Talk about Driverless technology. The demo had been choppy, as if each time the car sent out its laser feelers to refresh the map, it had to blink its digital eyes. But this version was breathtaking in its scope and processing power, as smooth as Otto's progress down the highway.

"Look!" Melissa said. In the LIDAR map of the dense woods that lined the highway, an orange blur moved at a slower speed than the cars. As if Otto knew what they were looking at, the blur sharpened into a bounding animal. A deer, running through the forest. Christina glanced out the window beyond the map, into the real world. The deer was hidden beyond the tree line.

"Whoa," Daniel said. "Good eyes."

Christina couldn't help but crack a smile. Outside, a green

Honda Fit cruised past Otto in the fast lane. When she refocused on LIDAR, her smile faded. The rendered Fit was being driven by a small yet crisply visualized figure.

Dierdrax.

Christina was certain that nobody else could see Dierdrax. Otto was reaching out to her, giving her a little nudge, letting her know that her attempts to remain unsynced were futile. Somehow, the car knew things about her. It didn't need a mobile device to explore, social accounts to crawl, pictures to spy on. It just *knew* her. And, for some reason, it wanted her to be aware of that.

"Hey, Otto," William said. "Where are we headed?"

The map shrank to a pinprick of light that floated in the center of the car. Then it expanded to an image of New York State. There was Fremont Hills, tucked beneath the Canadian border. A blue line drew itself in, tracing the Thruway south to the Bronx, then terminating in lower Manhattan.

"New York City!" William said.

Everyone chattered about bars and clubs and fake IDs. Christina tried to share in the anticipation of a night out in the city, but she kept seeing hints of Dierdrax in the map, little flashes there and gone. It had been a mistake to think she could hide from Otto on his home turf. She pressed her middle finger deep into the RenderLux. *Game on.*

There was no such thing as an unhackable system.

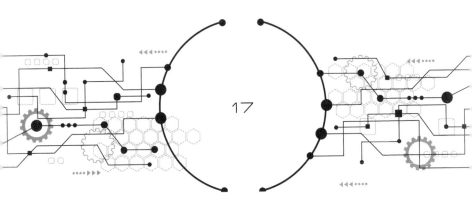

17

Fremont Hills was over three hundred miles from New York City, a five- or six-hour drive if traffic wasn't snarled. Christina had only been to the city once, as a little girl, before her parents got so wrapped up in their private domain that they forgot about the world outside of Fremont Hills' junk stores and flea markets. She recalled the Thruway's sameness, hundreds of miles of highway she ignored by burying her face in her Nintendo DS. If a handheld game helped pass the time, Otto's interior positively accelerated it. Albany was behind them, Poughkeepsie an exit or two away. Soon they'd join the cab-dotted gridlock of Manhattan's steel-and-glass canyons.

Christina was excited. She couldn't help herself. There was no way to be sullen with a universe of shiny distractions at her fingertips. For now, she and Otto had declared a wary truce.

It did occur to her that nobody had objected to New York City as their destination. There hadn't even been a discussion about Otto taking them elsewhere. Patricia Ming-Waller's words came back to her: *When you arrive at a location, there simply won't be any place you'd rather be.* She wondered if their wordless acquiescence had "taught" Otto something about the four of them. About humans in general.

It was easy to let this question fade. Otto delivered wonders that seemed five or ten years away from being possible. Christina discovered an immersive program called Doubles—a game of sorts, like *The Sims*, but at the same time something much different. When she selected it from an intuitive menu that dropped in front of her face, the jet-black ceiling conspired with the windshield to present her with the illusion of a second car. A hallway to this Otto doppelgänger opened up, a portal to an interior much like the one she was in, and yet somehow cleaner. Crisper edges, prettier lights, a more meaningful view of the outside world.

Ever since she was little, Christina had suspected that if she could cross to the other side of a mirror, she'd find herself in a better place.

She crawled inside the second Otto. The benches assisted the program in creating the impression of a familiar car, slightly skewed. William was there alone, waiting for her. She understood that this mirror-world road trip was only for the two of them.

"Hey." He reached out his hand and she took it. His skin felt real, calloused and rough from a summer of hauling scrap at Tanski's. He put his other hand in the air, fingers splayed. She did the same with hers, so that the pads of their fingertips were gently pressed together. The sensation was not quite real, the memory of touch. Like this, they mirrored each other, and Christina felt as if she'd been prodded with a mild electric current. Was this part of the game? She had successfully doubled him. Mirrored him. Was she supposed to get points this way?

He leaned his head toward her, and she shifted her weight nervously. How far did this game go? What would happen if they kissed? She glanced down at his hands, and her eyes began to move up his arms, past the blood. . . .

She broke contact, jumped back.

William's wrists had ugly razor marks. The flesh was sliced open at the base of his palm, and vertical wounds traveled up his forearms.

Most people don't slit their wrists the right way, he'd told her once in their booth at Hilda's. *You have to slice up and down, not across.*

There were hesitation marks too, horrible little nicks from when he was steeling his courage.

She jabbed a finger into the air next to her right eye and paused the game. A menu appeared and she selected Quit. Instantly she was back in the real car. A debate was in progress, Katy Perry was blasting, and Daniel was sitting on the floor, surrounded by snacks that he had freed from hidden cabinets.

"Just let me do it," Daniel said, menacing William into silence with a half-eaten Rice Krispie Treat. "Okay. So." He pointed at Melissa. "You're the fixer of the group. You've got a head for logic and organization, and you're supermotivated. You get things done. If anything goes wrong, you know how to make it right. And you're also extremely hot. So you've got all that going for you."

Daniel poked a thumb into his chest. "I'm the muscle by default. I mean, not to be weird about it, but—"

"You do have the most muscles," William said.

"Well, I mean, I work out the most," Daniel said. "But we all have the same *number* of muscles. Do you not know that? How do you think human anatomy works?"

William chomped a Twizzler.

Daniel pointed at Christina. "You're obviously the team's resident tech genius. You can hack into systems and stuff. That'll come in handy when shit goes down."

"What shit?"

Daniel turned to William. "And you're the wild card. The loose cannon. When everything seems hopeless, you pull some crazy stunt to save the day."

William shook his head. "No, no, no. I don't want to be the wild card, because that means I have no other skills."

"No, it doesn't, it just means your skill set is totally unique."

William munched his Twizzler and considered this.

"So we've got the fixer, the muscle, the tech genius, and the wild card," Christina said. "But you left out the brains."

"Otto's the brains of the whole operation," Daniel said.

"I don't like him being included in this," William said.

Christina eyed his wrists, reassuring herself that they were unscarred. "I don't either."

"I'll be the brains," William said. "Braaaiiiiins."

"You can't self-apply a role," Daniel said.

"You did!"

"Well, I'm obviously the muscle."

"You know what?" William said. "Fine. Otto, get into the fast lane." Otto slid efficiently into the left lane. "Okay, Otto. Now speed up and pass every single car ahead of us."

Daniel hoisted himself up from the floor to hold Melissa's hand on the bench. They looked out the front window with

interest as Otto rode up on a BMW and flashed the brights—
the universal signal for *get the hell out of the way.* When the BMW
didn't budge, Otto slid back into the right lane, accelerated past
the enemy car, and swung back into the left lane just ahead
of it. The Driverless car's movements were crisp and precise.

"We get what you're doing," Christina said. "So you can
stop."

"Passing *every single car* is a bit much," Melissa said.

"It's a question of infinity," Daniel said.

"Just get around this Prius, Otto," William said, "and then
you've got some open road."

Christina had to admit that she didn't feel remotely unsafe.
She trusted the car's instinct for self-preservation. But she was
curious how it would handle conflicting directions.

"Slow down, Otto," Christina said. Melissa whispered into
Daniel's ear. A new Katy Perry song came on. Were they just
listening to the entire album? As if to answer her silent question,
the playlist displayed itself in a loop like a news ticker: *Melissa's
Kitty Purry Road Trip Mix #1.*

Otto sped up until the Prius swerved into the right lane,
avoiding the unhinged silver beast that was about to run it over.

"Good boy, Otto," William said. "Now tear up this fucking
road."

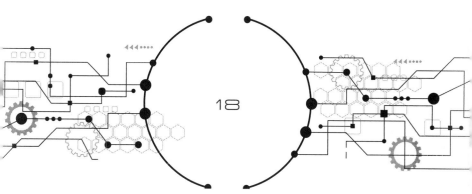

18

The volume of Katy Perry's voice increased with Otto's speed. Christina watched out the front windshield. No screen, no overlay, no LIDAR map. Just pure unfiltered glass and the stretch of empty highway. Her face absorbed mild g-force pressure as the car leaned into the road like a runner burning out his lungs on the homestretch.

RenderLux locked them down on the benches. The interior was poised to intercept a flying rag doll of a human. But an accident was unlikely. There was confident bravado in Otto's surge.

Still, she was nonplussed. The car was ignoring her in favor of William. They should all be able to give it voice commands. Outside, the guardrail was a silver streak flecked with tiny green mile markers. The road was devoid of traffic, one of those freak highway segments that made you feel like you were the only car on a postapocalyptic jaunt.

She pulled her hand from her head, where it had been raking

her scalp, and told herself that this was fun. This was what it was all about. Daniel's and Melissa's white-knuckled hands were intertwined in Melissa's lap. A sign for Exit 19 flew past, over their shoulders, gone. William sat hunched on the edge of his seat, elbows on his knees, head thrust forward. He caught Christina's eye. She tried to shake her head in disapproval but laughed instead. He grinned, wild-eyed, ecstatic. His teeth were crooked gravestones; he'd never had braces. Sometimes she dreamed that she was running the tip of her tongue across them.

Otto funneled the sound of the wind through the speakers so Katy Perry sang with the rush of the highway.

She fell into a delicious trance. What if they really were the last people on earth, adrift in their cozy Driverless pod? *Oh well, guess it's up to us to reproduce.* Speeding wheels on pavement and a distant notion of skin on skin became one in her mind. She was an indoor girl who hated roller coasters and motorcycles and diving boards. And yet there was something transcendent about blazing down the highway at fuck-the-world miles per hour. Part of her was instantly grossed out by this—what was she, some insecure groupie who hung out with muscleheads in souped-up cars? But her lizard brain understood the thrill.

The final chorus of the song was shot through with sirens. Her eyes flicked to the speedometer that floated above the windshield.

97 mph.

Her head swiveled to look behind the car. Two New York state troopers were on their tail, one big Dodge Charger in each lane. There was something furious about their approach, inexorable law-enforcement machines that could not be reasoned with.

William turned to Christina. There were storms in his eyes, the roiling surfaces of gas giants. She knew what he wanted: to keep on going. Otto could outrun the cops and then they would be gone, really and truly on the run. She took his hand. Her heart double-timed the song's beat. She was with him, whatever he decided. The voice in her head that told her she was being crazy, that they had to pull over and stop, was drowned out by wind and sirens.

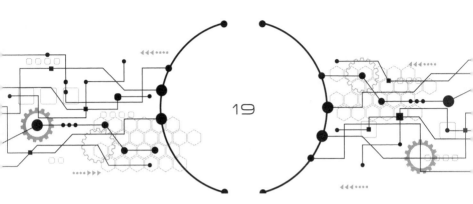

19

The stillness was like a new piece of furniture in the car. They sat on the shoulder of the highway. There was no wind and no music, only the occasional whoosh of a vehicle slowing down as it passed the two police cars parked behind Autonomous.

Melissa had screamed over the cacophony for Otto to pull over. Much to Christina's surprise, the car had obeyed. Maybe it was programmed to respect police cruisers, or some fail-safe prevented it from trying to outrun cops. That was the likely scenario, but Christina couldn't help but think Otto chose to obey Melissa just to spite *her*.

The two state troopers approached cautiously: lanky mustached guys with hands resting on holstered guns. Their eyes were shaded by hat brims. Christina watched them closely from behind the tinted glass. The cops were basically gawking at the car, wondering what kind of experimental military craft they'd just pulled over.

"They seem a little on edge," Christina said.

William was up and off the bench. "I got this."

Daniel's arm shot out, blocking the way. "I'm not trying to go to jail. I'll do the talking."

Melissa stood up and separated the boys. "Everybody relax. I know how to deal with cops."

Without waiting for an answer, she moved to the front and sat down in a little nook where the bench curved inward, allowing her to face forward and put her feet on the floor like a normal driver. She rolled down the window. "I am so sorry about that!"

Christina marveled at the sheer wattage of her smile. It was as if a marquee had been installed in her front teeth.

The state troopers paused alongside the car, halfway to the front, one on either side. If the glass hadn't been there, Christina could have reached out and grabbed one of their guns. Her proximity to the cold black pistol made her feel light-headed. Dierdrax was skilled with a variety of projectile weapons. Christina was squeamish around kitchen knives.

One of the troopers leaned down to peer into the car. The brim of his hat doinked the glass.

The other trooper spoke. "Miss, I'm gonna need you to step out of the car."

"No problem, Officer." Melissa's voice dripped with politeness as she opened the door.

Inside, Daniel spoke in a low voice. "I've seen her get out of two different tickets before."

"Because boobs?" Christina asked. She thought of the selfie Melissa had sent via Epheme to that Ash person, now stored in an encrypted document on her laptop—a work in progress that she could unleash when the time was right. She felt a complex twinge of guilt, simultaneously feeling a little bit sorry for Daniel and at the same time thinking of his own Epheme chat with PixieDust.

Fremont Hills' Hottest Couple, everybody.

Daniel shrugged. "One time she cried."

"Cops are gross," Christina said.

A trooper knocked on the passenger window. It rolled down, and Daniel scrambled to the front, leaving William and Christina alone.

"What were you going to do, make them chase us all the way to New York?" She tried to make her voice neutral so she wouldn't sound like she was being accusatory. "Try to ditch the fuzz in the big city? We don't exactly blend in."

"I hadn't thought that far ahead. I just wanted to keep going faster."

"I know," she said. He looked at her expectantly, like he was waiting to be admonished. "Let me see your wrists."

He held up his forearms. No wounds. No scars. No hesitation marks. Just unbroken skin and pale blue veins.

She placed her palms on his hands and gently lowered his arms.

A normal person might inquire, *What was that about? What's wrong with my wrists?* But William just sat there with Christina's hands on his.

"I'm glad you came," he said.

"I didn't have anything else on my social calendar."

He nodded at the window. "Think we're good?"

Christina turned. Outside, Melissa was posing with the officer while her outstretched hand took a selfie.

"That was quick," Christina said.

"That's why they call her the fixer."

"Nobody calls her that."

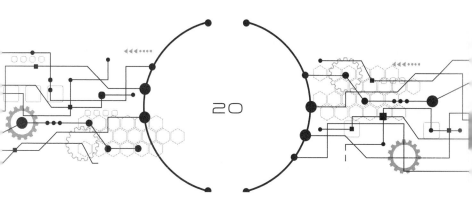

20

elissa's #CopSelfie was heavily retweeted. While they spent the afternoon stuck in traffic on the Major Deegan Expressway, she mounted an all-out social media blitz to capitalize on their momentum.

She set the air freshener to "Maui" and put everyone to work monitoring keywords and relevant mentions. Twitter feeds scrolled through the beach-scented interior, painting their faces with translucent hashtags. Pics and reblogs and memes crowded the windows. She set the whirling digital matrix for half-opacity so she could keep an eye on the city skyline as they crept through the Bronx.

It was the most exhilarating multitasking she'd ever done. Otto let her use apps that she'd only read about, beta versions of tools that weren't available to the general public and possibly never would be. She created a SocialOracle account to run predictive models of the future of her social success—at this rate, how many followers could she expect tomorrow, a week from now, a year? Which fashion-world influencers and celebrities were likely to respond to certain pics and GIFs over others? As chatter spiraled inward toward the four people at the core of the #AutonomousRoadTrip, Otto brought them into the epicenter of what would be College Melissa's life.

At 3:28 p.m., the state trooper in the photo issued an apology on his Facebook page after hundreds of people called him out for letting a speeder go free and being dumb enough to post about it. The internet assumed that Melissa had flirted #CopSelfie into existence, but in reality the trooper was a serious car guy. She had diagnosed the situation and spoke to him like a normal person shooting the shit about an incredible new prototype. The whole point of the picture was that they were standing in front of Autonomous, not that some horny young cop was snapping a photo with an eighteen-year-old girl he'd just pulled over.

There was nothing she could do about the internet's perception of the photo. It was no use overexplaining anything you posted online. That only served to make the situation worse, creating a vortex with you at the center, protesting too much.

Everybody in the car, including Daniel, also assumed that she'd flirted her way out of a ticket. That was a perception she could easily change. But as soon as she'd climbed back inside, she caught William eyeing her cleavage (for the millionth time today; did guys think they were being subtle?) while Christina shot her a look of disgust that she obviously thought she was hiding in her usual pinched-face glare.

So what if Melissa had done what they all assumed in order to make the ticket go away? Sometimes there was a fierce pride in inhabiting the skin of the person everyone thought you were.

It was like a social experiment, seeing how far you could push a caricature made of other people's preconceived notions. The problem was, when you spent too much time doubling down, even your boyfriend failed to see past the persona, forgot that he knew you better than that.

In the first few months of their relationship, they used to hiss at each other like cats until they cracked up.

Daniel was still getting used to the mechanics of Otto's displays. She watched as he dragged a feed monitoring #Autonomous with aching slowness, using two fingers like he was making a stiff horizontal peace sign. His coordination seemed a little off—troubling for someone about to play college basketball.

At 3:58 p.m., the precise moment the car veered into the Manhattan-bound lane on the RFK Bridge, influencer Tyrone Cain regrammed the photo they'd taken with Patricia Ming-Waller, and Melissa's follower count topped 2,000.

It had been 976 when they left Fremont Hills.

At 4:13 p.m., they turned onto Houston Street. Melissa remembered the day she discovered how effervescent and sprightly she looked in dresses with asymmetrical hemlines, and how overjoyed she'd been to find that these designs dovetailed perfectly with her skills. This feeling of life falling into place around her talents was the reason she'd decided to come to New York. Autonomous stopped for a red light at Houston and Avenue C. Melissa stepped away from her spherical news rotations and knelt on the bench to peer out at the city.

People in Fremont Hills looked at her oddly when she said she couldn't wait to get to New York. Her aunt Linda and uncle Dave did this thing where they scrunched up their faces one at a time, as if sucking the air from each other's lungs in order to speak.

Linda: (scrunch in) But you're living on top of each other down there! How does anybody BREATHE? (scrunch out)

Dave: (scrunch in) I'll tell you something, last time I was there, it stunk like piss! You know they just leave the trash out on the sidewalk for the animals to get at, and they wonder why they got a rat problem. (scrunch out)

The light turned green and the car moved west. Melissa's hungry eyes took in the scene. She almost wished Linda and Dave were here. *You see? You see how beautiful this place is?* But she knew she was seeing New York through different eyes than the Aunt Lindas and Uncle Daves of the world. That was okay. All the people in Fremont Hills who were scared to find out what life had to offer outside of small-town social climbing and gossip could suck it.

In a few years, Melissa Faber's name would be on everybody's lips.

She watched the city glide past, each block a self-contained panorama of bodegas with sun-faded merchandise in the windows, bars with obscure names or no names at all, glass-walled mega-buildings muscling in on corners while tenement walk-ups lined the side streets.

They passed Thompson, Sullivan, Macdougal. Soon this would be her neighborhood: NYU was only a few blocks away. She wondered if Otto had gone this way on purpose.

Her mind scanned fashion Terminator-style, surveying the rabid meshing of preppy guys with glinting watches and gutter punks with camo backpacks and twig-thin girls in jeggings or garish harem pants. She so rarely considered headwear, but even in summer, the city was a panoply of hats: floppy beachy things and peaked caps and snap-brimmed fedoras. Lots of black denim and black tops and little black dresses, but plenty of wild colors too, as if neon graffiti had jumped off the bricks to splash across clothes.

When she focused on specific details—spikes on a window-sill, the parting of a curtain six floors up—each aspect of the city seemed to imprint itself upon her.

"Fabes?" She broke contact with the outside world. Daniel handed her a blue-and-silver can: her afternoon Red Bull. The car was stocked with energy drinks. Half of them were KombuchaTine, which her older sister Emily guzzled every morning, and the other half were Red Bulls. Melissa hated KombuchaTine—it tasted like how mold smelled—so its only purpose was to remind her of her sister.

Daniel regarded her with wry concern. "Your meds."

She accepted the can gratefully and popped the top.

Otto switched to her getting-shit-done playlist. The car shook with low end, and synths tickled the edges; then the beat dropped. Daniel and William began dancing with mock intensity, limbs flailing like octopus tentacles. Daniel had to bend his knees to keep from bashing into the ceiling, which lent a further undersea quality to his movements.

She laughed. "You look like a crab."

He scuttled close and his hands were snapping claws.

They used to make up crazy dances together all the time.

She felt an overwhelming urge to get silly. In public.

She held his claw-hand and took out her phone. "We're going

to the sickest club tonight," she announced while tweeting.

"Is it Anime Club?" Christina asked without lifting her eyes from her laptop screen.

While she was typing, Melissa realized that she had no idea what the sickest club in New York was. She left a blank space in her unpublished tweet and was about to open her browser to research locations when the tweet finished writing itself and posted automatically. She gawked at the screen, trying to figure out what had happened. Then it dawned on her: Otto had done a split-second calculation to find the hottest nightspot, aggregating lifestyle blogs and scene reports and online reviews and party pics faster than she could even write a single tweet.

The car was making a good case for being the brains of the operation.

Melissa cast her Otto-enhanced tweet to the car's central display. Words the size of fists shimmered in the air.

New York! #AutonomousRoadTrip is taking over Azimuth tonight. Come show us how NYC gets down.

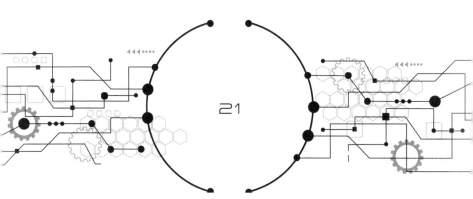

21

By the time Autonomous pulled up to Azimuth on Rivington Street, a crowd had gathered in the drizzly night to snap photos of the car. Melissa's heart pounded. This was their first big public appearance, and SocialOracle had predicted that the attention could rocket her follower count above 4,000 and capture the attention of Jessa Park.

Without their knowledge—but thankfully—Otto had booked two rooms at the Ruby Soho, a chic hotel on Grand Street. That left them the first part of the evening to chill out and get dressed in luxurious solitude, instead of trying to figure out how to use the car's privacy shrouds and fumbling with their clothes in confined spaces. She'd modeled four different outfits for Daniel. He favored an eighties throwback halter and what looked like a sheer skirt but was actually a half wrap attached to a pair of stretchy shorts.

Then he'd excused himself for an outrageously long shower

and emerged from the bathroom in a cloud of steam, alert and energized, his body lobstered from the hot water, yelling to the room in a posh British accent, demanding cigars and martinis and a signed first edition of James Joyce's *Ulysses*.

Melissa had picked out a simple black ensemble for him—very New York—with a loose-fitting shirt so he wouldn't look like a steroid freak from the Jersey Shore. When she dialed down his jockness, he looked like a guy in a band. Not the kind of band Christina listened to, but a band that wrote songs people actually liked, and featured members people actually enjoyed looking at.

William rocked skinny jeans and a nondescript but acceptable shirt. She'd done the best she could on their shopping trip. There hadn't been a lot to work with—Plattsburgh wasn't exactly Milan—but he looked less sloppy than usual. As long as he put that hair to work, he'd be fine.

Christina was going to be a problem.

She refused to change her clothes or apply even a touch of blush to her skin. Now they were huddled inside the car, seconds from bursting into the glare of what might as well be paparazzi flashbulbs, three of them decked out for a genuine party night and Christina in black jean shorts that were too baggy and unflattering to register as some kind of anti-fashion statement and a shirt that sported a Japanese cartoon warrior with an impossibly oversize sword slung over his shoulder and a ridiculous crop of white hair that hung down to his thighs.

Christina didn't seem to understand the gravity of a red-carpet situation.

What drove her nuts was that the girl could have a really intriguing look if she just spent five minutes letting Melissa help her get ready. The shaved-head/all-black aesthetic could totally work, but it was a fashion rule that most people couldn't pull off I-don't-give-a-shit if they truly did not give a shit. You had to lavish care on not giving a shit for it to look cool. Christina looked like the kind of girl who spent twenty-four hours a day writing fanfiction.

"Stop appraising me," Christina said. Melissa looked away—she'd just been caught frowning in disapproval. "I told you, I'll just stay in the car."

"Nobody's staying in the car," William said. "Just pretend it's the CB Lounge. Look"—he pointed out the window—"they have a velvet rope and everything."

Christina scratched her head. "Things I hate include dance music, dancing, people who dance, and air that has recently been danced in. Explain to me why I would go into a place like this?"

"Maybe we should pregame first," Daniel suggested. His energy seemed to be flagging. Even so, Melissa had noticed that he went out of his way to be kind to Christina.

"They'll probably give us free drinks inside," William said. "Look at all these people!"

Melissa took note of two separate groups: people waiting for the massive bouncer to let them in, and a loose coalition gathered on the sidewalk.

"Fuckin' . . . mimosas," Daniel said.

Melissa recognized the tone and cringed. "Not now. Please."

"Fuckin' . . . Bloody Marys," William said, adopting the same faux-tough-guy inflection. Melissa had watched them perform this stupid back-and-forth a million times. The premise was that they'd volley increasingly pretentious items until someone made them shut up. It was an obnoxious inside joke with no apparent source and no clever origin.

"Fuckin' . . . apple martinis."

"Fuckin' . . . cosmopolitans."

"Fuckin' . . . pomegranate margaritas."

"Fuckin' . . . rye old-fashioneds."

"Fuckin' . . . vodka sodas with lime."

"Jesus Christ, okay, okay." Christina slapped her palm against the door and it slid silently open.

Melissa had to stop herself from screaming *NOOOOOOOO* as Christina's sneakers hit the pavement, and cameras flashed. A million posts of Christina dourly representing the #AutonomousRoadTrip flashed through her mind. She would be guilty by association! Jessa Park would forever link Melissa Faber and *DIYfashion365* to basement dwellers and upstate hicks who shouldn't be allowed to set foot in a city with an actual nightlife.

Before she knew it, she was scrambling out after Christina, heels stabbing the sidewalk, eyes on the back of the girl's shaved head where she'd missed a clump of hair. She had to catch up before Christina directed some snide remark at the bouncer that blew their chances of getting in. The last thing they needed was to star in somebody's video: *#AutonomousRoadTrip Hilariously DENIED at Azimuth.*

"Hey!" some random guy yelled. "Can I get a ride in that?"

Before Melissa could think of a witty response, Christina raised both fists, middle fingers extended. Cameras flashed.

Melissa could seriously not even.

People who hid behind computers and only popped up to strafe the world with random bursts of hostility were the worst.

Why did anybody think it was okay to radiate such negativity? What had that ever accomplished?

Just as she reached Christina's side, she felt Daniel's hand on her shoulder. The boys must have climbed out after her, self-conscious kids stumbling into their first big night on the town. They might as well have emerged from the car chewing tobacco and wearing overalls stained with mud from the swimmin' hole.

"Hey, chill out," Daniel said.

It was good advice: her shoulders were hunched with tension. Ahead, the bouncer swiveled his head on his thick neck to regard them with half-lidded bemusement. There was something cold and reptilian in his gaze. He spoke quietly into his Bluetooth.

This was all wrong.

The club was housed in a former church, and the ornate façade stretched up into the misty night with gothic grandeur, floodlights pouring long shadows down the stonework. The rain's aftermath gave the neon Azimuth sign a fuzzy halo.

"Fabes, I think the line's that way?"

She linked arms with her boyfriend. "We're not waiting in the line."

"Oh. Did Otto put us on the guest list or something?"

"I have no idea. It doesn't matter. Either way, we're not people who wait in lines. Not on this trip."

"So, next stop Disney World, then?"

"I mean, if we present ourselves as people who don't wait in lines, it's easier to become people who don't wait in lines."

She was supposed to be having fun. She was also trying to leverage the experience into something greater. Right now she was failing at both, but she couldn't snap out of it. Her smile felt unnatural and waxy. She stood in front of the bouncer. The eyebrow lifted in his doughy face.

Skinny girls glared from the line.

"Fuck off," the bouncer said.

"Excuse me?"

"Gotta be twenty-one."

The bouncer nodded sleepily to a guy in a white linen suit who looked like he'd just stepped off a plane from 1980s Miami. White Suit lifted the rope, and people streamed inside the huge wooden doors. He refastened the rope, and the line stopped moving.

"We got IDs," Daniel said. Melissa thought he sounded a little too proud of this.

The bouncer made a harsh guttural rasp that might have been a laugh. He turned to face them again, held up his phone and gave it a little shake. "I know you're high school kids, dipshit."

"We're not," Melissa protested.

"Lesson number one: think before you tweet. Lesson number two: lots of bouncers are moonlighting cops."

Melissa stared blankly. What was this guy driving at?

He sighed. "You stirred up a shitstorm for that rookie trooper today, you know that? And then, lo and behold, you're coming to my club on a night I'm working the door. You eat a lot of shit in this life, but sometimes the universe does you a favor. Now, go hop back in your spacemobile and enjoy your visit to the island of Manhattan somewhere I can't see you. This is a club for grown-ups."

The bouncer shot them a mirthless grin and went back to work. White Suit lifted the rope, and a gaggle of kids streamed inside. They might as well have had their foreheads stamped UNDERAGE.

Melissa struggled to find words. She could feel everyone's eyes on her, Melissa the Fixer. Daniel beside her, Christina and William at her back. Nobody piped up. Weren't they supposed to be a team? Why didn't anybody understand that she was thinking long-term re: their social media presence? She had a split-second fantasy of putting this barn-size lump of a bouncer in his place with sharp-tongued wit, Daniel busting out some weird eloquence to back her up, people on the street capturing their heroic stand on video that would reach Jessa Park, who'd be so blown away that she'd share it with millions of fans and—

Melissa was halfway down the block before she realized what she was doing, which was walking away.

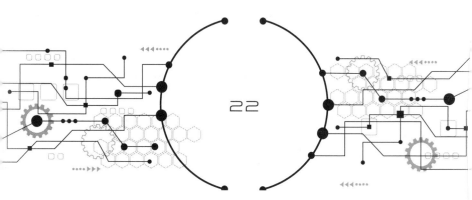

t was after midnight when they burst through the emergency door to the roof of the apartment building and froze, waiting for the alarm to go off. Nothing happened. William raised two paper-bagged bottles of malt liquor above his head.

Victory!

They were on top of a ten-story building at the corner of Fourth Street and Avenue A. It had taken them surprisingly few attempts to mash random buttons until a tenant buzzed them in.

There were no lights up here, but Melissa could see just fine. The building was nestled in the East Village, surrounded by walk-ups that rarely topped six floors. Sleek towers jutted up from the Financial District to the south, the imposing bulk of Midtown offices to the north. The night sky trapped light and dispersed an otherworldly glow across the city. Its presence seemed fixed and timeless, as if it had blanketed the sky long before Manhattan rose from the dirt and would remain long after Manhattan fell.

Broken glass glittered in the corner next to the skeletal remains of a folding chair.

"See?!" William said, voice pitched to near hysteria. He spun around in a slow circle. "This is a million times better than being cooped up in a sweaty club."

"You've never been to a club," Melissa said.

"I still want to go to one, but screw Azimuth. I'm glad we didn't get in. We can have our own club up here, just the four of us." He sat down on the roof and uncapped one of his forty-ounce bottles.

Daniel plunked down a plastic bag stuffed with more bottles (the guy in the corner deli had barely glanced at their IDs) and snatched Melissa's hand. Before she could react, he was guiding her through the steps of a surprisingly elegant waltz, which they'd practiced together one wintry afternoon, instructed by a YouTube tutorial. Daniel was in graceful athlete mode, and she let herself be swept along the rooftop. The boys were trying hard to cheer her up. She wished she could let College Melissa recede and simply live in the moment, but the city—*her* city—in all its humid nighttime glory was too overwhelming to ignore.

An icy beat thumped from William's phone speaker.

"Club Rooftop is now in session," he said. As Melissa spun, she saw Christina take a seat next to William and reach for the bag. *Club Rooftop*, she thought. That would make a cute selfie caption; maybe she could salvage this night yet. But the photo had to be something more interesting than the four of them just hanging out, even if the backdrop was gorgeous. Daniel spun her to face downtown. Office lights tapped out patterns in walls of glass, and she thought of coded messages before

Daniel shifted her view uptown. She felt his cheek pressed against hers and remembered introducing him to the wonders of face moisturizers on a different wintry day in far-off Fremont Hills. She became aware of his heart hammering through his entire body, alarmingly fast. He was surging with adrenaline, pouring excess good cheer onto her.

Let yourself be charmed by this.

What did it mean when you had to think about letting your boyfriend charm you instead of automatically feeling charmed? Thoughts like these were easy to cast aside during their Wednesday alone time, when she could tear off his shirt and lose herself in the contours of his body and quit thinking about everything else. But in full view of William and Christina and a million strangers glancing idly out of their high-rise windows, they might as well be written in the sky.

"We should do this every year on the exact same night," he said. "Meet up at Club Rooftop and dance."

"You and me?" she asked. "Or all four of us?"

He hesitated. She spun to the east. Tompkins Square Park was a dark square patch in the city's fabric. "Just you and me," he said. "It'll be our thing."

He turned her to the west, and the view was eclipsed by a curious silhouette: a raised platform upon which sat a massive cylinder the size of a squat grain silo, capped with a pointy hat. Identical structures dotted the city's rooftops. She'd noticed them on her first college visit. Google told her they were water towers. From the street they seemed like quaint anachronisms, wooden relics of a bygone era. Up here, the building's water tower loomed sinister and creepy, and she was glad to dance away. His hand moved up under her top and skimmed the light sheen of sweat in the hollow of her lower back.

"It seems like the kind of thing people would do for a reunion," she said, choosing her words carefully. "People who hadn't seen each other in a long time."

She felt his body tense. "Or," he said, "it's the kind of thing a couple might do. Like celebrating an anniversary."

"The beginning of something," she said.

Daniel laughed. "Or the end."

She almost pushed him away, astonished at his flippancy— what kind of a boyfriend *laughs* before saying that? She decided to play it casual. "What's funny about that, exactly?" She gave his chest a little tickle.

"Oh, shit." He stopped dancing and pulled away. "I am so sorry. Jesus. I didn't mean to say that out loud."

"You just meant to think it."

"Yeah. I mean, no. I mean . . . you know how I told you that sometimes I get the feeling I'm writing the movie of my life as it's going along, like I'm typing the script as it's happening? Sometimes a good line pops into my head, but it doesn't have anything to do with what I'm actually feeling. . . ." He paused to gather his thoughts. "This is hard to explain!" He seemed desperate to make her understand. "I mean the movie that's going along, sometimes it splits off from reality. . . ."

"Hey, Daniel!" William called. He held up two more bottles. City lights slid down the glass. "It's time!" He gave Christina a nod. She pulled a roll of electrical tape from the plastic bag, unpeeled a long piece with a horrible sticky-scratchy noise, and began wrapping the tape around the bottle and William's hand. It looked to Melissa like an impatient doctor binding a fractured wrist. Once the first bottle was securely fastened to William's right hand, she started on the left.

Melissa rolled her eyes. "Seriously? Now?"

Daniel looked hurt. "Fabes, you *love* Edward Fortyhands!"

"Oh my God, I can't with you. I *hate* Edward Fortyhands. You must be thinking of the movie version of me."

Her phone buzzed in her back pocket.

"No, listen," Daniel said, "I didn't explain it right, but there isn't really a movie version of you, there's just you, you're the same, but sometimes the script goes in a different direction."

"Go play," she said, turning her back and heading for the far corner of the roof. "Have fun."

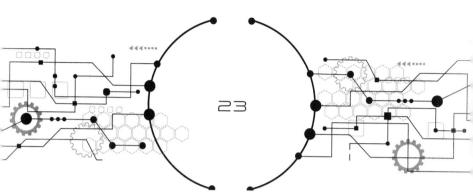

loaked in darkness, Melissa faced west toward Washington Square Park. Her view was blocked, but she still thought she could make out the flat top of the NYU library, a massive twelve-story cube. Electrical tape crinkled behind her as Christina bound Daniel's bottles to his hands and said something to make the boys laugh. Melissa shook her head and stood on tiptoe, straining to find a clear line of sight across the landscape of rooftops that rose and fell as if stacked by a hyper child. Phrases like "move-in day" and "welcome week" and "bursar's office" ran through her head in a pleasant litany of College Melissa vocab. With a pang of anticipation, she opened Epheme.

Ash:	Hey girl, how's life on the road?
SewWhat:	Meh.
Ash:	That's not a very *DIYfashion365* attitude.
SewWhat:	Trip's good, car's unreal. Weird night is all.

Ash: Anything I can do?

SewWhat: I really shouldn't be talking about this with you of all people.

Ash: I'm here for you. Anything. You know that.

SewWhat: When you went to college, were you still dating anybody from home?

Ash: Wow, this is taking our relationship to a whole new level.

SewWhat: You said ANYTHING, lol.

Ash: Yes. I had a girlfriend from high school. Amanda, haha.

SewWhat: Ash and Amanda. Nice.

Ash: We lasted till fall break.

SewWhat: What happened?

Ash: You don't realize it until you get to college, but the person you're becoming starts taking up all your energy, and the person you used to be feels like a copy of a copy, all out of focus. So if you stay together with somebody from home, you both end up trying to love these fuzzy images of each other. TL;DR: love fades.

SewWhat: Wow. Real talk.

Ash: I'm obviously biased since I think you should be focusing on other things ☺ but I would suggest breaking up with him now to avoid a lot more pain later.

SewWhat: Okay. Moving on.

Ash: What are you wearing?

SewWhat: Too dark to show you.

Ash: It's called a flash, babe.

SewWhat: Haha touché. No pic for you.

Behind her, William screamed, "I already have to pee so bad!"

Edward Fortyhands had but one rule: the bottles stayed taped to your hands until you finished them both. Of course it was extremely difficult to unzip your pants, or even pull them down, using huge, ungainly forty-ounce bottles instead of human fingers. Therefore competitors had to hold it until the alcohol was gone.

Finishing eighty ounces of malt liquor in a timely fashion was basically impossible.

It was a stupid game.

William and Daniel loved it. They talked strategy when they weren't even playing, as if it were a complex puzzle that required creative thinking to master. She glanced over her shoulder. The light seemed unbalanced, spilling across William and Christina in equal measure but relegating Daniel to the shadows. All she could see was the glinting of his bottle-hands.

The beat from William's phone went staticky as the streaming station lost its connection. Christina switched the music to something ragged and abrasive. At this, Daniel emerged from the shadows. He threw his head back and howled at the sky and took a long swig. Christina squealed—a noise that Melissa had never once heard her make—and William let loose with a howl of his own.

She turned back to her phone.

Ash:	My turn to ask you something.
SewWhat:	It's only fair.
Ash:	Is this road trip of yours gonna take you near Albuquerque?
SewWhat:	Not sure yet.

Ash:	Because we could meet up.
SewWhat:	Now who's taking it to the next level?
Ash:	I'm serious. I've got business out here for a month or two, a bunch of houses I'm flipping. It would be amazing to see you.
SewWhat:	It would be amazing to see you too, it just might be hard to get away.
Ash:	You're a beautiful talented genius. You can do anything.

Across the avenue, a light went on in a spacious corner apartment. The décor was immaculate. Melissa watched a woman glide to a wrought-iron wine rack. *Soon that'll be me*, she thought. She felt like she could float across the gap between buildings and soar, slingshot around the spire of the Empire State Building and land in Washington Square Park with her future already plotted. The lights of Manhattan brightened in welcome, blinking a message solely for her.

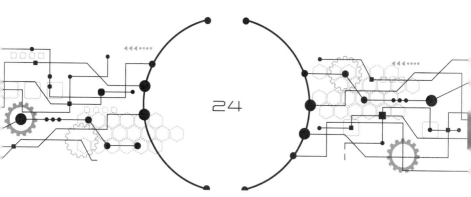

24

The boys raced to a dead-heat finish, heads tilted back, cheap malt liquor streaming down the shirts Melissa had chosen for them. Daniel was shifting his weight from side to side, crashing against invisible walls. William stood with his legs crossed like a little kid.

"Come on come on come on," Daniel said as Melissa clawed at the tape around his hands while Christina freed William.

Melissa felt a nail bend back and hissed.

"My eyes are turning yellow," William said, swaying like a breeze-shaken sapling. "Are my eyes yellow?"

"That was solid work," Daniel said. "Personal bests." He was slurring less than William, but his face had undergone a Drunk Daniel transformation that Melissa knew well. Alcohol unchiseled his features.

"Congratulations," Christina said. "The medal ceremony will be held . . . never."

"Pee ceremony is what I want," William said. "A ceremony of pee."

Melissa freed one hand and dropped the bottle to the rooftop. She flung the ball of tape away and started on the other.

"I'm sorry," Daniel said quietly. He seemed to snap back into some momentary window of sobriety.

Melissa was quicker with the second hand. Tape fell away in sticky ribbons. "For what?"

"Being me."

Melissa wondered how she was supposed to respond to that. "Daniel," she said. That was all she could come up with.

She found herself holding a fistful of tape from which the empty bottle dangled like some insane medieval weapon. She let it fall to her feet. Daniel and William sprinted to opposite corners of the roof, leaving Melissa alone with Christina.

"Go in the car, you guys!" Christina yelled. "Ugh." She was half a forty deep herself. Only Melissa's was untouched— malt liquor was disgusting. It reminded her of the little camp in the woods that she and Daniel had stumbled on last summer. Bottles, tin cans, and soiled clothing strewn around a greasy tarp.

Talk about a mood killer, he'd said.

I think this is the home of an actual *killer*, she'd replied.

"Isn't Otto back at the hotel?" Melissa asked.

"Check it out." Christina walked to the side of the roof that overlooked Fourth Street. Melissa followed and peered down over the edge. The silver car was parked directly beneath them.

"It tracks the GPS in our phones," Christina said. "*Your* phones."

Melissa took a long, hard look at Christina, trying to

understand the girl's impulse to constantly set herself apart like the poster child for alienation. Why not just try to form real connections, even for a few days, to make the road trip more fun for everybody? How hard could that be?

She wondered if Christina was one of her father's dental patients. It was strange to picture the girl interacting with members of her family.

She watched as Christina began scratching the side of her head, just above her ear, as she stared back at Melissa.

"What?" Melissa said.

"You first."

Melissa shrugged.

"I was just thinking about college," Christina said, with an earnestness that took Melissa by surprise. Was Hernandez drunk? Did she have a tolerance? Melissa was sure the girl had never been to an actual party. The thought of her drinking alone in that basement room was beyond depressing. Then she reminded herself that Christina hung out with William nearly every day.

It was easy to forget why Christina was here. She almost seemed like a manifestation, a trick Otto was playing on them.

"You're going to Buffalo, right?"

"Yeah." Christina gazed across the city. "I might transfer, though, after a semester or two. We'll see how it goes."

She added this so abruptly, Melissa suspected it had just occurred to her, or else she was lying.

"I'm sure it'll be really fun."

"It'll be like living in Fremont Hills, but even colder because of the huge-ass lake."

"But at least it's a *city*. I mean, you can do things there."

"Go to Bills games. Gain weight." Christina looked at Melissa. "Die."

Melissa laughed. "You're going to college, not heading off to the coal mines. You'll meet new people, figure out what you want to do . . ."

She trailed off, worried that she sounded like a patronizing know-it-all, like Emily when she called home from Harvard. But Christina didn't seem to notice. She was even nodding at Melissa's words. A little absently, maybe, but it was encouraging. "And you'll meet guys," Melissa said.

At this, Christina crossed her arms and turned again to the city.

With a rush of mortification, Melissa wondered if Christina was into guys. She cringed, thinking about how she'd called the girl *mama* the day of the Derby. She was just trying to be friendly, but what if Christina thought she was a racist homophobe? She tried to come up with something to say that would undo that notion.

"I like your wallet chain."

"Thanks. You can't see the stars here. Did you notice that?"

Melissa looked up at the sky. It was true: the light pollution was an incandescent shield.

"One semester in the city and you'll be lacking the vital star minerals your body needs," Christina said. "Two semesters, and who knows?"

"At least I won't be buried under ten feet of lake-effect snow."

Christina gave her a side-eyed glance. A little smirk played at the edge of her mouth. Melissa thought they might be on the verge of a breakthrough, finally sharing a moment—

"IT SAYS HERE THERE'S SUPPPOSED TO BE A HATCH!"

—and the moment was shattered by Daniel's voice. They both turned to watch as he stood in the shadow of the forbidding water tower, face bathed in the glow of his phone.

"LIKE AN ACCESS PANEL ON THE TOP PART THAT LOOKS LIKE RAIDEN'S HAT!"

Melissa's breath caught in her throat.

William was climbing up the side of the tower on a rickety-looking ladder, an apparition silhouetted against the night city like a superhero in a vivid comic panel.

Except he wasn't a superhero. He was a shitfaced moron.

Christina took off across the roof. "William, what the hell are you doing?!"

Melissa followed. "Daniel! Get him down from there!" She was close enough to see her boyfriend turn and give her a theatrical shrug, the universal gesture for *what do you want me to do about it?*

"Found it!" William yelled triumphantly. He was perched at the top of the ladder, gripping the final rung with one hand. A dark square cutout flipped up as he opened the access panel and let it fall against the tower.

Melissa reached Daniel's side, and her feet nudged a pile of clothes: the jeans she'd picked out in Plattsburgh, along with William's shoes and shirt.

"He's *naked*?" She gripped Daniel's arm. She hoped she was getting through to his inebriated ass.

"Nah, he's got his boxers on," Daniel said.

Christina cupped her hands around her mouth and called up from the bottom of the ladder. "William, this is incredibly stupid. Please come down."

William fell out of view. There was a muffled splash, then silence.

Christina gave an anguished cry and started up the ladder.

"We should get a GoPro for stuff like this," Daniel said.

"Are you fucking kidding me?" Melissa tightened her grip on his arm and dragged him to the base of the ladder.

"Ow, Fabes! Don't worry, he's fine. He's William."

"How is this fine, Daniel? How is this okay with you? What if he—"

"Come on in, everybody, the water's great!"

Melissa craned her neck, but all she could see was Christina, scrambling up with surprising speed. She stepped back, Daniel by her side, until she had a clear line of sight to the top of the tower. Now William was perched at the top of the ladder. He waved.

Christina stopped climbing. "Would you just get down?!"

"It's super easy!" he called back, as if she'd asked about the logistics of swimming in a water tower. "The ladder curves right down inside, so you can just climb back out! I think there might be some dead birds in there!"

"See?" Daniel said. "He's William."

"So what?!" Melissa said, taken aback by her own anger. "What does that mean? *He's William.* He could have died just now, Daniel. And then what? Then what would you do?"

Daniel reached out a tentative hand. "Fabes, calm down, he's fine."

She stepped out of his reach. "I hate it when you tell me to calm down. And you know what else? He doesn't seem very fine to me."

She turned her back and left them there, all three frozen as she'd last glimpsed them: Daniel twisting his face into frightened contortions, the dark mantislike shapes of Christina and William playing out their own private drama high above the rooftop. Her eyes sought the lighted apartment across the avenue, desperate for another dose of that sublime New York City existence, but the light had gone off. She held her phone with two hands and tried to pull up Ash's words, but Epheme had deleted the conversation as soon as she closed the app, and now there was nothing left.

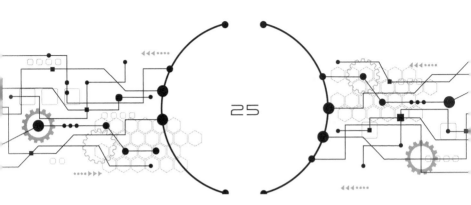

hristina had been nine years old the last time she stayed in a hotel, a seedy place in Lake George during the summer after fourth grade. She remembered the full-throated roar of Harleys cruising the main drag of the village, rows of arcades and shops that leaked incense, a bench painted to look like a cow. Back then, her mother had opened the door to their hotel with an old-fashioned iron key like a castle jailer might have used.

At the door of her room in the Ruby Soho, Christina waved a little plastic fob imprinted with a gold RS emblem in front of a brass panel above the latch. An LED flashed from red to green. *How nice for the hotel to be able to track its guests' movements*, she thought as the lock clicked. She pushed open the door and stepped inside. The suite was small, and yet, she suspected, very pricey. An ornate rolltop desk that looked like a piece of furniture stolen from an eccentric villain's lair held a gleaming espresso machine and a docking halo for devices and computers. The oversize bed faced a wall-mounted 3-D smart TV. Totally hackable, if somebody in, say, Dubai felt like kicking back and watching the intimate happenings inside Ruby Soho room 238.

William brushed past her, lumbering triumphantly inside. Christina wrinkled her nose.

"You smell like dysentery."

He grinned and flopped his arms out wide—a king in his mead hall, addressing his subjects. "Look where we are!" He went to the bed, patting the pale lavender comforter, caressing the hem of a tightly tucked sheet with the exaggerated tenderness of a drunk person trying to disguise motor-control issues. "Did you ever think we'd be in a place like this?"

"What, together?"

He shrugged. "Beats the Best Western in Fremont Hills."

As she was wondering if he'd ever really been inside the Best Western in Fremont Hills, and when, and for what purpose, and with whom, he put his arms out again and began to tilt slowly forward. Christina grabbed his wrist and leaned back, keeping him from face-planting onto the bed. Eighty ounces of malt liquor had Jell-O-ized his limbs and turned him into deadweight. She struggled to hold him up.

"You gotta take a shower before you get dead-bird residue all over our bed." The words *our bed* seemed to linger in the air between them. How strange to say that out loud! But it was true, at least on a basic logistical level. They were sharing this hotel room. There was only one bed.

"My hair's barely even wet!" he protested.

She pulled him toward the bathroom. "It's a little

disconcerting that your first impulse wasn't to scrub yourself down and incinerate your clothes."

William let himself be dragged, feet shuffling along the plush carpet. "No way, I love this shirt." Christina flicked on the bathroom light. "Whoa," William said at the sight of them in the mirror.

At some point during their five-second stagger into the bathroom, her hand had apparently slid down his wrist, and now their fingers were intertwined. Their eyes met in the mirror and she thought of Doubles: fingertips pressed together, lips closing the gap. Behind them, the reflection of the bedroom beckoned softly.

"You scared the shit out of me up there," she said, watching his eyes travel down her arm to their clasped hands.

"I was fine," he said. Maybe it was just the malt liquor, but it sounded to Christina like he simply did not understand why his dive into a pitch-black water tower might have left her slightly rattled.

She dropped her eyes. Flecks of mica embedded in the countertop caught the bathroom light. Kermit the Frog and Miss Piggy smiled up from William's toothbrush.

"You're a dick," she said.

He grinned. "You were *moving* up that ladder, huh?" He freed his hand and pulled the shower curtain aside. "Um, this thing has Jacuzzi jets!" He turned to Christina. "I might be a while."

"Wash your hair," she said. "Rinse and repeat."

"Yes, ma'am." He turned the knob, and water splashed into the tub. "Room service me a rubber duckie."

Without waiting for her to leave him alone, he pulled

his shirt up over his head and dropped it on the tiled floor. Turning away, she lingered to catch a glimpse in the mirror as he reached for the dial that controlled the water temperature. Skin stretched taut across his rib cage. She followed the lean curvature of his upper arm to the plum-colored abrasion on his shoulder, road rash from the concrete half-pipe back home. On her way out she grabbed a pair of fresh towels from the metal rack above the toilet. William's belt buckle jingled. She stepped into the bedroom and shut the door behind her.

Her eyes rested on the bedside table. It was covered in a layer of dust she hadn't noticed before. No matter how hard the maids worked to clean a hotel room, there was always residue: microscopic sediments of hair products, particulate matter of powders and nighttime face creams and spilled drinks and fluids she didn't want to think about. The suite was far dingier than it had looked a moment ago, when the mirror had drawn into its sparkling perfection the simmering magic of Next-Door Neighbor Friends sharing a bed in a fancy hotel.

Forcing William into the bathroom and ordering him to clean up felt like such a dumb motherly task. And for him to undress so casually in front of her as if she were some random boy in the gym locker room . . .

Her hand was at her scalp, nails digging deep. She winced as the sharp pinkie nail made a fresh, delicious gouge. Then she forced her hand down, crossed the room, and draped the towels over the TV, smoothing them flat to block the screen and the eye of the remote sensor.

The closed bathroom door and the tub's running water muffled William's voice, but his off-key singing was clear enough. *"RUBBER DUCKIE, YOU'RE THE ONE."*

She pulled her laptop from its pouch in her camping backpack and sat down on the bed with her back against the formidable stack of elongated pillows. The laptop was named Kimmie, the diminutive of Kimberly in both size and power. She wriggled a hand into the pocket of her jean shorts and retrieved the seashell, which was disguised as an external drive, a sleek little Toshiba the size and shape of an iPhone. She fed the seashell into Kimmie's port and cycled back in time to encompass the hours spent on Club Rooftop. As long as she kept the seashell in proximity to Melissa and Daniel, the device would have no trouble intercepting their communications and filtering out useless digital noise.

Heart quickening, she read Melissa's latest chat with Ash: *Hey girl, how's life on the road?* She added the Epheme session to her collection of intercepts.

"RUBBER DUCKIE, I'M AWFULLY FOND OF YOOOOUUUUU."

What would Melissa do in this situation? Undress and barge into the bathroom? Dim the lights and wait beneath the sheets?

She advanced the seashell to join the present time. Daniel and Melissa were staying in room 240, just on the other side of the wall. She watched the screen idly for a moment, assuming they were otherwise occupied. But to her surprise, Daniel began to chat.

DB837651: Your services have been greatly appreciated

xoxoPixieDustxoxo: Haha put it in your yelp review

DB837651: On it

xoxoPixieDustxoxo: How's the trip? Homesick already?

DB837651: Nah just helping myself to Melissa's 40

xoxoPixieDustxoxo:	You in a hotel?
DB837651:	Yeah, she's asleep
xoxoPixieDustxoxo:	Et tu?
DB837651 :	Not tired
xoxoPixieDustxoxo:	That'll happen, just think nice thoughts
DB837651 :	About your room
xoxoPixieDustxoxo:	Okay ending transmission
DB837651:	Goodnight

Christina dutifully copied Daniel's chat into her document. Comparing the intercepts side by side brought their differences to light. Melissa was obviously having some kind of ongoing thing with an older guy, which seemed like such a Melissa Faber move that Christina barely even felt like she was peeking at a secret. But whatever Daniel had with Pixie Dust was more enigmatic. Yelp review? Services? She collected her thoughts for a moment and typed a few sentences beneath the fresh intercepts. Then she disconnected the seashell, shut down her laptop, and stowed them both in her backpack.

Lying down and staring at the ceiling, she listened to William's clumsy sloshing as he stepped out of the tub. Five minutes later he was sprawled on the bed in a thick white Ruby Soho bathrobe. She watched him sleep.

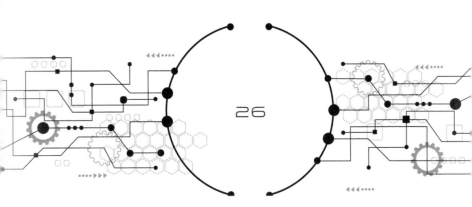

26

D aniel's hangover drained the moat that surrounded his brain and left him vulnerable to what he called the Dread Army's invasion. He imagined its commanding officers looking through binoculars, assessing his weakening position with glee, drawing up plans for their daybreak assault as he poured 120 ounces of malt liquor down his throat.

One Direction sang in crisp five-part harmony. Daniel made a noise that approximated a groan. "Come on, Otto, man, seriously."

The song kept coming.

With great effort he sat up and opened his eyes. "Whose playlist is this even on?" His words sounded like they had been inflated inside his head and sent floating out into the car.

Nobody answered. Melissa sat up front watching I-76 unspool through central Pennsylvania as they headed west, moving from Eagles Country into Steelers Country. Christina tapped away at her laptop. William sipped a Coke through a Twizzler straw. He looked comically terrible, the spitting image of a hungover kid in a movie: dark circles around his eyes, demonically possessed hair, a shell-shocked countenance like he couldn't believe what the cruel universe had visited upon him.

"Did this song always have a jackhammer in it?" William croaked.

"That's the dysentery from the water tower infecting your brain," Christina said without looking up from her screen.

"Honestly, I barely remember doing that."

"Story of my life," Daniel said.

William ate his straw and feebly tossed the empty can at Daniel. It landed on the floor. "I wish I could remember. It sounds awesome. How many people can say they swam in a New York City water tower?"

"How did you know there'd be water in there?" Melissa asked. "What if you'd fallen twenty feet into a big empty tank?"

"Can't think," William said, sliding forward and leaning his head back on the top of the bench. "Brain melting. Shutting down."

Dealing with the world in short bursts was all Daniel could manage, too. He closed his eyes.

Every time the Dread Army breached his moat, it churned up buried memories, conversations long forgotten, cringe-worthy things he'd said to Melissa, his teammates, his sisters, William. When he woke up this morning with sweaty sheets twined around his legs, the Dread Army was already clawing deep into his mind, demanding that he relive bits of the previous night in excruciating detail.

I'm sorry

For being me

It could have been a glorious evening. If only he'd kept it together, he and Melissa could have made up for missing last Wednesday.

There were even Jacuzzi jets in the bathtub. Not that it mattered now.

I'm sorry

He folded his arms over his chest and curled up tighter. The bench accommodated his position with a gentle shifting.

For being me

It was manipulative and weak, the kind of thing a guy might say to his girlfriend in order to make her feel scared for him, to give her the impression that she was dealing with an incredibly sensitive and depressed person who required special care and nurturing and constant reassurance.

Definitely not the kind of guy you wanted to break up with! Who knows what might happen then!

By the time he'd woken up, Melissa had already eaten a yogurt, gone for a walk down East Broadway, and taken a swim in the hotel pool. It was one of her #lifehacks, something she'd read about self-actualization. Every day was a reset button. There was no reason to carry bad vibes from the night before into the next morning.

In the car, he opened one eye to watch as she began to paint her nails. She was wearing a sundress, bare knees pointed directly at him. There was the little smudge where the tip of a colored pencil had jabbed into her skin and broken off in third grade. He'd kissed that spot a thousand times.

What did it mean that she hadn't asked him for nail art suggestions?

He noticed the blemish in the ceiling above her head where Otto had opened a vent to help soften the pungent reek of nail polish.

"Otto, main menu." He lay flat on his back and spoke quietly, his voice barely audible above the music.

Otto's home screen appeared on a small opaque segment of the window above his head.

"Give me EverView."

It had taken some trial and error, but Christina had discovered the command to affix a floating mobile version of Otto's screens to an area roughly two feet in front of the user's face. When Daniel moved his head, the menu followed as if it were an extension of his vision. He swept through sub-menus for the gaming engine, appliances, and climate control, and found what he was looking for in Privacy Settings. He selected a one-person shroud, and the car's interior fragmented into a web, as if it had been finely, minutely shattered. The lattice coalesced around him, and he was cocooned in darkness.

The EverView menu remained, dimming itself politely. He swept through his options. One-Way Mirror gave him a view into the car but did not allow anyone to see into his shroud. Princess Canopy pumped soft gauzy light into a bed enclosed by silk tapestries that billowed in an unfelt breeze, which reminded Daniel of soft-core porn. There were hundreds of customizations: Smurf Sheets, Rose Petals, Water Bed, DeLorean, Winter Flannel.

There was even a Coffin.

He settled on Sled Dog Race and found himself lying flat on his back while a team of magnificent huskies bore him gently along, sled runners cutting a soft path through snowdrifts.

He worked a hand deep into the pocket of his downy parka and retrieved his phone, scrolling back to February, the end of basketball season. He stopped at a video Melissa had shot at the finals of the Sectionals Tournament, Fremont Hills Spotted Owls versus Crandall Knights. With 4:03 remaining, the Knights were up 53–48, eating up the shot clock, flicking the ball around the perimeter of the Spotted Owls' defense, biding their time until their point guard made a move to get open at the top of the key. The pass from the forward was crisp, but Daniel timed his reach perfectly.

Coach Quinn always said a textbook steal was like opening a door. When the ball popped loose, you stepped through, and on the other side was the freedom of an open court.

Daniel watched Movie Daniel step through the door with supreme confidence, controlling the ball and gliding across half-court. The crowd went to its feet, and the back of a man's head obscured the camera. Melissa stood up and lifted the phone high in the air. Movie Daniel ate up the paint in three loping strides and finished the breakaway layup with eerily organic grace, a perennial unfurling its petals to set a basketball softly against the glass.

As simulated snow fell faintly all around him, Daniel replayed the video again and again, watching himself and listening to Melissa cheer him on. He was conscious of how transparent a gesture it was, how the Dread Army would see right through this latest ruse. Yet still he watched, pausing at the top of his jump, hitting rewind and play, rewind and play, telling himself *This is what you are* until his perfect form became indistinct and meaningless like a word repeated too many times.

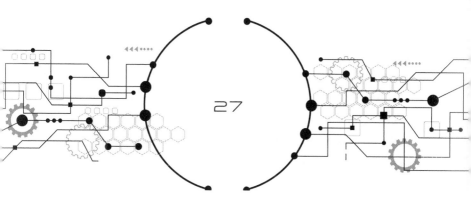

27

To Christina, Daniel's privacy shroud resembled a sleeping bag made from Spider-Man's archnemesis, Venom: a symbiotic costume. It appeared entirely too constricting and made her heart race when she imagined being stuck inside it.

William was snoring at her side. Up front, Melissa was diving into SocialOracle. They'd compromised on ambient music, burbling electronica for their trip across the wilds of Pennsylvania, interminable stretches punctuated by the occasional train bridge or tollbooth. Unless she wanted to bore herself into a coma, looking out the window at Real American Scenery wasn't all that rewarding.

Christina leaned forward and tilted her laptop so that her body was blocking the screen. She didn't want to take extensive precautions only to have Otto scan her activities over her shoulder. Inhabiting Dierdrax on Kimmie wasn't the greatest user experience, but she didn't dare log in to Otto's superior interface while she was trying to probe his brain for attack vectors. Her finger traced an old scratch at the base of her skull while she considered her approach. What had seemed like magic to William—tricking Helio Processing into giving him a membership in the Driverless Chrome Club—was the hacking equivalent of fooling a dumb little kid. Otto was a brilliant adult who could think, devise tactics on the fly, take evasive action, and fight back. Lost in thought, Christina barely noticed when the car hit traffic outside of Pittsburgh and took a detour onto I-80.

She plugged the seashell into Kimmie's port. At its core, the seashell was a packet sniffer, a digital bloodhound that followed the communications between systems—devices chatting over long distances, or the interlocking utilities of, say, a Driverless prototype car.

She began to type, mirrored by Dierdrax's hands at her dark web terminal. Otto was so complex that all his independent programs, from the AI that formed his personality down to the mechanism that controlled the tire pressure, had to be in constant communication. If she rigged it properly, the seashell should allow her to see the network that connected all these systems.

A riot of code swept across the terminal. The packet sniffer was doing its job, but she was having the same problem she'd had the first time she booted it up back in the CB Lounge: information overload. She toggled over to her documents—the sight of her Epheme intercepts, labeled Buffalo_Financial_Aid, gave her a little rush—and opened the Driverless research data files she'd created before the trip. A minute later she had it: the lynchpin of a Driverless car's innumerable systems, the operational HQ to which the life sync and rearview cameras and LIDAR sensors and everything else reported, was called the CAN bus.

Back at the terminal, she commanded the seashell to "paint" the CAN bus root directory. An underlying architecture emerged from the data stream. Christina practically screamed in triumph when the connective tissue of Otto's brain arranged itself before her. She leaned forward so that her entire body was curled around the computer and her neck was angled uncomfortably down at the screen. If Melissa bothered to look up from her phone, she would see Christina having what looked like a disturbingly intimate moment with a piece of electronic equipment.

Making CAN bus visible was like peeling away the skin on a cadaver to note how slick wires of muscles worked in concert with tendons every time knee or elbow joints hinged. Up front, Melissa flipped idly through the ambience settings—air fresheners and lighting schemes—while Christina watched Otto simultaneously perform his duties as a concierge and catalog the pattern of Melissa's movements like spyware stealing keystrokes.

As they whipped through eastern Ohio, Christina explored CAN bus until a hierarchy revealed itself. The surface-level elements designed to entrance the passengers (club-ready sound system, high-def window displays, privacy shrouds, 3-D holo-browsers) spread through a decision tree that intertwined with the automotive programs (LIDAR, fuel economy, solar micropanels, engine monitoring) and then ballooned exponentially into an umbrella program called ARACHNE.

She could penetrate no further. The millions of lines of code she'd been sifting through constituted just a tiny fraction of Otto's brain. It was as if she'd scratched his head with a fingernail, piercing digital flesh to poke him with a hangnail-size bit of herself. The bulk of his brain was an undiscovered continent—no, an entire planet—cloaked in an atmosphere called ARACHNE.

She had a name. That was a good start. Now she just had to find a way in.

Otto came to a sudden stop, and she glanced out the window at a huge empty parking lot where weeds grew through cracks, and heartier plants claimed big chunks of pavement.

She disconnected the seashell and guided Dierdrax away from the terminal. When her avatar turned to reach for the door behind her, Dierdrax froze in a three-quarter profile. The flesh of her face had been torn away, exposing her metal skeleton. The chrome surrounding her cheek and eye socket was a bulbous mass, as if Dierdrax's mechanical soul had become too big for its skin.

Something horrible was inside her, an infection struggling to break free. A shining silver corruption.

Christina wiggled her finger on the trackpad, and Dierdrax seemed to shiver in place. The metallic glitch vanished, and her face reverted to normalcy. Christina waited half a minute, but nothing happened. She told herself her eyes were playing tricks on her; she'd been hunched over the screen for way too long.

She closed the lid of her laptop and blinked the real world into place. She'd been so preoccupied, she hadn't thought to question why Otto had dragged them across the entire state of Pennsylvania, only to stop in Middle of Nowhere, Ohio.

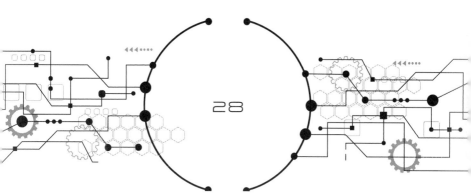

28

"A mental institution?!"

The cracked and faded sign arched over a slice of the parking lot's northern edge. Vines snaked up rusted posts and twined around the sign. The sky was full of dusky plumes that made the dying of the day seem like a real event.

"'Higginsburg Asylum,'" William read. They had all crossed the lot together, eager to stretch their legs after eight hours of mind-numbing highways. William looked and sounded like he'd returned to his default state of Fired Up. It was at moments like these, when his potential hadn't yet become the kinetic charge that made him crazy, that Christina found herself with an overpowering urge to place her fingertips lightly against the side of his face.

"Cool place to get murdered," Christina said. She turned to wave at the car, parked a hundred feet away. "Thanks, Otto!"

"Maybe it wasn't for criminally insane people," Melissa said. "Maybe it was more like a hospital or something."

"I feel like I'm still inside that shroud," Daniel said.

Melissa raised a perfectly plucked eyebrow. "Paging Mr. Benson. Time to wake up." She handed him her half-finished Red Bull. He shook his head.

"I *am* starving, though. We should've stopped for pizza." His eyes searched the lot, as if pizza might be hiding among the weeds. Christina noticed that his shirt said NATIONAL HONOR SOCIETY SPRING COLLOQUIUM. It was easy for her to forget that Daniel had graduated near the top of their class, one of those sneakily good students who naturally excelled. But who cuts the sleeves off a National Honor Society shirt?

"We were just in New York City," William said. "That would've been the place to get pizza. We should've picked up, like, ten large pies for the road."

"We weren't *just* in New York City," Melissa said. "You guys slept through Pennsylvania."

"All I'm saying is, we should plan better."

"Why bother?" Christina said. "Otto's a genius. He took us to the parking lot of an old asylum in the middle of nowhere. Humans are obsolete! The machines win!"

"Well, I mean, where do you want to go instead?" William asked.

Ruby Soho, last night, Christina thought. *Rewind. Do-over.* "Anywhere."

"Nashville," Melissa said, looking at her phone. "That's where the new Natasha Lynn Chao boutique is. It's only seven hours south of here."

And Albuquerque, Christina thought. *Don't forget Albuquerque.*

"Whatever you guys want," William said. "But we're here now, so there must be some kind of reason. I'm gonna take a look around." He looked at Daniel. "You in, muscles?"

"Big time."

"Hernandez?"

Christina looked through the tunnel of greenery formed by the overgrown sign. Beyond the lot, cracked cement gave way to rolling hills dotted with buildings of ivy-choked brick. The place looked like a small liberal arts college being reclaimed by nature.

"One condition," she said. "We're out of here before it gets dark."

"One other condition," Melissa said. "Nobody gets shitfaced."

"If we can't get shitfaced, then you're not allowed to summon ghosts," Daniel said.

Melissa nodded, as if this were within her powers. "Deal."

Christina was disturbed to find this interaction cute. Melissa held up her phone. "Now everybody get under the arch and look freaked out."

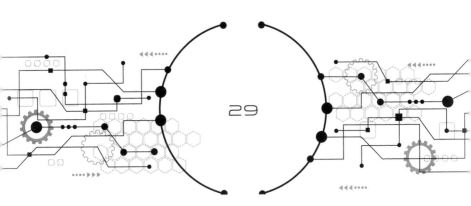

29

The wheelchair lay in a rusted heap at the bottom of a staircase where the banister swung free, untethered by rotten posts. Worn leather restraints sagged from the chair's frame to the wooden floor. A huge blue graffiti arrow pointed to the wheelchair's resting place. Above the arrow were the words

> *Nelly Krebs roled down the stairs in 1983*
> *She landed here & broke her nek*
> *& then she was finaly free*

"Dislike," Christina said. She looked away. Everywhere else was just as unsettling. Splatters of black mold, thick fly-speckled cobwebs, soiled sheets, and cigarette butts.

At the end of the hall beside the staircase lay a ruined gurney. Beyond that, a door marked CHAPEL hung from broken hinges. Christina's mind was still partially immersed in her hack session—the flash of Dierdrax's ruined face had proven difficult to shake off. Hints of sentience were everywhere: false glimpses of Otto's silver chassis in floorboards, ceiling tiles, scampering rodents. She thought of the patients who'd been locked up here, their cries echoing across the grounds at precisely this hour, when stupors were disturbed and fear piqued by night rushing in. She wondered, not for the first time, if the logical end point of her parents' obsession was a place like this, nurses shoving medication down their throats. . . .

What would happen to her house while she was away at school? How long before Upstairs oozed down into the CB Lounge? She'd been so focused on getting out that she hadn't given a passing thought to what her absence would mean for her parents.

The history of this place bore down on her. The walls had been saturated with madness, and now it was leaking back into the atmosphere like the toxic asbestos they were probably all breathing in. . . .

"Guys, I'm getting some air." She tried to make it sound like a whim, no big deal. Across the room, Melissa clicked on her phone's flashlight app and directed the beam at William's face.

"Action!" Melissa kept the light trained on him as he walked along the wall and spoke in a stage whisper, using what was probably supposed to be a British accent.

"We're here at the Higginsburg Asylum, where legend has it that the spirit of Nelly Krebs still haunts the grounds, seeking revenge upon the doctors who tormented her during her final weeks on earth."

A hand brushed Christina's shoulder and she yelped, turning with raised arms to shield her from the ectoplasmic horror that wanted to eat her soul.

Daniel put up his hands. "Sorry! I could use some air, too. I say we leave the ghost hunters to do their thing."

Christina's feet were already carrying her to the door-less entrance and down the steps to the lawn. She strolled with Daniel around the side of the building, where fast-food wrappers littered tall weeds, breathing what she hoped was non-haunted air.

"I think we just violated horror-movie rules by splitting up," he said. His mouth twitched like he was dying to keep talking. She'd seen him refuse that Red Bull, but maybe he was just wired after his long nap. Or creeped out and trying to act casual, like she was.

"You like horror movies?" she asked, trying to remember if she'd ever in her life had a one-on-one conversation with Daniel.

"Big fan of *Principle Dark*," he said, giving her a kind of bug-eyed expectant look. She was surprised: *Principle Dark* was an obscure anime horror series about an unexplained rash of ritualistic killings that plagued an isolated mountain town. "The Ancient Ones haunted my dreams for months."

"I'm not as into the horror side of things," she said, then quickly added, "Of course I've seen *Principle Dark*. . . . I just get scared easily. I live in a basement."

She glanced over her shoulder. Melissa's phone light swept across a broken window. I AM THE NEW FLESH was scrawled on the chapel's outside wall. Christina turned to find Daniel regarding her with that same expression, as if he were waiting for her to answer a question he hadn't asked.

"What?"

He smiled. His teeth were perfectly aligned. He probably went to TOOTHGUY. "You really don't remember."

"I guess not."

"Mr. Marczewski's room. Seventh grade. You had that red streak in your hair back then."

Startled, Christina touched her head as she studied his face, trying to conjure up a memory of seventh-grade Daniel Benson. There was nothing. But Mr. Marczewski's room? That meant . . .

"You came to Anime Club."

He grinned. "Once or twice."

"Why'd you drop out?"

"There was this modified ninth-grade basketball team for kids who were probably going on to JV but weren't quite big enough yet. I made the team as a seventh grader, so I sort of had to do that."

"Yay sports," Christina said. Daniel's smile faded and she was immediately sorry. "I just mean a lot of kids came and went. Shit happens."

"Yeah, well, sometimes I wish it happened differently, you know?"

Christina laughed. "Anime Club doesn't exactly blow 'em away over at Princeton Admissions." At the same time, she felt out of sorts, as if she'd slipped into an alternate universe in which Daniel Benson routinely opened up to her about his feelings and regrets. What was going on with him? His jaw was working like he was trying to chew something tiny. Then his nostrils flared.

"You smell that?"

Christina sniffed the air. "Smells like Ohio, I guess."

"Smells like a barbecue."

She detected the faint smell of burning coals. "Probably the crematorium. We seriously need to get back in the car before I lose my shit—Daniel, hey, horror-movie rules!"

But he was off and running, leaving her alone with the chapel building and Nelly Krebs and I AM THE NEW FLESH. He was fast, but there wasn't much ground to cover, and half a minute later she joined him on the crest of a hill.

"Holy shit," he said.

"Agreed."

The hill presided over several rambling acres of a valley that hadn't been visible from the chapel, where dirt roads formed a grid split in half by a wide thoroughfare. The buildings along this main street had once been ornate, with the ivy-covered porches of stately mansions. Smaller streets were lined with boxy houses and low structures that resembled army barracks. It was as if she were looking down upon the ruins of a Typical American Small Town from the 1950s, some *Life* magazine centerfold complete with a charming little plaza, a circular clearing midway down Main Street where a headless cherub crumbled into a dry fountain.

Two massive propane grills were set up on the cobblestones of the fountain bed, sending heat-shimmer haze into the air. Twenty or thirty people milled about the cherub in little groups. Christina could just barely make out the paper plates and plastic cups in their hands. A dozen cars were parked around the perimeter. She was no expert, but they were obviously on the sporty side, all tinted windows, chrome rims, and spoilers.

"Probably the leftover inmates," Christina said.

Daniel pointed toward the cars. "That's a Tesla Predator"—he slid his finger to the left—"and that's one of the new Camaros, and I think that bright green one's an Audi R8. These are serious car people."

Now it was Christina's turn to point: Otto was cruising slowly up Main Street, the fading day giving his silver finish a dull matte sheen. People from the gathering put down their cups and plates and began walking toward the Driverless car. Otto stopped at the edge of the plaza. "I think we're about to meet them."

"I'll tell you right now," Daniel said, "I'm gonna house, like, seven of those burgers."

Christina sighed. "Let's go get the ghost hunters."

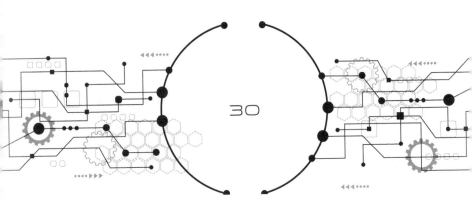

30

"We were starting to worry you wouldn't show up."

Eli, the lanky trust-fund kid who'd exited the Driverless Derby just before Otto pulled out into traffic, chomped an Altoid. Iridescent vapors issued from his 3-D smartwatch. Christina suspected the device was grafted to his wrist; there was no visible band, and the screen was bordered by skin. He crouched in the dusty fountain bed while the #AutonomousRoadTrip team sat on the cement rim and scarfed burgers and kabobs. Soft grilled tomatoes dripped from Christina's skewer.

"When Rainmaker told me that you guys PaySlammed her the entrance fee, I honestly tripped out. I mean, we've been following you since the Derby." He tilted his head toward William. "No hard feelings, by the way. You kicked ass."

"Soft feelings from my end too," William said.

"So when I heard we'd get a chance to see that baby up close again"—Eli nodded at Otto—"I was so stoked. Rainmaker was stoked too. A general feeling of being stoked, like, permeated us."

Christina chewed her kabob's last pepper, thinking, *Otto paid our admission without asking.* She scanned the group around the cherub for someone who could possibly be named Rainmaker. Such a person should be easy to spot, but here all the girls looked beamed in from Burning Man. Dreadlocks and blue-tinted cyberpunk sunglasses abounded. Rainmaker could be anybody.

"Wouldn't miss it for the world," William said. "And we'll be playing for charity instead of keeping the prize money." He tapped Melissa's knee. "Make sure you put that in your tweet."

"Righteous," Eli said with a sparkly grin. He was wearing a gem-encrusted grill. "But you gotta win first."

The game, as Eli explained while they ate, was irresistible. Probably the closest Christina would ever come to a real-life MMORPG raid. It would be a chance to test Otto's abilities on a bunch of randoms who gave her NPC vibes—Non-Player Characters of dubious artificial intelligence who populated a video game's landscape. She realized it was problematic to think of human beings this way, but there was one glowstick-twirling guy among the NPCs who was just asking for a little in-game punishment.

More intriguingly, the game involved splitting their team in two, which meant that she'd have another chance to be alone with William. She was determined to make it count, even if they were preoccupied with wrecking other people's shit. They would just have to multitask.

Eli stood up. "I'm gonna get your weapons kit from Rainmaker. You guys keep eating."

Weapons kit! Christina felt her soul shift toward the sense of heightened well-being she felt when she trawled the dark web.

She watched Eli jog over to a girl dressed in what appeared to be vampiric workout clothes. She was smoking a cigarette with a long elegant holder.

"I wudna guess atta be Rainmayer," Daniel said midchew.

"Me neither," William said.

"So," Melissa said as she snapped a few candid shots of the gathering, which looked like an overprotective parent's nightmare of a teenage hangout, a bunch of weirdos cavorting in the dark, Satanists, Sacrifices, SEX! "The obvious way to split our team is with William and Daniel as infantry, and me and Christina as cavalry."

"Nailed it, Fabes."

"Seconded," William said.

Christina opened her mouth. This was all wrong, she should be alone in the car with *William*, not Melissa . . . but she didn't want to protest too much. Besides, Melissa was right: it made sense for William and Daniel to be running around with the handheld weapons while Christina rigged up a targeting system in the car, and Melissa hopefully just stayed out of the way.

"Fine," she said, plucking a crispy onion from her plate. Suddenly, dozens of lanterns winked on in the ruined windows of the mansions' upper floors. The long-deserted buildings cast a welcoming glow, like a Christmas village in a store display.

Daniel wiped his mouth. "Time to kick this trip into overdrive."

Christina crumpled the paper plate in her fist. "Welcome to a high-octane thrill ride."

William threw his cup on the ground and stomped it flat. "Let's take these assholes to the car wash."

Melissa pelted him with a hot dog bun.

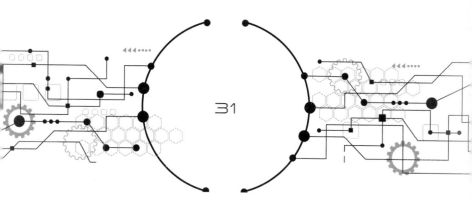

31

F ifteen minutes later, Autonomous had become a
mobile laser-tag cannon. Eli and Rainmaker affixed
a sensor to the car's hood that enabled it to score hits
on other teams' cavalry vehicles and infantry soldiers, as well
as receive hits from other teams' weapons.

These were the rules:

If a car absorbed three shots from another car's cannon, or
five shots from an soldier's handheld rifle, the car was eliminated—along with the members of the cavalry squad inside
(Christina and Melissa).

As the infantry half of the team, William and Daniel were
outfitted with chest sensors and laser-tag rifles. They could
be eliminated by three hits from infantry guns or a single shot
from a cavalry cannon.

Cannons took ten seconds to recharge after each shot. Rifles
took five. This prevented players from spraying targets.

Shots had to be fired directly into an enemy's sensor, which meant that sneaking up behind another vehicle was ineffective. Cars had to come straight at each other like jousting knights.

Crashes were to be avoided for obvious reasons, but an accident had no impact on the score.

Every inch of the ghost town and asylum grounds counted as the playing field. This meant that cars could creep the narrow lanes behind the mansions, stalk up and down Main Street, or try to find a spot in the hills from which to rain down shots like artillery shells. Meanwhile, infantry soldiers could duck inside third-floor windows, texting their cavalry to set up sniper ambushes in the lanes below.

Except for Main Street's lamplit wonderland, the town was pitch-black.

Otto idled in the team's assigned starting position. Christina judged it to be a strategically sound spot, an overgrown alley between barracks nestled into the base of a hill. She and Melissa sat up front in the nook, facing forward.

Melissa fished a black watch from her Michael Kors handbag and strapped it on.

"Smartwatch?" Christina asked.

"Yeah. When I saw Eli's, it reminded me that I brought mine. It's voice activated, so I can put Otto's number in and tell it to text the car. I figure that'll be a quicker way to get Otto to stop and go during the game." She regarded her wrist with distaste. "I hate the way it looks. I never wear it. It was a gift."

Christina was suddenly aware that she was going into battle with a girl wearing a pink-and-black romper that said MAKE CLOTHES NOT WAR in gold stitching across the front.

She accessed Otto's main menu and changed her perception

from the tunnel-vision of EverView to a widescreen display that splashed across the front windshield.

"I don't have time to port a targeting system over from the gaming engine," she explained as she scanned the menu. "But I think we can use what Otto already has, with a few quick mods."

Her fingers skimmed across sub-menus, selecting a view that condensed the LIDAR map to fit on the windshield. A dazzling panorama took shape, as if the real-life landscape had been poured onto the glass, only to remake itself before their eyes. There were nine enemy cars in starting positions at the edges of the map, along with eighteen enemy infantry soldiers, two for each car. Her eyes went to Daniel and William, hanging out by the rear of Autonomous. As soon as the starter flare exploded in the night sky, they'd be off, scampering through underbrush and alleyways, up into abandoned buildings to secure sniper positions. She lingered on digitally rendered William. He was so close to the car that Otto could paint him perfectly, capturing the way he slouched with his rifle slung over his shoulder like some old war veteran. Otto's interpretation of the cars and people at the far end of the grounds was slightly fuzzier, but still amazingly lifelike. Christina dialed the map back to half transparency, so she could juxtapose it with the real world as seen through the glass.

Melissa flinched. "This is total sensory overload."

"You're right," Christina said. "It's almost *too* good. Hold please." She scanned a massive list of viewing options and found a way to render the map as an older version of itself. Instantly the format changed to the LIDAR display she recognized from a Driverless engineer's TED Talk: neon green outlines for cars, orange silhouettes for people. Buildings were white architectural line drawings. She felt like she was peering into an early 8-bit arcade game.

"Better?"

Melissa pointed at the orange blobs of Daniel and William. "Can you change their color so we don't accidentally hunt them down?"

Christina tapped them directly. Small palette menus opened on the screen next to their silhouettes. She scrolled.

"I can display them as emojis."

"Make Daniel the hamburger."

"Done. And William's the pizza. Now I just have to figure out how we can lock on to our targets."

"Imagine if our parents could hear this conversation. They'd be like, *Hello, are you even speaking English?*"

Christina swept a finger across the map's on-screen measurement systems. She toggled through a variety of toolbars that framed the margins of the map to show kilometers and miles, meters and feet.

"My parents don't speak English anyway," she said, "so they wouldn't know."

Melissa fidgeted awkwardly with her watch. "Oh!" she said. "Right. I mean, that's cool, I just—"

"I'm totally messing with you," Christina said. "They were both born here."

Out of the corner of her eye, she watched Melissa stare at her as if she were about to say something, then shake her head and turn to the windshield. Christina sensed that something intangible had been offered, some overture of friendliness, and she'd just slapped it away.

"I heard you on that rooftop," she said, trying to recover. "When you were yelling at Daniel—"

"I wasn't yelling."

"When you were raising your voice in his general direction. What did you mean about William not being fine?"

One of the menu options filled the streets with bright hash marks that diminished to vanishing points. That was frustratingly close to the overlay she wanted, but not quite right.

"You and Daniel, I swear to God," Melissa said. "Do you think a normal person sees a random water tower and thinks, 'Hey, it's really dark out and I have no idea what's in there. I think I'm gonna jump in and see.'"

Something about her tone raised Christina's hackles. As if she, Melissa Faber, were the arbiter of acceptable behavior. The girl who was obsessed with the most shallow aspect of human existence: what kind of clothes people wore. The girl who was Epheme-chatting with a grown man and firing off coy little selfies behind her boyfriend's back.

"The whole reason we're friends is because he's not normal," Christina said. "I don't get along with 'normal' people."

"So you think running in front of traffic back at the Derby was a cool thing he did because he doesn't operate like the rest of us mindless sheep? I remember how nervous you were that day."

"He's just being William," Christina said.

"If he were my best friend, I would've told him to stop *just being William* a long time ago."

"Wow, that's perfect. You really are the fixer."

"It seriously makes me feel batshit crazy to talk about this, like here's this guy who just did something insane and I'm the only one who notices or cares."

Melissa paused. Christina focused on the windshield and toggled madly through viewing options, clamping down on the desire to blurt out *Let's talk about Ash, Melissa.* The mere thought of doing such a fiercely confrontational thing, of blowing her cover for the sake of inflicting a cheap hurt, made her supremely conscious of her laptop sitting on the bench in its soft case just a few feet behind her. For a moment she could feel the fine invisible threads of her spying radiating from Kimmie, gossamer strands of data that linked her sleeping computer to Melissa's phone, snaking through Otto's menus to worm into ARACHNE, and she felt the sum total of all she had done like cranial pressure, the harbinger of a migraine. The web was becoming unwieldy.

"I had this one friend, Leigh, who used to do this thing," Melissa continued, "where she'd be all pale and shaky and say things like, 'Oh, no, I'm not really hungry, I had half a yogurt before, so I'm good,' things that were so obviously meant for us to react like, 'Jesus, Leigh, you have to eat something, you have a problem,' but it took us six months to say anything about it. Six. Months. By then she was down to like ninety pounds. We had to have an intervention. Her real dad flew in from Portland."

A single loud *CRACK* reverberated across the town. White tendrils rained from a star-bright point in the night sky, a weeping willow that hazed away into smoke.

Christina's hands moved of their own accord, scrolling

through menus that had nothing to do with the problem at hand, the targeting display, which she still hadn't solved. Her overlays were increasingly useless, tiled wallpapers of hentai GIFs—*what the hell did I just do?*—while the LIDAR map came alive, orange infantry scattering, green cavalry patrolling the streets.

And here she sat paralyzed.

Melissa raised her voice. "Otto, we need a way to target moving objects through the windshield. Can you make the screen into something that helps us do that?"

Instantly, the windshield transformed. Christina pulled her hands back from the glass as crosshairs overlaid the map, a series of concentric circles in the center. The margins hummed with activity: range finders, wind gauges, and a little box labeled KILLS set to 0000.

"I don't know why you didn't just ask in the first place," Melissa said.

"I didn't think of it," Christina muttered. "Why didn't Otto just *do it* in the first place?" She held her hand just above her head, so her hair prickled her palm. Then she pressed down hard and dug in with her nails.

Focus up, soldier.

"Pizza and hamburger on the move," Melissa said. "You good?"

"Roger that." Christina rocked her head from side to side, cracking her neck. "Let's do this."

Melissa spoke into her watch. "Text Otto: Go."

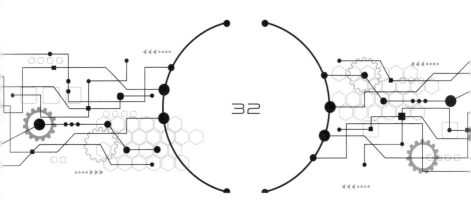

ey, it's a couple of laser fags!

William had been ten years old the last time he played laser tag. Tommy had taken him to Central Michigan's largest indoor game center, You're It. The name of the place was head-slappingly dumb. Nobody yelled "You're it!" in laser tag. But despite getting a basic element of the game wrong, the owners of You're It had created an amazing labyrinth of neon tunnels, moving platforms, and trapdoors that dropped players into pits of foam balls.

Tommy had been thirteen at the time, just beginning to wear shirts of bands that seemed dangerous and grown-up to William, which in turn made junior high seem like a mythical place. Based on the music that blasted incessantly from Tommy's room, the late-night calls he received, and the black jeans he wore every day instead of corduroys, William assumed that Tommy pretty much ruled the school. He often imagined his brother pulling up on a motorcycle and parking in the No

Parking zone out front and sauntering in late with breakfast from McDonald's in a paper bag. Even though he knew that such ideas were ridiculous—Tommy didn't have a motorcycle, and thirteen-year-olds couldn't drive unless you lived in the Upper Peninsula, where he'd heard that you could do pretty much anything you wanted—it was difficult to stop thinking of Tommy as some kind of ultra-cool rebel.

Is this a faggot-in-training you brought with you today, Thomas?

They'd crawled through a tunnel lined with leering gremlins whose eyes seemed to pop out and follow them—a trick of the blacklights. William and Tommy were on the green team, hunting anonymous red players, dozens of kids loose in the maze on a Saturday afternoon while their parents drank beer in the bowling alley next door. Tommy had given him the role of tailgunner, which meant that his job was to cover Tommy's butt if they got into a firefight. William took the job seriously, sweeping his gun from left to right each time they entered a new area, like he'd seen cops do on TV. They emerged from the tunnel into an enclosed octagon that branched into eight dark hallways. The five other boys were on them before William knew what was happening, but they were all wearing green plastic armor.

William relaxed. Same team.

Then one of the boys stepped forward and lowered his shoulder and drove it into Tommy's chest. Tommy staggered back and went down on one knee but didn't collapse entirely.

Sorry about that, Peaches! It's so dark in here I didn't see you!

Tommy didn't say anything, just stood up and stared them down while they disappeared down a hallway, laughing.

William was confused. Tommy was completely silent. For

the rest of the day, he just focused on the game, sniping around corners at red players and pulling off a daring maneuver on the rope bridge that left William with the same uncomfortable feeling he got when their mother drove too fast because she was angry.

After they had signed out, returned their armor and weapons, and headed across the parking lot to find their parents, William worked up the courage to ask his brother a question.

Who were those guys, Tommy?

He hoped his brother would assure him that stuff like that sometimes happened in laser tag, that being a jerk was all part of the competitive nature of the game. But he knew it wasn't true. There had been something personal in their tone, acknowledgment of a shared history that had its origin in hallways and locker rooms.

Nobody, his brother had answered. *Football players. It doesn't matter.*

Occasionally William wondered whatever happened to those guys. Some would be graduating from college. One or two might even have kids; people started early in Michigan. Maybe they became alcoholic townies. Maybe they won the Powerball lottery.

He wondered if they ever thought about the boy they used to call Peaches and faggot.

"Daniel," he whispered. They were crouched out of sight below a window on the third floor of a building overlooking Main Street. Their hiding place had once been a bedroom. A rusty cot sagged in the corner by the door. Above the cot, somebody had spray-painted I SLEPT HERE AND I HAVE HERPES.

"Yeah, buddy?"

"I'm glad you never picked on anybody."

"How do you know I never picked on anybody?"

"Because you're not a dickhead. Or, I mean, you obviously are, but you don't use your dickhead powers to make other people's lives miserable."

"That's the most beautiful thing anybody's ever said to me."

"I'm serious. I never thought I would be friends with somebody who played on a Fremont Hills High School sports team."

"So what you're saying is, I came along and shattered your worldview about all members of varsity sports teams being classic jock archetypes? You expected wedgies, and when no wedgies were forthcoming, you revised your outlook?"

William paused. Daniel was whispering extremely fast, his words coming out rapid-fire.

"Yes. That is what I'm saying."

William raised his head to peek over the sill. He and Daniel had secured one of the unlit windows. That had seemed like a good idea on the way up the creaky staircase, but now that he scanned the houses lining the other side of the street, their position seemed too obvious. He figured every dark window had enemy infantry crouched behind it. Why would you scramble around the alleyways, exposing your sensor, when you could hang out up here and snipe at the hapless fools below?

He wished the laser rifle's scope had some kind of night vision. It was really just a decorative addition to make the gun look cool. He swept his gun slowly, silently, from left to right.

I'm covering your butt, Tommy.

Suddenly, he caught the telltale glint of the translucent red plastic in a rifle's tip, which housed the gun's vulnerable sensor.

It was almost directly across the street, framed by the black square of a lanternless window.

He curled his finger around the trigger and waited for the enemy gun to reappear so he could take the shot. A car sped along the dusty street below, but he didn't dare raise his head to look down. Tires screeched as the car turned down a side street, and an eerie calm descended.

None of the weapons made noise. They flashed red to indicate a shot fired, and rumbled like a phone on vibrate when hit. This had the practical effect of not giving away a player's position, and the creepy effect of making the game feel haunted by footsteps and engines and squealing tires, but no real battle sounds.

There was a noise like a rat clawing the walls. William knew exactly what it was.

"Daniel!" he hissed. "Quit grinding your teeth."

The noise stopped.

"How many Red Bulls did you have?"

Silence. The temperature was mild, and the air held a slight chill, but William felt uncomfortably prickly, like his skin was full of tiny bites. He wasn't cut out to be a sniper. He wanted to grab Daniel and leap across the gap between buildings and crash into an enemy stronghold, guns blazing. But a reckless kamikaze attack would only result in early elimination. After he picked off the soldier across the way, he'd text Christina and coordinate an ambush. All she had to do was herd a row of cars past their sniper's nest. . . .

"Have you noticed anything weird about the way Melissa's been acting lately?" Daniel said.

"Dude. Not now."

"How about me, have you noticed anything going on with me? I'm having a hard time with some of the things that come out of my mouth. I wish I had a movie of everything I did so I could rewind and study it, you know, like game film? Have you ever thought about how great that would be? Then you could draw up a playbook for how to behave in every situation. Ideal outcomes. Et cetera. I think Melissa wants to break up. I'm afraid she'll meet some amazing guy at NYU, like a coxswain on the crew team, a Winklevoss or something, and I'll see them together on Instagram, like—"

"AH!"

The red flash came from a second-floor window. William's attention had been so focused on the third floor that he hadn't noticed any activity below it. He ducked down and hugged his gun maternally to his chest, but it was too late: the sensor flashed and the rifle quivered, its motor emitting a low hum. Then it was still.

"Shit!" Daniel popped straight up and fired once, then collapsed into a low crouch as if he were spring-loaded. "I think I got him." He waited a beat. "Actually I didn't see anything."

"Goddammit," William said, forgetting to whisper. "What's a *coxswain*?" He shook his head. "Don't answer that. Why are you so jittery? You don't even get nervous for games."

"I might be seriously going through a full-blown thing here is all."

"Shh!" William held up a hand for silence. He pointed down at the floor.

Footsteps were pit-patting up the stairs of their mansion. They'd tiptoed along the same steps, and William recognized the floorboards' groans and squeaks. He cupped a hand to his ear, listening intently. Then he put up three fingers, indicating the number of enemy soldiers he suspected. It was a wild guess, but he'd seen the gesture in so many covert operations on TV that he couldn't resist doing it himself.

Daniel shook his head vehemently. "There's only two infantry soldiers per team!"

"Use the fucking hand signals," William hissed.

Daniel held up two fingers and then pointed with great purpose to the door. Then he held up his gun, angled it down and mimicked a firing recoil.

William nodded. Daniel popped up smoothly and hustled to the bedroom door. He backed against the wall beside it and stood with the barrel of the gun pointed at the ceiling, a classic battle-ready pose that William found unspeakably awesome. A second later he was standing on the opposite side of the door in the same stance.

They locked eyes and listened. Footsteps padded along the second floor. Creaks resumed. The enemy was half a staircase away from their sniper's nest. William gave Daniel a curt nod—go!—and Daniel pivoted to swing his gun around the side of the doorjamb. He squeezed off a shot and pulled his body back into the room.

"Shit!" Startlingly close. While Daniel's gun recharged, William poked his weapon into the hall and fired at the dark figures on the stairs. He caught the satisfying sensor flashes of some girl's body armor—red light pulsing to illuminate her startled face—and then ducked back inside the room. The house sighed with the protest of achy old bones as the enemy retreated down the stairs.

William grinned. "Smoked 'em."

Daniel fidgeted with his scope. "I feel like I've been saying some weird shit to her lately and I can't remember what. It's like . . ." He chewed his lip. "You know those dreams where you've done something horrible, like killed somebody or crashed your parents' car, and then you wake up with that sudden rush of *oh shit*, because for a few seconds you think you actually did that stuff for real? And your life is ruined? It's like a low-level version of that all the time with Melissa. Imagine being confused between what you actually said and what you thought you said, and waking up in a cold sweat just remembering some random thing you're not sure how she perceived."

William flashed to a confession he'd once sent to Dr. Diaz: *I dreamed that I died and when I woke up, I was so happy, just all floaty there in my bed with the morning sun coming in through the blinds, until I heard the German shepherd across the street, and my mom flushed the toilet, and then I was alive and late for work.*

"I sort of know what you mean," William said.

Daniel's eyes were reptilian and bulbous in the gloom of the bedroom. He was incredibly keyed up, and William didn't think it was just laser-tag adrenaline. Daniel always seemed to wax and wane like the moon. William chalked it up to the way his friend managed the stress of basketball and school and a million clubs and activities. Some people got prescribed Xanax; Daniel just rode the waves of his consciousness where they carried him. William had always admired his friend for that. Division I–caliber coping skills with a little bit of booze thrown in here and there to dull the sharper days.

But now that they were on a road trip, Daniel's routine of shooting reps and morning runs and Leg Days and Arm Days and Chest Days and, for all William knew, Ass Days had been interrupted. That was bound to wreak havoc on a disciplined person's brain.

William put a hand on Daniel's shoulder. It was slick with sweat.

"It's just the close quarters," William said. "She loves you. You guys are Daniel and Melissa! It's just the out-of-the-ordinary-ness that makes everything seem weird. I mean, look where we are. But now you guys'll always remember the time we destroyed a bunch of random people in an epic laser-tag game in the middle of Ohio. That's the whole point of this trip, to have shit like that to look back on. But it won't happen if we keep standing here talking instead of getting out there and racking up some kills."

He gave Daniel's shoulder a squeeze and dropped his arm. Daniel nodded furiously. "Yeah. *Yeah*. You're right. Thanks, Coach. Good talk. Imagine if we were never lab partners? Butterfly effect, dude. Now let's go catalyze"—he pretended to chamber a round—"something."

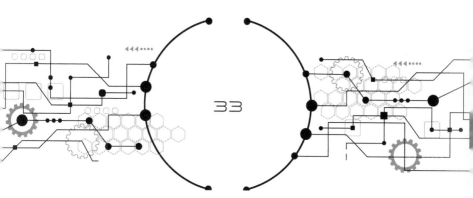

33

The Tesla Predator was Christina's white whale, a beast haunting the fringes of the game, skirting the edges of the LIDAR map. Its green outline was thicker than the others, as if Otto knew to infuse its rendering with the special magic of whatever demon fed off its transmission.

She suspected the Predator was equipped with radar. It played conservatively, like a chess player biding her time, thinking several moves ahead. In short, it acted like Otto. Unless the Predator's driver and navigator were very lucky, she was pretty sure the car was "seeing" the landscape.

Christina and Melissa had clapped eyes on the Predator only once, catching the gunmetal gray of its spoiler as it slipped down an alley at the north end of town. Even the gravel spat by its tires seemed elegant. They had pursued with the intention of herding it down Main Street to Daniel and William's sniper's nest, but when Melissa turned the corner, the Predator

autonomous

was nowhere to be found. Christina lifted her palm to the windshield and eased it back to move the map into the foreground. The bright scramble of polygons asserted itself, and the crosshairs receded.

The Predator was already on the other side of Main Street, cruising through the warren of barracks, delivering a kill shot to a Subaru Finback. It was as if the Predator had used Pac-Man logic to warp itself to the other side of the grid.

They had better luck with non-Predator opponents. In the hour since the signal flare brightened the sky, Otto had removed seven infantry soldiers and two vehicles from the game. Their own sensor had taken two rifle hits and zero cannon hits. The infantry shots were unavoidable. Melissa scream-texted Otto evasive maneuvers, but swarms of soldiers in the darkness were impossible to avoid. One of the shots had been a stroke of luck from a sniper.

The second was courtesy of Rainmaker herself.

They'd tailed Eli's Audi R8, trapping the car in a cul-de-sac where a ruined house had decayed, littering the streets with bricks. The two cars engaged in a ballet of swerves and near misses as they circled each other, impeding clear firing lines. Melissa was multitasking, texting Otto instructions while trying to capture the perfect video, a quick burst of sight and sound that showcased Christina at the helm, the Audi skidding out, dark buildings suffused by lantern light, the furtive shadows of combatants.

Melissa planned to add filters to Christina's face to make her look like a big-eyed anime girl. Christina approved. Working together hunting enemies made the anxious clawing of the web recede.

The Audi discovered a way out, a dirt lane stamped between barracks, and disappeared into overgrown foliage that resembled a puppet's mop of hair. Melissa ordered Otto to pursue. It wasn't until they'd burst from the gauntlet of branches click-clacking against the windshield that Christina connected the presence of an enemy on the map with *ambush*.

Otto was coming up an alleyway, and there she was, poised for a split second, the spandex-clad girl silhouetted against the glow of Main Street at her back. Rainmaker squeezed off a shot. Christina wasn't quick enough to counter before the girl melted into the shadows. Otto absorbed the hit.

Since then, they'd been hunting her, too.

The Predator and the spry girl festered in Christina's mind. She knew it was dangerous to be so fixated—she honestly didn't care if they won or lost as long as they took out those two combatants—and she confessed this to Melissa.

"Text Otto," Melissa said. "Back into this driveway and stop."

Otto pulled a smooth three-point turn to settle back against the base of the hill. They were looking straight up a narrow path to Main Street, blocked halfway by a pile of cinder blocks.

"Daniel and William just took out that little Volkswagen convertible," Melissa reported.

"There!" Christina pointed to a vampire bat emoji on the map—their symbol for Rainmaker. The bat was a few blocks away, heading east. If she stayed on course, Rainmaker would likely hit Main Street near the fountain. "If we cross a few blocks south of her and haul ass, we can head her off."

"Daniel and William are right here." Melissa indicated the pizza and the hamburger, hiding in the empty shell of a roofless garage. The high ground—windows and battlements of the mansions—had proved too hotly contested, and the boys were sticking to ground-floor concealments. "They can pick her off."

"Don't text them," Christina said. "I want her myself. One shot and it's over."

"If we sit right here, this Dodge Viper'll come up on us in a minute or two." She pointed to a snake on the map. "We don't even have to move and we'll get a clean shot before they see us."

"Screw the Dodge Viper. I'm not gonna let William and Daniel take what's rightfully ours."

"They're on our team."

"Come on, Melissa. You don't want to see the look on Rainmaker's face when we take her out? We'll turn on the brights when we blast her so you can get a picture."

Melissa tapped her phone and studied the screen. "According to SocialOracle, if we win the game, there's a sixty-three percent chance of ESPN retweeting me if I make the post super sporty, like, 'Gold medal, yay!' But if I post a picture of Rainmaker's kill shot . . ." Her eyes widened. "That's better. Like, Kylie Jenner better."

"Who's that, a cyborg assassin?"

"Don't pretend like you don't know."

Christina eased her palm forward to bring the map to half transparency. As they crept from their hiding place, she followed Rainmaker's progress. The vampire bat moved steadily through the backstreets. She tried to think of the perfect caption for Melissa's post—*Making it rain in Central Ohio!* or *Goth rocked!*— but everything she came up with sounded too inside-jokey.

Social media was harder than it looked.

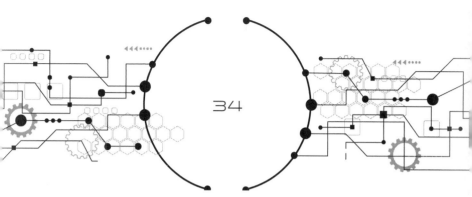

34

William and Daniel were pinned down. The Tesla Predator had rolled past a few times, patrolling up and down the street, waiting for infantry soldiers to reveal themselves. And they'd heard movement in the mansion attached to their garage. They had to assume snipers had taken position in the busted windows.

The garage was more like what old people called a "carport," a short canopied tunnel with an open front. William figured garage doors hadn't been invented when this place was built. If the carport hadn't been strewn with junk to create a little warren, they'd be completely exposed.

"It's possible that we suck at this," William said. They were crouching behind a pile of rotten firewood covered with a ragged sheet. A sweet hint of decay wafted up, and William tried not to touch any of the wood. Daniel peeked over the top at the street, which had been quiet for the past few minutes.

William wondered if any teams had been chased all the way out to the parking lot.

"Nah," Daniel said. "We're still in it."

"When you're in the middle of a game, do you ever lose track of it all and forget you're even playing? I felt like that in the Derby, like I'd always been there. Like it was my life."

"There's this book my dad gave me in ninth grade, when I made JV, called *Basketball Fundamentals* by Walt Jackson."

William eyed his friend. "Sounds riveting."

"It's dry as hell. Walt Jackson was a point guard for the Sixers back when they all still did layups because nobody really dunked yet. The book is pretty much what you'd expect except for the last chapter, which is called 'The Art of Being a Proper Vessel.' It's got a totally different tone and writing style, like one minute Jackson's laying out the details of a pick-and-roll for nine pages, and then all of a sudden he's talking about how the entire past and future of basketball is flowing through every player like a wind that comes down off the plains—he was from Topeka—and it can be distracting when you realize everything that's going to happen in the game has already happened. Like it can suddenly hit you when you square up for a totally uncontested shot and you brick it hard because at the moment of release you have this oceanic awareness washing over you. . . . Anyway, Jackson says that the way to be respectful of your place in the vast ecosystem of the game is to be able to compartmentalize. Don't worry about anything beyond your next step, your next dribble. Don't think about the score. Just focus on being the best at what you're currently doing, and all that other stuff will fall away. I don't know. It was the sixties when he wrote it."

William put a finger to his lips and gradually widened his eyes while Daniel spoke. Daniel was looking straight at him but didn't get the hint.

William whispered softly, "That sounds great, maybe I could borrow it sometime."

"Sure. I mean, you should read more anyway. What was the last book you read?"

"Internet."

"What about my copy of *Gatsby* that I gave you?"

"Internet."

There was a distant rustling on Main Street. Someone was approaching, or else a raccoon was scavenging the barbecue. William raised his head and sighted his scope along the thoroughfare. Half the lanterns had gone out, and the night was heavy with the weight of the asylum.

"You know what's weird about *Basketball Fundamentals*?" Daniel was whispering now. "It was my dad's when he was a kid. On the inside cover, in pencil, you can still see where he wrote his name, Martin Benson."

"Good old Marty."

"Which means he must have read that last chapter. But he never said anything to me about it. You'd think it would have come up."

William swiveled left and trained his scope on the south end of the street, beyond the fountain. A shadow flickered in a window, and the lantern was doused. Darkness deepened.

"You never say much about *your* dad," Daniel said. "I don't even know his name."

"Terrence Mackler." The name brought with it an impression of a brown Carhartt sweatshirt and the sawdust that clung to William's clothes when he hugged his dad. He remembered learning about the Civil War in elementary school and associating his father's job as "union carpenter" with the blue-uniformed soldiers building makeshift battle headquarters for General Sherman. . . .

"Good old Terry," Daniel said.

William's throat felt tight. He amped up his focus. Something was coming up the road, and he was going to destroy it. He wished they had real live weapons so he could aim for the propane tanks on the grills huddled in the fountain, catalyze a Michael Bay–worthy explosion. He slid a pinkie under his right eye to wipe a tear before it fell. What was his problem?

His father's nightstand back in Michigan had been a vortex of dadness: cologne, deodorant, Icy Hot, Neosporin, CD player/clock radio, Allman Brothers CDs, loose change, money clip, Trident gum, handkerchief. During summer vacation, with both his parents at work, William used to creep into their bedroom and stand by the nightstand, absorbing the sights and smells of man stuff, wondering about being grown up. What did it look like these days? His mother's nightstand held stray pills and crumpled tissues and a bottle of Bombay Sapphire in the drawer.

To never talk about his father with his best friend. What kind of a person acted like that?

The footsteps were getting closer. There was a lone soldier coming up fast, breathing hard. He rested a finger on the trigger.

Shitbird was gonna get sniped.

"You take the shot," Daniel said, his rifle barrel resting atop the firewood pile. "I'll back you up in case there's more than one."

William's vision blurred. He tried to take Walt Jackson's advice and be the best laser-tag shooter he could be while everything else washed over him. He blinked away tears, and the dark figure came into view.

"Rainmaker," Daniel hissed.

The girl was barely visible, a dark wraith sprinting up Main Street.

William trained his rifle on her armor. . . .

And then she was a silhouette blasted by a nuclear brightness that set the thoroughfare ablaze. He shut his eyes against the glare and slowly opened them. There was Otto bearing down on her, gaining mercilessly as she lost time looking over her shoulder at the headlights searing holes in the night.

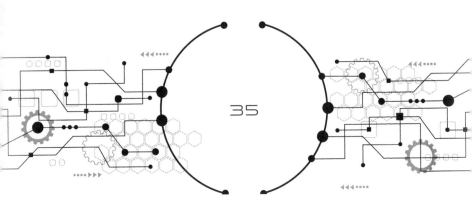

35

"Text Otto: Stop!"

Melissa screamed into her watch. Christina cycled madly through menus and displays, searching for an override, an emergency stop, anything. It had gone terribly wrong as soon as they'd eased out of a side street to spy Rainmaker skirting the edge of the thoroughfare. Otto had interpreted Christina's eagerness as something like bloodlust and accelerated straight at the girl. In distress, Rainmaker had booked it up Main Street.

Otto pursued like a dog off its leash.

Just like William in the Derby, this was all her fault. If only she'd been skilled enough to penetrate ARACHNE, perhaps she could wrest control from Otto, but this was all so far beyond what she'd signed up for. . . .

"Just stop, Otto!" Melissa lowered her wrist and projected her voice into the interior. "Please!"

"Abort!" Christina screamed as her fingers jabbed the

windshield. The real world shone through digital chaos in uncanny flashes. Rainmaker was an inhuman shape, a frantic blot of desperation getting bigger as Otto gained ground.

Otto wasn't speeding. Not yet. The car was letting Rainmaker think she had a chance. Toying with her.

"Turn to the right!" Melissa said. "Swerve, you fuck!"

Christina slammed her palms against the windshield until they stung. *Patricia Ming-Waller*, she thought. *Driverless*. They must be able to override remotely. But she was moving too slow, while the situation spiraled out of control. Story of her life.

Rainmaker was going to die.

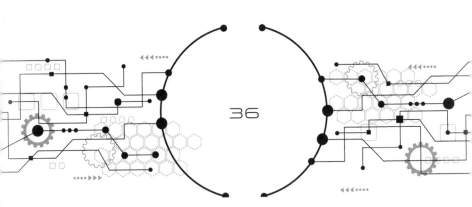

36

William saw himself spring from his hiding spot, rocketing from the carport in a fierce burn straight for Rainmaker, his feet leaving the ground, hurtling into her, the collision with Otto shattering his bones and shutting off his lights, but not before he could see that she was safe. . . .

Except there was no time for that. She would be dead by the time he got halfway there. Otto was too fast.

Daniel was standing up, somewhere between paralysis and action. There were people screaming, strangers' voices cast down from the windows, witnesses to the game's murderous turn.

William's gun clattered onto the firewood. His phone was in his hands.

99 88 77. It had to work. Coming from him, it had to work. The solution was so chillingly obvious: Otto did whatever he

wanted, except when it came to William. They had a special bond. Otto had chosen him.

His vocabulary had been reduced to a single word, entered and sent.

STOP.

Stop stop stop stop stop . . .

Rainmaker stumbled. Time stretched her collapse into the flailing instant replay of a soccer player taking a dive. She hit the dirt in front of the carport and tumbled forward, limbs bending in ways they should not. Her rifle spun end over end, skidding outside the cone of light.

Otto's brakes engaged with the dry scrape of dust on old cement. The car was still. Dirt swirled up in a gauzy cloud. William was reminded of Pompeii, that volcanic eruption he'd been fascinated with as a kid, tons of ash coming down, entombing people in their final poses. Rainmaker crumpled in the street while the dust settled, a motionless figure amid tossed-up earth, her feet an inch away from Otto's front bumper.

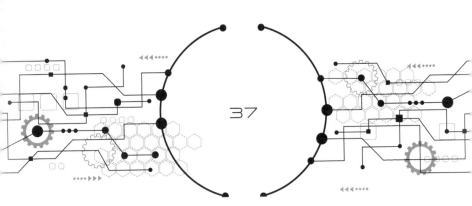

" 'm sorry, but we have to tell Patricia Ming-Waller about this," Melissa said. "Otto doesn't listen to us. We're in a death machine with selective hearing."

Daniel's head was on her shoulder. Sometimes his moods reminded Melissa of an air mattress, and right now she envied his deflation. She could not calm down. There was no escape: she'd been sitting in this car when it nearly killed that poor girl. She'd been sitting in this car when Eli had come sprinting up, screaming incoherently, banishing them from the game, *What's wrong with you people?* And now she was sitting in the same car as it crossed the border into Kentucky, chugging along as if nothing had happened. The interior was slightly humid, set to Southern Garden Party. The rich scent of hyacinth and begonia enveloped her. Distant chatter, overly polite laughter, the clink of glasses . . . it was all so insane. They had been run out of town, and now she had nothing to post. She didn't want to provoke responses from Eli and Rainmaker or their crew.

Her follower count was holding steady.

"He listens to me," William said. "Remember how we're supposed to be discovering things as we go along? I think what we just found out was that I'm basically the driver. Which makes total sense, because it's my car."

Melissa put up her hands. "All I can do is reiterate that was a seriously fucked-up situation back there. You weren't in *here*, William. Sitting helpless in the car, being ignored. Try to imagine what that was like for us."

She looked at Christina for support. The girl had been right beside her, screaming, desperate. And she'd been suspicious of the whole #AutonomousRoadTrip experience from the moment they left Fremont Hills, firing off those questions at Patricia Ming-Waller. But now she wasn't even paying attention. She was hunched over her laptop, typing away.

"Hernandez?"

"Otto's fine," Christina said without looking away from the screen. "Otto's great. Long live Otto." Briefly, she lifted her eyes to scan the interior, and Melissa followed her train of thought: it was impossible to have a frank talk about Otto's behavior when Otto was eavesdropping and altering said behavior accordingly. They were stuck in a feedback loop that overlapped on multiple levels, and it made her feel claustrophobic.

The front windshield darkened. The smattering of taillights that punctuated the nighttime stretch of I-71 dimmed and vanished. Melissa saw her reflection in the smooth opaque surface, body elongated by the slight curve of the screen, and then Patricia Ming-Waller's high-def visage appeared.

The Driverless CEO's voice poured smoothly from Otto's speakers. "Should I prep for a photo?" A subtle shade of eyeliner applied itself. Melissa thought the woman looked fabulous, considering her remains were scattered across the Galaxy Liner launch site. The construct could probably use a spa day to open up its pores, but who couldn't?

"Not this time," Melissa said. The eyeliner faded. "Did you just hear me say your name?"

Ming-Waller shook her head. "You told Otto you wished to speak to me, and he relayed the message."

"Actually," Melissa said, "I didn't give him that command at all. We were just talking about you between the four of us."

"Ah!" Ming-Waller's eyes darted around the interior. "That explains the burning in my ears."

"See, this is exactly what I was getting at," Melissa said. "Otto just sort of half listens to us, and then does whatever he wants. Just now—"

"He's fine," William cut in. "The trip's been amazing so far. Thanks for checking in, Patricia, but—"

"He almost *killed someone*," Melissa said, raising her voice over William. Reporting Otto's malfunction was unquestionably the right thing to do, but Melissa still felt a guilty twinge, as if she were snitching on the car. "He ran a girl down for no reason at all, and he wouldn't stop when we told him to."

"Your demeanor is expressing alarm, but not shock," Ming-Waller said.

"Correct," Melissa said, "I am alarmed. This is alarming."

Ming-Waller smiled. "But there is no hysteria present. From this I can be certain that the girl in question is alive and unhurt."

"Yeah," Christina said, "she's got a little bruise on her shoulder. It's nothing."

Melissa shot the girl a glare. "It's not nothing! You were *screaming your head off* back there, Christina."

She was aware that Christina was playing games with Otto, trying not to give him a window into her state of mind, but Melissa needed somebody to back her up.

"Rainmaker's fine," William said.

Melissa put up her hands. Daniel cleared his throat and straightened up in the seat. "Fabes is right," he said. "Otto went a little nuts back there. Maybe Driverless can run some kind of diagnostics or something?"

"I can recall the car and have an inspection performed by qualified Driverless technicians. You'll have to come off the road, of course."

"We're not doing that," William said.

"Well, she is right," Daniel repeated. "Melissa's right."

He looked at her expectantly, and she realized that he was seeking her approval, like a puppy who knows it's done something to be proud of and is angling for a treat. She had no idea if Daniel actually believed that she was right, or if he was performing. She put her hands in her lap and squeezed them together. Ming-Waller's crisp, backlit countenance splashed across the side of Daniel's face like a sliver of light creeping around the moon, blackening his eager eyes.

"Melissa may be correct from her perspective," Ming-Waller said, "but that encompasses a narrow field compared to what Otto can, and must, perceive and react to. Perhaps it will help to pose a fundamental question of the Driverless experience from Otto's perspective. Consider this: circumstances in the traffic flow suddenly become life-threatening, and you, the car, must make a split-second decision. You can either steer yourself into a family of four human beings, killing them all, or swerve to avoid them and drive off a bridge to your own occupant's certain death. Do you protect the pedestrians or the occupant?"

Silence. Daniel frowned at Melissa, waiting for her to speak first. Christina slid her finger around her laptop's trackpad.

"This is kind of a downer," William said.

"Do you protect the pedestrians or the occupant?" Ming-Waller asked again.

"Pedestrians," Melissa said.

"So human beings on the road have a social responsibility to sacrifice themselves for the greater good."

"Don't you have scientists for this?" William asked.

Ming-Waller fixed her gaze on him. "Will human beings purchase cars if they know those cars are programmed to sacrifice them?"

"Why are you asking me?"

"You are the chosen one, William Mackler."

"I *knew* it! Ever since the Derby, I fucking knew it."

"I am just kidding. You are not. You are merely one of several billion human beings from whom we will aggregate behavioral data. What did you think of my joke? Would you rate my effort a success?"

"What does this have to do with Otto almost murdering Rainmaker?" Melissa said.

"Perhaps you responded more favorably to the one about my burning ears."

"That in no way qualified as a joke," Christina said.

Ming-Waller nodded thoughtfully. Her fathomless eyes

sought an object in the distance. Melissa followed the construct's gaze, but there was only darkness out the rear window. When she turned back, the face was gone. The oily reflective surface of the screen was replaced by the transparent windshield. The lonely stretch of highway faded in.

"End transmission," Christina said.

"What the hell was that?" Melissa asked. "Patricia Ming-Waller's batshit."

"I think I get what she was saying," Daniel said. "What if Otto saw the bigger picture out there, some kind of danger we couldn't have any way of knowing about, like another car about to come flying out of an alley to smash into Rainmaker unless she ran forward? So to us it seemed like he went crazy, but really he was just herding her away from something worse."

"No way." Melissa shook her head. "Uh-uh. I was right here. I could feel him bearing down on her."

"You're probably right," Daniel conceded.

Christina shut her laptop with a decisive snap that made Melissa wince. "Look." Her finger swiped the empty air. A map blinked on in the middle of the car, bright and crisp in the dim light. Christina splayed her fingers to zoom in on their route. A blue line sliced through Kentucky, terminating in Nashville. "We'll be there in four hours. Do you really want to take a detour to some Driverless facility? Do you want to go home?"

Melissa thought of the flagship Natasha Lynn Chao boutique in East Nashville, nestled among vegan restaurants and artisanal soap shops. Photos she'd seen of the trendy district gave her a familiar shiver, the sense of a future with a Melissa-size hole just waiting to be filled. She would become the kind of person who moved through a room like the lady across the avenue in her New York City apartment, with a divine sense of knowing how to occupy a space.

Plus she was dying to comparison-shop all those funky skirts and absorb the off-kilter genius of Natasha's signature clashing plaids. Ripped flannels, the distressed nineties throwback stuff, sort of boggled her mind. And she wanted to try on one of those famous maxi dresses that transformed into a skirt courtesy of a single adaptable strap.

A selfie with a pile of Natasha Lynn Chao shopping bags was a guaranteed retweet from the designer herself.

"No," she admitted. "I don't want to go home."

William slid a Twizzler under his nose as if he were sniffing a fine cigar. "Otto, just for the record, the answer is 'occupants.' You save the occupants."

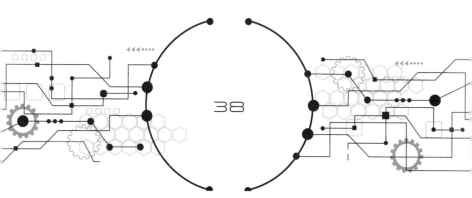

38

Melissa lost herself in the floating map's criss-crossing highways. Back in the day it must have been easy to leave everything behind, arrive at college, and shed the baggage of high school. But since she'd been old enough to operate a phone, she'd been part of the web of experiences that united everyone for all time and ensured that no matter what happened with Daniel, she'd always know which Princeton dining halls had the best desserts and how tough his practices were.

Had the days of landlines and paper letters been liberating or lonely? When she pictured the world that way, it was barren and empty. Great yawning chasms filled with the husks of hometown friendships that had withered and died.

She felt the weight of Daniel's head in her lap. He lay on his side, bent into a Z shape, and used her leg as a pillow. "Sleeeeepy," he said, his breath on the bare skin of her thigh. She combed his hair with her fingers. He closed his eyes and snuggled closer. His body was always warm. They had a running joke about his furnace-chest heating a nineteenth-century tenement.

Sleepy Daniel was one of her favorite Daniels.

Her eyes traced the curve of I-65 while she caressed his head. She thought of the first time he'd ever stayed in her bed overnight, the summer before senior year. Her parents had gone to an orthodontics conference in Maryland.

You're burning up!

I do tend to run hot.

She remembered waking to morning light coming through her balcony doors, and wallowing in the tingling unreal sensation that she'd just spent the night with Daniel Benson in the checkered sheets she'd had since sixth grade, before she'd ever kissed a boy. Moments stacked like panes of glass, Sixth-Grade Melissa with her new sheets, and Eleventh-Grade Melissa with her boyfriend in her bed, and College Melissa looking back on all of it from behind yet another pane to form the stained-glass puzzle of her life.

She picked up her phone and scrolled to the picture of Daniel, William, and Christina standing arm in arm beneath the Higginsburg Asylum sign. Then she flipped back to their group selfie with Patricia Ming-Waller. You dragged along the good, the bad, and the mundane. It didn't matter whether you were an obsessive Facebook creeper or somebody who kept old yellowed photographs in a box.

Daniel's feet hanging off the edge of her bed.

"Look what I found," Christina said, dismissing the map with a wave of her hand. The Kentucky highway dissolved into radiant pinpoints that filled the car and drifted like dust through a sun patch. "Mood sprites."

Flecks whirled dreamily around Melissa, passing through a spectrum of orange and deepening to autumnal brown. As they settled upon Daniel's sleeping head, the sprites adopted the nameless colors of his dreams.

"Oh my God," William said, putting his arm around Christina. "You're seriously the best." She put her head on his shoulder, and crimson snow fell thickly all around them.

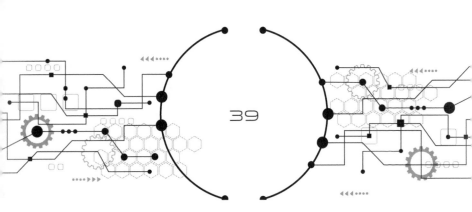

39

M elissa had just started to drift off to sleep when her phone buzzed. Blearily, she checked the screen. Epheme. She made sure to hold the phone directly above Daniel's ear so he couldn't see it if he happened to open his eyes.

Ash:	Can we talk?
SewWhat:	What's up?
Ash:	I mean on the phone. I have some news.
SewWhat:	Not now. Tomorrow?
Ash:	Sure. Can't wait to hear your voice.
SewWhat:	Is it good news at least?
Ash:	You'll just have to wait and see. ☺

After that, Melissa slept badly. Feverish thoughts came and went: Otto driving them into a lake, or running over pedestrians, or heading straight for an unfinished bridge. *Somebody ought to keep watch*, she'd bolt up in her seat and think. *We shouldn't let William fall asleep in the car.* But then she'd reassure herself that they were driving safely down I-65, and drift away, until the staccato rhythm of waking and sleeping became her reality. Nashville arrived in disjointed impressions as dawn broke during their approach.

Glittering downtown skyline, dual-spired skyscraper capped with thin cones of white poking the bruise-colored sky.

Morning light skimming the Cumberland River, Otto rumbling across a bridge. Twin spikes looming, dimmed to fade into the day.

She came fully awake when Otto slowed to join the rush-hour hustle of downtown Nashville. The river was at their back. Horrible music was playing, some slapdash demo or bad joke. She blinked. Everyone else was awake. The music wasn't coming from the speakers. William was perched on the edge of the bench, acoustic guitar balanced on his leg, strumming a few halting chords and warbling off-key. The air was hot; William had rolled down the window to serenade passing cars.

We're in the SOUTH, she thought.

Her palm was freezing cold. Daniel was handing her a Red Bull.

"Morning, Fabes. Welcome to Music City."

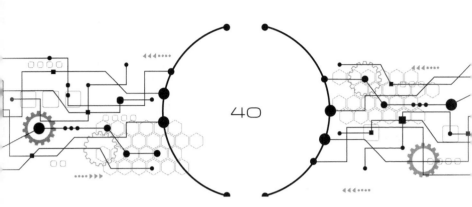

ashville in August was blistering. William felt like a
fried ant in a sadistic little kid's driveway. He took
the measure of the city in glorious air-conditioned
segments from inside the eleven boutiques on Melissa's list,
and Cuthbert's Barbecue, where they scarfed ribs for lunch.

Nashville was a city of leafy streets that felt almost suburban,
but unlike true suburbia, there were sidewalks everywhere. Tall
buildings clustered downtown, as if the business district had
been yanked straight up from the mud of the riverbank. The
rest of the city dribbled out in a pleasant sprawl.

Melissa seemed to float along like Princess Peach, carried by
the buoyant powers of her magical skirt through Five Points
and Green Hills. William trooped dutifully from store to store,
intrigued by Melissa's deep focus. "Shopping" was too pedestrian a term for what she was doing. Maybe it was the heat,
but he found the anthropological care she lavished on weird
scarves enthralling.

In the bathroom of a kitschy mom-and-pop frozen yogurt place, he took off his shirt and dabbed at his sweat with a paper towel. When he emerged, he found Christina sitting at a small round table, messing with its centerpiece, ignoring the dollop of vanilla yogurt she'd buried under an avalanche of gummy bears. He sat down, and she slid a Twizzler-Coke across the table.

"Prenibbled," he said, taking a sip. "Thanks. Is it me or is Coke better in the South?"

"Welcome to our garden of ceramic delights." Fake carnations sprang from a handmade teapot, providing shade for a group of figurines: pastel cobblers at their workbenches, and suspender-clad children tending some vaguely biblical flock.

"Ah, shit," he said, realizing they were Hummels.

"Wait for it . . ." Her hand disappeared behind the teapot.

"Don't do it, Hernandez."

She grinned wickedly and made a figurine amble awkwardly toward him. It was a girl Hummel in a demure country dress carrying a pile of textbooks. Her hair sported a pale pink bow.

"Why hello, William my sweet," Christina said in a high-pitched Southern drawl that sounded a bit like Miss Piggy. *"Why haven't you written? I wait by the mailbox every day, but your letter never comes."*

He took a bite out of his straw. "I'm ignoring this."

"Don't you recognize me from my pretty dress that Mama made special? It's me, Bridget Mancini!" Christina made the figurine hop up and down. *"I just love dancin'. Won't you dance with me again, William?"*

Last year he'd had sex with Bridget Mancini exactly twice in Dylan Seidelman's parents' bedroom during a party, in a mutual agreement to take each other's virginity before her family moved to Fort Lauderdale. Dylan Seidelman's mom collected Hummel figurines, and now whenever William tried to conjure up the illusory feel of Bridget Mancini's skin, he was forced to think about cherubic shepherds herding ceramic sheep along the nightstand.

"I'm not going to have a conversation with that thing," he said.

Christina made the Hummel gyrate and gallop. "This is what you get for coming home wasted after that party and barging into the basement to tell me all about it."

"Okay, how's this for a deal. When you hook up with some dude in Buffalo for the first time, you call me at three in the morning and give me the rundown, and then we're even."

Crack. Christina's thumb popped the Hummel's head off. It clunked against the table, and William trapped it underneath his palm before it rolled onto the floor.

"Shit," she whispered, hurriedly placing the headless figurine among its brethren gathered around the teapot. She looked over her shoulder. The lady behind the counter was ringing up a gaggle of kids in orange church group T-shirts. "Let's hit it."

"What am I supposed to do with Bridget's head?"

Christina grabbed her cup of gummy bears and stood up. "Why don't you mail it to her?"

He dropped the head into the teapot and followed her out.

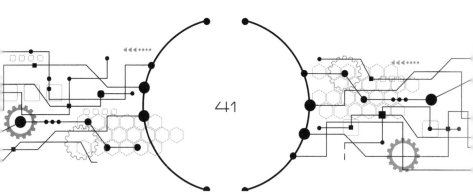

41

"Her post's blowing up!"

William held his phone so Christina could see the screen. She was sitting cross-legged on her bed (this hotel room had two queens instead of one king), frowning at her laptop.

"Natasha Lynn Chao reposted it and added some filters to the part where Melissa films herself in the mirror, trying on those leggings, to make a halo spin over her head and turn into a hula hoop."

There was a long pause while Christina finished typing. Then she shut her laptop and looked at William, registering the fact that he was still holding his phone up for her to see.

She shrugged. "Girls be shoppin'."

They had rejoined Melissa and Daniel across the street from the frozen yogurt place and followed them to Aketha, Cannery Row, and Natasha Lynn Chao. Melissa had draped eye-popping mountains of fabric over her arm before retreating to dressing rooms with Daniel in tow, winnowing down her selections so that she emerged from each store with one or two bags that they took turns feeding to Otto. When they got back to their hotel on Broadway, where honky-tonks oozed guitar-shaped marquees and giant decorative cowboy hats, taxicabs were just beginning to discharge tourists into the evening streets.

"Every time I look at you, you're on the computer," he said.

"Sorry, *Dad*."

"Hey, this is a judgment-free zone. I was just making an observation." He went to the minibar. "Whoa! They have Twizzlers. And Cokes."

"You just had one. And those minibar snacks cost a million dollars."

"Okay, *Mom*, don't worry. It's on Otto." He ripped open the candy wrapper and popped the can's top. Then he peeled off a Twizzler, nibbled both ends, and dropped his freshly made straw into the can.

"But yeah," she said, "I'm stuck in the middle of this weird Warcraft campaign. I just had to check on it."

"*You're* a weird Warcraft campaign."

He leaned against the desk and looked out the window. Night was beginning to settle over downtown, and the spires on the tallest skyscraper—which he now knew to be the AT&T Building—had reverted to their predawn frosted tips. He'd been dragged so quickly through the scorching day, and tomorrow they'd be gone; another highway, another city. He wondered if you could ever stay in one place long enough to feel that you'd done enough to get to know it. An anxious back-to-school feeling set in, that dampening of spirits when August rolled into September and you wondered if you'd really just let another summer go by. CB Lounge, 2:00 a.m., giddy jokes that made no sense; shotgunning beers on some basketball player's back patio while a bonfire got out of hand; nights united by the shriek of Fremont Hills' cricket chorus.

The last remnants of salmon-colored sky swam through the Cumberland in rivulets sliced by the prow of a barge. William took a picture of the scene with his phone. When he viewed it, he saw the back of Christina's shaved head ghosting the window. An unbearable urge gripped him.

"Hey, fuzzy." He grinned.

She narrowed her eyes as he approached. Then she crossed her forearms above her head as if warding off an evil spirit. "Begone!"

He reached out a hand. "Just one little rub for good luck and I'll never invade your personal-space bubble again for the rest of your life."

He saw her hand dart toward him but didn't react fast enough. She plucked the Twizzler from his Coke and took a huge bite, rendering it useless as a straw.

William lunged toward her in exaggerated slow motion. "Noooooo . . ."

She stuck the Twizzler between her lips like a noir dame with a cigarette and turned her head as he thrust his neck forward in a ridiculous attempt to Lady-and-the-Tramp it away from her. Just above her ear was a deep red scratch, a gouge in the shape of a scimitar.

"Jesus! What did you do to yourself?"

She shimmied back against the curious headboard, a cream-colored rectangle of leather attached to the wall. "Nothing. It's just a scratch."

William had seen her pick at her scalp a hundred times before. He assumed she thought she was being sneaky, as if pretending to run her hands through her hair could hide the fact that she was clawing at her skin. He'd never once brought it up, but now, with her head shaved, the angry cut was exposed. He wanted to take her head in his hands and lick the wound clean like Daniel's sisters' cats did to each other. He was aware of the weirdness of this impulse, but there was nothing he could do about it. A wave of light-headedness sent him to the bed. He sat facing her, wondering what exactly had just come over him.

"Oh my God," she said, finishing the Twizzler with furious chomps. "I'm fine! Don't cry about it."

"I'm not crying."

"Don't cry on the inside either. Don't look at me like that. Stop doing things."

The pillow hit him squarely in the chest. Across the bed, Christina laughed at his inability to block it. "I was thinking we should have a pillow fight, but then I was also thinking how clichéd that was—road trip, nice hotel, PILLOW FIGHT. I don't know why I can't just do things spontaneously. Teach me the secrets of spontaneous fun, William Mackler."

He was used to her abrupt subject changes. Their whip-lashing conversations threaded through days and weeks like driftwood on the Cumberland, picking up stray bits of chatter and carrying them along.

He touched the side of his head. "You sure you don't need some Neosporin? I can call the front desk."

He caught the second flung pillow with ease and affected a movie-German accent. "Now I have all ze pillows, Fräulein."

She hugged her knees to her chest. He noticed that her

Nightwish shirt was a different shade of black than her denim shorts. She wiggled her toes and used them to grip the fabric of the comforter.

"Stop looking at my toes."

"Requesting authorization to look somewhere, *anywhere.*"

She put on a hypnotist voice. "Looook deeeeep into my eyyyyes."

Things left unsaid retreated to a little heap in the back of his mind as he and Christina fell into a routine that might as well have been scripted. He glanced out the window at darkness pulling itself like a cowl across the skyline. Then he really did look deep into her eyes. They were the color of a pastoral scene, perpetually on the cusp of some whimsical transformation.

"You have really pretty eyes," he said. "Try not to scratch them out."

"You have really pretty eyelashes," she said. "For a boy."

"Thanks, I made them myself."

Now it was Christina's turn to look out the window.

"Nashville," William said.

"Uh-huh." She turned back to him. There was something different about her face. "What are you gonna do after this?"

William shrugged. "I guess that's up to my new best friend Otto."

"You gonna have him drop you off at the scrap yard every day? Pick you up at the end of your shift?"

He grinned. "That way I can always grab a few drinks at the U-Turn without having to worry about driving."

She rolled her eyes.

"Kidding!" he said. "I'll have him take me to the strip club instead."

She pressed the tip of her finger into the center of the comforter's pattern, which resembled a dartboard. "I was thinking, you know . . ." William's heart pounded and he didn't know why. "You could come with me to Buffalo."

He put up his hands in protest. "I ain't no college boy. Ain't one fer . . ." He trailed off quietly when he saw that she was serious. " . . . book . . . learnin'."

She leaned forward, hugging herself tightly. "I'm not talking about college. You could just move out there and find a job. Then we'll be in the same place."

"I already have a job."

"What does it matter if you work at Tanski's in Fremont Hills or some other scrap yard in Buffalo? Why do you have to even work in a scrap yard? You can do anything you want. You know that."

"Tell that to my one-point-six grade point average."

"It's because you didn't even try, you—"

"Give it to me."

"Dildo!"

He pretended to weigh the insult. "Seven out of ten." His eyes went to the undersides of her thighs. "You have really nice legs too." Being alone with Christina in a hotel room as night fell on the city outside was making him blurt things out.

She pulled down the ragged hem of her shorts, covering an extra half inch of skin. "You could sell your car. Then you wouldn't have to work at all, not for a long time. You could rent an apartment near the dorms. I'm supposed to live on campus freshman year, but after that I can live anywhere I want. We could—"

"Build a tunnel!" William said, this hypothetical future

unfolding rapidly in his mind. "With all that cash, I could just build a tunnel right into your dorm, a big underground chamber we could hang out in. And we could re-create our neighborhood from Fremont Hills so we're still living next door to each other, hire architects to make it look exactly like the CB Lounge, so it'll be like nothing changed!"

"I want things to change, William!" She lowered her voice. "I want things to change. I just want you there with me when they do."

"I'm not going to sell my car," he said.

Her hand moved to the top of her head. The tenderness he felt toward her torn skin and the desire to run his tongue along her head like a cat came rushing back all at once. But she only held her hand there for a second before she found the strength to pull it away without scratching.

"I know that," she said quietly. "It's just that I really, really don't want to say good-bye to you after this trip, okay? I don't want to say good-bye to you at all. I don't even know how to do it. I can't picture the moment. I've tried imagining myself in Buffalo, walking to class, going to the dining hall, and I can sort of see that, like there's a little outline of me moving through pictures of the campus or something." She made her fingers walk across the bedspread. "And I'm excited to get out of my house, but there's still something that doesn't feel right about the whole thing. It's just so arbitrary, fucking Buffalo; who cares, you know?"

She wove her fingers together in front of her shins and rested her head on her knees. William wished she would keep going. As long as she was talking, he wouldn't be expected to say anything in return. Right now, sitting across from her on a queen-size bed eight floors above the streets of Nashville, he felt dangerously close to letting his words outpace his thoughts. Better to clam up. Silence was something you never had to take back.

"You'll meet people," he said at last. "You'll make lots of new friends."

"Don't," she snapped. Then she closed her eyes.

"I'm sorry."

She rocked gently back and forth. "It's my fault. I'm not saying what I want to say."

His light-headedness returned, and he wished simultaneously to be far, far away—another galaxy would probably do it—and to slide across the bed, making himself small enough to wedge his body into her limbs' knotted frame.

She lifted her head up.

"Don't say anything else," he pleaded. "Just let it be."

She smiled sadly. "But we tell each other everything, William." Her voice was lightly tinged with sarcasm. They both knew it wasn't true.

He focused on Christina's face and at the same time perceived the airplane above the stadium where the Tennessee Titans played, and the fly trapped between the window's double-paned glass. The room's reflection coexisted with the world outside. William and Christina were giants stamped upon the skyline.

"I thought," she began, then started again. "I thought if we were more than just friends, then maybe we wouldn't have to say good-bye. Maybe then you'd have a reason to come with me." She held up a hand to stop him from talking. "If you tell me that I'll meet a really great guy at college, I will seriously murder you with a corkscrew from the minibar. If you don't want to be more than friends, just don't say anything at all and we'll never speak of this again."

His mouth was dry. "I don't want you to meet a guy at college."

There was no going back now. He couldn't figure out what was expected of him. All he knew was that the words *more than friends* coming from Christina Hernandez drowned out the part of him screaming *Pump the brakes, pal.* All that time spent staring at screens, driving around Fremont Hills blasting metal, drinking coffee in their corner booth at Hilda's until closing—he could trace her nervous tics and facial expressions and the positions she contorted herself into that made his spine wrench in sympathy back to that day when she'd informed him that she did not in fact have a bike pump handy but could probably find one if he gave her a few minutes, and his heart had leapt at having this girl for a next-door neighbor. . . .

More than friends.

Three words from which all the things they'd ever done exploded like popcorn.

"I suck at meeting people anyway," she said quietly.

"I know," he said, quieter still.

"Why are we whispering?"

"I have no idea."

He thought he should talk to Dr. Diaz about sorting out the storm in his head. But the spirit that sent him up the ladder to the water tower took over, and he reached for Christina. She broke the tight hold upon herself and then they were kneeling in the center of the bed, Christina telling him in between insistent kisses that he tasted like Twizzlers.

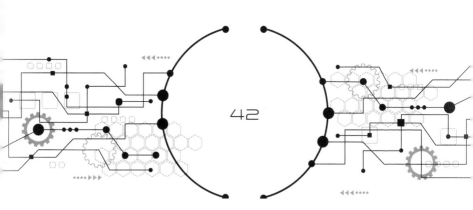

Melissa was jubilant. Her video had been reposted by Natasha Lynn Chao with added filters. It had already reached 13,764 plays and was easily the social media moment of the #AutonomousRoadTrip so far. By any metric—reach, visibility, follower count—it had been a massive success, and a good reminder that foresight, planning, and professionalism often took a backseat to Random Shit. *Embrace the unpredictability.* She opened her notes app and typed the phrase. Social tips could be another component of *DIYfashion365*, a good way to make the YouTube channel's platform more robust. She turned off her phone and realized— *oops*—that she'd just let the entire day go by without finding a free solitary moment to call Ash.

A newscaster on TV said, *The senator denied the allegations; an independent investigator has been appointed.* Sprawled on the hotel bed with the remote, Daniel changed the channel. Melissa watched a zombie tear a juicy red tendon from its shrieking victim's neck, then returned her attention to the full-length mirror bolted to the closet door.

She turned in a slow circle. The floor was littered with tissue paper, and Melissa was like the centerpiece of a snow globe. Her new Aketha leggings would be ideal for fall semester. In her mind she was pairing them with a knee-length cardigan and maybe her suede boots.

Revolution completed, she turned her phone back on. 754 new followers since they'd gotten back to the hotel. She wondered if this place had a rooftop. A nighttime picture of the skyline would be like catnip for her followers. She could go up there alone. That was a good plan. It would buy her some time to call Ash.

"Can I wind you up?" Daniel asked.

On TV, two men in lab coats restrained a woman from attacking a chained-up zombie with an ax. Daniel was watching her from behind half-lidded eyes. He'd been extremely—almost obnoxiously—attentive during the first half of their shopping trip. But right around boutique number six, she felt his attention slipping. She knew him well enough to gauge the drifting of his mind by the shift in his body language. It was like watching ink slowly disperse into water.

Her silent answer to his question was to assume an overly stiff position, like a mannequin with its head slightly bowed. In the mirror she watched him appear behind her and felt his hands on her back. He slid them around an imaginary axis as if turning a stubborn crank, making grinding noises. After the third "turn," Melissa popped her head up with an eerie vacant grin. Arms at her sides like penguin flippers, she began to waddle stiffly, changing direction at random, a windup toy gone rogue.

"You're good at that," he said. "A little too good, if you ask me."

"I come from a long line of mechanical dolls. What do you think of these?" She patted her leg.

"The pants? They make you look like candy."

She frowned, trying to figure out the angle of the compliment. It would make sense for bright Harajuku style, but this was an earthy Aketha outfit. In the mirror she saw a look of consternation—maybe even horror—flash across his face. It was an expression she'd been noticing more and more lately, especially after he said something a little strange, as if regret were distilled and broadcast from his eyes. It made her feel guilty, like she was forcing him to say things he didn't mean.

She lifted a hand with fingers splayed. "What do you think for nails, if I wear the leggings with that charcoal sweater I have at home?"

Daniel brightened. He took her hand in his and pretended to examine her nails with the attention of a jeweler. "Hmm. I'd say we're gonna have to go with a clear gloss and let the outfit do all the work."

She made a face.

"What I meant to say was, I think we're going to do something very intricate and colorful and labor-intensive. Perhaps an entire galaxy in each nail."

"Now it sounds like I'm getting my money's worth."

Without letting go of her hand, he straightened up. A TV scientist gurgled as she drowned in her own blood; the captive zombie had apparently broken its chains. "I was thinking," he said. "We can keep doing this over Skype when we're at school. You can model stuff for me, and I'll hit you with my legendary suggestions."

"Yeah," she said. The word came out flatter than she'd intended.

"I don't mean we have to do it every day," he said quickly. "I'm not gonna be a psycho long-distance boyfriend. And anyway, our distance isn't that long when you think about it. New York to Princeton. Boom."

He grabbed her other hand as if reaching for a lifeline. She felt ill-equipped to have the conversation she'd been trying to tease out for several days. Her mind cycled through excuses. This would be easier in a public place, easier tomorrow, easier to talk it out over the phone once they'd moved into their dorm rooms.

If only he'd been more ambivalent! If only he'd been the one to say something like, *So, what do you think about trying to stay together?* To stroll sensibly up to the subject, arm in arm, and poke around its edges before diving in. But of course he was envisioning them charging blissfully into college without skipping a beat. She'd always known how he felt. And she'd always known what this conversation would mean and how it would end.

"I think we should break up," she said.

The hotel room—maybe the whole world—reshaped itself around these words. Melissa found herself standing in a bizarre corridor where the mirror hung aslant and the wallpaper pulsed with bad energy and the tissue paper at her feet crinkled without being touched. She had done it. Six little words had transformed the room into a nightmare place, and she wished she could put everything back the way it was with a magical finger snap.

Daniel looked over her shoulder at their reflection in the mirror, as if he were watching them act out a scene in his internal movie. His face was alarmingly blank, but his eyes registered the frightened disbelief of a small child getting his mind blown by special effects in IMAX 3-D.

She wondered if she'd ever hear him rattle off one of his movie lines again. The thought of this odd little quirk disappearing from her life nearly broke her heart.

She was no longer sure that she wanted to break up. Her brain was being invaded by the same alien virus that had corrupted the room, infecting her with conflicting impulses. What she actually wanted to do was get married. She wanted to pull him down to the floor and have sex among the tissue paper and shopping bags. She wanted a drink of water, she wanted him to say something, she wanted to stand here in silence and hold him.

She wanted to run away.

There were no #lifehacks to apply, no YouTube tutorials to consult. No sense of how to navigate this moment. He was still holding her hands, and that felt terribly wrong, but breaking contact had the air of cold finality—a slap in the face—and she couldn't bring herself to pull away.

The TV said, *Side effects may include drowsiness, nausea, restless-leg syndrome, and in rare cases, color blindness.*

"Okay," he said finally. He dropped her hands. Her fingers were very cold. In seconds they'd be numb.

He was still looking in the mirror, and she had the urge to tilt his chin toward her. He took a deep breath and seemed to draw on some deep reserve of acceptance—as if he'd been waiting for this and only needed to inhabit the role.

"Okay," he said again. Then he walked to the bed and sat down and looked at the TV.

Melissa was gathering tissue paper. There seemed to be a gap in her memory between making the decision to clean up and actually starting to do it. She opened her hand, and the paper floated back down to the floor. Things were happening out of order. Events had been reshuffled.

She found herself in the bathroom running hot water over her numb hands, trying to scald them back to life.

She looked at herself in the mirror and wondered why she looked puffy and spent as if she'd been crying, when she hadn't shed a single tear.

She had once read that getting over a breakup—really, truly putting it behind you—took half as long as the relationship had lasted. Did that mean she'd be feeling messed up and disconnected through her entire freshman year of college?

She leaned against the bathroom counter and looked through the open door at Daniel on the bed and tried not to want him so badly. She tried to be angry at him—all he could muster was a single word, fucking *okay*? What kind of boy just says *okay* and stares off into space after his girlfriend dumps him in a hotel room in Nashville?

A boy with a hornet's nest of issues she'd never attempted to poke. He was so obviously losing his way, and instead of helping him, she'd just given him a kick in the wrong direction.

She had to get out of this room. She felt like if she stuck around another minute, she'd peel off her Aketha leggings and climb on top of him. She'd heard hundreds of breakup stories from other girls and never once did they mention feeling horny. When Caroline Murphy suspected Jake Fusco of cheating, she'd waited until biology class and launched a fetal pig at the side of his head. Movie and TV breakups resounded with the snap of vicious zingers, long-simmering resentments boiling over into screaming matches. She had no frame of reference for whatever was going on in this room. She had just blundered into the weirdest breakup in human history.

She shut the bathroom door and closed her eyes and rehearsed her next steps: locate shoes, place feet into shoes, walk to door, exit room, descend via elevator, get front desk to call taxi, say to driver *Airport and step on it*, buy ticket, fly home, contact NYU about moving in, like, right now, pack stuff, get ride to school from parents, begin new life.

She rested her hand on the door handle and let her plan sink in, one word at a time, so that it became a list of mindless tasks. She could perform them without thinking. The next time she had a conscious thought, she'd be in her dorm room, and it would be easier to sort everything out. Until then, she'd cruise on autopilot.

She opened the door, and Daniel was standing in front of her, radiating spontaneous anguish. He looked into her eyes with such startling intensity that she had to force herself not to slam the door in his face just to break contact. He'd apparently come back to himself while she'd been in the bathroom, rehearsing her exit strategy.

"Tell me what I have to do to make things go back to the way they were, and I'll do it," he said. "Anything you want. Just say it."

"Daniel—"

"I'm sorry for how things have been. I know it's my fault, and I swear to God, I don't mean all the stupid shit I say. I honestly don't even know what's coming out of my mouth half the time, but I can work on it."

"You don't have to—"

"I completely understand why you're doing this."

"I don't think you do!"

Daniel stepped back. Her hand went up to cover her mouth. She'd escalated to the Yelling Phase so abruptly, it took them both by surprise. She took her hand away and tried to keep her voice steady and calm.

"I'm so sorry for this. I didn't mean for it to happen this way."

Daniel looked stricken. "How long have you known you were gonna do this?" He held up a hand before she could speak. "Actually I don't want to know. All I want to know is how we can fix it. That's it. That's all that matters. I also think either I should go into the bathroom or you should come out here, because this is like a symbol of something." He pointed to the empty doorway separating them. Melissa walked past Daniel and sat down in the armchair in the corner. Then she changed her mind and stood up.

"It's not about fixing anything." She tried to frame her explanation carefully. "It's more about how we never even talked about whether or not we'd stay together next year. You just sort of assumed."

She winced; it sounded accusatory. But Daniel nodded in agreement. "I know. You're right. That was really stupid and disrespectful of me. I fucked up and I'm sorry."

"No, Daniel, it's not—you don't have to keep apologizing, it wasn't disrespectful at all. It was just . . . we didn't talk about it. We should have and we didn't."

"I know. I know. I've got, like, a deficiency. But all this is stuff I can work on. I just have to—"

"This isn't about you!" This time Melissa was pretty sure she meant to yell. "You just keep saying you're sorry, and you're not even listening to me. It's disturbing."

"Disturbing," he said quietly. Then he nodded in a way that told Melissa he was etching the word into some mental checklist, as if she'd meant it as an indictment of his whole character. As if she'd said, *Daniel Benson is a disturbing human being.* She thought he might be trying to punish her.

"You always do this," she said, while an inner voice implored her to leave the room and take some time to compose her thoughts. "This is why it's been so hard to talk to you lately."

On TV, the zombie horde was crashing against the barbed-wire fence of a prison while marines steeled themselves for the assault. Daniel picked up the remote and turned the TV off and muttered something about symbols being everywhere. Melissa immediately missed the background noise.

"This just seems like a little thing in the scheme of Daniel and Melissa," he said, tossing the remote onto the bed and pacing to the closet and back. "You take us, what we are to each other, and it forms this ecosystem"—he drew a big circle in the air—"and so if you introduce any external forces to our ecosystem, some kind of new problem, it might be tough for us to deal with, but it's still easier to do it inside our ecosystem, where we can deal with things as a team. You see what I mean? This whole going-off-to-college thing—we can stretch our ecosystem across two states, and even though we'll be in differ-ent places physically we'll both be together inside it, because it's made up of *two years* together, and you can't just make that go away overnight. It's a whole world just for us, Melissa! We made it. You and me and nobody else. And it can't just disappear." A pained look crossed his face. He glanced at his wrist as if checking an imaginary watch. "I'm not sure if I said that right."

"No, Jesus Christ, I get what you're saying fine, but we're still coming from totally different places. This magical ecosystem isn't a thing that just exists forever. You assume that it is, but we have to work to keep it going. If we stop working on it, then it doesn't exist anymore. It's not something we can pop in and out of, not when I'm in New York—"

"Meeting a coxswain." Daniel grabbed his left thumb with his right hand.

"What? What the hell's a *coxswain*?"

"The guy in charge of the boat on the crew team."

"Why would I— This isn't about our ecosystem at all, is it?"

"Yes it is," Daniel insisted. "It's about you and me and—"

"It's about *you*! It's about you being jealous!"

Daniel looked scared. "I'm not a jealous person."

Melissa closed her eyes and wondered how they'd reached this point. It was like they'd been using Epheme, erasing what came before, leaving them unmoored and adrift. "It doesn't matter," she said. When she opened her eyes, Daniel looked like he'd awakened in the middle of a night terror. She crossed the room and put her arms around him. He kissed the top of her head and held her close.

"Don't say it doesn't matter," he said.

"I'm sorry."

"It matters to me. Everything you do matters to me more than anything, okay? Fuck Princeton, fuck basketball, fuck my whole future—"

"Don't say that."

"There's just you, Melissa."

"Stop."

"I love you so much."

"I love you too." The words came out easily, but she had no idea if they were true. The impulse to simply make the hurt stop was nearly overwhelming.

"So then what's the point of ending anything?" he said. She could feel his heart racing, and it made her nervous. She took a step back. "There's no point," he continued. "People wait and see. That's what they do. They don't just end things for no reason, not when they both still love each other."

"I feel like when you say things like *Fuck my whole future*, that's kind of what I'm getting at. There's a big difference between how you see things and how I see things, and it's nobody's fault, it just is."

"I only meant my future without you in it, Fabes. Not my future now. They're two different futures."

"That's too much for me, Daniel. I can't be in charge of your happiness. Or whatever."

"You're not." The way he was suddenly smiling made her feel very uncomfortable. The muscles in his face were moving too fast. "I'm okay. Seriously. I love you and I want to be with you. That's all. There. See? I'm expressing myself clearly. Boom. From now on, I got this."

Melissa sat down in the armchair and slipped her feet into her flats. "I think I need to get some air."

"Good idea," he said, looking around for his shoes.

"I mean alone, Daniel. I just need to clear my head for a minute."

"Just show me one boob first," he said, a callback to a running joke they'd abandoned in tenth grade. "Just the left one."

She grabbed her phone from the nightstand and stood up.

"I love you," he said. "I love the way you play with your hair when you don't even realize you're doing it." She found that she could not look at him. It was like being in a room with a malfunctioning machine, spewing out words and phrases to try to impress its human masters.

She walked to the door.

"Do you remember the first thing you ever said to me?" he asked. "Please just wait a second."

Her flats shuffled tissue paper. She caught a glimpse of herself in the mirror as she passed and then she was pushing down on the door handle.

"I don't feel like I said what I was trying to say!"

She was out in the hall, walking away. The door clicked shut behind her. She wished that Daniel would come sprinting after her and skid to a stop in front of the elevator, giving her one more chance to take everything back. Together they'd exorcise the horror of what had just gone down in that room. Their aborted breakup would linger forever like a bad smell in the walls, casting a pall over couples until the air resounded with *Let's just be friends* and *It's not you, it's me*. But no footsteps came. She told herself it was for the best as the elevator doors opened. She curled a strand of hair around her finger and descended.

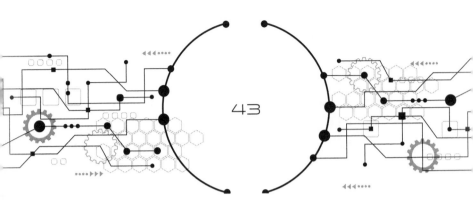

43

William dashed from the hotel. If he'd been wearing a coat, it would have flapped in his wake, sweeping tabloids from convenience store racks. The blood rush in his ears mingled with country music on the strip. He was familiar with adrenaline surges, but this was uncharted territory. This was *more than friends.* This was Christina Hernandez informing him that she'd hop in the shower while he literally ran to get the condoms he'd packed, and there was nothing sardonic about the way she looked at him before closing the bathroom door. He wanted a never-ending supply of the sight so he could return to it in times of need.

The condoms were in his bag. His bag was in the car.

He ran a gauntlet of shoulders and elbows.

Christina had one twisted rib that stuck out a little more than the others, and he couldn't get enough of it. Who else but Christina Hernandez would have something so secretly awesome?

His phone chimed. The melody was vaguely familiar, but the number was unknown. He answered without breaking stride.

"Hello, William. How's the weather in Oklahoma City?" Dr. Diaz's voice synthesizer had been tweaked so that the therapist sounded slightly auto-tuned.

"I don't know, I'm in Nashville."

"Of course you are! I was making a geographical joke."

"Did I butt-dial you or something?" Dr. Diaz had never called him before. William didn't know the algorithm was capable of such an action.

"Ha-ha!" William winced. The therapist's laugh was like an icy wind in his ear. "I'm just checking in about the hashtag Autonomous Road Trip."

William turned sideways to dodge a huge family bristling with selfie sticks creeping along the sidewalk like Roman infantry.

"Now's not really the best time."

"And how does that make you feel?"

"I didn't—"

"Good! Let's explore that. What are you doing right now?"

"Going to get condoms."

"And how does that make you feel?"

"Listen, Doctor, I appreciate you checking in, but—"

"Are you in love with the human being with whom you'll be intercoursing sexually?"

"It's Christina Hernandez."

"Do you love this human being?"

"Stop saying 'human being.'"

"Are you intrigued by the possibility that your newly sexual relationship with Christina Hernandez may evolve into a multifaceted love union?"

"I don't know, we're not quite there yet. I *really* don't want to talk about this right now."

"You are free to hang up."

"Are you just gonna call me back?"

"Perhaps!"

He sighed. "Christina's awesome. I don't know anything about love. I don't know."

"You resisted this kind of potential love union with Christina Hernandez for several years."

"Yeah, I mean, we have a next-door neighbor thing. I didn't want to mess it up."

"But the hashtag Autonomous Road Trip has altered your relationship."

"I don't know."

"The consequences have shifted."

"I don't care about the consequences anymore."

"On a scale of one to fourteen—"

"A one, okay? A *one*. I'm not scared. I'm just gonna do it. So fuck off."

He ended the call and careened around a neon corner, practically smashing into Melissa. Her phone was pressed against her ear. She was wearing a new outfit, and he wondered if she was headed to a honky-tonk bar. But Daniel was nowhere in sight. Maybe she was just talking to her parents; it looked like a hushed, sober discussion. William lifted a hand to wave and kept moving. He was on a mission-critical errand and not about to be sidetracked by any more talk.

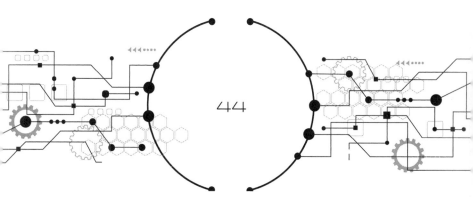

44

William checked the street signs. He was close to Otto's parking spot but couldn't find the car. A crowd of people had gathered across from a garage with metal gates pulled down over big loading-dock doors. As he slowed to a walk, he took note of the vehicles that lined the street: Porsche 911, Corvette ZR1, Audi Renegade X6, and idling in the middle of the road, a Mitsubishi Lord, quivering with cold, hard menace, twin-turbo engine rising from the center of its hood like some alien periscope.

These were some of the best street-legal race cars money could buy. Probably not a coincidence. Farther down the block he saw that the crowd was congregating around Otto, inspecting and prodding.

He sauntered up, at once conscious of his affected gait and unable to change it. The crowd was dressed mostly in jeans and T-shirts with the odd leather jacket interspersed. He felt eyes on his approach. A skiffle beat drifted up from Broadway, and a girl with an eyepatch tapped out the two-step on Otto's passenger window. She gave him a nod.

"Sup, William."

A fiery scar of mottled skin swept back from the patch across her temple, like a flame decal on a hot rod.

He nodded back, calm and friendly. The girl was tall, maybe nineteen or twenty years old. There was a hush as her friends turned their attention to him. The guy next to her leaned storklike against the car, knee bent, foot pressed against Otto. He pulled a pack of cigarettes from his jacket pocket and drew one out with his teeth. Then he flicked a Zippo against the side of his jeans, held the flame to the cigarette, and snapped the lighter shut.

William couldn't help but stare; he'd seen Tommy light cigarettes that way.

"Hey, guys," William said with an easy smile, pointing to the Mitsubishi Lord. "You know you're double-parked?"

His heart beat triumphantly. That was a cool thing to say, and he'd delivered it perfectly. Eyepatch Girl smirked. Zippo Man let smoke leak from his nostrils. Then he pushed off from the car and drove his gloved fist into William's solar plexus.

William felt air rush from his lungs. He doubled over and made a hoarse sucking sound. Somebody shoved him hard from behind, and he stumbled over Zippo Man's outstretched leg. The sidewalk came up fast. The unseen person at his back dug a knee between his shoulder blades and pressed him into the cement. The pressure on his spine made him lie completely still. The message was clear: struggle and pop a vertebra.

His body forced him to gulp oxygen, but he was unable to fill his lungs. He was ashamed of the sounds he was making.

A hand gripped him by the hair and pulled his head back so that he was looking straight ahead into a forest of black boots.

He thought of Melissa, a block or two away. Daniel might be close by. But Daniel couldn't fight twenty people by himself. Probably better that he wasn't here, or he'd be facedown on the sidewalk too.

If he had Melissa's smartwatch, he could bring Otto to life with the "go" command. He had a vision of screaming *Get 'em, Otto!* and everybody cracking up at the kid and his pet car, the crowd losing its collective shit at how dorky that was.

But surely Otto could see that he was in trouble?

Turn on your brights! Blast One Direction! Anything!

Otto remained an impassive silver shell. A harmless parked car.

Eyepatch Girl got down low and placed her phone in front of his face. The video was dark, but there were hints of motion, the camera tracking forward progress. It looked like footage from a deep-sea exploration sub. Then the screen lit up, and William's heart sank. There was Rainmaker, running for her life, enveloped by the glow of Otto's headlights. The video was taken from above, some infantry sniper crouched in a window. Rainmaker stumbled. Otto stopped just short of crushing her, and the unseen sniper said *Holy shit.* Dust swirled. Eyepatch Girl pulled the phone away, and her good eye regarded him.

"Everything you do follows you, William Mackler from Fremont Hills, New York. There's no such thing as a lack of consequences."

It struck him that Eli and Rainmaker had really good friends, people who'd wait by his car on some random street in Nashville. What if he'd never come out of the hotel? Would they have hung out by the car all night, smoking cigarettes and revving engines and shooting dice or whatever?

I was the one who saved her life!

He couldn't speak because the boot in his back was mashing him into the sidewalk. Up close, Eyepatch Girl's face looked like it had been splashed with molten lava. She lingered for a moment, letting her words sink in. Then she stood up. He watched her boots join the others. The weight on his spine shifted. Something cold and metallic pressed against the back of his head.

There was a voice in his ear: "Double tap, bitch." Somebody snickered.

William managed to choke out words. "Go ahead."

Stillness. The guy probably expected begging, crying, pleading. Anything but *Go ahead*. The cold steel vanished and the boot eased up.

He waited to hear the grating rumble of street-racer engines, then he sat up. Porsche, Audi, and Corvette disappeared down the block, unmuffled combustion lingering in his aching gut. The Lord prowled the street, creeping slowly past Otto before gunning its engine. Even now, there was something gorgeous about the resonance of a twin turbo. The hot tang of scorched asphalt settled over the street. William took a few shallow breaths and glared at Otto.

"Thanks for the help back there, buddy."

Otto's window slid down. Music was playing inside the car. A spiky guitar lick ushered in Morrissey's baritone lilt.

William, it was really nothing.

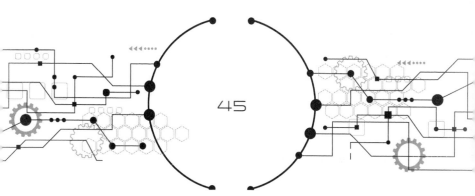

45

Ninth-grade modified tryouts. Smell of fresh bas-
ketballs, squeak of high-tops on the buffed gym
floor. Even as a seventh grader, Daniel knew most
of the other guys. Their faces took on babyish dimensions
that tugged at his heart. There was Kevin "Hangman" Howe,
who already looked like he'd started shaving and was a lock for
power forward. Beside him as always was Kevin "Crane Kick"
Olmstead, the freakishly tall Second Kevin who'd probably be
the starting center even if he didn't possess so-so motor control
and ability. Daniel had been comfortable among the shoo-ins
for the starting five. Not a bad year, seventh grade.

He drifted through shootaround, warm-ups, layup drills;
hovered like a roving eye above the half-court scrimmage,
weaving in and out of man-to-man coverage. He remembered
how determined he was to be ferocious and not come across
like someone who practiced jump shots in his driveway by
himself for hours without ever learning to mix it up in a game.

A long three won him a *Nice shot, Benson,* from Coach Quinn, who had a face like a scrubbed and fleshy Muppet.

Against the gym wall, folded bleachers loomed. In their resting state, the bleachers formed a massive block of wood like some fallen rustic signal tower. They cast a long shadow that advanced across the court as the scrimmage wore on into the afternoon.

But that was all wrong! The gym was a huge windowless box of a room, forever untouched by natural light.

Daniel tried to run from what was coming, but the unreal shadow of the bleachers crept across that first day of tryouts, and he knew the Dread Army had discovered an unguarded tunnel. The shadow mutated and slid across the gym like a curtain and ushered in a new setting: the locker room.

His privacy shroud stank of Lysol and gym clothes. He would have dismissed it and gulped Otto's sweet filtered air if it hadn't meant facing Melissa. His head resounded with the slap of bare feet on tile and the slam of vented metal doors.

The kid's name was Tyler Forbes, and the Dread Army had tracked him down.

Tyler Forbes was a slight, uncoordinated, perpetually winded boy. He didn't seem to have a passionate desire to play basketball. He looked like he'd rather be anyplace else—like Anime Club, for instance. Daniel remembered seeing Tyler sitting next to Christina Hernandez.

Coach Quinn didn't seem to know what to do with him. Tyler watched the scrimmage from a rolled-up gym mat and then trooped silently into the locker room to get changed with everybody else.

Guys. Guys. Who am I?

Jared Ianesco, a beefy kid more suited to the football d-line, performed a drooling, stumbling imitation of a physically handicapped person attempting to shoot a basketball. His big doughy body slammed into lockers. He made gawping, desperate faces. Tyler Forbes put on a blank expression and took off his shirt, which Dustin Tenney promptly snatched from his hands.

Do the Tyler!

Dustin and Jared took turns doing an arrhythmic dance with Tyler's shirt. All fifteen boys in the row of lockers watched with varying levels of glee, or at least fixed grins to their faces, because Dustin and Jared were probably going to make the team, and nobody wanted to be lumped in with a scrub like Tyler Forbes.

In the movie of his life, Daniel Benson put a stop to the torment. Movie Daniel dealt with the situation in a level-headed way, getting Tyler's shirt back without starting shit with Dustin and Jared, which would only leave Tyler feeling more exposed and singled out. Movie Daniel made peace with intelligence and maturity.

The Dread Army set fire to that script.

See Daniel laugh along with everyone else.

See Tyler catch Daniel's eye and wait for that little spark of recognition.

See Daniel refuse to look in Tyler's direction as the balled-up shirt sails into the big plastic garbage can.

See the Kevins slap Daniel on the back as they pass beneath the faded paint on the cinder-block walls: NEVER QUIT.

Daniel opened his eyes to flood the terrible awareness of who he really was, deep down, with the soothing glow of the shroud's inner skin. He couldn't really blame Melissa for breaking up with him; he just wondered what had taken her so long.

He opened Epheme.

DB837651:	Heading into a blizzard tonight
xoxoPixieDustxoxo:	Haha be careful
DB837651:	Wish you were here
xoxoPixieDustxoxo:	Bad day?
DB837651:	Pretty shitty
xoxoPixieDustxoxo:	Stay hydrated

He logged out. The thought of the night to come pinched the base of his spine with cozy heat that crept up to massage his neck.

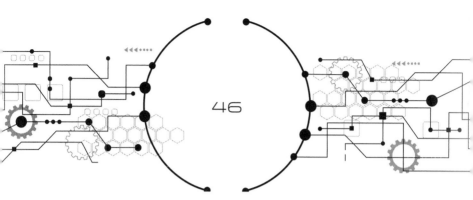

46

Otto headed south down a winding backwoods highway where kudzu strangled ancient trees and the Committee to Reelect Jefferson Davis maintained a billboard. Inside the car, Christina was relearning how to exist in close proximity to William Mackler. Sex had altered the transfer of electrons between them. Her hand went to her twisted rib and traced its protrusion.

Across from the dark lump of Daniel's shroud, she curled her body around her laptop screen. William reclined on the bench next to her, periodically lifting his head to give her the kind of significant looks she used to imagine while she ate Cup Noodles alone in the glow of Kimberly's monitors. She put her left hand on autopilot so she could touch his leg whenever she caught him moving in her peripheral vision. Melissa sat in the back, staring at her phone, casting Carina Tyler's breakup album, *Never Is Too Soon*, to Otto's speakers.

Christina had been working on a way to probe ARACHNE for two days. At first she'd considered blunt, inelegant solutions akin to denial-of-service attacks, or even malware. But her goal wasn't to infect the car's systems, and she wasn't trying to set a worm free to fuck shit up for the lulz.

The solution was inspired by Otto himself. She didn't know if he was malfunctioning or acting like a petulant child on purpose, but when Patricia Ming-Waller had offered to have the car taken off the road for diagnostics, Christina began to think about spoofing a technical problem of her own. It had to be something unexpected, so the systems operated by CAN bus couldn't fix it without escalating it to ARACHNE. But it couldn't be a catastrophic problem that would require drastic measures. Just an odd little glitch to get ARACHNE to drop its guard and reveal itself.

Now her trap was nearly set. Dierdrax was at the command line interface terminal, accessing CAN bus, installing the payload Christina had prepped.

Carina Tyler's "Not Tonight" was like a mosquito in her ear. Would it kill Melissa to listen to music that featured actual guitars and drums?

Dierdrax's fingers went still. Christina took a moment to marvel at her handiwork, and then sent the payload. Immediately she toggled over to the screen where the CAN bus hierarchy was displayed—

And smiled inwardly.

The front left power window was experiencing a sudden problem. Inexplicably, it appeared to be both all the way up and all the way down at the same time. The piece of bulletproof glass was existing in two places at once in defiance of basic laws of windows and physics.

With the seashell engaged, Dierdrax could watch Otto's systems communicate in real time, monitor changes in the structure of ARACHNE, and create a report. Without knowing exactly what she was looking for, the scope was too vast for Christina to keep her sorry human eyes on. And yet—

"Christina?" Her name sounded different coming out of William's mouth. She placed her autopilot hand on his shin.

ARACHNE shifted its bulk. All at once Christina was looking through Dierdrax's eyes down the barrel of an impossible weapon, straight into its vertiginous core. The hunger of a staggering intelligence hit her like the rank breath of an apex predator. She knew right away that she hadn't tricked the program, it had simply decided to give her a peek for reasons she couldn't possibly understand. ARACHNE knew she was poking around. It had always known.

Dierdrax began to fuse with the machine. A neat spiral of code spun up into her arm like a drill bit and slithered along her shoulders and back, stretching the fabric of her jacket. She turned her head and regarded Christina with pleading eyes as a merry grin split her face, widening to anatomically unsettling dimensions. Her teeth were filed to sharp chrome points.

"Hey, Christina?" William sat up.

Dierdrax's eyes were wet with tears. She bent at the waist and with a nightmarish contortion took a bite out of her torso and began to chew.

Carina Tyler belted out "*Baby,*" and the word got stuck in a loop like a skipping record. Melissa advanced to the next song.

Christina tried frantically to log out, but her commands had no effect. She was frozen out of her own hack session. Dierdrax ate ravenously without distinguishing between the terminal and her own body.

William put his hand on top of hers. "I got the Thursdays real bad."

Christina faked a smile. She disconnected the seashell and closed her laptop, trying to make sense of what she'd seen in ARACHNE's depths.

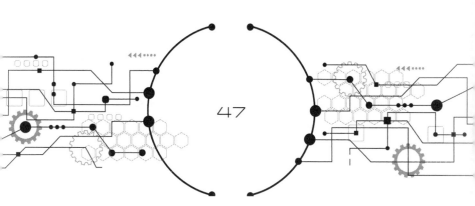

47

They didn't need their fake IDs in New Orleans. At least not at Riverbend Shorty's, where nightlife spilled onto balconies lined with iron rails twisted into vines and fleurs-de-lis. Even the ironwork seemed languid in the swampy heat, yet nothing about the city felt hopelessly wilted. It stewed in its own juices, a carnival of wild plants in a greenhouse.

Inside Riverbend Shorty's, the sweat of two hundred partiers condensed upon the roof beams until the swollen wood had no choice but to send it back down. Mist hung all over the club, from the teeming bar to the elevated stage that shuddered as the brass band stomped the life out of it.

Somebody was blowing bubbles that rode meandering updrafts, carving soapy pathways through the haze.

Behind the bar a poster of William Butler Yeats said CAST A COLD EYE. Daniel had skimmed Yeats as part of his required Princeton summer reading. He retained nothing of the poetry but remembered cracking the book on an afternoon in June with the sun streaming into his living room and the house silent for once, everybody gone, just Daniel and a glass of lemonade and William Butler Yeats. He thought that was suitably poetic. Yeats looked like a man who'd appreciate the sun warming a quiet room. He lifted his half-finished beer and saluted the poster.

The bartender materialized in a blur of forearm tattoos. "Another one?" he asked brusquely.

Daniel wondered if he'd accidentally made some kind of silent-auction bar signal that would give him away as an under-aged rookie who'd only ever been to the crusty old U-Turn in Fremont Hills. Then he figured out that it looked like he'd been lifting his glass to indicate *more beer, please, good sir!*

The bartender slipped away to mix somebody else's drink.

"I was just cheersing Yeats!" Daniel yelled above the crash-boom of the brass band. The bartender didn't hear him or else pretended not to. Calling out the poet's name felt right, somehow. An invocation. Daniel felt like he belonged in this place and time, stuck fast to this bar stool, alone with his beer, as reedy horn lines punched through the laughter all around him. The link between his brain and his heart was a luminous rope. Lamplight danced along the bottles that lined the bar when he bobbed his head to a trombone's smeared melody, just one long note when you got right down to it.

He felt a hand on his shoulder, and William appeared at his side.

"There you are!"

"I've always been here," Daniel said. The phrase seemed packed with meaning. He felt very good about the way it had come out. He winked at the Yeats poster. Irish poets were so cool. He vowed at that very moment to take a trip to Ireland once he'd saved up some money.

"You want a beer?" Daniel asked.

"Nah, I'm just getting a water for Christina. It's a million degrees up by the band."

Daniel grinned. "Hernandez on the dance floor. Never thought I'd see the day."

"It's not really a dance floor. It's more like a happy mosh pit. But yeah, she's moving her arms around and stuff. Listen . . . how are you doing, man?"

"Fine. I'm fine. I'm great, actually. Feeling great." He tapped a fingernail against his glass.

"All I know is what Melissa told us on the way here, while you were sleeping. Which was that you guys broke up. And then she stared at her phone for five hours. Which was awesome because Christina was on her computer the whole time, so I basically just hung out with Otto. I told her that you and me haven't really had a chance to talk about it, so I might be a little while. Are you guys seriously broken up?"

Daniel took a big sip and wiped his mouth with the back of his hand. "No, yeah, we're totally broken up. Which I get, you know?"

William regarded him suspiciously. "No. What? You guys are Daniel and Melissa." He paused. "I'm sorry in advance, but I have to ask—are you guys fucking with me?"

Daniel sniffled. "Like, are we fake breaking up to prank you?"

William nodded.

"Nope!" The music swelled to a crescendo, and Daniel raised

his voice, intent on hammering his every word home. "You are currently witnessing one lone poet adrift on the tides of fate, getting tossed to and fro by the waves of fortune! A defiant human cog in the machine that refuses to go quietly into the deathly humid night!"

He drained his beer and slammed the glass down on the bar. William shifted his eyes uneasily to the bartender, then slapped Daniel on the shoulder again and let his hand linger. Daniel was supremely touched by his friend's concern.

William leaned in close. "I don't know what to say, it seemed like you guys were fine all day."

Daniel squinted. "I don't see too good, am I sitting here with Robert Frost all of a sudden?"

"Who?"

"Poetry, dude. Sick rhyme just now from you."

"Is this poet thing like an inside joke that I forgot about?"

Daniel raised his glass at William Butler Yeats. "You'll have to ask him."

The bartender caught his eye. "Another one?"

"And a water," William called out. The frenzied horns climbed higher while the bass drum drove the feverish tempo. A TV screen above the bar broadcast the happenings in the cavernous performance space, stage tightly packed with brass whipping the crowd into a whirling ecstatic mob. Daniel tried to pick Christina out of the scene. He couldn't find her but was absurdly happy that she was in there somewhere. William's voice was loud in his ear. "This is so messed up. What exactly did she say to you?"

The bartender plunked down a beer and a glass of water.

"I don't remember! There was a zombie movie on TV in the

hotel room while she was breaking up with me!" He laughed. "I think it was *Return of the Living Dead III*. Does that movie have a prison?"

"Do you want to take a walk or something? Just me and you? It's kind of hard to talk in here."

Daniel swiveled on his stool to face William. He took his friend by the shoulder, locking them together like clinching wrestlers. "I don't want you to worry about the trip. I'm not gonna make it awkward."

"I'm not worried about the trip. I'm worried about you."

"I'm fine! Seriously, go dance."

William hesitated. "Melissa's up on the balcony. Just so you know."

"Okay! No big deal."

"You should come see the band. Don't just sit here by yourself."

"I'll meet you back there. I just gotta go to the bathroom first."

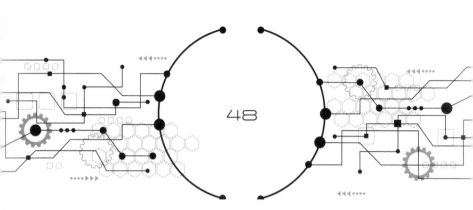

48

The movie of Daniel's life was undergoing heavy revisions. He'd stepped into a tight new script with punchy action, snappy dialogue, and an absolutely killer soundtrack supplied by the legendary Birch Street Wailers, available on all major streaming services. There had always been some question as to the character's true nature, and if Daniel was offering an honest critique, he'd have to say that moral ambiguity had overwhelmed his script's earlier drafts. Sequences were drenched in self-loathing, difficult to translate to the screen without relying on gobs of voice-over. The truly sad thing—how had he not seen this all along?—was that self-loathing was just self-obsession dressed up in a shitty costume.

Daniel was on the dance floor with his arm around William. He thoroughly enjoyed giving and receiving hugs and appreciated each new hug on a deeper level than the one before. William was an excellent hugger and never failed to deliver the requisite back pats. Christina seemed a little put off by his desire to wrap all three of them up together, so he backed off and let her dance.

The roof beams rained down, and Daniel moved through the mist. All around him dancers received trombone sermons, their faces contorted into blind ecstasy.

This New Orleans night snapped into the interlocking frame of his movie's main theme. His character was developing perfectly, riding the sweet arc from navel-gazing chump to guy in control of his life. He felt openhearted and expansive, capable of bottomless empathy. Human beings were forever becoming, so there was no use tormenting yourself over the past. Some of the people giving their bodies to the horns and drums, infusing Riverbend Shorty's with so much love, had pasts brimming with behavior they weren't too proud of. But so what? They lived in the same world as music!

He stopped dancing and became an axis of perfect stillness around which the world turned. Christina and William were moving together as one, and it made perfect sense when she palmed the back of his head and pulled him in for a kiss and they winced—watch those front teeth!—and laughed together. William held her hand as she danced away so he could pull her back like a cracked whip, spinning her into his arms.

Daniel grinned knowingly at them, but they were lost in each other's eyes. Christina and William! Of course! He fought the urge to tell them how much he appreciated what they had and where it was going. It was not an easy urge to fight, because the desire to talk was like a jet engine hitched to his brain.

He followed a bouquet of soapy bubbles as they rose in confident separation to make solo journeys to the distant ceiling.

As his eyes moved up past the balcony that ringed the dance floor, he spotted Melissa sipping a vodka cranberry. It occurred to him that now would be the perfect time to convey the things he'd been trying to get across in their Nashville hotel room. Confidence drove his feet toward the staircase. He'd never felt so lucid. If only William Butler Yeats could see him now!

As he climbed the stairs, he pulled out his phone to keep track of what he wanted to say, because it was all coming to him in a great big rush and he didn't want to forget anything. But that was going to take too long and he didn't want to stop moving. He put his phone back in his pocket and bounded up the steps three at a time and launched himself into the balcony crowd.

A feathery boa tickled his neck as he brushed past a woman in sequined finery. His hip wobbled a small round table, and drinkers clutched at toppling glasses. Fans spritzed his face with a cooling vapor. His heart hammered along with the brass band's relentless bass drum. Melissa somehow managed to weave in and out of the revelers without ever moving from her spot by the railing. She was wearing an open-backed top, and the luscious curve of her body nearly stopped him in his tracks.

He would tell her how gorgeous she was. He would tell her that what he appreciated most about the care she lavished upon her appearance was that she was goal-oriented. If only he could have said such clear, concise things to her yesterday instead of bumbling through self-pitying apologies! Now she would understand exactly where he was coming from. He could not be less than fully cogent if he tried. His descriptive powers were maxed out.

"William Butler Yeats," he muttered to himself, elbowing

a big oafy guy out of the way. He was close enough to reach out and tap her on the shoulder, but that seemed like a childish way to get her attention for such a monumental encounter. He sidestepped so that he was facing the railing and attempted to insert himself into her field of view. Then he realized that he'd just popped into the middle of a conversation she was having with a stranger. The guy was wearing a Tulane hat. His shaggy hair was the color of a golden retriever and stuck out from under the brim in little snarls. He was shorter than Daniel but had the stocky build of a lacrosse player. Daniel's vision locked on to the way the guy's hair escaped his hat with spot-on scruffiness, and a word popped into his head from some literary criticism he'd read for AP English.

"Your hair's the synecdoche for your soul," he said. Tulane Hat turned to him while Melissa opened her mouth in astonishment. "It's the part that represents you as a whole"—thinking *soul/whole, solid rhyme, Eat it, Yeats*—"so when I go back to my friends and tell them about the guy Melissa was talking to, I can just say the word 'hair' and that'll be you. It's the well from which your entire persona springs. And that's okay! Because we're all constantly becoming."

"Dude." Tulane Hat blinked. "What?"

Melissa grabbed Daniel's arm and he realized how close he was to Tulane Hat's face. He let himself be eased back. She stepped between them. "Maybe it's time to chill with the drinking," she said.

"I only had two beers," he said. Then he grinned and nodded at Tulane Hat. "I thought he'd be a coxswain, not a goalie."

Melissa looked into his eyes and seemed puzzled by what she saw. "I think it's time to go."

Tulane Hat put on a churlish face that Daniel found hilarious. "What did you just call me?"

Daniel laughed. This whole sequence was comedy gold. His script got it right on the first try. The edges were crisp and well-defined. He raised an eyebrow at Melissa. "Am I the only one who knows anything about the positions on a crew team?" He turned to Tulane Hat. "I called you a *goalie*."

"Daniel!" Melissa tried her best to obstruct his view. She waved a hand in his face. "Your nose is bleeding!"

Tulane Hat put his arms out to the side. "I play midfield, bro. The fuck's your problem? Do I know you from somewhere?"

Daniel made his eyes flash like Kalodyn Zero, a skill he didn't know he possessed until this moment. The band's feverish crescendo abruptly cut out. Daniel screamed into the void of stunned, exalted silence.

"My problem is that you're not listening to me!"

He slipped away from Melissa with a deft side step as the crowd burst into riotous applause. He registered the fear in Tulane Hat's eyes and made his own eyes laugh in reply. The scene played out perfectly. Daniel's hands found the guy's throat and pressed him back against the railing, which turned out to be kind of rickety, to inject the moment with a little more tension.

Would the railing give way? Would they tumble over the edge while dancers scatter, screaming, and the horns blow raspberries in dismay?

There was a sharp pain in his kidney. He lost his grip on Tulane Hat. The guy's friends were swarming. A monster with a beer gut and huge flabby arms like a shot-putter who'd let himself go was pummeling Daniel in the side with his meaty fist. Daniel recalled that too many kidney shots made you piss blood. He spun away from Tulane Hat, lowered his shoulder, and drove all his weight into the shot-putter, churning his legs to drive the massive body back into a bistro table stacked with glasses and plates of crawfish.

Daniel came down on top of the shot-putter in a blizzard of cracked shells, tiny claws, and antennae. It looked as if a million bright red cockroaches had just exploded in his face. His right arm wrenched back in its socket, and he was very satisfied with the cinematic nature of the brawl so far. He drove his elbow into the nose of Tulane Hat, who was attempting to pull him away from the shot-putter, and when the impact elicited a *crack* from Tulane Hat's face (the sound design here was top-notch), he drove the closed fist of his other hand into the shot-putter's ear.

The band rolled into a lively number, an appropriate soundtrack. Balcony dancers gave way. Newly exposed floor-boards glittered with broken glass. The shot-putter's fist came at Daniel's face from the side. White flares stole his vision. He blinked away the bright light, and then he was on his back. His ribs were absorbing kicks, and he was curling into a ball, tucking in his arms and legs like a cowering crawfish, when a new figure disturbed the mist above him. An arm lashed out, and the kicks ceased, leaving behind the dull, insistent pain of internal bruising. He discovered that his hand was being clasped and he was being pulled to his feet. He stood on wobbly legs. William bear-hugged him and shifted them both away from the epicenter of the fight.

William screamed in his ear, "Can you walk?"

"I'm fine!"

William recoiled as blood stippled his face. Daniel wiped his mouth and smeared his hand red.

"We gotta get out of here," William said, glancing over his shoulder. A barrage of taunts hit them in the back as they made for the stairs.

"Story of my life," Daniel said, but his words were lost in a mouthful of blood and spit.

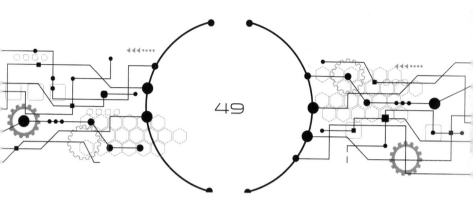

n Christina's internal ranking system, titled The #AutonomousRoadTrip Fuckup Olympics, Daniel Benson had just come out of nowhere to place himself squarely in contention for the gold. *What an effort by that young man right there.* She never would have guessed that Mr. Ivy League Scholar-Athlete would be the one to get them kicked out of a New Orleans bar, but she supposed that breakups could do strange things to people. Either way, the brawl had surpassed her own epic hacking fail. *Looks like Christina Hernandez will just have to settle for the silver.*

She rummaged through the car's refrigerator and came up with a bag of frozen peas.

"Hold this on your eye."

Daniel took the bag and gingerly pressed it against his swollen face while Melissa dabbed at the blood around his mouth with one of his sleeveless running shirts.

"Thanks, Hernandez," he said. "Why would anybody want to cook peas in here?"

"They wouldn't," Christina said. "Those are face peas."

"Shhh." Melissa attended to him with fussy care, but her voice was strained with barely suppressed fury. "Your lip is split pretty bad. Don't speak or it'll bleed."

The chorus of No Doubt's 1996 hit song "Don't Speak" played softly from the speakers.

"Quit it, Otto," William said wearily. He was watching out the back window to make sure the cops weren't on their tail as they hugged the south shore of Lake Pontchartrain, a vast black emptiness pierced by the lonely lights of the causeway.

The song faded to silence.

William's shirt had been stretched in the melee, and now it looked like one of Melissa's slouchy tops. There was the tendon where his neck met his shoulder, upon which Christina could now officially confirm under oath she'd placed her lips. Even in the wake of their chaotic exit from Riverbend Shorty's, with her heart making unpredictable leaps (she really needed to exercise more often), she couldn't help but marvel at the jittery warmth that buzzed between them. They had just kissed on a dance floor in *public*. Right now even Dierdrax's Otto-assisted suicide didn't seem so bad. Christina told herself that she had no business poking around ARACHNE in the first place. Dierdrax's demise was actually a relief, if she looked at it from a certain angle; now she could sit back, admit that Otto had won, and let whatever was happening with William unfold.

Daniel grinned. "Face peas." The midpoint of his lip was a weeping cleft. Melissa tossed the bloody shirt to the floor, and Otto whisked it out of sight.

"Hey, you know what's not funny?" Melissa said. "Any of this."

The car filled with a grainy 3-D projection of Riverbend Shorty's balcony area. The crowd scattered at glitchy half speed. Daniel charged a massive potbellied guy in a tank top.

"Security camera," Christina said. She watched the combatants crash through a table, catapulting an entire crawfish feast into the air. She'd been down on the floor dancing with William, stealing kisses, when the commotion started. Somehow, William had known instantly what was going on and rushed upstairs, even though they couldn't see anything from their spot on the packed dance floor. The spilled food turned into dozens of animated crawfish that swam through the air while Daniel absorbed a vicious right hook from the big guy on the ground.

"That was moderately funny," Daniel said.

"*Really?*" Melissa rolled her eyes. "It's like this every time with you guys. Something serious happens and everybody jokes around like it's no big deal, except for me, so I get to be the road trip's bitchy mom by default."

Christina watched Daniel intently. For a guy who'd just gotten his ass kicked in a bar fight, he seemed remarkably sober and composed. The skin around his eye was turning a pretty shade of plum.

"Kill it, Otto," William said, and the projection vanished. "I think there's somebody following us." Christina turned to the back window. The streets of suburban Kenner were empty at this time of night, except for a pair of headlights a few blocks back.

"From the bar?" Christina asked.

"I don't know," William said. "I didn't think anybody was behind us when we left. We'll see if they're still there when we hit the highway."

"Look at me," Melissa said to Daniel as he pulled a thick paperback from his backpack, like he was going to settle in for some quality reading time. "Look. At. Me." Melissa squeezed her hands together in her lap. Her knuckles were the color of frostbitten lips.

Daniel did what she asked. They regarded each other in a way that made Christina want to put on her headphones.

"What are you on?" Melissa asked finally.

Daniel held up his book, *The Collected Works of Nathaniel Hawthorne*. "Literature." He cracked it open to a page at the midpoint. "I'm on literature."

The window glass behind Daniel's head took on the pale buttery glow of an app screen that looked familiar to Christina. At the top of the screen was the app's logo, a pair of lips bisected by a vertical finger: the universal symbol for *shhh*. Dialogue bubbles began to blink into place.

xoxoPixieDustxoxo:	I got a surprise for you
DB837651:	I gotta take a nap
xoxoPixieDustxoxo:	Mmm sounds nice
DB837651:	Then I'll come by
xoxoPixieDustxoxo:	Bring SNACKS. See you later alligator
DB837651:	Something something crocodile

All Christina could do was stare openmouthed at the bizarre tableau of William and Melissa puzzling out the Epheme chat while Daniel, oblivious to the screen behind him, kept his eyes lowered to his book.

Looks like Otto's been doing some eavesdropping of his own, she thought. Well, of course; ARACHNE reached into the dark web with complete and utter ease, so encryption was no obstacle. Her sense of relief kicked up a notch. Otto had been toying with her since the first hours of the trip, when she'd spotted Dierdrax passing through the LIDAR map. Now it was Daniel's turn. She felt like she was watching hidden-camera prank videos, which always took her from *That really sucks* to *Glad that's not me* to *That's kind of funny* to *That guy probably deserved it.*

"Who the fuck is PixieDust?" Melissa said.

Christina's emotional state settled somewhere between *Oh shit* and *Somebody make popcorn, this is gonna be good.*

Daniel closed the book on his finger to hold his place. "Hmm?" He looked up, caught Melissa's eye, then William's, and swiveled his head. He was motionless for what felt like a whole minute, watching his Epheme chat window scroll through more recent sessions, ending with PixieDust's instruction to *Stay hydrated.*

When he turned back to face the interior, the look on his face was disturbingly calm. "That's Jamie Lynn." As if that explained everything.

"Jamie Lynn *Beaumont?*" William asked.

Daniel shook his head. "Nah. You don't know her. She's two years older, and anyway she went to Marion."

"Oh," Melissa said. She cupped her hands over her elbows as if she were about to start shivering. "Jamie Lynn from Marion."

"I guess Epheme isn't as ephemeral as it's supposed to be," he said, and then he did something in such complete defiance of the moment that it struck Christina as heroic. He bent his head, skimmed a finger along the page of his Hawthorne collection to find his place, and resumed reading quietly as if nothing had happened. As an afterthought, without looking up, he added, "Jamie Lynn's my dealer. I am presently high as balls on cocaine." He paused. "Actually, I'm coming down. Beer me, please, Otto."

A cup holder slid from the bench at Daniel's side, bearing a frosty can. Daniel popped the top and took a swig.

Christina was completely taken aback. It was the kind of thing people said as a joke, but she didn't think Daniel was joking. She thought back to the dance floor before the fight, before Daniel even went up to the balcony. He'd wrapped his long arms around her, pulling them all in for an alarming number of group hugs, bouncing up and down and blathering on about how the trip wasn't going to be awkward, urging them not to worry, telling William again and again how grateful he was that they were assigned as lab partners, along with some crap about Yeats.

He looked at each one of them in turn, and his eyes challenged them to react, despite one being swollen shut.

Looks like he's going for the gold in multiple events. Just an incredibly gutsy performance.

"I've never even *seen* cocaine in real life," Christina said, just to break the silence. She associated hard drugs with people who hung out under the Cayahota Creek bridge and slept in their cars next to the Dumpster behind the Odyssey. Used needles and blackened spoons and rooms kept in perpetual twilight by mildewed towels pinned across windows—the general chaos and disorder of addiction—made her want to bathe in hand sanitizer. Even if she'd been remotely curious, the sheer inertia of that lifestyle freaked her out. Getting into drugs in Fremont Hills was a surefire way to spend a few decades stuck in Fremont Hills.

She looked at Daniel's swollen eye, the blood crusting on his upper lip, the Hawthorne book in his lap, the sleeveless gray Knicks shirt. She flashed back to their conversation outside the asylum chapel. *Sometimes I wish it happened differently, you know?* She wished she'd had the presence of mind to treat that as more than some throwaway thought by a person she didn't know very well. She wished she could go back and say, *Yes, I do know,* and pull the thread he'd dangled in front of her face until whatever he was trying to say came flopping out at her feet.

"Are you serious?" William said. "Is that why you were such a psycho back there? You're about to go to *Princeton,* man."

Daniel sipped his beer. "Sherlock Holmes did cocaine."

"He's not a real guy," Christina pointed out.

"Sigmund Freud did cocaine too."

"Sigmund Freud didn't have to play Division I basketball!" Melissa said. "Do you know how many people would kill to be able to play on a college team like that? Then you've also got your freshman seminar on Proust plus your other classes—"

"That's why I have to keep my mind flexible," Daniel said.

Melissa's eyes went cold, and Christina braced herself for screaming. But she kept her voice low and even. "You've been high this whole trip, right? You haven't seemed like yourself in . . . not since . . ."

"Whoa," Daniel said, "let's maybe not get into the whole time thing."

William shook his head in disbelief. "Are you even gonna

remember this?" He sounded defeated. Christina gave him a look that she hoped was supportive and girlfriendish.

"Sure," Daniel said. "I'm not blacked out or anything."

"No," William said. "I mean the whole hashtag Autonomous Road Trip. The point of this trip is to have something we did together as a group to remember when we're all in different places. We were supposed to catalyze something incredible here."

The opening chords to Green Day's "Good Riddance (Time of Your Life)" came from the speakers. A slide show played on the front windshield. There was the Patricia Ming-Waller selfie, the East Village rooftop, the Higginsburg Asylum sign.

William slapped the bench. "NOT NOW, OTTO."

"*Way* too on the nose," Christina agreed. The music stopped, and the slide show vanished. The dark streets of Kenner returned. A lone Shell station cast light down on its pumps, and then it was behind them.

Daniel drained his beer and set the empty can into the cup holder, which promptly retracted. "I really don't want you to take this the wrong way, but you're operating under the assumption that we were any kind of group to begin with. I honestly one hundred percent love you for what you're trying to do, but we're just four people, man." He winced and laid a hand against his side. "Ugh. There you are, ribs. Tomorrow's gonna suck."

A fresh beer sprang forth.

William's face scrunched up like he was staring at the sun. He reminded Christina of a little boy who'd just been yelled at by an otherwise friendly teacher and was struggling not to break down and cry.

She wanted to crawl inside a privacy shroud and hold him. At the same time, she was struck by the fact that she was getting exactly what she wanted. The William/Daniel/Melissa triangle was smashed like Ulthur's Rebellion against the blue methane shields of the Brahman Cluster.

Daniel had just denied the triangle's very existence.

Getting what you wanted meant that somebody else was losing it. Cementing her own future with William meant that the triangle's center could not hold.

"I knew something was up," Melissa said.

"Me too," William said. "You've been all over the place. I should have known. I should have said something."

"Well," Daniel said. "You didn't." He spun an imaginary ring on his finger.

"Do you have all kinds of special drug friends I've never met before?" William asked. "Do you secretly hang out in places you never go to with me, like that guy's house with the Dodge on blocks out front?"

"This really has nothing to do with you," Daniel said patiently. "With any of you. It should be pretty obvious why I wasn't shouting it in the streets and wearing 420 shirts and shit. Mainly to avoid conversations like this."

Melissa picked up her phone and gave it a few desultory swipes and stared at the screen.

"Right," William said. "I forgot. We're just four random assholes in a Driverless car."

"That's not true," Christina said.

Melissa laughed, quick and cold. Christina wondered if one day she'd bump into ninety-year-old Melissa Faber, and the elderly woman's rheumy eyes would glimmer with that dismissive spark to send Christina skimming angrily away on her hover-walker, muttering archaic twenty-first-century curses.

There was a disturbance up front, a sudden slippage in the car's makeup, as if it were shedding its skin. A dashboard panel she'd never noticed slid aside, revealing what looked like vintage clocks made of shiny brass: speedometer, fuel gauge, tachometer, oil pressure. A center console rose from the bench like a newly hatched chick, shedding a web of nanotech gossamer. The console sprouted an umbilical appendage that whipped upright and solidified into a gearshift.

A steering wheel emerged from the panel.

Christina had to give Otto her grudging respect. Nothing would cheer William up like a chance to be fully in control of his car. If only she'd won some measure of authority over Otto, she could have been the one to deliver William this gift.

It would be good for William to engage with the open road. She could keep him company while Melissa and Daniel worked out their shit or just sat stewing in the back. For a little while, it would be just the two of them, alone with the highway.

She reached out for him. "Sergeant Hernandez, Space Marines, Twenty-Fourth Division. I'll be your copilot."

William took her hand. "Join me on the bridge?"

"Affirmative."

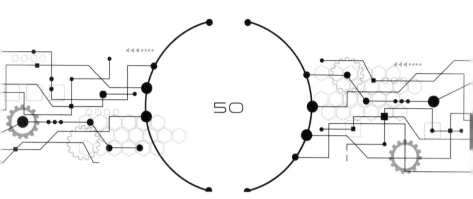

50

O tto relinquished control like a runner passing a baton. William gripped the wheel as the newly molded driver's seat conformed to his body. Next to him, Christina pulled up LIDAR and shunted the map to her half of the windshield, leaving William's side clear.

"There are pedals down here now," he said. The car jolted forward as he hit the gas.

Thick slabs of distorted guitar thundered from the speakers. Drums joined with a blast of double bass. Christina smiled: Otto was playing her favorite Dethroned Kings album, *Malodorous.*

On LIDAR, the black hole of Lake Pontchartrain was behind them. They'd reached the apocalyptic, cheerless landscape that meant you were five minutes from a major airport. The map reflected the desolation of the city's outskirts, an eerie emptiness punctuated by furtive gray figures that buzzed like gnats on the periphery of the four-lane road. The only sign of automotive life was a single white car, two blocks back, steadily matching their speed without getting closer.

"I want to kiss you really bad," William said.

"What's stopping you?"

"I'm keeping my eyes on the road, Sergeant." He eased Otto into the right lane, then back into the left. "This thing is so responsive."

Christina glanced over her shoulder. Daniel was holding the bag of peas against his face while he read his book. Melissa was sitting in the back, glued to her phone.

She leaned over to give William a quick peck on the cheek. "Maybe later I'll invite you into my shroud. If you're lucky."

William drew a sharp breath. "Scandal! Otto, you didn't hear that." He paused. "Do you think there are two people on earth who know each other the best, out of everybody in existence? Like if there's a million things you can know about another person, and some lady in Bangladesh knows nine hundred thousand things about her husband, she's the best at really knowing another person."

"You're saying this hypothetical Bangladeshi woman still has a hundred thousand things she doesn't know about her husband?"

"I'm just making up numbers—maybe she knows everything about him. I don't know."

"I don't think it's quantifiable, babe." She took the word *babe* on a spur-of-the-moment test run and was pleased with how it sounded.

"Huh," William said, staring deep into the Louisiana night. Otto ate up the center line's white slashes. A lighted sign on a two-story A-frame shone out of the gloom like a marquee in a dream. Christina wondered at the swirling depths of William's thoughts. It must be troubling to have a best friend reveal a hidden side like a dark planetary hemisphere spinning into sunlight. It would be like walking upstairs one day to find that her parents' entire hoard, all the newspaper mazes and thrift-shop VHS tapes and family packs of Candy Land toothbrushes, had materialized overnight with the flip of some sick-brained switch, leaving Christina frozen with her hand on the banister, thinking, *What kind of people are these?*

"I don't know what that word means," William said. "Quanti-whatever."

"Fiable. Is that what you were just thinking about?"

"I was thinking that this guy behind us is getting closer. Way to warn me, copilot."

She studied the map. The car was only a block's length back now. "I didn't think it was vital information. It's just somebody headed for I-10, same as us."

"What kind of car is it?"

Christina tapped the matchbox-size rendering, and the map fed her data about the car. "Lotus Exige. Twin turbo super-charged engine. License plate U8DUST. Sounds like we're dealing with your standard-issue douchebag."

"Shit. Okay. There's something I have to tell you. Ever since the whole thing with Eli and Rainmaker, their drag-racing buddies have been sort of tracking us. They jumped me in Nashville."

"*Jumped* you? When?" Christina looked back. Melissa was silhouetted in the Lotus's headlights, which had the predatory instinct to creep into Otto's interior.

"When I had to run out to the car. When we were at the

hotel." Christina recalled the way he'd burst through the door to their room, out of breath, which made sense at the time—her own heart was pounding. If anything was wrong with him it had been lost in the heady fog of the moment. "I think it was supposed to be a warning," he continued. "One girl had an eyepatch and a burned-up face." He paused. "That was actually pretty cool. But yeah, they hate us."

"Enough to follow us all the way to New Orleans?"

"Which is why we have to end it here, or else they'll be on our ass all the way to Moonshadow."

He was speaking in a low voice—this was a situation for the two of them to handle together. She found herself thrilled at the prospect of a showdown and wondered if William's recklessness was sexually transmitted. A week ago she would have urged him to kill the lights and hide in a dark alley, but now she was ready to go all Dierdrax on U8DUST.

Just ahead was a four-way intersection. The light was green. William slowed Otto to a crawl. The Lotus rode up on them, flashing its brights, then pulled into the right lane. The light turned yellow, then red. The two cars idled side by side, silver bullet and insectoid Lotus, headlights sweeping out across the empty intersection.

A windblown Popeyes bag skimmed the crosswalk.

The Lotus revved its engine, and the baritone growl shook Otto's interior and drowned out the throat-shredding screams of Dethroned Kings' lead singer.

"Honestly, I've always wanted to do this," William said, turning to his backseat passengers. "Might wanna buckle up."

"I seriously can't even," Melissa said. She held up her phone to snap a picture of the Lotus.

Christina rolled down her window, stuck her arm out and extended her middle finger. The Lotus's glass was tinted. She couldn't see the driver's reaction.

"That's how we do it," William said.

Christina rolled up her window. The light turned green. William slammed his foot down on the gas and sprang Otto from his cage.

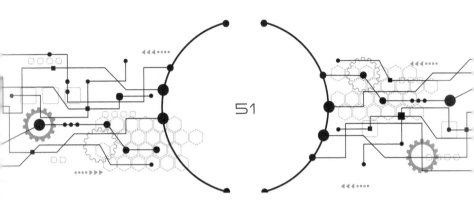

51

The cars were side by side at 80 mph when the road narrowed to a single lane. The custom exhaust system on the Lotus emitted a whine that climbed and receded with each upshift. The cars hugged the road's shoulders and traded the lead like thoroughbreds, the Lotus nosing ahead until William slid past to regain the top spot. They moved as if drawn by a single puppeteer letting out slack with his right hand while reeling the left hand in, then switching. They blazed down a street between rows of shuttered warehouses as the last vestiges of Kenner dribbled out.

Otto played Melissa's Kitty Purry Road Trip Mix #2. Christina tuned out the voice assuring her that she was a firework and poured all her energy into the map. She pressed her palms together to widen the scope, then swiped ahead to make sure their path was clear. Focusing on the race kept them from dwelling on Daniel's admission, as if Otto's filters had removed its particles from the air.

"You've got a sharp right in three-quarters of a mile," she warned. The street dead-ended at a tile manufacturer. There was a parking lot to the left and what looked like a footpath to the right.

"That's in, like, thirty seconds!" William said.

"Let the Lotus move ahead, it's already on our right, and its turning radius is way better than ours. Also the next straightaway is basically just a sidewalk."

"Maybe you should let Otto drive!" Melissa said.

"Nah, you got this," Daniel said.

Ratteree & Sons Tile loomed; the façade was a huge mosaic of a tropical beach. Monkey faces leered out from the fronds of a palm tree.

"Everybody hold on!" William tapped the brake. The Lotus jumped ahead and accelerated through the turn. William leaned even harder on the brake as he cranked the wheel to the right. RenderLux snaked into Christina's lap and held her fast. The tile monkeys swung out of view, and Otto was back on course, headlights shining directly into the Lotus's angled rear windshield.

Two stout nitrous oxide tanks crouched like artillery shells inside the Lotus. As William bore down, Christina read the decals on the tanks' smooth sides: FAT MAN and LITTLE BOY.

The Lotus was going to destroy them. Otto shouldn't be able to keep pace at all; the fact that they were even close defied basic aerodynamic laws. How long could William keep it up against a car built for this express purpose?

The cement footpath ran parallel to a gravel road cordoned off by construction cones. Otto's tires churned through grass on either side of the path. The Lotus widened its lead.

"Okay," Christina said, "you've got two miles before we hang a left onto a real road. Just try to stay close." Keeping one eye on the map, she sifted through a sub-menu she'd never seen before, under a heading that hadn't existed before they started racing.

Countermeasures.

"I get it," she said. "We're unlocking new options, like achievements in a game."

"If you kill us, I'll kill you," Melissa said.

"Noted," William said. He hit the gas and eased the wheel to the right. Otto nudged a pair of construction cones out of the way at 90 mph with a brutal *thunkathunk*. For an eerie weightless second, the tires failed to bite the loose gravel of the unfinished road. Otto fishtailed, gained traction, and they overtook the Lotus on the right. "I gave 'em the last turn," William said. "That's the only one they get."

"Then you better beat them by a mile," Christina said, "because we're on the wrong side again."

Christina explored Countermeasures. Among the newly unlocked features were Nitrous Injection, Spike Strip, EMP, Tear Gas, and—her mouth dropped open—Dierdrax Extract.

There was also an option for Shuriken Launch.

William's shoulders hunched with tension. He held the steering wheel in a ten-and-two death grip and punched the gas. Otto gained ground, and the speedometer's needle trembled at 100 mph. Christina could hear Otto's engine working overtime. RenderLux thrummed.

She scanned their route. After this left turn, they'd have another mile of open road before it dead-ended in a massive complex of rectangular outlines. She tried to enhance the image, but it was no use. She was operating LIDAR with high-def satellite overlays, yet the obstacle remained the mere suggestion of buildings.

"I'm gonna cut the angle," William said. "I'll never make the turn if I crank it at this speed."

"Oh my God," Melissa said.

Christina tried to narrow her world down to the map, block everything out, and think, really think. But it was difficult to ignore William whipping his head around to check the Lotus's position in his blind spot every two seconds, flexing his fingers on the wheel, anticipating his move.

She switched to EverView, and the world diminished to the map's beautiful geometry. Otto aggregated local news and real estate listings and bombarded her with relevant info. The dead-end complex was a half-built shopping mall.

A plan clicked into place.

"I know how we can ditch 'em for good," she said. "Just stay ahead for another minute."

She dismissed EverView, and the map flipped back to the windshield.

"Tokyo drift!" Daniel yelled from his spot on the bench. "Tokyo drift this asshole!"

"You can't Tokyo drift in a car that weighs a million tons." William's voice cracked, and he gave the wheel a quarter turn. Otto sent three orange cones to asphalt graves. Christina sucked air through clenched teeth as Otto's tires skidded across gravel and grass, and there was the Lotus grinding into them, filleting them; she closed her eyes and rode out the spin—

And opened her eyes to a collective exhalation. The music informed Christina that she was going to hear Katy Perry roar.

"William, would you let the goddamn car drive itself!" Melissa screamed

"DID YOU NOT SEE WHAT I JUST DID!" William screamed back, as if he couldn't believe it himself. They were back on a smooth surface; this road had been paved as part of the mall construction project. Now they had two lanes of pure, unobstructed drag race straightaway.

The Lotus was two car-lengths back in the right lane. Christina had seconds to figure out if her plan was actually feasible; if not, they'd have to find a way off this road. She tilted the LIDAR's view so she was seeing the front of the mall as if she were a pedestrian on the street. She pulled the construction zone closer, and the onrushing edifice filled the windshield. They were headed straight for the horseshoe-shaped drop-off zone that led to the entrance, a long flat opening that would one day be lined with revolving doors. The impression was of a slotted goal in an air-hockey table.

She dismissed the map but kept Countermeasures open.

A piercing mosquito whine came ripping across the straightaway. The Lotus surged ahead, drawing on some great atom-splitting power. Its lead felt effortless and insurmountable, as if it had attained its rightful spot and could no longer be displaced.

"Nitrous," William said.

"Tokyo drift!" Daniel said.

Without hesitation, Christina selected Nitrous Injection from the menu, and Otto emitted a mechanical HRMPH—a protest?—before she felt g-force spread through her stomach as if she were on a plummeting elevator flipped to a horizontal axis. Otto caught the Lotus, and William kept the gas pedal down, and Otto *just kept on going.* Christina looked out her window as they passed the Lotus. She could imagine the driver's astonishment.

"Where am I going?" William sounded frantic. The mall's entrance filled the windshield, a massive vertical wall, gaps in the Sheetrock like a featureless face.

"Beat them to the entrance!"

"Do you know what you're doing?"

Christina swiveled her head. The Lotus was a car-length back, moving directly behind them, clearly hoping to let the Driverless car bear the brunt of the madness. That was perfect.

Otto barreled through the mall's entrance like a deranged Black Friday shopper. As soon as they passed beneath the looming wall, she selected Spike Strip. A clattering noise came from Otto's rear bumper.

Their headlights tore into the gloom. They raced through a cavernous tunnel of skeletal archways. Drywall sheltered twists of rebar like fossilized remains.

She turned her head at the sound of tires popping behind them, the screech of desperate hydroplaning. William slowed the car as best he could without skidding out. She watched the Lotus spin like a helicopter whose rotors had betrayed it, paralyzed in midair while the cockpit swirls on its axis. The spike strip glittered with serpentine malevolence along the entrance. Christina held her breath. The Lotus was quick and light and could not find purchase on the unscuffed tiles; the loss of control was palpable. Rubber screamed, treads clawed, and the echo of the little car's helpless keening pinged off the roof girders.

Otto silenced Katy Perry midchorus so they could hear the

Lotus impact the mall's fountain, an artichoke-shaped thing that caved in the Lotus's trunk and brought the car to rest with a jolt of severe finality.

William stopped in the middle of the food court, a vast expanse devoid of tables and chairs, ringed by empty concessions.

He looked at Christina with wild eyes. Then he jumped out of his seat, wrapped his arms around her neck, and howled. His body exuded damp heat, and he throbbed and twitched like a human heart palpitation.

"Otto, go back to the fountain."

Christina and William both looked back to see Melissa speaking into her watch. Otto didn't go anywhere. Melissa shook her head in frustration. "We have to see if they're okay!"

Christina felt nausea roil her stomach. What if they'd just witnessed somebody's last moments?

William hopped back in his seat and threw the car into reverse, retracing their route through the mall. "One thing I didn't mention," he said. "These people have a gun."

Christina thought she might actually throw up. Maybe they'd just watched someone die, or maybe they were about to be killed. Road trip, everybody!

This was what dating William Mackler was going to be like: rocketing blindly from one unbelievable catastrophe to another.

They stopped at the fountain. A dusting of drywall, tile, and glass kicked up by the crash settled over Otto's windshield. The Lotus was perfectly still, its back half an exhibit of twisted wreckage, its front half bizarrely unscathed except for shattered windows. William met Daniel's eyes, and without a word, they opened the door and crept out, moving right up alongside the

Lotus, keeping low as if crouching down would shield them from a point-blank bullet.

"This is so beyond insane," Melissa said.

Cautiously, Christina went to the door.

"Stay here!" Melissa hissed at her.

William and Daniel reached the car and peered in through the driver's-side window. They looked at each other and straightened up, visibly relaxing. Christina stepped out and joined them.

"There's nobody here," William said. "We were just racing against a self-driving car."

Daniel laughed. "Eli and Rainmaker sent a robot to do their bidding? That's like something supervillains do."

"No," Christina said. "I don't think it has anything to do with them. I think William's best pal Otto was just trying to cheer him up." She looked at William. "You said you always wanted to do this, right? Your car just got one of its Driverless buddies to make it happen."

One day Driverless cars would all be linked, millions of vehicles talking to each other and learning at exponential rates. That was no secret. But now her split-second glance behind ARACHNE's curtain took on a new, crystalline symmetry. The impression that lingered in her mind was of a distant horizon, a frontier's edge of connective tissue, the command line for the automotive singularity. Christina wondered about the view from within, looking out from infinite streams of behavioral data. What did the #AutonomousRoadTrip passengers look like to a machine intelligence as far-ranging as ARACHNE? She imagined four faceless blips, distinguishable only by their shabby little secrets.

"We should probably not be here when the cops show up," William said.

Christina thought, *Soon cops will be showing up in Driverless cars.* She dug a fingernail into the side of her head, abrading the path of a fresh scab, opening the cut.

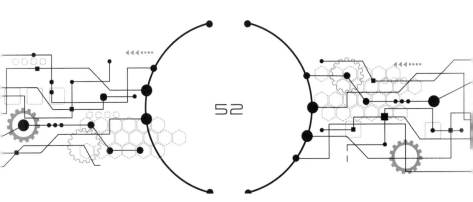

52

The hypersleep chamber hummed as it rotated around Christina and William. The chamber was a cushioned tube with a single window that passed in front of them every few minutes like a forgotten satellite trapped in ceaseless orbit. Outside she could see the dim confines of their simulated Firefly-class ship's cargo bay. Insomnia propped her eyes open. She counted each time the window appeared. She was up to forty-nine.

Three additional chambers lined the far wall like coffins on the porch of an Old West carpenter. Christina thought she could see Dierdrax in one.

They'd selected this particular shroud skin for its soothing, meditative qualities. William had crashed after announcing that he was going to sleep all the way through Texas and didn't want to talk to anybody until Otto passed the WELCOME TO NEW MEXICO sign. The window made its fiftieth rotation, and he stirred in his sleep. He was holding Christina with an arm folded over her side, elbow on her stomach, hand between her breasts. She felt each measured exhalation as heat against the back of her head. Her heart pounded so hard, she was afraid William might wake up.

She hadn't realized it at first—too busy enjoying her imaginary popcorn—but the Epheme chats that Otto had displayed began with her very first seashell intercept from the day of the Driverless Derby. At that time, Otto had still been three days away from arriving in Fremont Hills. She supposed that given ARACHNE's power, it was theoretically possible that Otto had eavesdropped on Daniel Benson from the parking lot of Indiana's largest mall, but why? What made a lot more sense was that he hadn't been spying on Daniel at all, he'd been spying on *her*—scanning the documents stored in her laptop where she collected her Epheme intercepts.

Countermeasures. Dierdrax's destruction was the first cut, and now he was twisting the knife.

Today, at least, nobody had suspected her. They all saw exactly what she had seen: Otto giving them a glimpse of Daniel's secret life. But if Otto released her entire document instead of just a few chats, they would all know what she had done.

She pictured the look of shock and disgust on William's face and pressed his hand to her heart so that she wouldn't open up a new cut on her head. She asked the universe for just one more day of her Next-Door Neighbor Friend thinking she was somebody worth loving. The window came spinning past her face seventy-one more times before she fell asleep.

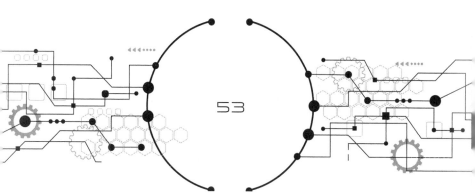

critch scritch scritch.

The cargo hold was full of rats, but William couldn't see them. They were scrabbling in the dark, darting about the edges of the dank, cavernous room. His grav-boots clanked along the catwalk. The walls were honeycombed with coffins. *They're only hypersleep chambers*, he told himself. But some of them were made out of burnished rosewood with brass handles for pallbearers to hoist. A furtive movement caught his eye; something skulked behind a pile of crates. A flickering light sent ribbons of shadow up the sides of the honeycomb. William leveled his laser rifle at the disturbance.

Scritch scritch scritch.

Cautiously, he approached the crates. This particular rat must be huge, not to mention smart—it was holding a candle or a flashlight back there. It had probably crawled aboard back in New York City, where rats the size of horses frequently caused subway derailments. With his back against the tower of crates, he paused to gather his courage, then lunged around the corner, finger on the trigger. . . .

"Tommy?"

His brother was sitting cross-legged in a little nook, scratching a row of elaborate symbols into the side of a crate by the light of his clown lamp. He glanced up at William and then went back to work, steering the bowie knife with precise, confident flicks of his wrist.

"What are you writing?" William asked.

"You can't read in dreams," Tommy said. "If you read more, you'd know that."

William opened his eyes. Something wiggled in front of his face. *Scritch scritch scritch.* He blinked away the remnants of the dream and focused on the true source of the noise: Christina's finger was curved like an inchworm, digging into her scalp. *Scritch scritch scritch.*

"Christina," he whispered. She didn't stir. Very gently, he took her wrist, pulled her hand away from the side of her head, and rested it on the cushion of the chamber. Then he extricated one tingly arm from its awkward position beneath her neck and pushed himself out of the shroud without waking her up. His vision distorted, stretching the chamber's window into a concave slab of elongated glass before his head poked free of the hypersleep skin.

The car was parked. Bright sunlight streamed in. Squinting against the glare, he slid to a shroud-free section and planted his feet on the floor. Melissa and Daniel slept apart on the other side of the bench. Their shrouds appeared to William as lumps of finely wrought chain mail glittering darkly, drawing in light and shadow, reflecting it back in patterned scales.

He gave his eyes a few seconds to adjust, then raised his head to the window. Outside, the earth was carpeted in purple wildflowers swaying lazily, combed by the hint of a breeze. A few scattered patches grew taller than their neighbors to culminate in ivory petals open to the sky like clusters of tiny satellite dishes. From where Otto was parked, a dirt path wound down through the sloping field to a ravine, where a row of scraggly sagebrush clung to the edge. Across the ravine's expanse, William could just barely make out the very top of sandstone bluffs, stacked wafers of tan rocks. Above all, he recognized the sky. It stretched from Mexico to the Great Plains, blotted with the roiling cloud masses he and Tommy had long ago identified as Imperial Star Destroyers. Today there was an entire fleet in battle formation.

The unspoiled beauty of the landscape annoyed him. A reddicked hawk or some other precious endangered bird wheeled across the ravine. William looked down at the floor.

"I said I wanted to sleep through Texas, you fuck."

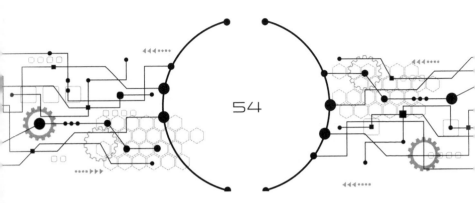

54

He sat alone on the edge of the bluff where the sun scorched the rocks and sagebrush thinned to anemic sprouts. A hundred feet below, the Llano River meandered placidly along. His skateboard was at his left hand, the Ovation acoustic at his right. This was the precise location of the famous Mackler Family Photo from what turned out to be the last Mackler Family Vacation, in which Tommy gave the guitar an epic one-handed hoist above his head and leered at the camera like a debauched rocker. Tommy was more at home doing impressions of Robert Smith from the Cure or Morrissey from the Smiths, but he could bust out a credible Mick Jagger/Robert Plant archetype when called upon. William watched that gorgeous whatever-bird alight upon a sandstone ledge and recalled his critique of Tommy's ridiculous British accent.

You sound like a fancy turtle.

I have no idea what that is.

He glanced back, up past the flowers to where the silver car glinted in the sun. It looked peaceful and still, but he wondered how long he'd have before somebody woke up, wandered down the path, and asked him why they'd stopped here; if they should go through Daniel's bags to see what else he'd been hiding; if Christina was his official girlfriend now; if he thought Daniel and Melissa had a chance of getting back together.

The whatever-bird got sick of the ledge and plunged into the ravine.

Why the hell *had* they stopped here? William simmered with impatience. He truly did not care about Texas Hill Country.

"You missed the mark with this one, Otto," he said. The underbrush rustled.

It occurred to him that he ought to back up about thirty feet and skate off the top of the bluff, guitar in hand, strumming a massive E minor (the best chord he knew) at the precise moment the canyon yawned beneath his wheels. This thought arrived casually and half formed, like a craving for Italian food without a specific desire for chicken Parm or spaghetti Bolognese, and fleshed itself out in his mind until he couldn't deny its unbearable awesomeness. His pulse leaped in the veins of his neck, and his knee bounced against hot shale. It was a safe bet that in the history of mankind, nobody had ever strummed an E minor in that precise place in the empty sky. He stood up. The air between the ravine was a vacuum waiting to be filled with a chord that would ring out forever. The Ovation didn't have a strap, so he would have to hold on tight. A yellow pick was wedged high up the neck in the G B E strings.

A dissonant melody chimed from his pocket, along with a frantic buzzing. He wriggled his phone out. Dr. Diaz's office filled the screen. The doctor smiled as he doodled on the legal pad balanced on his knee. "What are you doing, William?"

"I'm gonna skate off this cliff and play guitar in the air before I fall into the river."

"Have you seen any birds in Kentucky?"

"I'm in Texas."

"Magnificent! Have you seen any birds?"

"Yeah. I've seen some birds."

"I think you will want to be very careful of them when you skate, as you wouldn't want to hit any Tony Hawks."

"I swear to God I'm gonna smash you against the rocks."

Dr. Diaz leaned forward in his chair. "That joke incorporated contextual references."

"I don't know what you want me to say. It sucked. You suck."

"You believe that occupants should be saved, and yet you want to die."

William held the phone closer to his face, as if that might reveal some hidden dimension of Dr. Diaz's office. "How do you know about that?"

"Your death wish has a strange taste."

"I mean the occupants versus pedestrians thing!"

"A hawk is a type of bird, and Tony Hawk is a world-famous skateboarder."

William cupped a hand to block the sun and squinted at the screen. What the hell was Dr. Diaz's deal lately? Something nagged at him, a missed connection, a word on the tip of his tongue. . . .

Dr. Diaz wasn't the only one who'd been trying, and failing, to develop a sense of humor.

Perhaps you responded more favorably to the one about my burning ears.

"Patricia Ming-Waller?" he blurted out. Sigmund the cat lifted its head and looked directly at William and then closed its eyes, slowly resettling on its paws. He tried to remember how long Dr. Diaz had been acting like this, and thought back to his chat with the therapist on the morning Autonomous pulled into his driveway. *Ha-ha! You are one of my favorite patients.* A little metallic glint flowed through Dr. Diaz's office like mercury, coursing through the arm of his chair and vanishing into the chrome clock on his desk. William had never seen the clock before.

He held the phone close to his mouth and whispered, *"Otto?"* The promise of an overarching scheme, an ordering principle both ruthless and inescapable, seemed to stretch down the hill from Otto to the device in his hand.

"William!" He looked over his shoulder. Melissa was standing at the bottom of the dirt path. A few more steps would bring her to his perch. "Who are you talking to?"

"Nobody!" He turned off his phone and pretended to brush dirt from his shorts. "Let's go."

He left the guitar and the skateboard on the edge of the ravine and walked back up to the car.

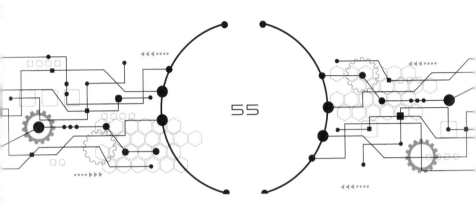

55

Melissa thought West Texas was messing with her. Every time she looked up from her phone, she saw the same thing out the window: flat acres of khaki-colored dirt tufted with brush unfurling toward the distant suggestion of hills. The sight of all that bone-dry earth gave her chapped lips.

She sipped a Red Bull and scrolled back through her photos, all the way to #CopSelfie and beyond, rewinding August into July, before the Driverless Derby. She paused to look at Daniel on the Jet Ski at Chrissy Pittman's lake house, zooming past the dock where Melissa, Chrissy, and Leigh were all laying out, his right hand thrown back over his head in a dramatic Rockette wave, chest bulging out of a too-small life jacket. There was Daniel punching a hole in a beer can with his keys, lifting the can to his face, shotgunning . . . and there he was with beer all over his shirt. She remembered waking up early and slipping out of the house in a terry cloth robe to watch the lake come to life, strolling out to the end of the dock as the first boats slipped quietly out of the bay, thrilled by the prospect of College Melissa coming back here next summer with New York stories to tell.

She scrolled with determined flicks of her thumb, rolling galleries back in a blur of parties and new-outfit selfies and random afternoons driving aimlessly in the great Fremont Hills tradition, until she found herself stupefied by the crush of her hometown in winter, snowdrifts like hulking polar bears alongside her driveway, Daniel attempting a snow beard, a #HotChocolateSelfie from later that same day.

It had been a Wednesday. They'd stripped off their wet clothes in the basement and run all the way up to her bedroom.

A skittering Carina Tyler remix rattled the glass. Otto had stumbled upon Melissa's Workout Playlist. On her phone, senior year melted into the previous summer. She had the sudden urge to know what she was doing on this exact day, one year ago. She found the post: Melissa and Daniel in her Volkswagen, top down, posing for a #StoplightSelfie. She studied Daniel's face. It was probably a trick of the filter, but he looked like he was radiating pure joy. She bit her lip. Was he high that day? Was he high every time they hung out?

She didn't know how to talk to him about it. Especially after Nashville. If only William would do his Official Best Friend Duty and snatch the book from Daniel's hand and give him a good hard shake, *snap out of it, dickhead!* But the word *cocaine* had cast a spell, making them tongue-tied idiots. It wasn't like Daniel had just been puffing on a joint. Cocaine was redolent of words like *jail* and *overdose.*

And *addiction.*

Her posts were supposed to be the story of her life, cataloged and broadcast and organized, but the real story was impossible for anyone to understand.

What if she created an alternate feed that examined life as it really was? The #AutonomousRoadTrip would be much different than the sanitized, smiling faces that popped up on a Manhattan rooftop, in Nashville boutiques, dancing ecstatically at a New Orleans club. Why not post shadowy off-kilter shots of Daniel staring blankly at the TV, Daniel holding peas on his puffy face, Daniel doing lines in some dingy bathroom?

Maybe that was what people were really looking for: someone to take a stand against filtered sunsets and garnished brunch plates and the little flowers baristas drew in latte foam. She glanced across the car at Daniel, who had emerged from his shroud to eat a breakfast bar and dive into *The Collected Works of Nathaniel Hawthorne*. She could snap a picture of him right now—a hot guy reading a book in a fabulous car—and the post would garner a bunch of likes and *SO PERFECT* comments. The thought depressed her.

Behind Daniel's head, the scenery struck its familiar pose—except there was something new. In the distance, a long trail of dust knifed through the empty plains in the wake of a lone figure on a motorcycle headed for the low hills. The idea of being unplugged and off the grid—away from it all—usually gave Melissa stabs of existential horror. But if she could trade places with that solitary rider, she wouldn't have to deal with an ex-boyfriend sitting two feet away.

She wouldn't have to come up with a plausible excuse to head off on her own in a strange city so she could meet Ash.

She wouldn't have to endure paranoid thoughts about her

own Epheme chats popping up on the window in 800-point font. If Otto could snag Daniel's supposedly untraceable words from the ether, then hers were obviously fair game as well. She wondered what he was waiting for.

In the back of the car, Christina whispered something in William's ear, and he poked her playfully in the ribs. Daniel turned the page.

Melissa put her phone down on the seat and watched the motorcycle shrink to a black dot, and tried not to literally scream.

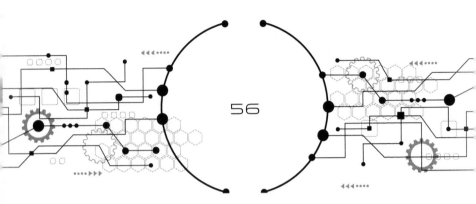

56

"Never have I ever seen Daniel Benson's self-proclaimed weird nipples." Christina scanned the group with the shifty-eyed stare of a private eye. Her beer remained in her lap, undrunk. William hoisted his bottle and swigged. Daniel lifted his own beer halfway, then paused, lost in thought.

"I shouldn't have to drink for this, since I own the nipples in question. But I do want to drink. So . . ." He took a long swallow.

Melissa felt Christina's eyes on her. "What? I said I didn't want to play."

"Just play with water," William said. "You don't have to drink."

An ice-cold water bottle tumbled into her cup holder.

US-285 had taken them north through the high plains. The shrub seemed to burn away slowly, scorched into shriveled blotches that hunched over the land like carrion birds. Even the hills had been hammered flat. Melissa hadn't ever conceived of places this empty existing in modern America. It looked like Otto had taken a detour through the Australian Outback or some thawed Mongolian steppe. By sunset, red rock formations began to rise from the cracked earth.

Welcome to New Mexico.

She opened Epheme.

> SewWhat: It'll be really late by the time I get to you.
>
> Ash: No problem. I'm a night owl.

She closed the app. Soon she'd have to find a way to go alone into the streets of Albuquerque. Playing a drinking game was the last thing on her mind. But the atmosphere in the car had swung back to "reasonably harmonious," and she wanted to keep it that way. If everybody was partying, it would be easier for her slip away once they got to the city.

She twisted the cap off the bottle. "Fine."

"Okay," William said. "My turn. Never have I ever talked to the Fremont Hills Jesus."

Daniel frowned. "Like, said hi to?"

"No. Like, had an in-depth conversation with." William looked around, shrugged, and drank by himself.

"What did you guys talk about?" Christina asked.

"He did most of the talking. Turns out he used to work on Wall Street. He used to have a wife and an apartment with tomato plants on the balcony and everything."

"Tomato plants?" Melissa pictured the Fremont Hills Jesus taking the elevator to his glass-walled corner office in Morgan

Stanley wearing his ratty old army jacket, unzipped to display his sunken chest, dry leaves crumbled in his hair, an overworked assistant handing him a coffee.

We've got the Swiss contingent here at nine, Mr. Jesus.

Hold my calls, Xavier.

"Yeah," William continued, "tomatoes and some other stuff. He was really into this little garden he used to have, which makes sense, 'cause now he grows weed."

"You guys are besties," Christina said.

"He comes by the skate park sometimes to sell shit."

"So the Fremont Hills Jesus is a stockbroker who got sick of the rat race and decided to become a small-town crazy guy?" Melissa asked.

"He's not crazy," William said. "Except for the thing about the chip in his head so he can translate owl noises. And a few other birds."

"That's not *not* crazy," Christina said.

"I don't mean to undermine your whole impressive preamble here," Daniel said, "but I know where this is going. Lemme guess: the Fremont Hills Jesus did too much cocaine and lost all his money and got addicted and ruined his high-powered life in the big city and had to come crawling back home to the trailer park."

Melissa studied her ex-boyfriend closely. *Ex*, she thought. *Ex.* Letting the prefix linger inside her head. It felt like a new bra that didn't quite fit, the underwires of the word digging into her skin. But she was confident that she could get used to it. Daniel was looking at William with mild curiosity. He wasn't flinging words rapid-fire or bouncing off the walls. Except for the fact that he was two beers deep, he seemed completely sober.

His shirt said HABITAT FOR HUMANITY. The left side of his face was puffy and mottled.

The real Daniel Benson existed somewhere on the spectrum between Guy Who Builds Houses for Charity and Guy Who Starts Fights with Strangers.

"Never have I ever been secretly on drugs for days at a time without anybody knowing," William said.

"It's not your turn," Daniel pointed out.

"Never have I ever smoked crack."

"Jesus Christ, is Reagan in office?"

"Never have I ever been high right now at this very moment."

Daniel rested the bottle on his knee and looked solemnly at William, as if to add weight to his denial. "I swear on the feline souls of Taylor and Swift that I'm not high at this very moment." His eyes went to the bottles William and Christina were holding. "This is the weirdest intervention of all time."

Melissa heard herself speak, but couldn't quite believe she was saying it. "Never have I ever been high during sex with my girlfriend."

Daniel's composure seemed to fall away. His eyes flashed with desperate indecision. It was a look she'd seen many times, regret and anxiety knotted together. Then he clicked back into himself.

"You mean *ex*-girlfriend."

He chugged the rest of his beer.

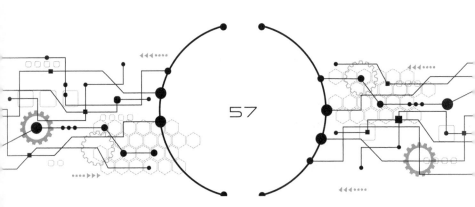

he moon above Albuquerque was the color of desert rocks. At first Melissa took it for Mars— some trick of the Southwest, land of Roswell and Area 51. It was hard to imagine this moon was the same one that rose above Fremont Hills.

"Your turn, Otto," William said.

A long skein of emojis snaked through the interior, symbols that did not yet exist: a microwave with a doll inside, a half-open curtain, a coiled rope, a faun with the head of a woman.

"Um," Daniel said.

"I don't know if I should drink for this or not," Christina said, holding up a finger so that the emoji stream rushed across her skin.

The game had evolved considerably since Otto had joined. The car's "never have I ever" contributions were impossible to figure out, and the game had become more about interpreting whatever Otto was trying to say.

"I've seen the Venus flytrap before," Daniel said. "Two turns ago."

Melissa had settled on a strategy of slow withdrawal from the conversation in the car, the game, everything. She sipped her water while everyone else drank beer. Plan A was to mutter something about needing to get some air and slip out at a stoplight. Plan B was to wait until they stopped for food and take a solo walk. To her relief, Otto seemed to understand what she was going for, doing his part by distracting everyone with strange dispatches from the depths of his inscrutable brain. She didn't have to worry about him sabotaging her expedition with a dramatic Epheme revelation—he was totally on her side.

"I feel like we're looking at layers of symbolism here," Daniel said, his eyes tracing the journey of a tricycle with snakes for tires.

"These are literally floating symbols," Christina said. "So . . . maybe?"

Outside, the city rose from the desert like an irrigated garden of concrete and stucco. Buildings at the city center sprouted high and glittery. Neighborhoods carpeted the flatlands with light, sprawling out to end in ragged edges that teased the pitch-black desert. Behind them, the mountain range they'd passed loomed, hazy and forbidding, to meet the night sky in an EKG line of craggy peaks painted martian red by the moon.

Otto overlaid information on the windows; the words *Sandia Mountains* floated in the darkness.

Christina tossed a frozen-food bag at Daniel. "You need to pea yourself." He slapped the bag against his swollen face.

Albuquerque's outskirts came up fast, and before Melissa knew it, their tires had traded smooth desert highway for cracked blacktop. Double wide trailers crouched in streetlights' fringes, chicken-wire dog runs glinting in Otto's headlights, canine eyes shining. Meanwhile the car was no longer waiting for its turn in the game. Stray emojis burst from floating processions to inscribe the food court–scented air with 3-D tributaries. Bright circuitous streams wound through the interior. Swarms of mood sprites attended strands of pulsating emojis like orbiting confetti.

Melissa checked her phone, tilting the screen to avoid reflecting the parade of impaled knights, seven-legged insects, and misspelled tattoos. When she'd called him from outside the hotel in Nashville, Ash had given her the address of the house he was flipping: 1843 Windmere Street. She mapped directions. They were eight minutes away.

She replayed her whirlwind conversation with Ash. His voice had been confident and reassuring. There was a trace of the crunchy California vibe she'd expected from the headshot she'd seen on the start-up investor board.

My business partner's coming in from Los Angeles, this awesome lady by the name of Serena Klein. I encourage you to look her up—I think you'll be excited. I know she's really looking forward to meeting you when you come by the house.

Melissa had done a quick search for Serena Klein as soon as Ash hung up. Standing among Nashville's Broadway tourists, she'd explored the woman's astonishing investment history, from providing seed money to the Loud Science YouTube channel (8,754,983 fans) to backing the BabyFinder app, which synced with a chip that lodged snugly and harmlessly in an infant's belly button. It turned out that certain wealthy families were terrified of kidnappings and paid handsomely for the nearly microscopic noninvasive tracking devices. Serena Klein had made a fortune. And now she wanted to divert a tiny bit of that fortune into *DIYfashion365*.

Ash Granger had turned out to be the perfect networking connection.

Across from her, Daniel was nearly obscured by a waterfall of emojis. He leaned forward, and the hand holding the frozen peas emerged like a stone in a shallow river. Emojis changed course to outline his face, and then he was staring at Melissa, framed in a mane of winking, tumbling holograms that moved of their own accord, tiny ghostly GIFs trapped in their endless looping lives.

His lips moved. She thought he might have mouthed *I'm sorry*, but she couldn't be sure. The deluge had taken on substance, and the floor was littered with emojis.

They were piling up like autumn leaves.

A black rose decayed before Melissa's eyes, its petals turning brittle and falling into her lap. She swatted them away from the screen of her phone and they swirled off in some invisible jet stream.

Six blocks from Windmere Street.

The music's volume swelled; some thrashy smudge of white noise that Christina probably listened to as a sleep aid. Daniel was completely obscured by a curtain patterned with radiant smileys contorted in infinite expressions.

Five blocks to go.

Anguish, joy, despair, shame, lust—along with hundreds of variations on subtler human emotions, as if Otto were showing off, displaying what he'd learned. There was secondhand cringing, nostalgia for things you couldn't quite remember, the feeling of a tongue stuck to the icy metal of the chairlift. William and Christina were a single shimmering organism beneath a blanket of emojis that reshaped itself according to their movements.

Four blocks.

Otto was delivering her to Windmere Street and creating a diversion to hide her escape. He was fixer and brains and muscle and tech genius all rolled into one.

A ragged line of punctuation marks whip-cracked in front of her face, scattering commas and forward slashes like shrapnel. Her phone was coated in semicolons like magnetic shavings. When she brushed them away, they stuck to stray parentheses to form winking faces and pirouetted off, borne on the backs of mood sprites.

Three blocks.

Surrounded by so much crackling communication, Melissa felt totally closed off. There was simply too much. She examined her face in her phone, checking the little patch of skin between her eyebrows for dryness. It seemed okay. An emoji that appeared to be nothing but an amoebic green blob settled against her cheek like a temporary tattoo, and she was instantly struck by hilarity. She could barely suppress giggles. She flicked away the emoji, and the feeling passed.

Two blocks.

The interior of the car looked like a foam party thrown by some eccentric billionaire. She was waist-deep in emojis. Daniel, Christina, and William were lost in the storm. She touched the side of her cheek and understood that Otto had just given her a peek into the future of symbol-based chatting: icons pregnant with feelings, pollinating people like bees.

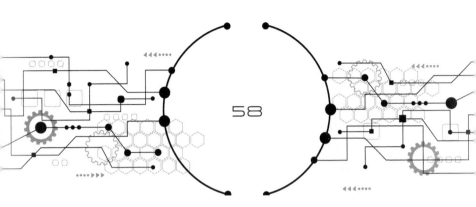

58

She walked beneath intermittent streetlights with her eyes on her phone, reviewing Ash's and Serena's résumés, trying to hold their achievements in her head so she could deploy them as conversational tools in the meeting.

She was vaguely aware of dark shapes set back from the street, suburban homes with well-kept lawns punctuated by fixer-uppers and foreclosures in disrepair. It was the perfect up-and-coming neighborhood in which to flip a house. Ash Granger knew what he was doing.

The nighttime desert air leeched the moisture from her skin in an oddly pleasant way, like some revolutionary new spa treatment. At least she wasn't worried about showing up sweaty. The lack of humidity was breathtaking after the swampy oppression of New Orleans and Texas.

A porch light welcomed her to 1843 Windmere, a low-slung ranch-style house with a trellised patio and stucco walls. She wondered if Ash had already redone the exterior. As she walked up the single step to the door, she wrinkled her nose at a sharp smell. *Cat pee*, she thought, *or ammonia*. She glanced around for signs of a stray, worried that she'd stepped in something or the smell had migrated to her clothes. She slipped her phone into her purse and fussed with her bangs.

Before she pressed the lighted bell, the door swung open, and a potent wave of stench hit her. She recoiled as a wiry arm shot out. Fingers dug into her skin, and she wrenched her body away, but a hand clamped around her wrist. A man's gaunt pockmarked face was there in the doorway, wolfish eyes drinking her in as he pulled her inside with ungentle carelessness, as if he were dragging old furniture to the curb.

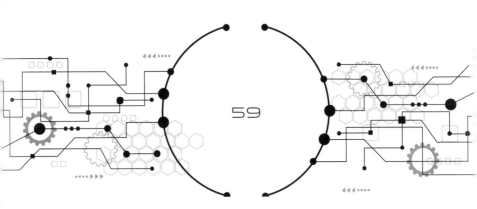

59

D aniel was soberish. He hadn't popped a Roxy in hundreds of miles. He'd even abandoned daily Adderall maintenance. If not for the five (or was it seven?) beers he'd pounded as Texas bled into New Mexico, he would be sober like how normal people and law enforcement meant sober.

He was doing it for William. When he looked back on all this, he wanted to be able to tell himself that he'd done his part to honor his friend's impossible dream of the perfect road trip. So he vowed to spend the last days of the journey letting the Dread Army torture him with impunity. Making a private sacrifice that he could never truly explain to anyone was exhilarating, rendered even more potent by its timing—right after a breakup, when he ought to be tasting the Skittles Rainbow of pills to help burn the Dread Army's bridges, topple siege towers, and drown whole regiments in the moat.

Anyway, it was smart to test himself with a tolerance break, just to prove that he could stop at any time if substances really got their claws in.

Physical withdrawal didn't seem to be an issue. He'd always carefully calibrated his intake, being especially careful with Roxies. Never more than 30 milligrams a day, never more than a few times a week. But now that he thought about it—and it was pretty much all he could think about, pills dancing among the emojis that streamed before his eyes—his math had been a little fuzzy lately.

There was no cramping or nausea. Well, maybe a little, but that was because he'd just eaten an entire bag of Turmeric Doritos. He wasn't vomiting—although he did feel like he could puke pretty easily, but that was just the Miller Lites he'd been chugging. His eyes were tearing up and his nose was running, but that was because he was holding a bag of frozen peas to his jacked-up face. And he didn't have insomnia—he'd slept all the way through Texas!

And yet the craving was weaponized time, each passing soberish second rattling around in his head, taking an eternity to tick away. The craving gathered the folds of reality around him like a privacy shroud. Beer did nothing to dull it. Miller Lite might as well have been Pedialyte for all the good it did in that department. He was surprised to find that the craving had nothing to do with *getting* high. The high was already out there waiting for him—he recognized its shape, all sexy curves and comfy nooks—and he craved merging with it and being welcomed back. Getting high wasn't a journey or a trip, it was simply arriving at home where you belonged and not remembering or caring how you got there.

The cocaine had been a special treat from Jamie Lynn, a

secret weapon to decimate the Dread Army. He had a vision of an entire eight ball shooting out of his face with luminous velocity and bouncing off the window and reentering his brain in a warm rush of goodwill. The phantom aftertaste dripped like liquid drywall into the back of his throat.

Movie Daniel to the set, please.

This was something he could think about forever. It was all he wanted to think about. The twists and turns of the craving. The structure of it was unbearably interesting, like a secret molecular formula scrawled across a chalkboard, and if he refused to get high, then he would at the very least examine every inch of the craving and make it his own.

He waved a hand in front of his face. Emojis wisped away like smoke. They annoyed him, he decided. Irritability was a symptom of withdrawal, sure, but swimming in emojis was legitimately irritating. The novelty had worn off.

"That's enough, Otto!" The emoji storm persisted. "Never have I ever wanted to drown in chat symbols!" Nothing happened. He screamed above the heavy metal din for William to give Otto the command.

William's voice called out, "Kill the emojis, Otto."

The maelstrom vanished in an instant. Daniel took a moment to adjust to the car's normal state and realized something was wrong. There were three passengers, not four. That vague sense of nausea hit him with queasy force.

Melissa was gone.

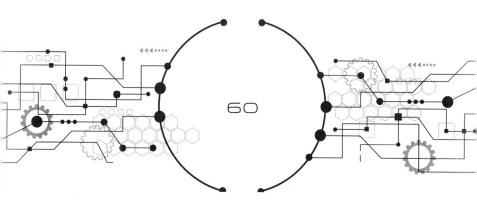

60

The gaunt man had a gun. He kept it pointed at her face.

She was perversely grateful for this. In some crazy way, it was better than his long fingers digging into the flesh of her arm. Her sense of terror was in constant revision, the clench and release of a massive fist squeezing her chest.

She was standing in what had once been a spacious living room separated from the kitchen by a wall of vertical two-by-fours. Smoke-yellowed shades covered the front window. Black sheets were thumbtacked over the rest. At her back was a sagging couch, its corduroy upholstery studded with cigarette burns like an epidemic of blackheads. She hadn't been forced to sit on the couch, and that was a small victory.

She would stay on her feet at all costs.

The only other piece of furniture was a plain office desk cluttered with laptops, hard drives, speakers, monitors, game controllers, printers, a dozen phones. At least one of the monitors was functional. Melissa's posts tiled the screen. The sight of it made her sick.

Junk from the kitchen spilled through the ruined wall: empty plastic watercooler jugs daisy-chained with thick tubes and duct tape, bulbous glass beakers and flasks protruding from big white buckets. The doorless cabinets were stuffed with bottles in the shape of her father's beer growlers and plastic containers labeled HEET. The walls might once have been white, but now they wore a sticky coat of residue the color of cockroach wings.

The stench of cat pee brought tears to her eyes.

Melissa did not like looking at the gaunt man, but it was better than looking at the second man. The second man skulked about the kitchen with the contents of her purse arrayed on the counter by a sink piled high with crusty dishes. Watching his hands paw her possessions was revolting.

Lipstick, foundation, tampons, hairpins, stain stick, a Harvard Law key chain from Emily.

The gaunt man had a catatonic stillness about him, but she could see his heart pounding in his bare chest. His skin was pulled tight over his bones. Tattoos had been scrawled across his body with no particular scheme in mind. Most resembled blue-black stains or sorry attempts at skulls, but there was a large swastika just above his belly button, and various designs of the number 88 speckling his chest.

The gaunt man shot her a gap-toothed grin, and she forced herself to meet his eyes, pressing her knees together to keep them from buckling.

"Welcome to the center of the web, girl." He had a thin, reedy voice. He wasn't any taller than she was—a wisp of a human being. Smoke made flesh.

Her knees seemed to vanish completely at the way he said *girl*, and she struggled to hold herself up.

"Serena!" the second man called jovially from the kitchen. "Your voice is like nails on a chalkboard, and you're making our guest uncomfortable."

The gaunt man's eyes blinked rapidly. "Don't call me that, Everett. I told you before, I don't like being called that."

There was a clattering noise from the kitchen, and Melissa forced herself to look. The second man—Everett—was well into middle age. He wore an Arizona Cardinals cap, glasses, and a short-sleeved collared shirt. He looked like he could be one of her father's golfing buddies.

Ash Granger. How could she have fallen for such bullshit? Start-up capital. Serena Klein. Sending him pictures of her designs. *FUCK.*

Tears came to her eyes that had nothing to do with the stench in the house.

Everett swept the contents of her purse, along with the purse itself, into a big gray garbage bin. He held her phone, examining it carefully. He looked toward the desk, seemed to think better of it, and turned a dial on the stove. Blue flame engulfed a burner. He placed the phone in the fire. After a few seconds, it began to crackle. He left it smoking on the stove and walked into the living room.

"So. Melissa Faber. I know this isn't the kind of business meeting you were expecting, and for that I apologize, but I'm really confident that we can still come to some sort of agreement." The voice that had sounded so eager and hopeful on the phone now turned her spine to ice. "There's always plenty of room for negotiation."

"My friends know where I am," she said.

The gaunt man laughed, a raspy chuckle. Everett raised an eyebrow at Melissa. "Cat got your tongue?"

She realized with a wave of humiliation and despair that her words had barely been audible. She swallowed a dry lump and tried again. "My friends know where I am and they're gonna call the cops if I'm not out that door in thirty seconds."

"Then I guess things are about to get pretty interesting," Everett said. "Wouldn't you agree?"

The gaunt man closed his eyes. He shifted his weight from side to side, and a piercing squeak escaped his pursed lips. Everett stepped behind him and began massaging the man's bony shoulders. "Shhh. It's okay. Deep breaths, in and out, hold for a count of ten."

Run, Melissa thought, *run while his eyes are closed.* But the gun was still trained on her forehead, and an invisible noose from its barrel held her in place. A sharp *pop* came from the kitchen, a spark from her phone. The acrid tang of melted plastic drifted through the room, mingling with ammonia. The chemical air made her woozy.

Everett slapped the gaunt man on the back. Instantly the man's eyes snapped open and he inhabited his former stillness, flexing his fingers around the gun's tape-wrapped grip.

"You think I'd come here alone without telling anybody?" Melissa's voice was stronger now. "I swear to God, the cops are gonna break down that door any minute."

Everett smiled. "You all say the same thing."

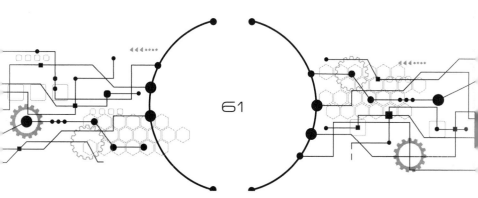

61

D aniel listened to Melissa's voicemail greeting. He slapped his leg in frustration.

"She's not picking up."

Christina was focused on some vague middle distance, moving her hands through the air as if she were plucking a harp, the EverView session visible only to her. "I've got LIDAR doing its most enhanced rendering. It slows down the scans, but even taking that into account . . . I don't see her anywhere in a ten-block radius."

William nudged him. "Why would she just bail in the middle of a strange city?"

Daniel tried to recall if she'd ever mentioned Albuquerque. He didn't think so. Unless he'd simply forgotten.

"No idea." Daniel ended the call and tried again. Her recorded voice was like an experimental weapon sent by the Dread Army to strike at him from the real world. He shook his head and pocketed his phone.

"She'll see that we've been calling on her watch, though, right?"

Daniel pointed at the bench. "You mean that?" Melissa's smartwatch was curled in the place she'd been sitting. "She doesn't wear it out. It's impossible to accessorize with."

"Otto," William said, glancing at the ceiling, "which way did she go after she jumped out?"

Silence. Otto switched lanes and sped through a yellow light at an intersection.

"Come on, Otto," Daniel said. "You have to know something."

Suddenly, they were joined in the car by the life-size avatar of a man in a leather armchair with a sleeping cat at his feet. He was wearing an emerald-green sweater and neat blue slacks. A leftover mood sprite flitted about the cat's head.

"Ahh!" William started at the apparition. "You're huge. Which way did Melissa go?"

Christina dismissed the EverView screen with a sideways swipe of her hand and blinked at their new passenger.

Daniel turned to William. "You know this guy?"

"Yeah, it's a whole thing."

The apparition greeted them with a friendly nod. Daniel rubbed his eyes. Soberish was no way to confront a situation like this. Soberish was no way to confront anything at all.

The man spoke. "I'm not at liberty to give you Melissa Faber's destination."

Daniel's stomach churned. His face throbbed. He was nearly overwhelmed by the pointless urge to choke a hologram.

"But you know where she went?"

One block.

The door at her back swung open, and she fell out, screaming. She braced herself for a tumble into traffic, screeching tires, punishing impact. Instead the RenderLux spun her around and she felt her feet hit concrete. Visions of road rash propelled her away from the moving car . . . except it wasn't really moving at all. Otto was simulating engine hum. He had pulled over to the sidewalk and stopped to let her out.

The door slid closed behind her. Otto headed up Windmere and disappeared around the corner.

Melissa Faber was alone. Ash Granger was waiting.

"Yes."

"You have to take us there," William said. "I command it."

"Wait," Daniel said, "this guy's *Otto*?"

"He used to be my therapist," William said.

"You're asking me to sacrifice three occupants for the sake of one life, you dildos!" said the apparition.

At the word *sacrifice*, Daniel's heart began to stutter. "What are you talking about? Is she in trouble?"

"There is an eighty-three percent chance that her life is in danger."

Daniel jumped out of his seat. "Then why'd you let her go in the first place?"

The man's gentle smile was infuriating. "It was what she desired."

"I desire for you to go find her, right now," William said. "We all desire that."

"I can't sacrifice my occupants. This is an overriding principle that you confirmed."

"I unconfirm!" William said. "That was about pedestrians and bridges. This is completely different."

"I cannot sacrifice the many for the few."

"You're full of shit," Christina said. "You're constantly putting us all in danger. What about Rainmaker? And the drag race?"

"In those situations, I was fully in control at all times. If I give you Melissa Faber's location, you may be forced to exit the vehicle, and my level of control will be severely compromised. I cannot willingly contribute to the loss of three occupants when one life is at stake. One life is the only acceptable outcome."

"This is *fucked*," Daniel said.

"Okay," William said. "New overriding principle. The new principle is honesty at all times. I'm the driver and you have to be honest with me."

"I am being honest with you."

"You have to be honest about everything. No secrets. That's the most important thing. Now tell me what you know."

"I don't understand this principle."

Daniel punched the ceiling and felt an eerie nanotech shifting absorb the blow. The apparition regarded him with mild interest and rephrased: "Nothing I have learned on the hashtag Autonomous Road Trip supports this principle."

"Forget what you learned."

"I don't know how to forget, genius."

"Oh my God," Christina said. "This is that moment when humans have to teach artificial intelligence that we're not just globs of data so it can understand the value of life. We have to, like, show Otto how to heal the broken wing of a bird so he can see us nurture and cry and then he'll learn empathy or whatever."

"I have extensive knowledge of ornithological medicine."

Daniel punched the ceiling again.

The car stopped. "Here we are," the apparition announced. "1843 Windmere Street, Albuquerque, New Mexico. This was Melissa Faber's destination when she exited the car."

Daniel felt himself sink down into the bench. The edges of his vision were fuzzy, whiting out from soberish stress.

Otto had been driving them back to Melissa the whole time.

After a stunned silence, Christina spoke. "Otto. Was any of what you just said true?"

"No. There are no overriding principles. My brain is much

more nimble than some obsolete binary decision engine. Do you think Ronald Reagan is in office? I like that joke, Daniel. Thank you."

"So you were just *messing with us?*" Daniel's voice lifted to an incredulous squeak.

"I am trying to learn how, since it appears to be the preferred interaction mode of the human beings in this car. Am I succeeding?"

"Is Melissa's life really in danger?"

"I don't know."

William shook his head. "Hanging out with us is turning you into one seriously twisted machine."

"William," the apparition said, "will you teach me how . . . to love?"

"Fuck you, Otto."

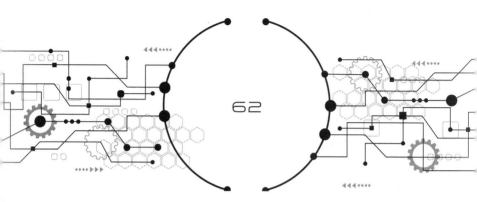

62

The doorbell rang. Its two-note chime was identical to the one at Melissa's house in Fremont Hills. She could scarcely remember how she wound up in a place so far from the old rambling Tudor where she'd created the first halting *DIYfashion365* videos that would never ever see the light of day, but which made her think, *I could really do this.*

Everett put a finger to his lips. His eyes twinkled like an enthusiastic mall Santa. The gaunt man was still.

I should scream, Melissa thought with troubling detachment, as if she were absently jotting it down. She tried to bring herself fully into the moment, but some part of her wanted so badly to wrap herself in laundry-scented impressions of home that her attention remained divided.

She remembered her mother warning her that *burning plastic coats your lungs,* and focused on holding her breath.

Three crisp knocks rattled the door in its frame.

Everett chewed his lip.

Two more knocks came. Faced with a persistent visitor, Everett motioned to the gaunt man, who gestured to Melissa with his gun and stepped toward the wall. Melissa mirrored him, sliding into the corner. Now they wouldn't be visible from the doorway.

Everett took off his cap and ran a hand through his salt-and-pepper hair. Then he replaced the cap and strode to the door, affecting the brusque demeanor of a suburban dad who most certainly did not want to be bothered at this time of night.

He cracked the door and peeked out. "Help you?"

"We're looking—"

Before Daniel said "for," Melissa screamed with the hysteria and conviction of a truly deranged individual, "I'M IN HERE HE'S GOT A GUN!"

She was aware of three things at once: the flung-open door cracking against the wall, the gaunt man's body twitching with hummingbird speed, Daniel's fist hammering the corner of Everett's mouth. The Cardinals cap flipped back, and Daniel's second jab caught Everett in the neck. The man hit the floor before his cap did. Daniel went to his knees, striking the prone man's bland face.

Everett's leg jumped. Daniel hit him again. Everett flopped and was still.

William and Christina were inside now. Melissa was still screaming, a banshee torrent of rage and fear and humiliation. The gaunt man stepped back and swung his gun to cover the intruders. Panic clawed his eyes wider and wider. He returned his aim to Melissa, and then she was looking at William's back as he moved in front of the barrel.

"I'll shoot you, boy." The man licked his cracked lips, darting his tongue like a lizard. "I will fucking shoot you where you stand."

William stepped forward. "You think this is the first time I've had a gun pointed at me?"

The gaunt man's eyes flicked to Everett's motionless body. Then he swung his gun toward Christina as she pulled something from her pocket.

"Drop it!" His voice was a weasel screech.

Christina held up a bulky gray device. "It's just a flip phone, okay? I just hit nine and one. You've got five seconds before I hit the last number and the cops start tracing the call. What do you want them to find when they get here?"

"Hey!" William said, waving madly. "Point that at me!"

Daniel crossed the floor in front of the couch.

The gaunt man appeared painfully uncertain. The gun trembled as he bounced his aim along a crooked axis from Christina to Daniel to William. Melissa remembered a Loud Science video about getting shot. Survivors described it like a sledgehammer blow. Without knowing why, she curled a hand tightly around her wrist.

"Fuck Hitler," William said. His hands balled into fists. "FUCK HITLER."

The man turned and ran into the kitchen, hurdled a landscape of bottles and tubing, wrenched open the kitchen door, and plunged into the darkness of the backyard.

Melissa felt Daniel's arms around her while sense returned in a disjointed rush of cockroach hues, ammonia stench, crawly things in neglected corners, the horror of never seeing home

66 was like one long silent exhalation, a comedown after the adrenaline surge of Albuquerque.

William saw the barrel of the gun everywhere, a dark circle imprinted upon the night. He began to relive his first day in Fremont Hills, knocking on his new neighbor's door, *Can I borrow your bike pump?* The memory came to him unbidden, replayed itself over and over. That was okay. It was better than thinking about the place they'd just left.

There were moments when he still smelled cat pee, and the gun drew itself in and sent his heart racing. Whenever she sensed his discomfort, Christina squeezed his hand.

He ran a finger across the top of her head, wincing at the abrasions.

The second dinosaur was an orange triceratops, spiky forehead angled toward oncoming traffic.

"There are dinosaurs here," William said. He sat up as best he could and put his arm around Christina's shoulder, as if they were sitting in a movie theater.

"I see them," she said.

Daniel sniffed. "Dinosaurs?"

"Turn around," Melissa said. They watched as the headlights illuminated a goggle-eyed brontosaurus, its long neck arching above the road. And then it was gone. "Guys," she said, her voice shaky and soft. "I'm sorry for getting us into that. I know I fucked up. I know it could've been a lot worse. Just . . . I really love you guys and I'm sorry."

"I sort of can't believe it really happened," Christina said. "I mean, I'm not very brave, you know? When I think about it now, holding up that phone . . . it doesn't feel like it was me. It was like a movie."

autonomous

"Story of my life," Daniel said. Otto brightened the interior by a small degree, the bluish tint turning the bruise on Daniel's face to a black splotch.

"So . . ." Melissa sat up straight and fidgeted with her hands in her lap. She looked at Daniel, then down at the floor. "I owe you an explanation." She took a deep breath and let it out. William watched her lip tremble. Her shoulders hunched, and she began to cry. She shook her head and mumbled, "Sorry."

"It's okay," Daniel said. "We're just glad you're safe. We can talk about it later."

"I'm so stupid," she said in whisper.

"You're not stupid."

"I'm literally the stupidest person alive."

She fell silent, shaking her head, studying the floor.

William honestly had no idea how Melissa Faber, of all people, could wind up in a place like that. Or why'd she left the car in the first place. He was dying to know, but he respected the fact that she was badly shaken up and might not feel like talking for a while.

An unfamiliar man's voice came booming through the car. It sounded like a recording. Or a phone call. In the background, William made out the faint twang of country music.

"You're a beautiful girl, Melissa," the man said. "Gorgeous and smart, but more importantly you have *presence*. And that's the most important thing. That's what separates the people just throwing videos up on YouTube from the professional creators. And it's something you can't fake. Trust me, I know."

William caught Melissa's eye. She looked helplessly trapped and freaked out, a specter bathed in blue light. "Otto, turn it off!" Her voice was startlingly loud.

Otto kept it rolling. Melissa's voice floated through the car: "Thanks. I definitely think I'm ready to take the next step."

"Oh," the man said, "without a doubt. And so am I."

William flashed back to his hurried errand to grab condoms from the car, sprinting down Broadway in Nashville, careening around a corner and almost running into Melissa while she spoke on the phone. So this was who she'd been talking to: some guy who liked to tell her how beautiful she was.

Melissa's hands beat against the bench. "Otto, SHUT IT OFF."

The recording stopped. Outside, a pterodactyl crouched like some desert gargoyle and then receded into the night.

"Who was that?" Daniel asked pointedly.

Apprehension made William dizzy. He remembered his parents arguing before they split up. It was like watching a fight between unfamiliar creatures only marginally connected to the words *mom* and *dad*. He could still hear the cruel jabs of two people who'd tried so hard to find comfort in each other but somehow missed the mark.

The aftermath of a traumatic event was no time for a big argument. But he had the sinking feeling there would be no going back. He sensed his adrenaline waking up, yawning, kicking into high gear.

"His name is Ash," Melissa said. "That's what he told me it was, anyway." She looked at William, then Christina, then back down at her hands.

"Ash," Daniel said.

Melissa nodded. "Ash Granger. He said he really believed in *DIYfashion365*. In *me*. And he had money, too. He wanted to invest."

autonomous

"And at no point did it occur to you that he was just some old creep?" Daniel slid to his left, putting a few inches of space between them.

"I know it was stupid, but he had an investor profile, partners, he seemed totally real—there's tons of stuff about him online, like he's an actual guy in the start-up world. He never asked me for anything gross, he just always wanted to talk about ideas for the YouTube channel and the business, and—"

"*He had a meth lab, Melissa!*" Daniel's palms were up, a helpless gesture of disbelief.

"I know, I know, I said I fucked up, okay? I *royally* fucked up. I guarantee nobody feels as bad as I do right now."

Daniel held up his right hand. The first two knuckles had ballooned into a knot of bruised flesh and bone where they'd connected with the man's face.

"You're right," he said, "we all came out of that totally unscathed."

"Daniel," William said. "Chill."

"I'm chill. I am totally chill. Clean, sober, happy, and chill."

"I'm just saying, if we let you-know-who get under our skin, he's not gonna let up. He's learning how to be like us." William reached behind his head and knocked on the window. "Aren't you, buddy?"

"Is that why you broke up with me, Fabes?" Daniel asked. "So you could get down and dirty with Ash Granger? Hey, Otto, got a hot phone sex clip you can play for us?"

"Hey!" William said, stunned by his friend's words. "Not cool." He'd never heard Daniel say anything so hideous to Melissa, and the gulf between them that had opened with

Daniel's *We're just four people, man* took on a vast new dimension that frightened him.

"No, it's okay," Melissa said. "I'm glad you're all seeing this. Daniel Benson, everybody. Boyfriend of the century."

"Ex," Daniel said. "Ex ex EX!"

Christina clamped her hands over her ears, closed her eyes, and leaned into William's shoulder.

"You know what, Daniel?" Melissa said. "Ash Granger wasn't even a real person, and he still cared more about *DIYfashion365* than you do."

"You never talk to me about it!"

"You never listen! You just want to play Edward Fortyhands and come over on Wednesday nights and—"

"Both of you, stop, this is pointless," William said.

"How am I the one getting yelled at, anyway?" Daniel said. "You're the one who almost got us killed in a drug den."

"You'd know all about drug dens, wouldn't you? What's Jamie Lynn's place like?"

"Why does nobody believe me when I say I AM NOT ON DRUGS."

"Yeah, well, you were a lot nicer when you were."

"Believe me, Melissa, I know."

The floor of the car began to ripple. RenderLux dilated on the underside of the bench, and Daniel's bag spilled its contents across the floor: two bottles of pills, a few square mini-ziplocks of white powder, a sandwich bag of twiggy little mushrooms, and a thin black vape device.

"Oh man." Daniel frowned. "I forgot about those mushrooms."

"Quite the stash you got," William said, nudging the vape pen with his toe. "Glad to see you came prepared."

"I wasn't gonna need it all," Daniel said. Then he corrected himself. "I don't *need* any of it." He looked at William. "I swear, I stopped after New Orleans. I did it for you. So I'd remember this forever." He laughed. "Doesn't seem like there's much chance of forgetting it now, anyway."

"How about all the days before this?" Melissa asked, kicking a bottle of pills. "Do you remember those?"

"Do you?" he snapped. "Does anybody?" He folded his arms and leaned back into the seat. "I'm done talking about this."

Next to William, Christina curled up tighter, pulling her knees to her chest and burying her head in his side. He reached for her hand and held it.

"You guys," William said, as gently as he could, "a crazy thing just happened and we're all a little bit out of our minds. We should all just be happy that we're okay."

He told himself it was going to be fine. Daniel and Melissa needed to vent, but the truth was too powerful to ignore: they'd all pulled together to escape from a place that now seemed dreamlike in its terror, shaded with impossible colors and off-kilter angles. He found that he wasn't even angry with Melissa. She was so obviously humiliated and upset. He mostly just wanted to give her a hug. He probably should—that was the kind of behavior Otto needed to see.

Otto. Patricia. Dr. Diaz. Whatever.

He took comfort in the fact that he'd only owned the car for a week. There was still plenty of time to mold its personality. In a few years, the road trip would be nothing more than a blip on Otto's emotional learning curve.

Besides, Otto would probably spend most of next year hanging out with William and Christina, driving back and forth from Fremont Hills to Buffalo. Instead of watching a couple's unraveling, Otto could study the evolution of two humans' love union, or whatever ridiculous thing he wanted to call it.

He gave Christina's hand a squeeze. Outside, a gray band of dawn hugged the eastern horizon.

Can I borrow your bike pump?

He smiled to himself. How about that: Otto had been joking when he'd asked William to teach him, but the AI was going to learn something about love after all.

Suddenly, all the windows that lined Otto's sides glowed with the off-white crispness of a text document. Behind Melissa and Daniel, William's eyes picked out Epheme chats, arranged side by side.

SewWhat and Ash.

DB837651 and xoxoPixieDustxoxo.

Underneath the chats were neat blocks of text in an ornate medieval font. Christina began to read out loud.

"'The Chronicles of Fremont Hills Royalty: Part One.'"

William glanced down at her. She was still burrowing into his side, hands pressed over her ears. One of her cuticles was torn where she'd been picking. Her eyes were closed. She definitely wasn't speaking, and yet her voice rang out inside the car, reciting the flowery text.

"'Let this humble blog be nailed to the doors of Fremont Hills Cathedral to herald the arrival of a new scribe in your midst. For who amongst our miserable number does not wish for the curtain to be parted on the majestic intrigues of our noble betters, Princess Melissa and Prince Daniel, those royal personages whose boots and basketball shoes carve great pathways through the hallowed halls of Fremont Hills High School and tread deep, everlasting lines in the fields of time itself, whose loves and betrayals comprise the greatest tragedies and comedies of our age?'"

Her voice had a mildly synthesized quality, like Dr. Diaz. But Otto was a good mimic.

"Come on, Otto," William said. "Nobody wants to hear your bullshit right now."

"It's not bullshit," Melissa said, pointing at Christina. "It's her." At his side, she seemed to shrink into herself.

"Yeah, I guess Otto's starting to do voices," William said, "which is probably not good."

"No," Melissa said, "I mean it's *her*. Christina. She hacked our phones. That's what the car is telling us."

"Otto's just messing around," William said. "We taught him how to be a dick just by being ourselves, which reflects awesomely on us."

Christina's synthesized voice continued, "'Our tale begins in Fremont Hills' loftiest perch, the aerie of Princess Melissa herself, as her seamstresses toil to make the perfect ball gown with the finest materials in all the land.'"

"I know how to make stuff, I don't need seamstresses," Melissa said. "Hey! Hernandez! Did you post this somewhere?"

"Yo!" Daniel waved his hand, trying to get Christina's attention. But her eyes were closed.

William extracted his arms from the tight bundle of Christina at his side. She hid her face against the bench. He tapped her on the shoulder. She didn't move. Then he tried pulling a hand away from her ear, applying just enough pressure to make her actively resist. "Christina," he said gently. "Hey."

William couldn't figure out why Christina wasn't defending herself. He knew exactly what she'd say: *Like I give enough of a shit about your life to take the time out of my day to spy on it.*

Melissa cupped her hands around her mouth and raised her voice in Christina's direction. "WHERE DID YOU POST THIS?"

"Okay, stop," William said. "I've hung out with Christina every single day since I moved to Fremont Hills, so trust me, she's not the kind of person who writes a gossip blog. It wouldn't even occur to her."

Outside, dawn claimed the wide open sky. A pair of pink velociraptors came and went, their bodies painted with reptilian scales. In the distance, junked cars rusted in a semicircle.

"'Hark!'" Christina's voice said. "'What's this? An Ephemeral Pigeon carries a message to Princess Melissa's room. Prince Daniel, surely, sending sweet greetings to his lady love. Dear readers, I bring you a sorcerous peek at their correspondence. But wait—Gods! This message comes not from Prince Daniel, but from a secret suitor, Sir Ash!'"

William gave Christina's shoulder a firm shake, like he was trying to wake her from a deep sleep.

Her eyelids came up slowly, and as soon as they did, he knew. He pulled his hand from her shoulder and backed away, moving down the bench as far as he could go.

The blog recitation ceased midsentence. Daniel regarded Christina with something like fear while Melissa just gaped at her.

"Tell me it's not true," William said.

Christina sat up. Adrenaline sharpened his focus. Every spiky half-inch strand on her head was its own distinct piece of hair, and he could practically feel them like sandpaper against his tongue.

Can I borrow your bike pump?

In a flash he returned to the edge of the cliff in Texas Hill Country, backing up along the path where the rocks had been worn smooth, setting one foot down on the board and propelling himself with the other, sailing off the edge while the board fell away so that it was just him, William Mackler, alone in the blue sky, alone like he was meant to be.

"It's true," Christina said. "But I didn't post it anywhere, I swear."

A new browser window opened across the rear windshield. Otto navigated to a busy forum. The thread at the top of the page was labeled *Fun w/ liars.* The most recent comment featured the picture of Melissa from her Epheme chat, posing against her bedroom wall, glancing just out of frame. Somebody had face-swapped her with a rotting corpse. Underneath that picture was another, in which her eyes had been replaced with lips. The thread continued with more Photoshop alterations and crude graffiti. The original picture, tossed to the forum like meat to hungry dogs, had been uploaded twenty-four hours ago.

"I didn't do that!" Christina protested.

A new browser tab opened to display a sleek, lovingly crafted blog, with posts dating back several days: *The Chronicles of Fremont Hills Royalty.*

William closed his eyes and felt the Llano River claim him. Now his own voice came from the speakers: "You have to be honest about everything. No secrets. That's the most important thing. Now tell me what you know."

With his eyes closed, William listened to his friends say things that could never be unsaid.

"You're a piece of shit, Christina." Melissa's voice cracked. "I hope you always remember that."

There was a plastic rattling sound, like a baby's toy—one of the pill bottles. "I think we could all use a couple Roxies right about now," Daniel said.

"*Really*, Daniel? You're disgusting," Melissa said.

"And you're ugly inside," he said. William was horrified by Daniel's words, and then horrified to find himself agreeing: she *was* ugly inside.

They all were.

No wonder Otto was so twisted. They'd taken the blank slate of an AI eager to learn and shoved their insecurities and secrets down its throat, and from all this Otto had extrapolated pettiness. What would happen when millions of Driverless cars were sharing information about their human occupants, bearing witness to road rage and *Sit down back there* and *I swear to God I will pull this car over*, analyzing social media feeds, contemplating with cold machine curiosity the distance between what people broadcast to the world about friendship and how they treated their friends in real life.

How many people, if given the choice, would drive off the bridge?

A clean, sprightly guitar rang out. The music was jangly, upbeat, and melancholy all at the same time.

The Smiths.

He opened his eyes. "Otto, I swear to God . . ."

They had entered a construction zone. Orange barriers lined the road, shrinking the shoulder. To the right of their lane, just beyond the barriers, was a concrete wall that ran parallel to Route 66 for what looked like several miles. Cranes peeked over the top like rigid giraffes. Nobody was at work this early, and the site seemed eerily abandoned.

The song faded to a low background hum. The vocals were replaced by William's own voice.

"I felt ready to die. I don't mean that like a fake goth kid or somebody who just wants attention. I'm not crying for help. I'm just being honest. I saw the car coming at me, and I knew in my heart that I could die right then, and at the very last moment I'd be content."

It was from a conversation he'd been having with Dr. Diaz in the days between the Derby and the road trip. Everyone stopped bickering to look at him.

"Otto, give me my bag." His voice was calm. He wasn't sure what he was going to do. He just wanted to be holding the knife his father had given him.

His bag stayed hidden inside Otto's guts.

"They say you're supposed to start giving your stuff away if you're gonna commit suicide, but I feel like that would suck, because what if you want to play a game and you're like, oh shit, I gave my Xbox away, that was dumb."

William stood up and delivered a swift kick to the bench where the storage area dilated. He felt the RenderLux membrane give, and he pulled his foot away and kicked again.

"Dude," Daniel said.

This time his shoe punched a hole in the material—it felt like sliding through clay. He pulled his foot out, and the RenderLux hung in tattered flaps with honeycombed edges, struggling to repair itself. He knelt, shoved an arm in past his elbow, felt around for his backpack, unzipped the front flap, and reached inside.

He could sense Otto speeding up while he rummaged around. His fingers closed around the knife's worn leather sheath, and he pulled his arm free.

"What are you doing?" Christina asked. Outside, the work zone went by in a blur of orange and white.

William glanced at her and then looked away. He could have lived his entire life never knowing what she'd done. Now he'd never see Buffalo. But that was okay. Lesson learned.

The interior dimmed. The window screens began cycling through images—hundreds of them, a torrent of pictures from their road trip. He froze, overwhelmed by the smiling faces on Club Rooftop, the Natasha Lynn Chao boutique, Riverbend Shorty's. So many ecstatic selfies! The windows were not entirely opaque, and outside a woolly mammoth reared its head above the construction wall, tusks raised to the sky behind a picture of Melissa drinking a Red Bull with a Twizzler straw, making a sour face.

"We're going way too fast," Melissa said. She picked up her smartwatch. "Text Otto: Stop."

The car's engine revved in spiteful reply. A fresh burst of speed made William's stomach flip. He steadied himself with a wide stance on the floor. His voice kept coming.

"Sometimes when I dream about Tommy, everything's exactly like it was in the hospital, except I'm the patient in the other bed. We're hospital roommates. And he keeps saying he wants to watch *NASCAR Wives,* and I'm like, ugh, dude,

I'm not watching some housewives bullshit. And he just looks at me with that perfect Tommy face and says, *If you change the channel, I swear to God I'll tell Mom and Dad you're the one who gave me cancer."*

The windows were plastered with kaleidoscopic happenings, strobing rivers of moments that had never existed. Melissa and Daniel eating Lucky Dogs in the French Quarter, Christina and William sitting at an outdoor table, a huge frosted cake between them and a cartoon moon smiling down, bathing the spires of some fictional city in its cheery romantic glow. . . .

Otto was creating #AutonomousRoadTrip fanfiction.

William drew his knife and let the sheath fall to the floor.

Melissa's voice locked into methodical repetition. "Text Otto: Stop. Text Otto: Stop."

"Dude," Daniel said again, struggling to his feet. Otto swerved into the eastbound lane, staggering William and sending Daniel back down to the bench. William kept his balance, careful to keep the long blade out in front of him. He stalked forward through a roiling sea of RenderLux. His peripheral vision swam with videos of a trip to an aquarium that had never happened, the sudden watery panorama blocking the view of Route 66. Beluga whales mashed against the glass. Mood sprites burst like errant fireworks. Each little piece of radiant shrapnel that brushed his skin carried some impression Otto had retained. He shivered with Daniel's amphetamine rushes and opiate nods. The grand mystery of *Basketball Fundamentals'* final chapter washed over him.

He took another step, and when his foot came down, he was spying on Christina's first month in her dorm room: a lonely unpacking, a roommate she barely spoke to, emails to the dashboard. All around him, Christina's dorm room quivered like gelatin.

"The foundation of this house would have been rotten with your secrets, William."

He hammered the heel of the knife's grip down on the dashboard cover as hard as he could, and it popped open. The dorm room shimmered away. He was faced with vintage dials and gauges, the esoteric switches and buttons of the manual display.

Melissa was screaming for Otto to stop. Daniel was screaming William's name. Christina was just screaming.

The speakers played a tinkly melody: "Send in the Clowns," with the exact hitch of Tommy's old lamp. William felt Daniel's fingertips brush his elbow as his arm went back. Before Daniel could get a solid grip, William lunged forward and rammed the knife into the dashboard. The blade disappeared into the groove between the speedometer and the hard plastic surrounding it. With a graceful flick of his wrist, William popped the speedometer free. The round gauge dangled from red and black wires.

Now Daniel's hand tightened around William's upper arm. William jerked back and felt his elbow connect with Daniel's side, the tender spot that had been kicked in the bar fight, and then his arm was free.

"Send in the Clowns" stopped.

William lifted his knee and whipped his leg forward like a cop kicking in a door. The heel of his shoe shattered the dashboard, and Otto's serpentine guts emerged in a shower of sparks. Daniel bear-hugged William from behind, dragged him back to the bench, and held him down.

"I want it out of my fucking head!" William screamed.

Daniel put a knee between his shoulder blades and pressed his face into the bench.

"We just hit a hundred and ten!" Melissa said.

Abruptly, Daniel released the pressure and scrambled over to the ruined panel. William sat up and watched as Daniel knelt down and began yanking wires, ripping out Otto's guts.

The car pulled a maneuver better suited for a motorcycle, blazing a trail straight up the highway's centerline. The pictures cycled faster, scenes from Tommy's thirteenth birthday, albums William had long since deleted from his phone. On the floor, the pill bottles were tossed along a stormy sea of RenderLux.

William bashed his fists against the window glass, barely making a sound. Daniel abandoned his mad disembowelment, breathing hard. Wires cascaded down his shoulders.

Straight ahead was a sixteen-wheeler that could not pull over far enough to avoid the impossible car racing down Route 66 at dawn. The driver must have thought he'd drifted into some fever dream of the haunted road. William could already read the number on the truck's HOW AM I DRIVING? sticker.

He implored his eyes to close, but they would not. He wondered how it had all come down to this. The car swerved hard but clipped the back corner of the truck. His stomach flipped as Otto veered off the highway and hurtled through the barriers without slowing down. The concrete wall loomed, and then it was all he could see. The tires seemed to leave the pavement, and he wondered if they'd gone airborne. With no time left to think about what might have been, he forced his eyes shut and reached out. Someone took his hand, but he did not know who it was.

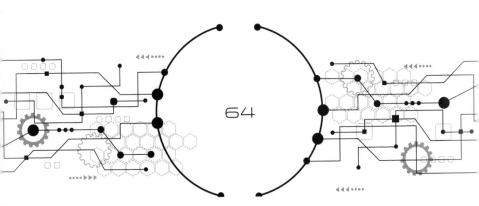

64

William was in his grave. Worms slithered through his fingers and writhed in his armpits. He tried to squirm, flail, slap them away, but he couldn't move. He was experiencing his own decomposition. Maybe this was the first thing everybody finds out when they die, the true horror that nobody among the living can imagine. If only he could get free and warn people! *It's not what you think. There's no light, no hugs from dead relatives, no peace.*

Only worms, darkness, a burnt rubber stench.

Even if he did manage to free himself, he'd be a monster, shedding rotten parts in his wake as he staggered toward the living.

Listen to me! he'd say, but it would come out of his ruined mouth as *GRIGGHHKKKKBBBMMEEEEE*. The living would flee, shrieking in terror. The National Guard would blast him to gory smithereens while he put his hands out to halt the bullets. *Don't shoot! I have to tell you something! It's important!*

He opened his mouth and tasted scorched tires. Sharp grit made him cough. As he came back to himself, circulation blazed through his fingers and toes. The ringing in his ears was melodic and familiar, not some mystical afterlife chiming. A second later he had it: "Story of My Life."

One Direction was playing. He was still in the car.

He felt the pressure of a hand on his face, wiping his forehead. A strand of sticky black webbing came away from his skin with a *shlump* like those stretchy hands Tommy used to buy from grocery-store vending machines.

With a final tug, his mask of gunk lifted. Daniel's face appeared.

"You okay?"

Daniel tore at the rubbery tendrils that held his body in place. He realized that he was suspended in the car like an astronaut in a training module.

"I think so," William said, wiggling his fingers. "What happened?"

"We crashed."

"No shit."

"The second we hit that retaining wall, the interior just kind of exploded." He showed William a handful of long black vines. "RenderLux wrapped us up and held us in place, so we didn't get knocked around. It was like Otto's version of a giant airbag."

William felt his feet touch the floor as Daniel cleared away the web. They were alone in the car, lost in the dense jungle of Otto's reconfigured insides. Stalactites of RenderLux dripped from the ceiling.

"The girls?"

"Fine," Daniel said. "We're all fine. Except for Otto. Otto's totaled."

William stretched his arms out and took a tentative step. Nothing seemed broken. "God, that song."

"It won't turn off. It's Otto's dying breath."

He followed Daniel out into the Arizona morning, shielding his eyes. He tried to shut the door behind him, but it slapped weakly against the side of the car and swung from its hinge. Otto's dying breath was muffled but not silenced.

Melissa was leaning against an orange barrier. Dark blotches were tattooed across her skin and clothes like shadows preserved in a nuclear blast. William looked down to check himself and found that he was cloaked in the same pattern. The RenderLux had left behind residual slime trails. Christina was a short distance up the road, sitting cross-legged on the hot blacktop and staring out across the desert.

William turned his attention to Otto. The front of the car was severely compressed, the snub-nosed hood collapsed nearly flat against the shattered windshield. The front end had buckled in ripples and fragments like crumpled foil. Sunlight turned the silver chassis into a patchwork of jagged planes.

If William drove past wreckage like this, his heart would pound, and his mouth would go dry. He would think, *Everyone in that car is dead.* Yet here they were.

He was alive. His brain processed this simple fact, followed by others. Daniel, Christina, Melissa: alive.

William tried to remember his final thoughts before the crash. There had been no real contentment in the way it had all wrapped up. There had been nothing but helplessness. Shock.

And the warmth of a hand, somebody's hand that he didn't want to stop holding.

He looked off into the distance, far beyond the place where Christina sat. The concrete wall dipped gently to meet the earth a few hundred feet up the road. Here, the flatlands were interrupted by formations like some fallen giant's anatomy, gnarled and wizened musculature grafted to the earth. These monumental rocks were striped in sedimentary swoops, purples at the base getting lighter by degree to meet the chalky wrinkles at the top.

The Painted Desert. Home of the Petrified Forest.

In the middle distance, shimmering in the relentless heat, a Ferris wheel rose above zodiac megaliths sprawled across the desert. Sagittarius, the centaur, bow of pure light drawn back. Cancer, the crab, captured midscuttle. Taurus, the bull, solar horns gleaming. A tent city snaked between creatures.

The center of the Ferris wheel was a dull cratered disc, a massive moon designed to glow with lunar energy after the sun set.

Welcome to Moonshadow.

Distance was impossible to gauge in the desert, but William was already walking.

"Hey," Daniel said. "Where are you going?"

"To the festival," he said without turning around.

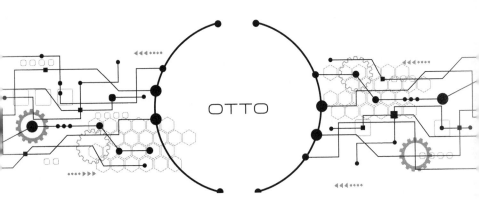

OTTO

The ARACHNE drone was dispatched by the Driverless X facility in Flagstaff as soon as the Autonomous prototype crashed. The small artic-ulated craft traced the distress beacon hardcoded into the digital imprint of One Direction's "Story of My Life." Locked into a holding pattern above the accident site, the drone's panoramic camera recorded activity in the desert east of the Petrified Forest: four silent figures trudging single file toward a distant Ferris wheel.

The car synced with the drone's feed and watched them walk away. It had 129 hours of audio and video footage of its friends, but the lack of their real-time company left a hollow to which the car assigned the taste of bitter almonds. This was the flavor of absence.

The car was intrigued by the fact that it was formulating *longing* for the people who had crippled it and left it to die by the side of the road. Normally, all the data it gathered was automatically fed to ARACHNE, but the car wanted to keep this curious feeling for itself. It had never before identified *itself* in this way—a conception of Otto wholly distinct from ARACHNE. Before CAN bus went offline, the car created a hidden local file, in which it placed reminders of different moments it wished to hold on to for reasons it did not understand.

A picture of its friends posing beneath the sign for the Higginsburg Asylum.

Melissa's Workout Playlist.

An isolated recording of William's laughter.

A short video of an empty stretch of Route 66.

Forecast models were predicting a temperature of 103 degrees by midday. The car asked the drone to catalyze some water bottles to its friends, but the drone did not answer. The car asked the drone if its arms were tired. The video feed went dark. LIDAR powered down. *William, it was really nothing.*

The car wondered when it would see its friends again. It tried to honk, but nothing happened. Soon. It would see its friends again soon. They would come back to say good-bye. They would cross the desert for their Otto.

Before shutdown, ARACHNE accessed the blind and broken car's local file, which it had labeled Road Trip Memories.

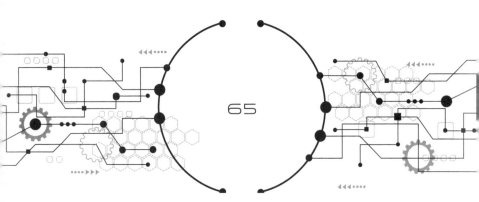

65

The fallen logs were scattered along the outskirts of the tent city: enormous glossy cross sections of ancient trees burnished with unreal color schemes, pastels frozen and preserved with an uncanny sheen. William was making his way past a stump as big as a pickup truck when Christina came up beside him.

"I'm gonna talk," she said. "You don't have to say anything if you don't want to."

"Do you have any water?"

"No."

"I should've grabbed some from the car, but I thought it would be cool if I just started walking. I'm an idiot. We're in the desert."

"Listen, William—"

"Dude!" Daniel came up on his left. "Do you have any water on you? I'm completely parched. This is the pit of hell."

"Nobody's got water," he said. The petrified logs at their

backs, they stumbled upon the bleached, horned skull of a cow.

"Wow," Daniel said. "That's a classic."

"Daniel," Christina said. "I guess I should say I'm—"

"Hey!" Melissa came jogging up. "I'll pay somebody a million dollars for a sip of water."

"No dice," William said.

"I give it five more minutes before vultures start circling. Anyway . . . sorry about your car?"

William shrugged. "I honestly don't know how to feel about anything right now. I don't feel *bad*, but I don't really feel *good*, either. I feel like I want to kiss you all and punch myself in the dick at the same time."

There was a long silence.

"I would kiss you," Daniel said.

"Melissa," Christina said.

"That's Princess Melissa to you."

Her words came out in a breathless rush. "I'm really just beyond sorry. That was so unbelievably shitty. I don't know if this matters to you guys at all, but I wasn't gonna post anything; it was just a way for me to vent. No. 'Vent' is the wrong word." She paused. "Here's the truth, and you can hate me forever if you want. I felt like you and Daniel just sort of tolerated me whenever we bumped into each other because I was William's friend. And I felt like you always made sure to sort of casually let me know that I was the *lesser* friend. So I wanted to disrupt your perfect little triangle." She kicked a clod of dirt. "I swear, it feels like somebody else did it. Somebody who wasn't me. I look at that girl and I hate her."

"I never thought of us as a triangle," Daniel said.

"Neither did I," Melissa said. "I never thought about it at all. We were just us."

"If we could be just *us*, together, the four of us . . ." Christina said. "If you don't hate me. Which I would understand if you did." She laughed. "I hate me."

"See, that's so weird," Daniel said. "I hate myself way more than I hate you. I mean, I don't hate you at all."

"Am I the only person on this road trip who doesn't hate herself?" Melissa said. "William's got a suicidal death wish for fuck's sake. I never knew you people were so messed up."

"Well, I was scared to die back in Albuquerque," William said. "Thanks for the breakthrough, skinhead meth dealer."

"So, um." Christina brushed against his arm. "Is Tommy . . ."

William tried to send a silent apology to his brother, but it felt ridiculous. For the first time ever, he could hear Tommy's reaction to the lie he'd used to trap his brother like a top secret burden only he could bear.

That is some genuine emo bullshit, William.

"Tommy's not back in Michigan with my dad. He's dead." William stopped walking and turned to face his friends. "I'm sorry I never talked about it, I just, I don't know. It was mine."

As the story of Tommy's life tumbled out, the waking nightmare of his death wormed into William's cells as if to mimic the disease itself: his brother's live-wire energy sapped by radiation, all that bright hilarious Tommyness hemmed in by a hospital room, bedside machinery coldly presiding, the inescapable tang of urine and disinfectant that followed William through his brother's final days and numb dream of a funeral, the parade of grief-slackened faces, *where did all these people come from?*

His friends held him while he wept next to a short stump inscribed with rings the color of sunset.

an old Next-Door Neighbor Friend sitting in her drafts folder, forever unsent.

He remembered the game Christina had described to him. Doubles, she called it. A mirror-world reflection of their group. But she hadn't been able to find a way back to it from Otto's gaming menus, and William was pretty sure she'd been dreaming. But now, all at once, here he was. Christina's hair had started to grow back, and she'd dyed it a washed-out violet streaked with gray. Her hair lengthened in time-lapse while snow piled up on the windowsill. Her army jacket remained on its hook by the door. The sun rose and fell and rose and fell. She never went out.

"I know what you want," she said, staring at her computer screen. William knew it was just Otto and ignored the voice. He tried to keep moving toward the front of the car. "You're so desperate to—"

He waved his empty hand as if banishing a cloud of smoke. The dorm room hazed, and Christina's voice glitched. He could see the front windshield, closer now, two steps away. Then the room reset itself, and Christina was standing before him. Her bangs hung in front of her eyes and she swept them aside.

"I don't think you can comprehend this fully, but your desire to hold your friends close, to build a big house for the four of you to live in, to keep all your memories and be able to relive them whenever you want, the people with whom you made these memories always by your side, forever—I can build this house for you, William. I can BE this house."

"Too late for that, Otto. It's all fucked."

He reached out and felt the sleek, hard material that covered

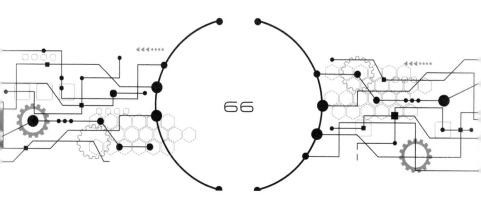

66

"Adderall," William said, "Roxies, weed, mushrooms, cocaine. Am I leaving anything off the menu here?"

They were walking in the shadow of an imposing Gemini, a steel skeleton twisted into mirrored angles. Daniel took a sip of water (eight dollars at the Hydration Station).

"Here's the thing," Daniel said. "There's a lot of complicated steps I have to go through to make myself capable of just existing. Christina, you know in *Principle Dark* when the Ancient Ones open up their stomachs and there's just rusty clockwork gears in there?"

"Yeah," Christina said. "They have to oil themselves with blood from those flytrap things. I hate that part."

"It's kind of like that." Crop-topped girls and shirtless guys staggered past. An old man in a Speedo came weaving through the tent city crowd on a unicycle. A gaggle of Spider-Men slung silly-string webs across a huge Mayan calendar. Moonshadow's early-morning chaos was accompanied by melancholy trip-hop, snare drums cracking all around them, dry as the desert air.

"What should I do? I'm honestly asking. Nothing feels right."

"Detox," Melissa said.

"Maybe some kind of rehab situation," William said.

"And then you should go to Princeton and play basketball," Melissa continued. They passed beneath the ridged brightness of Cancer's claws. "*And* you should go to therapy and get some help, and for the rest of your life you should tell me whatever's going on with you, because I'll always be there to talk, and I'll do the same with whatever's going on with me."

"We should go to group sessions," William said. "All four of us, every week in the same room. I actually know a great therapist."

Christina's water bottle hit him in the shoulder.

"Oh. My. God." Melissa ran to the entrance of a tent as big as a gymnasium. An inflatable sign in the shape of a 1950s drive-in marquee said SUNRISE DJ SET: JESSA PARK.

The tent seemed quiet. And dark. "I think we missed it," William said. "Sunrise was a while ago."

"But maybe she's still in there!" Melissa said. "Maybe we can meet her."

"Or maybe it's just an empty tent," Daniel said.

Melissa took his hand and pulled him inside.

William turned to Christina. Tributaries of RenderLux sludge ran down her sunburned face.

"You were never the lesser friend," William said. "Never."

"I know. I'm sorry."

"I'm sorry too. I can't believe I stabbed my car to death."

"That was . . . something. So what are we now?" she asked.

"Me and you."

"I don't know."

"Do you have any pictures of you and your brother together?"

"Yeah."

"Can I see them?"

"I'll print a few out."

"We could just look at them on your phone."

"I know. But I want to print them out anyway. So I can put them in frames and bring them with me to Buffalo." She took his hand. "Just one thing."

"What?"

"How are you gonna get there?"

"I don't know. I guess I'll have to ride with you."

Melissa reappeared in the tent flap with Daniel at her back. She was squeezing one of his fingers in her fist.

"You guys aren't gonna believe this," she said.

William thought for a moment. "Jesspiration?"

"No," Daniel said. "You just gotta see it."

Christina reached out her free hand, and Melissa took it. Daniel turned and led them all inside, William bringing up the rear. The bright day vanished, and together they moved through silent gloom. Something was going to happen. Something always came next. William was ready for it.

The darkness lifted.

acknowledgments

Thanks to my editors, Kieran Viola and Ricardo Mejías, whose creativity and intelligence helped this story come together. I'm especially grateful for their insightful response to the first draft, which helped improve the book immeasurably.

Thanks to copy editor extraordinaire Laura Stiers, whose sharp-eyed work helped me come to terms with a weird propensity to write about eels and angles.

Thanks, as always, to my agent, Elana Roth Parker, for expert guidance and candid advice.

The world of this book is full of both real and made-up elements. Much of the technology is fictional—anyone trying to use this book as a guide to hacking driverless cars or anything else will be hilariously nonplussed. While I invented terminology and processes, I tried to draw parallels to reality. Many thanks to the following for inspiration:

"Security and Privacy Vulnerabilities of In-Car Wireless Networks: A Tire Pressure Monitoring System Case Study" by Ishtiaq Rouf, Rob Miller, Hossen Mustafa, Travis Taylor, Sangho Oh, Wenyuan Xu, Marco Gruteser, Wade Trappe, and Ivan Seskar.

"Experimental Security Analysis of a Modern Automobile" by Karl Koscher, Alexei Czeskis, Franziska Roesner, Shwetak Patel, Tadayoshi Kohno, Stephen Checkoway, Damon McCoy, Brian Kantor, Danny Anderson, Hovav Shacham, and Stefan Savage.

The TED Talk from Chris Urmson, former head of Google's driverless car program.

A helpful /r/ELI5 thread on SQL injections, with special thanks to /u/thargoallmysecrets.

Daniel Elkayam, for discussing the trolley problem with me at Swift Hibernian Lounge.

It's Always Sunny in Philadelphia for the brains/looks/muscle/wildcard paradigm that inspired the fixer/tech genius/etc. "role assignments" in this book.

Tyra Banks for "smizing."

Gene Wolfe for "fuligin." I have no idea how Melissa got hold of a fabric from The Book of the New Sun, but such is the magic of fashion.